Oscar Wilde
Discovers America

A NOVEL

LOUIS EDWARDS

SCRIBNER

NEW YORK   LONDON   TORONTO
SYDNEY   SINGAPORE

SCRIBNER
1230 Avenue of the Americas
New York, NY 10020

SCRIBNER and design are trademarks of
Macmillan Library Reference USA, Inc., used under license
by Simon & Schuster, the publisher of this work.

For information about special discounts for bulk purchases,
please contact Simon & Schuster Special Sales:
1-800-456-6798 or business@simonandschuster.com

DESIGNED BY KYOKO WATANABE
Text set in Goudy

Manufactured in the United States of America

1 3 5 7 9 10 8 6 4 2

Library of Congress Cataloging-in-Publication Data

Edwards, Louis, 1962–
Oscar Wilde discovers America: a novel/Louis Edwards.
p. cm.
Includes bibliographical references.
1. Wilde, Oscar, 1854–1900—Fiction. 2. Traquair, William M.—Fiction.
3. Irish—United States—Fiction. 4. African American men—Fiction.
5. Master and servant—Fiction. 6. Authors—Fiction. 7. Valets—Fiction.
I. Title
PS3555.D945 O83 2003
813'.54—dc21   2002030879

ISBN 978-0-7432-3690-4

For two extraordinary families:

George and Joyce Wein

and

Alexa, Anj, and Ailey

*"He was accompanied by a business manager,
J. S. Vail, and by a black valet, W. M. Traquair. . . ."*
—RICHARD ELLMANN,
Oscar Wilde

*"I have . . . a black servant, who is my slave—
in a free country one cannot live without a slave. . . ."*
—OSCAR WILDE,
LETTER DATED JANUARY 15, 1882

Oscar Wilde
Discovers America

From the Atlanta *Constitution,*
July 6, 1882

Night before last, when Oscar Wilde's agent appeared at the union ticket office, he asked for three first-class tickets to Savannah and for three sleeping-car tickets. After Mr. Thweatt had supplied the agent's demands, the agent stated that one set of the tickets was intended for Mr. Wilde's valet, a colored man. Mr. Thweatt informed the agent that it was against the rules of the company to sell sleeping-car tickets to colored persons, and requested the return of the ticket, promising to refund the money, but the agent declined to do as requested. Mr. Thweatt then went into the sleeping-car where Mr. Wilde and his servant were and stated the case to them, but they both declined to change the programme they had marked out. Mr. Wilde said that he had never been interfered with before and persisted in having his darkey retain his sleeping-car ticket. Seeing all argument useless, Mr. Thweatt approached Steve Henderson, the porter of the sleeping car, and, soliciting his aid, posted him. Steve then went to Mr. Wilde's valet and told him that the train would go through Jonesboro, and if the people saw a negro in the sleeper they would mob him. This had more effect than all of Mr. Thweatt's talk, and in a few seconds the sleeping-car ticket had been returned and Mr. Wilde's valet had vacated the berth.

THE TOUR
1882

I

"America has never quite forgiven
Europe for having been discovered somewhat
earlier in history than itself."

—OSCAR WILDE

NEW YORK

BLOOD, coursing through William with a curious heat, burned his cheeks. Baxter was going to Europe tomorrow, and he was not. Just as, four years earlier, Baxter had gone to Harvard, and he had not. William brought his hands up to his face and felt the warmth of his envy pulsing there. Such emotion would have ruddied the face of a fairer man—Baxter would have been blushing—exposing his fury, but William, sitting across from his observant, judgmental father, enjoyed the refuge of his brown mask. Had William's gloom a glow and had Henry Traquair detected the source of his son's malaise, he would have, no doubt, lectured William about the perils of self-pity. His father, with the lone exception of pride, had never displayed, at least in William's presence, any interest in matters of the self at all. Perhaps this trait, William allowed, was an acquired one, the result of Mr. Traquair's life's work as a servant attending to the needs of others, a hazard of the job, as it were, like a coal miner's cough or a cotton picker's crouch.

For as long as William could remember, his father, who was now stylishly interrupting his own chatter (what was he talking about anyway—a Mr. Vail—who was this Vail and why should William care about him?) with perfectly timed double puffs of his cigarette, had been the senior servant in the household of Mr. Charles Gable, owner of a small but very profitable bank in New York City. Mr. Gable was a widower; William had no recollection of Mrs. Gable, though his own mother, Gloria, who was the only other full-time worker in the Gable household, occasionally spoke of her. A large portrait of Mrs. Gable hung in the grand entrance to the home, a three-story townhouse at 141 East Nineteenth Street in Gramercy Park—the only home William had ever known. Baxter, who was just a few months younger than William, was the Gables' only child. As boys growing up together in the same household, Baxter and William had been inseparable, sharing meals, mischief, punishment, and private tutors, who had taken them from simple addition through the mysteries of pi and beyond, from the English alphabet to Latin grammar, from the Greeks to Milton. They had found Hawthorne, Poe, and other more recent authors on their own; the tutors had evidently had a low opinion of American literature. William and Baxter had remained close even when they had gone away to separate colleges, Baxter, as expected, to Harvard, William to Bowdoin. (Mr. Gable had arranged William's matriculation to the Maine school, after having had no success in convincing his connections in Cambridge to accept William's application.) William still had the first of many letters Baxter had sent to him during their years of separation:

14 September 1877

Billy Boy,
    You wouldn't like it here. It seems no one believes in Plato at the moment. But I hear next semester that could change. Do classroom desks bother you as much as they do me? We students seem rather like sitting ducks—and, oh, how the professors do take aim.
        Terribly, shamefully happy,
        Ever yours,
        Baxy Boy

William had written back a letter of equal brevity and with just as delicate an admission of betrayal, because he, too, had settled in for four years of ecstasy. Yes, the initial disappointment at having been denied Massachusetts had been swept away early in his freshman year when a rolling wave had splashed him as he had stood on the rocky Maine coastline near Brunswick. The splatter of leaping and diving droplets had anticipated or possibly even precipitated his tears for the aggressive beauty of the great sea that had jumped up with such impetuosity to kiss the face of his youth. What a kiss! He could have retreated from the shore in time to save himself from a second dousing, but he had let the tide wash over him once more. Standing there in the arms of the Atlantic, he felt he had just learned what he might, in the future, expect of love—surprise and swiftness . . . and love of him—surrender. And college had been as breezy and romantic as that late summer day. But now those four years were done, and William had no idea where to turn for a pleasure that would match the stimulation, the intellectual and visceral orgy, that was academia and its environs.

Baxter had an easy answer: he was off to England, then France, Italy, Spain, and Germany—a yearlong adventure across the Continent. But William was expected to move to the South and become a teacher or to stay at home and become his father. He didn't feel inclined to do either, not because he feared failure, but because he dreaded success. They were such easy options. He knew he could manage either of them with little effort. He felt he had a certain aptitude for teaching. As a college senior he had assisted one of the best professors on campus with his survey course of American History. Logic told him he would become a teacher soon enough. But not yet. Not now. He needed a challenge. When he had left Bowdoin to come back to New York City, he had felt the classic depression of the recent undergraduate. The battle with adolescence essentially won, the confident, dangerously armed adult seeks a real war. When none is declared, a civil war as inevitable and debilitating as any other (was it the head versus the heart?) substitutes. Baxter had his war; he was off to conquer Europe. But what about *me*? William had moped, sighing like Sumter. Where is *my* continent?

And now, weary for the moment from the frustration that came of contemplating his predicament, William attempted to focus on the blurry image of his father in the small room at the back of the house that Mr. Traquair had long ago appropriated as his office and study. If his father refused to acknowledge the complexity of himself, William vowed he would try to see the man whole. Through a droopy-eyed gaze, across the smoke-filled room, he saw his father—puff, puff—sitting comfortably in his burgundy-colored leather chair behind his grand polished oak desk. William knew this pose photographically, could have painted it from memory had he the skill. But it struck him that he actually knew very little about his father. He knew the man's habits and his disposition. But who was he, really? A handsome fifty-year-old butler who had made a career out of studying, learning, and attending to his employer's needs? Was he simply that? Of course not.

But their countless, seemingly intimate conversations over the years had always resulted in William telling all and his father telling nothing. Lately he had begun to sense an annoying calculation in the way his father deftly guided their discussions away from himself. A father-boy relationship might have warranted such manipulation, William allowed, but a father and a young man, his son, must play by different rules. Yet even this understanding—that he and his father would soon essentially be equals—fresh as it was, had much more to say about William than about Mr. Traquair, so successful had his father been in maintaining the mystery of his being.

Prompted by a volume of poems positioned prominently on Mr. Traquair's desk, William remembered something of substance that he knew about his father: his favorite poet was Phillis Wheatley, the brilliant slave girl. William found his father's affection for Miss Wheatley displeasing—Phillis Wheatley: a poet held captive. The hopelessness of her circumstances both sickened and bored him, but apparently her situation and her achievement impressed his father. In the bitter tone of his dark state, William thought that Mr. Traquair adored Phillis Wheatley the way the oppressed always love their struggle and the symbols of it, with passion. But the idea of an enslaved poet, an imprisoned artistic soul, plunged William even farther downward, and he sank, as if through a trapdoor, to his depression's new, unsuspected bottom. *Poets should be free!*

"I *said*, 'William, why aren't you listening to what I'm saying?' That's what I just said to you," Mr. Traquair said.

William wondered, Did I just ask him what he had said to me? "I am listening, Father," he said, improving his posture. "Yes, now you have my attention."

"Do I need to begin again? Has even the gist of my words penetrated the mist of your meditation?" Mr. Traquair sounded more stern than usual. He was not a forceful man, merely a rigid one. William had always found the bass in his voice disconcerting, too strong for the delicately composed words he spoke through white teeth and perfectly shaped lips. The large size of his head, a bolder version of William's, also hinted at an aggression that William knew was not in his father's nature. In less melancholy moments, William had noted how his father's silver and black matted crown rested gently upon his head, accenting a regality that defied his station.

"Something about a Mr. Vail." William feigned interest.

"Right, right. Well, as I was saying, he came for a visit yesterday. Gable has known him since he was a child, possibly some relationship by marriage, though I remembered nothing of the young man when I met him. At any rate, I walked into the library to serve the brandy, and as I did, Gable says, 'Fine timing, Henry, right on cue.' And, of course, I'm thinking, Why should my timing not be fine after more than twenty years! I know how and when he likes his brandy served, what does he mean, my timing, why, I'm a veritable—why, were I a time-piece, my *brand* would be Gable. He must have sensed some confusion on my face and, I must say, he recovered nicely. 'We need your advice,' he said. A nice phrase to hear, my boy. 'We need your advice.' Listen for it in your lifetime, and try to be ready to answer its call. Not that I, mind you, held any conceit that I could truly be of much help to the gentlemen, but I stood ready to try. 'Mr. Vail,' he said, 'is in a bit of a fix. He's got a distinguished Englishman due to dock in New York harbor the day after New Year's, and the valet he had rounded up to attend to the man has mysteriously disappeared.'

" 'Disappeared?' I asked.

" 'Quite,' Vail said. 'Though not before my eyes. That reminds me of a ghost story I heard the other day—'

"Gable cut him off, thank goodness. Can you imagine? A ghost story? In the middle of my being asked for advice? 'Henry,' Gable said to me, 'we're wondering if you can suggest some good young man who'd be willing to look after the Englishman while he's here in the States. There will be some travel involved; no one's sure at this point how much. Right, James?'

"To which Vail says, 'Yes, we're hoping for a long tour, but there's no guarantee. Of course, there is a guarantee, but I'm not discussing that now. This is Mr. D'Oyly Carte's affair, as managed here by Colonel Morse.'

" 'Yes, of course,' says Gable, 'but that's more information than Henry needs. Can you think of anyone, Henry, any young man who might fill this position?'

" 'Yes, old boy,' says Vail to me, 'it seems I'm really in quite the spot.'

"I was really in quite the spot myself, son." Mr. Traquair paused here.

William, suddenly understanding what his father was intimating, said, "Father, you didn't!" He sprang up from his chair, hoping to display an appropriate sense of the shock he was experiencing.

"You will be seated," Mr. Traquair said firmly, and his son demurred. "Now, what I did was to make a suggestion that you, should you choose, be *considered* for the position."

"A valet, Father? Is that what you really think I'm suited to be?"

"A valet suits others. If you are to climb a mountain, at least have some idea of its height. Know your mission before accepting it."

"I don't need to know this mission because I'm not accepting it."

Mr. Traquair drew once, slowly, upon his cigarette and then spoke calmly and confidently. "William, in answer to your question, I don't know what you're suited for. And, frankly, neither do you. This mood you've been in lately is not attractive. And just what are you going to do when Baxter leaves tomorrow? He's backed up your foolishness through the summer and the fall, even put off his trip to keep you company—oh, I know these things, don't look at me that way. I should have said something long before now. I'm sorry I did not. When Baxter leaves tomorrow, you'll be very much alone. And your presence in this household, given your aversion to domestic duties, will amount to loitering. What will you do then?"

"Your suggestion is a rather extreme answer to that question."

"Perhaps. Perhaps not. But it is, nevertheless, *an* answer. *Your* response is as of yet forthcoming. It seems to me that you have joined me and Mr. Vail in being in quite the spot."

"What is it they say about misery and its company?"

"It would benefit us both if you would remember that misery is said to feel about its company the way I feel about you."

"You've got an interesting way of showing it. I'm not an indentured servant, you know. And didn't the war put an end to the other thing?"

Mr. Traquair's face grew dark at this remark, and he responded, "Mr. Gable's involved. Of course you'll be well compensated."

"But how is he involved? I thought you said this was Mr. Vail's affair."

"It is. What I mean is—and I suppose I should have said this earlier—upon my proposal that Vail consider you, Mr. Gable accepted the position in your name."

"Surely not, Father!"

"Well . . . at my suggestion that he do so. I didn't want Vail to find someone else and have you miss this opportunity. It has real possibilities. It's not permanent, but there is the chance for you to travel. Vail says maybe all across the country—if his man is successful with his lectures. I'd like to do that myself, some traveling. I did not imagine that you would object so strongly."

"Your imagination has never been your strong suit."

"True—but my reputation has *ever* been. And it is that which you are threatening now with your obstinacy. I gave Mr. Gable my word, and that—despite your high-and-mighty stance and your sense of self-importance, neither of which you would possess and be able to throw in my face at this moment were it not for my reputation and Mr. Gable's money, which sent you to college—well, I gave my word, and that, young man, *will* decide this matter."

"Father, you don't seem to understand my position."

"Don't qualify my inability to understand nonsense with the word 'seem.' I *don't* understand your position."

Upon hearing this statement, William paused and then suddenly found himself laughing. It occurred to him that he had gotten his own sensitivity to language directly from the man before him. Surely he had known this about his father and himself, an important trait they had in common. Maybe there was something more to Phillis Wheatley than he thought. Maybe he should look at her verses again. Maybe it wasn't her servitude, her suffering, that mattered to his linguistically perceptive and inventive father, who also just happened to be a servant. Maybe it was her poetry, her words. These four maybe's equaled one perfect squint through which his father, for the first time this afternoon, gained focus in William's eyes. With resignation and more than a little admiration, William sat back in his chair.

"I'm not agreeing, Father. But tell me about this Englishman. Who is he, the man I am to serve—I mean, the man whom, in deference to your stellar reputation, I am considering serving?"

"A young man by the name of Oscar Wilde. I only know that—"

"*The* Oscar Wilde!" William leaned forward, balancing himself against his father's desk, fingers pressed firmly along its polished front edge.

"*The*? Well, he's certainly *an* Oscar Wilde. I don't know that he's the only one."

"No, Father, he's the one! I'm sure. The papers have him arriving in three days' time. Don't you know who he is!"

"I suppose you'd know I was lying now if I pretended that I do know, so, no, I don't know who he is."

"He's the one. In *Patience*. The play. Gilbert and Sullivan. Oh, you never keep up with these things." Then he sang: " 'Twenty love-sick maidens we.' " His father still offered no countenance or gesture of recognition. "He's the *aesthete*. He's *Bunthorne*. But, what's more, he's a poet!"

"Oh, a poet," Mr. Traquair said with detachment. "At last a word with which I'm familiar. Am I mistaken, or are you excited about this act of betrayal by your tyrannical father?"

"You are mistaken. I'm not merely excited. I am ecstatic! Wait till Baxter finds out. He'll be mad with envy. Surely, he'll want to shoot me. I can't imagine anything better than that he'll want to shoot me."

"What nonsense you two talk," Mr. Traquair said.

"I must go up and tell him now. Excuse me, please, Father." William stood up quickly and was halfway through the door when his father's voice stopped him.

"Now, son, there are details to be considered."

"I know, Father. I promise I'll be right back down to discuss matters more thoroughly."

"Fine . . . fine," his father said, and William started on his way again.

"William . . ." His father spoke more softly this time.

"Yes." William pushed his head back into the room.

"I only wanted to say . . ." Mr. Traquair could not finish. He turned his head away from William, who understood the poignancy of the moment. Finally his father said, "You should be sure to take care in talking to your mother about this matter. You know how she was when you first left for school. And, you know, she's gotten attached again since you've been back home."

"Of course. Does she know about my appointment?"

"Oh, yes. She's already been out this morning to buy you some undergarments and a hat, I think."

"She's really the one, isn't she! I'll be, shall we say, less enthusiastic with her."

"Well—your enthusiasm is always welcome here, you know. Now off with you!"

As William dashed up the back stairs, he heard his own laughter, a sound that jolted him into perplexed contemplation of how quickly he had risen from the depths to the heights. All of his whining about Baxter's going to Europe without him was suddenly revealed as the childish complaint that it was. One would have thought it was his life's greatest tragedy—as if there were anything tragic about his life at all. Why, his whole life had been one privilege after another. Fine family, fine home, fine school. He'd known no real adversity. His entire existence had been, and something told him *would be*, the work of the better hand of Providence. The same for Baxter. They were the same, really, he and Baxter, in so many ways. They talked the same language, liked the same clothing (tweed in winter, linen in summer), had read the same books, wanted to meet Henry James, had confided in the other an overwhelming hunger for fame, possessed a modesty completely inconsistent with this desire, had confided in the other a wish to be in love, possessed a naivete that would complicate such emotion. Yes, they were the same— save the minor advantage or disadvantage (circumstances decided the matter) of the ability to blush. And William, as jubilant as the winner of a game of chance, rejoiced at the notion that now both he and Baxter had their own missions.

Completing a strategy in his mind for maximizing the drama of his news, he burst into Baxter's room. His friend, who was packing a small bag of books, sketch pads, pencils, and paintbrushes for his trip, started from the violence of William's entrance, dropping a book to the floor as a result. "Good God, Billy!" Baxter said, bending to pick up the volume, his long brown locks slithering from behind his ears as he leaned forward. "Melville might have broken my foot. What's got into you?" He stood up, waving the thick book in one hand and curling his hair back into place with the other.

"Oh, I don't know—let's just say I'm feeling too too utterly utter," William said, imitating the language from Gilbert and Sullivan's *Patience*.

Baxter laughed with recognition of the reference, his honey-colored eyes twinkling, brightening his handsome face. "Yes, that is a funny, funny bit, I agree. The cry of the aesthetes. I'll have to write you from London and tell you if any of it's for real."

"And when I write you in return, maybe I'll send you petals from a sunflower sniffed by the King of the Aesthetes himself."

"Oh, Billy Boy, do promise me you won't run around banging elbows with the crude hordes trying to get a glimpse of the Wilde man. What on earth could be more embarrassing?"

"Oh, I don't know—being his valet, perhaps?"

Baxter raised bushy eyebrows and let his slender frame go slack with puzzlement. "Well, I suppose you've got me there."

"Truth be told," William mused as he strutted around the room in a bouncy fashion, implying a superior but rarely used athleticism, "I should like more than anything to be his valet as he travels all over the country talking about art and making a complete spectacle of himself. It would be as much fun as anything I've done in my entire life."

"It might be at that," Baxter, flippantly changing his mind, agreed. "And—it would certainly simplify your gathering those sunflower petals." He laughed again and looked up at William, who had stopped his strutting and was smiling and nodding. "But, no, Billy!" Baxter said, understanding at last the truth hidden in William's jest.

"But, yes."

"But, how?" Baxter asked. "It's all too, well, too too utterly *bizarre*."

"It's the work of the two masters, Gable and Traquair. Of course, it's all a great big accident that they stumbled on to anything so bizarre, as you say—and so wonderful!"

"But it can't be true. Are you to know him, really?"

William cleared his throat for effect. "To *suit* him, my father would correct you."

"If one doesn't come to know a man while dressing him, 'intimacy' must be redefined." As if inspired by his own remark, Baxter drew closer to William, and the two, laughing, engaged in one of their frequent moments of conspiratorial affection. William needed only whisper his response. "I don't know about definitions," he began, before adding with a touch of solemnity, "but I think it may be *meaning* that I'm after."

"I must postpone my trip!" Baxter shouted.

"No, Baxter. No more. I'm on my own now. You're on your own. Besides, you can't keep Europe waiting. You've often said that she's the girl of your dreams. No doubt you're right. And while a long engagement may have the advantage of making the wedding night seem a week, it makes the marriage seem an eternity."

"Wilde?" Baxter asked.

"Traquair."

"Keep practicing, old boy. I don't envy you there, trying to measure up. They say he is quite the wit. You'll have to keep his knee breeches pressed, you know. I envy that even less. Whatever you do, you must promise to steal me a scarf. Some bright silk thing. Promise?"

"As good as done."

"And write to me all of his secrets, and years from now people will find the letters and there'll be posthumous scandals about us all."

"I shall steal a scarf and I shall write—that is all that I'll promise, Baxter. And you will write."

"I shall write, but my letters will surely be nothing compared to yours. You and Oscar Wilde, dashing all over the place, discovering America."

With that remark, William suddenly realized the larger implications of his impending association with Wilde. Together, they might be touring the entire country; that was what his father had said. The papers all but confirmed it as well. For the past few months, he had been yearning for a continent of his own, one to offer him the mystery and adventure Europe promised Baxter, and here, he understood now, it had lain before him all along—or even *behind* him, he considered, for hadn't it been the very thing that had pressed against his back, the thing that had propped him up when he had stood on that rock four years ago learning those first lessons of love as he kissed the coast of Maine? How unexplored is the familiar continent one calls home. Baxter had named her for him. America, William pondered. Might she be the girl of *my* dreams?

"Now mind that you don't trouble him too much," Vail said to William as they rode in the carriage on their way to the Grand Hotel at Thirty-first and Broadway to meet the poet the entire country was waiting to see. "These reporters have all but worn him to a frazzle, I suspect. There are probably some at the hotel right now. Even though his place of lodging is supposed to be a secret, word gets around. So be alert and ready to clear the room if necessary. You're a good size. That will help immensely. But I haven't prepared him for you. What I mean is, he knows only that you are a valet."

"As opposed to knowing that I am an *inexperienced* valet?" William asked with a smile, teasing Vail.

"No, he's aware of that. Let's just say that he'll be better informed once he's seen you. I know you'll be fine with him. As I've told you, Mr. Gable has spoken very highly of you. Once we get you settled in, I'm confident all will be well." Vail was only a couple of years older than William, twenty-four or twenty-five, but he had a nervous quality about him that made him seem older. He made William a bit uncomfortable with his habit of twitching his thin reddish mustache, and with the way he was constantly consulting his watch and tugging at the vest of his ill-fitting suit.

"Was Mr. Wilde expecting us before now?" William asked, referring to Vail's time-conscious anxiety.

"A bit. I do wish the driver would move this buggy along." There was a brief quiet moment before Vail, still fidgeting, began again. "Have you seen the papers? 'The Apostle of Art,' they are calling him. They don't know whether they love him or hate him. He's in for a round or two of joshing, that's certain. When the *Arizona* came into the harbor two evenings ago, those scribblers chartered a tug to go out to meet Wilde before he was even out of quarantine. That's when he told them he was disappointed with the Atlantic or some such thing. Disappointed with an entire ocean! How silly. Can you imagine that?"

"Indeed, I can," William responded contrarily, instinctively defending Oscar Wilde, sublimating his own affection for the Atlantic in order to counter the palpable dullness of Vail. "An *entire* ocean, as you stress, has the tremendous burden of sustaining one's attention. Its size, the best of its features, is also its handicap. Mere volume without substance is the very definition of 'vacuity.'"

Vail looked at William with curiosity. "Well . . . ," he said. "An apostle of the apostle. That should appease him. A tremendous egotist, you know. Did you see what he said at customs yesterday? The papers quoted it. It's gone all over the world by now. When the officer at the gate asked what he had to declare, Wilde said, 'I have nothing to declare other than my genius.'" Vail laughed loudly and elbowed William, who, having already read and appreciated the remark, was less overcome by Vail's clumsy restatement of it. "He gives them what they want. It's all good for this Aesthetic Movement, one must believe. And that means it's good for *Patience*. Colonel Morse tells me that Mr. D'Oyly Carte is thrilled to hear of all the publicity. He couldn't have done anything smarter than to book Wilde in America for this lecture tour to coincide with the opera. *Patience* is destined to run even longer now in New York and get proper treatment in other parts of the country as well. And Wilde won't do so badly himself. Ah, here we are at last."

As they exited the cab, William began to exhibit an anxiety akin to Vail's, slapping at the knees of his pants for no good reason. The new gray tweed suit he was wearing was flawlessly pressed; his mother had seen to that. He touched his cold face and hoped that the January chill had not dried his skin too badly. Why hadn't Vail informed Wilde that a large Negro would be assisting him while he traveled! Why shock the man—no doubt still weary from his voyage—any more than New York itself was bound to have already shocked him? But William, his legitimate apprehension about meeting Wilde notwithstanding, knew there was nothing overwhelming about his appearance, nothing other than something that might actually matter to Wilde. As he removed his hat, he caught a glimpse of himself in one of the many spotless mirrors in the hotel lobby, and he quietly acknowledged the stark truth of his reflection: William was beautiful. He had never dwelled on this fact, but he was aware of it. With an honesty that exposed the humble roots of vanity, he stared at his large, dark head, which was slightly dimpled at the temples, accentuating his forehead, forecasting his intelligence and relieving the rest of his face (ovular, wondrous eyes; the flaring, breathy nose; the full, ponderous lips; and the pointy, cheery, unchallenged cheeks—never cuffed, never kissed) of the burden of attending to all but one collective charge—beauty. Since childhood he had been praised as adorable; then handsome; now striking. Other adjectives, including pretty, had left him embarrassed throughout his life. Men and women alike had noticed his face, his form. (From the time he reached fifteen his shoulders, filling the breadth of the mirror into which he was gazing right now, had been as wide as his father's.) His appearance had always worked to his advantage; people simply responded to his unusual physical attributes with a remarkable attentiveness and kindness. Occasionally he had received slightly higher marks in college than he truly deserved; he had made friends easily all of his life despite possessing what he considered only a moderately friendly personality; in stores he was often served, out of turn, before others, and in restaurants more generously. He understood the shallowness of this feature of human nature—the granting of special privileges to people because of the way they looked—but he thought there was something deep and complex about the prejudice as well. A calm came over him now as he rested the weight of his anxiety upon the crutch of his comeliness. If Oscar Wilde, he reasoned, was indeed the great aesthete, the great admirer and champion of beautiful things, then William had nothing to be nervous about at all.

Wilde's two-room suite was on the first floor, rooms 142 and 143. Vail and William walked in through the door to 142 and were engulfed by smoke and laughter. Looking past the coatrack in the entrance hall and into the parlor, William saw at least twelve reporters busily penciling their pads between guffaws. All the men were standing and gazing down into the open, lamplit end of their semicircular cluster where, William presumed, Wilde was seated. He left Vail fumbling with the door and moved toward the crowd. As the laughter died, a voice rose up from the spot that was commanding the reporters' attention. William glided to its slow, rhythmic accompaniment.

"Genius is always *ostentatious*," he heard the voice say, lingering suggestively on the adjective. "It is by its nature so. Even a genius of subtlety is destined to show off that shyest, most demure of aesthetic traits. One of the marks of true genius is that it announces itself."

"Mr. Wilde, why are you wasting your time and your genius in America *talking* about art, when you could be at home in England creating it?" The question had come from the right side of the room, though William, whose eyes were shifting quickly in every direction, could not actually see the person who had asked it.

"Fair question. While I may be wasting artistic time here in America, I am, nevertheless, exercising my genius in the name of art. The only misuse of genius is the disuse of genius."

"Is there nothing that is impossible for the genius, Mr. Wilde?" another disembodied voice asked.

"An average man accepts the impossible. The dreamer ponders it perpetually. The genius dismantles it and keeps its useful parts."

The crowd chuckled. William, an umbral presence, had moved unnoticed farther into the dimly lit room. He reached the back of the crowd and waited for a thick puff of cigar smoke to pass and for Wilde to come into view. The man next to William turned to him with a look of confusion, and William wasn't sure if the look had been induced by his own sudden appearance or by what Wilde had just said.

He turned to look back in Wilde's direction, but now someone's head was blocking his line of vision.

"But, Mr. Wilde, can't a man practice his way to perfection, as is rumored?" a reporter wanted to know.

"Perhaps. But what is practice if not ritual? And ritual is the religion of redundancy. Besides, I can assure you that practice achieves perfection with far less frequency than does even the most indolent form of genius. Listen, gentlemen, enough on this issue. It's getting tedious. Let's say, for the record, that I've declared my genius in the name of Aestheticism, in the name of art. Rather like America declaring her independence in the name of Democracy, I'm anticipating the necessary struggle to establish the legitimacy of my claim. America, through force, had to persuade England of her position. I, with wit and no other weapons, am out to convince America of mine. I can't promise that there will be any less blood shed. Some of you have already started firing—I've read the morning papers."

There was another round of laughter. William was excited by Wilde's cleverness and his grace. As he considered these two of his own most prominent characteristics, he felt that Wilde, in defending himself, was also somehow defending him. Who were these unrefined men to challenge Wilde, his elegance, and his mission to make America more artful? The cigar smoker next to William cleared his throat and shouted toward Wilde, "I say, Mr. Wilde, how about taking a question from back here? I have one for you. They say you Ass-thetes are keen on flowers. Sunflowers, lilies, roses, and the like. Well, my editor was hoping you could define a flower for us."

"Define a flower, sir? I did not endure the Atlantic to be transformed into the dictionary of an anonymous newspaper editor."

Several reporters groaned. Then someone up front said above the others, "Oh, give it a go, Mr. Wilde. It'll make good copy. I can see it now: WILDE DEFINES 'ROSE.' The ladies will adore you for it. Don't define just any flower. Define a rose. Can you define a rose? What is a rose, Mr. Wilde?"

The entire room was silent, awaiting Wilde's response to this challenge. The smoker next to William who had first asked this silly question smirked, as if he'd defeated Wilde. William looked back toward the poet, whom he'd yet to set clearly in his sights, and he saw—just over a short man's shoulder, in a small space between the hips of two other men, then through the akimbo triangle of yet another—that Wilde was in the process of rising from his seated position. The crowd swayed back on its heels to make room for him. He was as tall as William, over six feet. His long black hair hung in fat curls almost to his shoulders. The face—its chin shocking in prominence—had the strange quality of a mask, as if it were ridiculously too large or attached a bit askew, covering somehow the countenance of the real Wilde. Perhaps this was why William concentrated on trying to see Wilde's eyes (which he could not) and why he was so eagerly awaiting the sound of Wilde's voice again. Wilde was smiling when he said, as he concluded his ascent, "A rose is . . . arose is what I did this morning."

The reporters erupted with delight. They had their quote. The smoker, triumphant just a moment ago, began a coughing fit, and both William—who could hardly contain his own laughter—and the man standing on the opposite side of the choking man rapped his back a few times. Vail motioned for William to open the door and usher everyone out. William jumped quickly down the short hall, waved all of the men toward him and, one by one, guided them out. He leaned back against the heavy door as it swung and rattled itself shut and locked. The metallic agitation passed into him, and his timidity returned, slowing his walk back to meet Oscar.

When he reached the edge of the main room, he stopped and intentionally shied himself out of conspicuous view. Wilde had again reclined casually on the sofa. "I was so hoping to have this day to myself," he was saying to Vail. "As you know, I need time alone to finish writing out my lecture. If I don't get it done, I might be forced to improvise. And as you may or may not know, Mr. Vail, improvisation requires twice the preparation of recitation. Yes, willful spontaneity requires great premeditation and tremendous effort—which is to say, it's certainly out of the question. So I was about to get out my papers, when suddenly there they were, banging on the door. It is probably difficult to believe, but the banging was worse than their actual presence. Needless to say, it was impressive banging."

"Yes, I suspected they might find you out," Vail responded. "Secrets always cause such trouble."

"I should certainly hope so," said Wilde. "Otherwise, what good would they be?"

"Not to contradict you, Mr. Wilde, but is trouble a good thing?"

"Trouble, taken in moderation, is indeed a very good thing, Mr. Vail. Contradiction is a troublesome thing, which, of course, makes it a good thing as well—if also experienced at properly spaced intervals."

"Agreed . . ." said Vail, with something in his tone that sounded to William more like disagreement or possibly mere confusion. In this state, Vail turned and faced him. "William, do come in and stop languishing there in the shadows. Let's have Mr. Wilde get a good look at you."

William slowly stepped into the light of the room, and Vail said, "Mr. Wilde, your valet, William Traquair."

William made an effort to stand erect, wanting to appear taller. He had been fretting about his size when he had exited the carriage, but now after having seen Wilde's impressive stature, he knew his own unusual height would not be imposing. William bowed his head slightly in the direction of Wilde, whose own head, William noticed with anticipation, was rising. Thinking he saw disappointment in the drop of Wilde's jaw, he was about to attempt to say something witty to win him over, but then Oscar Wilde said his name: "William Traquair. William Traquair, you are quite perfect!" Wilde turned quickly to Vail. "William Traquair is perfect, Mr. Vail. He is a veritable fortress. Why, if you'd had him here an hour earlier, as you promised, I think none of those reporters would have gotten past him to me. Would any of those reporters have dared to try to cross your guard, William Traquair?"

"They might have dared, Mr. Wilde, but if I am perfect, as you say, they would never have succeeded."

"Perfection!" Wilde stood up and moved to shake William's hand. "Vail, why did you not get him to me sooner?"

Vail began reaching into his vest pocket. "This watch has been the source of much consternation for me lately. It needs fixing. I can't tell you the trouble it has given me." Then, trying to recover, he added, "But trouble is good, is it not?"

"With your recent contradiction you've already met your trouble quota for the hour," said Wilde. William smiled and nodded gently at this remark, taking Wilde's contentiousness as confirmation of the righteousness of his own playful confrontation with Vail earlier. When Vail gave him a disapproving look, William waved his hand in mock apology.

"Well, he is here now," Vail said, "and being paid a wage I consider worthy of at least perfection, so I suggest you put him to work."

"I would wager this *is* work," Wilde countered. "And if it is not work it is certainly *laborious,* standing here being talked about while one is present. It is much more like fun to be talked about behind one's back. But to please Mr. Vail, Traquair, perhaps you should help me unpack the rest of my things and sort them out. My trunks are in the bedroom, the only proper place for sorting things out. Follow me, Traquair." William followed Wilde into the next room. "Traquair. That's an odd name. Do you like it much?"

"I suppose so. I have not given it much thought," William said.

"Well, Traquair is an odd name, but I say oddity becomes you," said Wilde, glancing back over his shoulder. "Vail said only that you were a special case. What do you suppose he meant by that, a special case?"

"I don't know. It sounds rather as if I were some sort of exceptional portmanteau."

"True," said Wilde, laughing. "And while is it perfectly fine being thought exceptional, being referred to as luggage is, simply put, dehumanizing. I won't hear of your being considered a special case, unless, of course, it pleases you." They stopped at the foot of the bed, where two tin Saratoga trunks and several bags were gathered. Wilde whispered, "If Vail had any poetry in him, I might guess that he was preparing me for your appearance—your eyes, your cheekbones, your elegant manner of dress. But that young man is not poetry. He is all improperly punctuated prose. He meant something else."

"I think he might have meant that I have been somewhat privileged in my upbringing and also in my education, where I was fortunate to have excelled. I'm certain he would think that I am special on that account. But I don't feel it, really. Special, that is."

"Then you must work at it. Not to feel is always a mistake. I am special, and I feel it intensely. Generally, it is this understanding that gets me through the day. If you have difficulty feeling anything, you should begin with this phrase: 'I sense a sensation that defies the senses.' Say that."

"I sense . . . a sensation . . . that defies the senses," William spoke slowly and tentatively.

"Now look at me when you say it," Wilde said.

Standing only about two feet from him, William looked Oscar

Wilde in the eyes for the first time. He was astonished and amused to note, first of all, that Wilde's eyes, like the soul of the country he had come to conquer, were blue but with a haunting infusion of gray. The eyes seemed in possession, like the man himself, of a language, a message, a story, even, that could be spoken or at least read. But they seemed, too, like all eyes, immutably mute, pained by their silence, as if they belonged to a man quite the opposite of Wilde, a genius not of language but of gesture. As William prepared to repeat Wilde's words—a strange phrase that magically endowed the unfeelable, the insensible, with power—he thought the eyes emblems of the idea Wilde had commanded him to utter. Something in him trembled, but his voice was steadier this time. "I sense a sensation that defies the senses."

"Yes," said Wilde, breaking their visual connection. "The more you say it, the closer you will come to comprehending the evasive sensation—whatever it is—and, failing that, you will at minimum conjure boredom, which, while unpleasant, is not the same as or as bad as numbness." William hummed the sentence to himself again.

"Here is one of my trunks. You must come to know it intimately. I suppose if you *do* have even the slightest hint of portmanteau within you, it should come in handy in these relations. Carry on. Now I'm off to entertain Vail, which is to say, I shall be right back."

Alone in front of Oscar Wilde's trunk, William felt thoroughly inadequate. Oh, his father would know what to do now, but William did not. (He was suddenly penitent, thinking of his recent impertinence toward his father.) He had enjoyed the contact with Wilde and even with the lively, raucous group of reporters; he was certain he would be satisfied with those benefits of the job. But this unpacking and tending to the wardrobe would take some getting used to.

He stooped and turned the key in the trunk's lock. When he lifted the lid, he was met with splendor. A sea of color, the contents of the trunk belonged to a man who would disparage—if it proved too calm, too monotonous—something as wondrous as an ocean. William saw greens, purples, yellows, dark reds, and blacks mingling in the forms of silks, velvets, and satins. Looking at the garments, which seemed to writhe in their collective sensuality, he felt as if he were eavesdropping on some pagan orgy—no, as if he had been called to officiate the proceedings and disengage the bodies. He closed the lid. Wilde, not expecting those reporters, must have rifled through the trunk earlier to find that gray-green scarf he was wearing and that black velvet coat lined with a fabric of pink flowers against a dark red background (William had noticed), leaving behind the entangled mass of shirts, stockings, and the unrecognizable rest of what he had just beheld. Or maybe things had simply been tousled about during the trip. He knew his job was, as Wilde had said, to "sort" these things out, and he believed he could accomplish that; he had always kept a well-managed wardrobe of his own when he was away at school. Lifting the lid for a second time, he found that he was less startled by the spectral blur. Feeling more motivated and more hopeful, he decided upon a course of action. He let his hand sink into the mix of clothes and removed the first thing he felt—a yellow scarf. Remembering his promise to Baxter, he smiled. He would gather all of the scarves together on the bed and then find a drawer for them in the dresser against the wall to his right.

Wilde rushed back into the room. "I told you I would return soon and here I am—a tribute to Vail's predictability, not my own. That man views everything through a sheath, a veil of business and money. My *l'art pour l'art* is in a battle with his *l'art pour l'argent*. Vail. More like Veil, *V-e-i-l*. The man is a walking homophone. But then, so am I. What about you, Traquair?"

"I was just starting to gather the scarves."

"No, your name."

"Oh, well, my given name is William."

"A name you share with both my father and my brother. The former is dead, and the latter continually rejects my insistence that he live. As I am hoping for better luck with you, I shall call you by your surname. Traquair. Henceforth, you shall be Traquair. I hope you are prepared to assist me in every way. We are up against a mighty mountain of ignorance, I fear."

"I . . ." said *Traquair*, "shall do my best. But judging from your handling of those newspapermen, you will require very little support."

"There are but few men who can withstand the force of real eloquence, and they are the few who happen to possess it themselves. None, other than myself, was in the room today. Or if he was, he chose silence. But then the truly eloquent never choose silence. Quiet rooms fear me. I know this. I suppose it is moral support that I am asking of you. 'Moral support.' That phrase is a near oxymoron, what with much of accepted morality being so shockingly *in*supportable and so much of the support one truly desires being widely considered *im*moral."

"I believe in your cause, if that is what you mean. I took this appointment mainly because I admire your poetry and agree with your position on the importance of the arts."

"I'm glad to hear that. I should hate to be attended by a *known* enemy—it so spoils the subsequent surprise of treachery."

"I can assure you of my loyalty, Mr. Wilde."

"You know only my poetry and my reputation—fabrications, both. Swear your allegiance after you have heard me lecture."

"But I already have—here, this afternoon, in the short time I have known you. All that you say has the ring of pronouncement. Life seems your lectern."

Wilde squinted, as if to examine his valet much more closely than he had until this moment. Then he smiled and said, "I have a feeling we are to be great friends, Traquair. How about you, are you feeling anything as of yet? Have you been chanting?"

"Yes, and yes again."

"You say that well. The affirmative must taste good upon your tongue. But then, there is no word as sweet as yes—except, of course, no. The proof is in the phrasing of the question. We shall talk more later, and I shall try to ask you only questions that will offer your tongue the pleasure of answering sweetly. But at the moment, I must get on with writing my lecture—my actual lecture, the one that people are paying to hear me deliver less than a week from now. Chickering Hall has no seats remaining, Vail has just informed me. Now they are selling standing room—which will increase the revenues, but diminish the mystique. I shall offer the hungry American masses 'The English Renaissance.' Let us hope they have had a bite before arriving at the theater. If you need me, I shall be at the desk in the front parlor. You are getting on nicely with those scarves. Don't mind if they wrinkle. I always tie them anyway."

Traquair stopped his work and stood erect—it seemed the valetlike thing to do. "Thank you, Mr. Wilde," he said.

"Oscar" was the reply.

PHILADELPHIA

15 January 1882

Dear Baxter,

Thinking of your being there, a world away, I'm reminded of the thing that came as such a shock to me when we first parted for college: the starkness with which separation can expose how close two people really are. Some queer science must be developed to explain that paradox, this odd fraternity of distance and nearness, and if science is unequal to the challenge, then I suppose we must turn to the realm of art, which, of course, brings us to the news of the day—Oscar Wilde!

You cannot imagine what he is like, so I shall tell you. He is the most evocative man I have ever met. Everything he says is smart and elegant, even the naughty bits, which despite your demand for them, I shall not record at this writing. The first words I heard him say were: "Genius is always ostentatious." Everything else he has said and done in my presence has supported this thesis.

His first lecture was a week ago today before a large crowd of New York's best dressed and most curious. From my post backstage, I saw your father in a very good seat up front on the center aisle. He smiled throughout Wilde's program. What a happy man your father is. He reminded me of you, and he was wearing that tie you bought him for his birthday a few summers ago, the blue one with the little white dots. (Forgive my noting such minutiae, but my current station has, regrettably, awakened within me a once dormant haberdasher's instinct for sartorial detail. I fear the valet's vice of idle chatter may be

in my immediate future.) I remember how much he liked that tie
when you gave it to him. He must have been thinking of you in
wearing it.

Others smiled during the lecture as well—some, I believe, were
merely amused by Wilde's knee breeches—but I did not feel the
speech was received as well as it might have been, which is a pity
because Wilde said so many beautiful things. He even had more
words about Gilbert and Sullivan. I am certain you have already
heard his much-repeated blow to them: Caricature is the tribute
mediocrity pays to genius. At the lecture he said, "You have listened
to Patience for a hundred nights and have listened to me for only
one." The mere mention of the play brought laughter from what was,
on the whole, a subdued audience. He continued, "You have heard, I
think, a few of you, of two flowers called, erroneously, I assure you,
the food of aesthetic young men. Well, let me tell you: the reason we
love the lily and the sunflower, in spite of what Mr. Gilbert may tell
you, is not for any vegetable fashion at all. It is because these two
lovely flowers are in England the most perfect models of design, the
most naturally adapted for decorative art. Let there be no flower in
your meadows that does not wreathe its tendrils around your pillows,
no curving spray of wild rose or briar that does not live forever in
carven arch or window of marble."

He has said to me that this is to become his main theme,
decorative art. He has sensed already that Americans have very little
"patience," if you will, for l'art pour l'art. When he reached the end
of the lecture, his words very nearly made me cry—and I already
knew what he was going to say because he had read much of the essay
to me earlier that day in a rehearsal at the hotel. It was the perfect
ending: "We spend our days looking for the secret of life. Well, the
secret of life is art." Some applauded; many yawned. They yawned!
Could it be that we do not care to know the secret of life, that the
only thing each of us really wants to know is the secret of his own life?
Tomorrow we are to leave by train for Philadelphia. Then a few days
later we're off to Washington and Baltimore, before heading
northward to Albany, Boston, and other points. Send a note
addressed to home. We will be passing back through New York a
couple of times next month, and I shall look forward to the physical
strain and subsequent joy that come of deciphering your scribbling.

On the subject of scribbling, I shall relate a secret that undoubtedly will be out soon, as everything about Wilde, it seems, is ultimately revealed. Wilde has received so many requests for autographs that he does not have time to sign them all. One day he called me into the room in the hotel suite where he does his work, and he requested that I sit at the desk and copy out his signature a few times until I had sufficiently mastered it. Of course, after the first try I had already achieved a startlingly accurate forgery. As you must recall, I have been signing your name better than you since we were twelve. If your memory fails you, here it is:

So since that first day I copied Wilde's mark, I have signed cards, handkerchiefs, leaflets, programs, and even a few pictures—prints of those taken of Wilde by the photographer Napoleon Sarony. No one is yet the wiser except you. Of course, surrogate autographing is a common practice among the very famous; deception, at least at this level, is not a crime. When Wilde beckons me to perform this service, he calls me his secretary. I suppose, in some small way, I am. The secret secretary. I assure you it is even more charming than it sounds, charming enough to unchain even the lowly role of servant from its traditional constrictions. Mercifully, I am not my father. But then, I suppose, if I'm really honest with myself, neither is my father my father; he's not the vassal valet that I, in meaner moments, pretend him to be. He's cleverly reinterpreted the manservant as minor master, as you and I have sometimes admitted during our fairest turns at assessing the worth of our fathers. Is it his manumission of the menial that I, in ironically slavish biological duty, am repeating? Dear me, if so, am I my father after all?

I began by telling you that Wilde is the most evocative man around, which he is. And for him, evocation becomes a sublime vocation. For me, when one includes the full range of my responsibilities, adjusting for sheer delight, vocation is more like vacation. Wilde's cleverness, we may justly conclude, has cast itself and a spell upon me.

> *Terribly, shamefully happy,*
> *Ever yours,*
> *Billy*

Traquair lay dozing on the living room sofa of the suite he and Wilde were sharing in Philadelphia's Aldine Hotel. He was awaiting Wilde's return from a reception at the home of Mr. Robert Stewart Davis, but fatigue from the train ride and from organizing and moving all of the trunks and bags was taking its toll. While his will to consciousness wrestled with the need for rest, his mind kept its own steady, swift pace. Its fluidity blurred his thinking, the way the train's speed had blurred his vision earlier. On the Pullman car, seated at a window directly across from Wilde, he had looked out at New Jersey and Pennsylvania and had fallen into the meditative state into which train travel always ushered him. A reporter for the *Philadelphia Press* sat next to Wilde asking questions about his impressions of America. Wilde, whom Traquair knew to be exhausted from the rigors of New York City (they had even missed breakfast in the rush to meet the train), was more than generous to the man with his comments.

"The relations between countries change over time," Wilde had said. "England and America are no longer mother and daughter or father and son. And they aren't sisters or brothers or cousins even, though perhaps one day they will be. No—currently England and America are lovers. Great, great lovers. Notice how we are constantly and enthusiastically exchanging passionate kisses of commerce and culture. My Irish blood aside, my very presence here in America is evidence of this romance. What am I if not a kiss? One long English kiss?"

Traquair had wanted the reporter to leave so he could talk to Wilde. He wanted to repeat the phrase that his meditation on the countryside passing by rhythmically outside the window was whispering to him: *Travel moves me.* Wilde would have appreciated that. But the reporter had kept Wilde busy, and Traquair didn't know when or if he would find the right time to mention it. He was only remembering it now that he was weary, and his pre-sleep state was imitating serious contemplation. Sleep moves me, he thought. Then: No, that is not true. Trains move. Thought moves. Moving trains is hard work. *Trunks,* not trains. Moving trunks is hard work. Thought moves but does not move me. Yes, it does . . . but it is not what I mean moves me when I say trains move me. . . .

"Tra-quair!" Wilde's voice wound its way through the maze of Traquair's mind. "Please, help me . . . with these things."

Traquair opened his eyes to the dimly lit room, quickly identifying his surroundings, remembering his charge. He sprang up and began removing Wilde's olive-green coat, which was sumptuously lined with the pelt of otter, the same fur that stylishly cuffed the sleeves and sashed the collar. Traquair adored the coat and treated it with care.

"I do not blame you for being asleep. I will soon join you."

"How was the party?" Traquair asked, prompted by the whiff of wine Wilde had just breathed his way. "Who was there?"

"The same people who are at all parties—everyone and nobody." Wilde yawned dramatically. "There were senators, but President Arthur did not attend as Mr. Davis, the host, had hoped. Many literary types, including my own publisher Mr. Stoddart—if a publisher can be considered literary—but Walt Whitman, who is aging and does not get out much, was not present. Stoddart has promised to do what he can to arrange a private meeting. The ladies were impressive. Their beauty was surpassed only but completely by a golden Persian rug that topped Davis's piano. There was a lone Fernlini chair that seemed unhappy, so, briefly, I sat upon it."

As they laughed together, the scent of Wilde's inebriation again sprayed Traquair, whose face tightened a bit this time in response. Wilde, who had stumbled a little with merriment over his silly remark, said, "Don't mind me tonight. I was overcome at the party by my own wickedness—which was uncommonly selfish of me, as I usually reserve the influence of my wickedness for others. I am generous that way, aren't I, Traquair?"

"I have found you generous in every way, Mr. Wilde," Traquair said as he removed Wilde's jacket, which he folded neatly over his left arm on top of the coat. Traquair took Wilde's arm and guided him toward the bedroom.

"I thought we had an understanding about formalities when we are alone, Traquair—there are to be none." Traquair did not respond to this comment. He sat Wilde—*Oscar*—on the bed and carried the coat and jacket to the armoire, where he hung them with the wardrobe. When he returned to the bed, he found Oscar lying across it. Traquair was surprised at Oscar's condition, because Oscar, he had noted, could drink a great deal and retain the appearance of sobriety. It must have been the tiring train ride and the length of the day that had forced him to succumb to the effects of whatever he had imbibed this evening.

Traquair bent down and removed Oscar's shoes, two perfumed

patent leather slip-ons with decorative bows, faintly spiced with per-spiration. Oscar shuffled his feet and said, "I was fine until I walked into this room. No one else is aware of my unfortunate crash. We will not be embarrassed upon seeing the hotel staff tomorrow, not any more than usual, I mean." Oscar's eyes were closed when he asked, "Are you looking at me now, Traquair?"

"I am disrobing you," Traquair said. "Yes, I suppose I am looking at you."

"I mean my face. Are you staring at my face?"

"No, I am not. Not just now."

"I thought you were," Oscar said dreamily. "Look at me. Bear wit-ness to this: the sleeper's mask is impenetrable by the outside world, even as it is invisible to the sleeper himself."

"Yes, but you are not yet asleep."

"That remark proves my point, for surely I am now quite asleep, though you cannot see it—and I cannot see the mask that you read as consciousness."

"It is not your face but your talking that I read as a sign of your consciousness."

"Had you heard much of the conversation spoken at tonight's reception, you would know that talking has little to do with con-sciousness."

Traquair smiled widely, but stifled his laughter, so as not to disturb Oscar's waking sleep. He put the clothes away and hurried back to the bed to assist Oscar, who was struggling with the covers.

"Oh, thank you, Traquair. We haven't had any time to talk today. Did you enjoy the train ride?"

"I loved it. Thank you for asking. I was thinking about it before you returned, as I was lying on the sofa. I wanted to tell you something I had thought about on the train."

"What were you thinking on the train?"

"Well, as I was looking out the window and saw New Jersey rushing by, I became excited about being on this adventure, and a thought was delivered to me through the sensation of advancing so swiftly on the train, a simple phrase—'Travel moves me.'"

"Love-ly," said Oscar, drifting. "Would that I were . . . travel."

"Would that you were what? You are mumbling words now, and they are not coming out right. My mind was just doing that to me, too, when I was fighting sleep on the sofa. Go on off now. Say good night, Oscar."

"'Good night, Oscar.'"

"'Good night, *Traquair*.'" His voice rose for emphasis when he said his own name. But there was no response.

In the morning Traquair, who had slept in the second bedroom of the suite, was the first to rise. It was nearly half past ten, much later than when he usually woke. He was surprised no one had come to disturb them before now. Then it occurred to him that, while he had slept, there might have been a tapping at the door. He dressed, checked on Oscar, who was still resting soundly, and went downstairs, where he picked up the morning mail and the newspapers. He had just finished arranging for a late breakfast and tea, when he bumped into Vail in the lobby.

"Good morning, William." Vail's raised eyebrows put Traquair on guard.

"Good morning, Mr. Vail."

"I dropped by to visit Wilde earlier, but there was no answer at the door." Vail idly tugged at the lower edge of his vest, not with his usual nervousness, but with something more like confidence.

"Mr. Wilde is busy editing his lecture for this evening," Traquair lied.

"I did not know that was something one could do in one's sleep," said Vail, refusing to play along.

Embarrassed momentarily, Traquair rebounded quickly with "One can't. Wilde can."

"Touché. But I would like to see him sign autographs and talk to reporters in his sleep." When Vail said this he nodded toward a couple of well-dressed women having coffee in the lobby and a separate group of three men who were smoking cigarettes. The women were clearly Wilde watchers, and the men were reporters. "I'll leave the situation in your capable, officious hands, William. I'm off for a walk and then to a luncheon with some old friends. Good luck." As he walked away, he waved a hand to Traquair without turning around.

Traquair stepped behind a large potted tree to avoid being seen by the reporters, one of whom he recognized from the press corps that had questioned Oscar during yesterday's arrival at the Broad Street Station, and to reflect on his predicament. He knew he would have a busy day with autographing and arranging the clothes for tonight's lecture. And he was concerned about Oscar's need for sleep and, once he awoke, for quiet. Charged with agitation and resolve, Traquair let his eyes wander. Across the bustling but strangely quiet lobby, he spotted John, an energetic young man he had met here yesterday. John operated a small shoeshine stand outside the hotel, but he occasionally came inside to solicit customers. When their carriage had arrived in front of the Aldine yesterday, John had left a patron midshine and come over to Traquair as he was loading the luggage onto a large cart.

"Fine coat you got there, cuz," John had said, smiling, shaking Traquair's hand and lightly pinching the lapel of his camel's hair topcoat. "Someday you got to tell me your secret."

"What secret?" Traquair had asked.

"The secret bout how to get me one of them coats, brother!" John's hand had come down hard on Traquair's shoulder.

"Oh—Brothers, indeed. Brooks."

"Well, Brooks, like I said, that shole is one damn fine coat."

Traquair laughed and, aiming to clarify his identity, said, "William—I'm—"

"Willie Brooks, I'm John Everest. Thought I knew you from cross the way, but then I got close and realized I don't know no niggers with no style like you, no class like you. Pleased to meet you. I gotta get back to my customer, but I'mo see you later. I'm always around."

John had drifted back to his station, but not before shoving Traquair gently back in the direction of his own duties. Traquair had hesitated, though, entranced by John Everest. In the course of their brief conversation, John had aggressively initiated a handshake, patted his shoulder with an unearned familiarity, and slapped his back good-bye. There was something in his animated presence, in his singular physicality, that appealed to Traquair, and, too, Traquair had marveled at the way meeting a complete stranger had suddenly transformed him into someone new. For the moment he wasn't William Traquair but, quite thrillingly, Willie Brooks.

Now, before he could step out from his hiding spot behind the tree and raise his hand to wave to John, the gregarious young man had already smiled at him and was trotting his way.

"Shine, Willie?" he asked, glancing downward.

"No, thank you, John." Traquair quickly considered his new friend's glaringly inappropriate attire—wrinkled jacket and ankle-high trousers that bulged at the knees—but he was persuaded by John's genuineness, his nakedness of spirit, to proceed with the idea that had formed in his mind. "But, John, you know I could use your help."

"Sho, Willie. I could see from way over yonder that you needed something." John leaned toward Traquair conspiratorially, letting his shoulder ride into Traquair's.

"I was wondering if you knew of anyone who could watch the door to the rooms of the gentleman I'm working for. You remember Mr. Wilde, the man you saw me escorting yesterday. I'd do it myself, of course, but I have a great many other matters to attend to today. Do you know of anyone?"

"Well, watching doors is simple. It's the folks who wants to go through em who is the problem."

"Very true. But the job does pay."

"Paying done solved many a problem. Paying good, a many mo. How much?"

"For the right man, two dollars."

"Sho nuff? I'm feeling mighty right myself. What you think, Willie?"

Traquair put his hands on John's shoulders and said, "I think—well, I think you look mighty right as well."

John grazed a soft fist across Traquair's chin, and they turned and started walking up to the suite. "As you say," Traquair explained, "it's simple. No one is supposed to know the exact room we're in, but they will find out. I stood at the door myself in New York just last week. Few will challenge your authority if you stand firm. Just tell the person presenting his card that Mr. Wilde is not receiving guests today because he is too busy. Gather the cards, and I'll get them from you at various times during the day. If anyone does challenge you, you can knock on the door, and I will take care of it." They arrived at the main door to the suite. "Do you think you can handle things out here, John?"

"Don't worry, Willie," John said. "I deals with white folks for a living, too—speaking of that—"

"Oh," Traquair said, reaching into his pocket. "Here's one dollar now. You'll get the other at the end of the day."

"Fine, fine." John and Traquair looked up and saw two men walking down the hall toward them. John said, "You go on in and take care of the gentleman. I'll handle this situation." Then he whispered to Traquair, "See, you and me's in the same game."

"I suppose we are in the same game," Traquair responded. "But I've only recently begun to play. I have a suspicion, John, that you are by far the superior player."

John smiled. "Oh, I'm not bad!"

Traquair opened the door quickly to escape the reporters. He stopped and placed his ear to the door to hear John say in a different tone of voice and with a more labored enunciation, "Master Wilde is too busy to recept today." Traquair grinned, waiting to see if he would need to intervene, but there was no knock at the door. He shrugged with pleasure at having relieved himself of this task and went into the bedroom.

Oscar was stretching and yawning when he entered. "There you are. I was calling for you."

"I went downstairs. Here are the papers," he said, handing the *Press* and the *Record* to Oscar. "You seem much better this morning."

"If I am indeed better, please don't tell anyone. People expect so much of me already."

"I only mean that you have sobered up since last night."

"Oh, that. A regrettable display. Please don't tell anyone about that, either—not because I fear embarrassment, but because people are bored by stories that reveal the dangers of pleasure, unless told by the most vicious and skilled liars or by saints. I'd rather not contribute to boredom or to the antipleasure movement."

"I have arranged for you not to be bothered all day. There's a nice young man guarding the door."

"How thoughtful of you, Tra."

"I ran into Vail downstairs. He was giving me a hard time about your still being in bed. Not that I told him so. He guessed it on his own."

"You didn't hit him, did you?"

"No."

"Pity," said Oscar. "If he starts in with me I might. Besides, why shouldn't one sleep until the afternoon if one cares to? I can assure you that the inferiority of the morning hour is confirmed by the mediocrity of breakfast. Oh—"

"Tea is on the way," Traquair anticipated.

"Tea. You've read my mind. At least the only thing in my mind this morning that's worthy of your perusal. 'T.' A single letter. Oh—"

"Yes, I do have the mail. Here are those that will matter to you." He handed a few envelopes to Oscar, who hummed a high note of appreciation. "I'll work on the rest later. Mostly autographs. I noticed a couple of requests for more flower wit. Your rose remark is not without its thorny repercussions."

"Oh, you know what to send them. What's that one thing we put together about the sunflower?"

"The sunflower emits no true light, but its radiance, nevertheless, forces our orbit."

"That's it. Did you say that or did I?" Oscar asked.

"It was something of a collaboration."

"Who could have guessed that in nonromantic matters, partnership would be so desirable?"

"We also said, 'While the sun flowers the heavens, sunflowers are heavenly.'"

"I like that less but, as we've said it, it's our duty to say it again. Use it if need be. You should have those words imprinted on some cards and sign them in advance to save yourself time with these tedious requests, Traquair."

"I don't find them tedious at all. To tell you the truth, I like the work very much."

"Don't tell me the truth, Traquair. If a man can't trust his own friends to lie to him, to whom is he to turn? Besides, there's so little mystery left in the world as it is, and truth is the death of mystery."

Three quick knocks sounded at the door. "Must be the tea," Traquair said, starting toward the door. "I'll be right back. Tea certainly has mystery in it, does it not?"

Traquair heard Oscar shouting to him, "Definitely, there is mystery in tea."

Traquair opened the front door and gladly accepted the cart with a tray of tea and biscuits from the young man making the delivery. When he noticed the reporters from the lobby trying to get his attention around John's outstretched arms, Traquair tried to hurry back inside. "Say, there! Hey!" they called to him.

Traquair rolled the cart just inside the door and turned to face the men. John stood to the side, looking defeated. "Yes?" Traquair said.

"Aren't you the one who was traveling with Wilde yesterday?" asked a reporter that Traquair did not remember seeing at the train station.

"How can I help you?" he asked, pulling the door behind him almost completely closed.

"Well, some of us have deadlines to meet and this fellow here says Wilde is busy and can't 'recept' today. Is this so?"

"That is correct."

"Well, it may be so, but it certainly isn't correct."

Traquair laughed, the other two reporters joining in, then said, "What John's words lack in grammatical proficiency, they more than make up in clarity and, as I've said, validity. You might ponder that on your way back downstairs. Good day, gentlemen. John will take your cards, if you care to leave them."

The men, apparently not caring to leave their cards or not having any, turned away and walked down the hall silently, as if they might indeed be pondering Traquair's words. John approached Traquair. "Damn, Willie. I don't know what you said, but I guess you told them a thing or two. Or three. Look like you not so bad yourself."

"I probably should not have done that," Traquair said as he opened the door to the suite. "But it was a more reasonable response than the other I was considering."

"What was that?"

"A punch."

"Unless you can punch like I just seen you talk, you might oughta stick to the talking. Besides, it looked like a knockout to me, anyway. Good work."

"Thank you, John. Coming from you—a man in the same game, as it were—those words have real meaning."

John nodded to Traquair with a puzzled look on his face, then asked, "Willie, what's your story anyway? Where you from?"

"New York."

"Ain't no niggers from New York. Where you *from*? I mean your people. Where they from?"

"Really, New York is where I've lived my whole life. My father and my mother have lived there their whole lives . . . I believe." Traquair felt suddenly flushed. His father's reticence over the years had left him embarrassingly uninformed.

"You *believe*?"

"Yes. That is my understanding." Mercifully, the stress of his mortification forced the memory of a fragment, an elliptical reference delivered once by a tipsy Henry Traquair to a twelve-year-old William. "Well—my father once told me about his brother, who is in the West some place, but I have never met him. Those are my people, as I know them."

"You must got some people you don't even much know about. You do kinda look like somebody I seen before. That's really why I stopped you yesterday, remember? I'm thinking we *must* know some of the same folks. You know ain't no niggers really strangers. I gots people and friends in Washington, Memphis, Atlanta, Mississippi, New Orleans, places like that, all down there still. Most of em trying to get up here. But you ain't from the South. You ain't got nobody down there. Hell, you ain't got nobody much of nowhere that you know of. Where y'all going with this road show when y'all leave here?"

Traquair was slow to answer, thinking about all the people he didn't have. "Well, all over, really. Washington, Baltimore, then back up north to Boston, various parts of New York, even out west."

"Befo y'all head out, you should go over that list of them places with me real good. I knows people everywhere, some kin, some not. I'll give you names of some folks in them towns you going to, and you can write em down. They'll show you a good time, and you might need some help sometime like you did today with me. You going south?"

"I believe we might get there this summer."

"That's where I can really help you out. I likes you, Willie. I likes the way you handles yourself. I think you gon make something out yourself."

"Let's hope it isn't a fool."

"Fools is underrated. I done knowed many and liked em all. Even so, that's not exactly how I sees you. You oughta make yourself out to be like that man you work with. What he is? A lecture? That ain't nothing but a talker. You can be that. Be a nigger one of them. Like Douglass. I sees it in you, the way you just talked out here."

"Traquair . . ." It was Oscar calling from the other room. "Where are you?"

"I'll be right there," Traquair yelled back to him.

"Don't let me keep you from your gentleman," John said. "But don't forget to get that list of them places together."

"I won't. Thank you, John."

"Thank *you*, cuz." John winked his right eye at Traquair, a new gesture in his repertoire of interaction, which, despite its less bodily emphasis, released the warmth of a hug.

Traquair went inside, pushing the tray in front of him. "Here I am!" he said loudly to Oscar.

"At last," said Oscar. "There was no need to press your point about the mystery that lies in tea by leaving me waiting. I thought I conceded just as much. But while you've been away, I've discovered that, in complement, at the heart of 'mystery' there rests a very vital 'T.' "

The next night Traquair and John sat sipping wine at the writing table in the living room of the hotel suite. Earlier, Traquair had watched Oscar deliver his lecture to a large but largely unimpressed audience at Horticultural Hall and then be whisked away by Vail, Colonel Morse, and Richard D'Oyly Carte himself, who was in town for the occasion, setting out for yet another reception in Oscar's honor. Traquair and Oscar had exchanged glances outside the hall, and he read Oscar's sharply arching eyebrows to say *Here we go again—don't wait up for me*. He had tossed back a perch-lipped, squinty-eyed *Go easy on the vodka*, and headed back to the hotel.

He had arranged to meet John after the lecture, and his newfound friend had been waiting for him in the lobby when he returned. John's enthusiasm upon seeing him (Willie, Willie—no one called him Willie!) delighted Traquair. And again he was fascinated at how something as simple as that could expand his notion of himself. He understood that, to John, he was not William Traquair, the bright, handsome, well-educated New Yorker. Nor was he Willie Brooks—he had gently cleared up the matter of his name already. No, to John, Traquair was, as Vail had put it, "a special case." Yet, whereas Vail's use of that phrase led swiftly to comic, portmanteau-ish dehumanization, John's appreciation of Traquair led to backslaps, shoulder-to-shoulder intimacies, imaginary hugs—in short, to an intensification of his humanity. As he sat readying himself to write out the list of acquaintances that John had promised to provide, he hoped the wine and the company might further endow him with the attributes, whatever they were, of a Willie. But just then, John disturbed Traquair's burgeoning romance with the idea that one could and should cultivate new selves.

"I been thinking, Willie, and I just don't know," John said, pouring himself a second glass of wine, the first having disappeared before Traquair could get settled at the table with his pen and paper.

As he wrote and underlined the heading *John Everest's Associates* at the top of the loose sheet of coarse white paper on the table between them, Traquair said, "What do you mean?"

"What do *I* mean? What do *that* mean?" John pointed at the words Traquair had just written. "That which you just wrote down. See, I don't know what you just wrote cause I can't read. And a whole lotta my friends can't read, neither. They rough, Willie, some of em. Not crazy or dangerous or nothing—they just not like you. They like me. That's what I mean, Willie. You and this man Wilde, y'alls got culture and class. So I been thinking, a fella like yourself don't want nothing to do with such folks, don't *need* to have nothing to do with em anyway. My friends . . . hell, I even got some people in my own family who I don't really think it would be right for you to know. So I been thinking, let's just let it be you and me who met like this and who was quick friends for some reason and leave it like that.

"Wasn't that nice how we met? Me thinking you was somebody I knew, but knowing really that I didn't know you, but that I just had to meet you cause it's not every day you see somebody like you. And then it was just like I knowed you my whole life, even though, shit, I ain't never met nobody like you before, I mean a real educated Negro man. But it was like I'd knowed you my whole life. I could tell you felt like that too, the way you trusted me to help you out yesterday. I could tell. And some kinda way in my mind, being round you like that, like this, just make a nigger feel like with a little luck he coulda been you. You know? Cause you is something and you gon be something else! And you don't need the characters I know in your life to be whatever you gon be. So I'm thinking, let's just let it be you and me and leave it like that." John drank what little remained in his second glass of wine and poured a third.

"I've been thinking, too, John," Traquair said, putting down his pen. "Well, not thinking so much as feeling, sensing things, as my friend Mr. Wilde has recently encouraged me to do. It is a practice that, in fact, is quite liberating. It may be that only after the mind has been emancipated from the tyranny of reason that we can finally sense the touch of truth. Truth may be purely a matter of the heart and not the head. And what I am sensing—what my heart is telling me— is that one day I shall look back on things and conclude that even though I set forth from New York by train a few days ago, my travels with Mr. Wilde did not begin in earnest until I met you. And so, you see, to continue to move forward purposefully, I must gather from you these references and in due course set out to make the most of them in the months ahead. If your friends share any of your delightful qualities, John, meeting them, like meeting you, will make me anew. Strange, but I am certain that if you deny me this opportunity, you will some- how derail my destiny."

"Boy, boy, boy," John said, palming the back of Traquair's head and shaking it gently. "You is something! And I damn sho want my friends to meet you, too, Willie. I want em to know you a person, a real flesh- and-blood person, not just something I made up. And to know you my friend."

As they worked together on the list, John glanced away whenever Traquair put his pen to the page. There was a moment when their eyes met and John said, "I can count ten times as good as most folks can, so I thinks that makes me even. A lotta people can tell a 'A' from a 'B,' but you'd be surprised how many people don't know what ten percent of nothing is."

WASHINGTON

MY DEAR *Carte* . . . Traquair watched, over Oscar's shoulder, the swift, steady movement of Oscar's hand begin a letter in its tight scrawl. Though he had mastered Oscar's signature, he still found Oscar's handwriting difficult to decipher. Usually he needed to know the context of the communiqué to grasp it verbatim—which today was the case. He knew that Richard D'Oyly Carte was to be the recipient of this letter and that the letter would be tinged with anger, expressing as it would Oscar's great disappointment in the overall management of the tour. Vail would come off badly, Oscar had implied to Traquair before he settled at the desk to begin composing the letter. Oh, there would be repercussions, Traquair thought. Turning to walk away, leaving Oscar to his task, he glanced back down and saw Oscar staining the gray paper with *Another such fiasco as the Baltimore business and I think I would stop lecturing.*

Entering his bedroom in the Arlington Hotel, Traquair looked across the room and saw on his desk a copy of the newspaper cartoon that had contributed to Oscar's uncharacteristically glum disposition. Traquair acquired a similar mood himself, his walk to the desk feeling more like a trudge, his descent into his chair, a slump. He sat staring at the illustration, which he had torn from the pages of the *Washington Post* the day before yesterday. Above an accurate drawing of Oscar holding a sunflower was an apelike rendering of "the Wild Man of Borneo" holding a ball or an orange. These offending words wrapped the images: "How far from This [the man from Borneo] to This [Oscar]?" Below those words and images, Traquair read:

We present in close juxtaposition the pictures of Mr. Wilde of England and a citizen of Borneo, who so far as we have any record of him, is also Wild, and judging from the resemblance in feature, pose and occupation, undoubtedly akin. If Mr. Darwin is right in his theory, has not the climax of evolution been reached and are we not tending down the hill toward the aboriginal start-ing point again? Certainly, a more inane object than Mr. Wilde, of England, has never challenged our attention, whose picture, as given herewith, is a scrupulously correct copy of a photograph put out with his sanction and which may be seen in all public windows. Mr. Wild of Borneo doesn't lecture, however, and that much should be remembered to his credit.

The cruel cartoon had appeared even before Oscar's lecture last night; the newspaper had never given him a chance. Not even Gilbert and Sullivan had struck such a blow. Caricature was homage. But what was insult? Envy, perhaps? Whatever it was, it had wounded Oscar and left him furious with the way Colonel Morse and Vail were handling his public affairs; he had to inform D'Oyly Carte that he thought the situation grave, thus the letter.

Traquair wasn't sure why he had kept the *Post* drawing, but the thought of coming across it years from now in the scrapbook he was keeping sealed his decision to be rid of it now. (In his mind he had already begun to construct a bed of nostalgia, a mattress filled with his favorite moments from the tour, upon which the old man in himself would one day recline.) With the precision of a seamstress, he worked his fingers quickly, folding the clipping twice, tearing it into small pieces. He thumbed the shreds into the wastebasket like lint or stray strands of thread, and then he sat down on the bed.

Oscar came to his door. "I'm done," he said softly.

"Are you pleased with it?" Traquair asked, referring to the letter.

"It's difficult to find pleasure in something one knows will displease another, but the letter I have written makes my point. I told D'Oyly Carte that if Morse or the disaster that is Vail cannot prove more com-petent, I shall discontinue the tour. Many of the things you do, Vail should be doing. Vail cannot do them, of course, because one cannot do anything if one is not present. I didn't mention how indispensable you've been. I don't want Carte to think he can use your abilities to let

Vail off the hook. Did you read that awful note Vail slipped under the door offering his boring apologies? It contained one misspelling and two misplaced apostrophes. In a world so filled with possessive personalities, it's odd that no one knows what to do with the apostrophe." Oscar's voice slowed. He sighed. "If you are asking me whether my letter to Carte pleases me aesthetically—no. Aesthetically, the letter is a failure. How could it not be? Good letter-writing requires congeniality among the head, the heart, and the hand. Today I know no friendliness within or without. Today we have no friends, Traquair. All are our enemies. I have wanted fame and I have got it, but how quickly it turns traitor and becomes notoriety. The price one pays for fame is one's obscurity—a seemingly worthless commodity because it is of true value only to the notorious, who, alas, have no real access to it. Today I know this." Then, Oscar brightened a bit. "Not that I flatter myself by saying that today I have truly achieved notoriety. I have not. After all, one must reserve some accomplishments for one's later years."

"Still, with your mood the way it is, I shall go out today," said Traquair, "and give you privacy, which is at least momentary obscurity."

"If you choose. But your presence, Traquair, is no imposition upon my solitude. The contrary is the case. As I sat struggling to write that letter, I was comforted by the thought that you were here. I knew that you were in sympathy with my situation and even sensed that you were concentrating on my troubles. When I wrote to Carte, 'I must never be left again—' a sensation, one of those that one can sense even though it defies the senses, came over me and I knew that my complaint on this point was false. I *felt* something. Now I know that it was you, Traquair. You have not left me; I have not this entire tour been truly alone. I understand that you are being paid to be here, but that fact has not kept Vail from abandoning me. Your presence was the unknown sensation that proved my words false—no small accomplishment."

"I shall at least take the letter to be posted."

"Yes, please do. And take your walk as well. I shall try to rest." Oscar walked over to one of the windows in Traquair's room. "It looks cold out. It may snow. Take a scarf and hat. Wouldn't snow be nice?"

"Yes, it would be quite nice."

"In London, if the sky looked like this it would surely rain. But raindrops lack the vanity of snowflakes, and this carelessness lessens their aesthetic value. Weather is more important than we admit. Climate forecasts temperament. Yes, snow is in order." Oscar turned and looked at Traquair, who had picked his coat up from the sofa and was putting it on. "Speaking of vanity, Traquair. It is a quality you must cultivate. You have such rare skin, your complexion, I mean. You must attend to it better. Do not let winter have her way with you. People will tell you not to care so much for your own appearance. But, as they are wont to be, people are wrong. They'll tell you it's self-indulgence or the crime they call vanity. But remember: Nothing defends beauty as does vanity. And acts of vanity, in their maniacal defense of beauty, are not acts of self-indulgence but heroic acts of altruism. So on your way out into the cold, you must visit my table and use some of my cream."

Traquair had stopped buttoning his coat. He had not thought about his dry skin since he had stepped out of the carriage with Vail on the first day he had met Oscar, which meant that Oscar had seen him this way for more than three weeks. His tactful, instructive way of mentioning that Traquair's skin was ashen was kind, but it did not assuage Traquair's embarrassment. With a studied casualness, Traquair resumed buttoning his coat. "Of course," he said. "I appreciate your generosity."

"If vanity is altruism, then generosity, too, is something else," Oscar said as he sat down gently on Traquair's bed. "Go now. The letter is on the desk."

"I'll take care of it," Traquair said. He went into Oscar's bedroom and sat down at the dressing table. In the mirror he examined his dry skin. Among the bottles of cologne and other toiletries, he found the cream he had seen Oscar apply to his own face. He opened the burgundy-colored jar and sniffed its contents. The white lotion was odorless, which disappointed Traquair; he had hoped for that subtle fragrance that Oscar sometimes sported, but that, he guessed, was probably the treasure held in the small, deep green, bulblike bottle to his left. He tapped the little flask playfully with his hand and, in the mirror, saw himself smiling. Then he dipped his finger into the jar of cream and began applying the soothing mixture as he had seen Oscar do. When he put his finger in for the third or fourth time, he noticed his hands, which were also dry, and he let out a little groan of distress. Before closing the jar, he rubbed some of the ointment first between his palms and then all over his hands. He was not going to wait for Oscar to comment on his hands, and from now on he would attend to them and to his face daily. Another quick look in the mirror told him he was all right now, and he headed out to drop the letter at the front desk and to see the nation's capital.

Traquair strolled down Vermont Avenue in front of the Arlington Hotel and then turned right onto H Street. Though he had his gloves on, he instinctively put his hands into the pockets of his bulky, warm overcoat. His right hand caught the edge of a folded sheet of paper, which he removed from his pocket. Opening it, he found the list of names of John's friends. At the top of the list were the names of men who lived in Washington. Traquair's eyes scanned down: Gus Holmes ("Gutter Gus"), Otis West ("O Tee"), Nathaniel Carmichael ("Nat Turner"). Next to each name and nickname, as John had dictated, Traquair had written the most accurate addresses John could remember. They weren't addresses, really, only phrases—"in front of Crystal's store on M Street" for Gus and "corner of Twenty-first and P streets" for Otis and Nathaniel—not home addresses, but cartographic clues, like longitudes and latitudes, leading one not to people and their residences but to destinations. Gus, Otis, and Nathaniel might have been geographical landmarks or possibly treasures, it occurred to Traquair. He had sudden visions of Baxter dashing out into the crisp London air for a walk past Buckingham Palace and running up the front steps of the British Museum, and he was overcome by his own rush of the adventurer's curiosity, the compulsion to visit and to discover.

At the corner of Sixteenth and H streets, he stopped and looked around in search of a friendly face he could approach for directions. His manner drew the attention of a man with a black leather briefcase, who stopped and asked, "Are you lost?"

"Not yet," Traquair said. "I'm staying there at the Arlington, but I'm trying to find my way to either of these two locations." He was pointing to the paper in his hand but, he noticed after a pause, the man was not looking at the notes.

"At the Arlington?" the man asked Traquair with something like disbelief in his voice.

"Yes. I'm traveling with a gentleman." Traquair almost stopped his explanation there, but could not resist elaborating for the man's benefit. "Oscar Wilde."

"Oh, really! I was at Lincoln Hall last evening for the lecture. Sad to say I was quite disappointed. Oscar Wilde is no Bob Ingersoll, which I suppose is unfair of me to say, but I did pay to see Wilde and I must admit I expected more. Ingersoll's agnosticism runs circles around your man's aestheticism. Even so, that awful thing in the *Post* on Sunday was trash. No doubt he's seen it?"

"Unfortunately," Traquair said.

"Well, do offer him my sympathy. These papers will do anything for attention. He must keep his head up. Washington is happy to have seen him."

"I will certainly let him know," Traquair said, without the slightest intention of offering Oscar a stranger's condolences. "Now—"

"Very good. Now I'm off," the man said, tapping his hat. And before Traquair could call out to him, he had strutted away.

Traquair decided to walk another block in the same direction he had been going. About halfway down the block, he saw a Negro woman heading slowly toward him. He waved to her with the paper in his hand. "Hello," he said. "I'm hoping you can assist me with finding my way."

"I'll try. Where're you going?"

He glanced at the paper then said, "I'm looking for Crystal's store."

"I know that place. If you walk back to Sixteenth, turn left and walk up to M, you would be right there."

"Wonderful. Thank you." Traquair started to walk away.

"Wait a minute," the woman called to him. "One thing, though. Crystal's is closed. I mean it's closed down for good."

"Oh. Well, then," he opened the sheet of paper again, "can you direct me to this corner?" He was pointing to the intersection where John thought the men named Otis and Nathaniel would be.

The woman raised her eyebrows. "Now that's a walk that'll warm you up. Keep going like you're going over to Twenty-first. At about Nineteenth you'll run into Pennsylvania, but don't let that bother you. Follow it over two more blocks and make a right at Twenty-first, and then just walk, walk, walk up to P. What you looking for on that corner? It might be gone, too."

"I certainly hope not. Thank you again."

Traquair followed the woman's instructions. At Pennsylvania and Twenty-first he saw a beautiful park a couple of blocks up ahead but resisted the distraction. Maybe he would stop there on his way back. It was only about three in the afternoon now, and he expected there to be plenty of daylight when he returned. He made the turn onto Twenty-first and continued to walk, walk, walk. When he crossed N Street, he grew excited at the notion that he was only two short blocks away from the spot where he might find John's friends; he experienced the same sense of wonder he had felt just before arriving at the train stations in Philadelphia and Washington, the thrill of almost being there. He had walked a longer distance than he had anticipated, but his legs were still moving briskly, having acquired an independent propulsive rhythm along the way. The little wine-induced prophecy he had shared with John came back to him, and he thought, faintly and instinctively revisiting that state of mild intoxication, that in life one travels upon invisible rails toward mostly unknown destinies. But then sometimes one knew—and now some whistle in his heart announced his imminent approach to one such stop.

Despite the cold of this late January day, two men indeed were standing at the corner to which he had been directed. They were in conversation, but Traquair, propelled by an unusual audacity that was fueled by a remarkable certainty (John had not given him a description of Otis and Nathaniel, but his instincts told him that surely they were the men who stood just a few yards in front of him), broke from all of his well-learned rules of decorum and interrupted the two strangers. "Excuse me. But I have a strong feeling that I know who you two men are." The men, who were in their late thirties or early forties, looked at each other with something like guilt on their faces, as if Traquair were a detective who had them cornered on an entirely valid charge. Traquair recognized their fear, so he widened his smile in hopes of calming them. "What I mean to say is, are you gentlemen"—he glanced down at his notes to remind himself of their full names—"Otis West and Nathaniel Carmichael?" Again the men exchanged suspicious glances. Traquair finally added, "Your friend John Everest from Philadelphia recommended that I look you up."

The men smiled at last. The short one spoke up, "I'm Otis and this is Nat, and why didn't you come right out and say you knowed John, mister? Niggers don't need no more surprises in this lifetime!" Otis and Nat laughed.

Traquair, grinning with embarrassment, said, "I'm sorry, but please forgive my clumsiness—which is surely due to my lack of practice at so brazenly approaching people I do not know. I offer this not as an excuse but merely an explanation. Additionally, I was very glad to see you here, as John had predicted you would be, and that excitement no doubt added to my bad form."

Otis howled loudly, then yelled through a chuckle, "Nigger, I ain't heard no apology like that since I had to answer to Lou-Ella on my wedding night! Things didn't go quite the way I had planned—not from a lack of practice like you, but mainly cause I'd been practicing too much. You remind me of myself, son." They all laughed again. "What's your name, boy?"

"Traquair . . . William."

"Well, Willie, if John is running with the likes of you up there in Philadelphia, he musta figured out a whole lot more than he knowed when he shipped his scrawny behind out of Washington."

"Ain't that the truth," Nat confirmed.

"You a regular Frederick Douglass," Otis said to Traquair.

"Oh, no, that compliment is too lavish for me even to consider accepting. But don't let my modesty deter you. Every man is due the luxury of his own opinions."

"See—that's what I'm talking bout. Just like Douglass. Damned if I know what *you* saying either. But the words is pretty enough to let you know they got something to em. That's a gift, Willie. Ain't it a gift, Turner?"

"Like frankincense and myrrh," Nat responded, answering, Traquair couldn't help but notice, to a different name.

"Now, nigger, don't go getting all poetic just because this young boy is here talking all good. Just nod your head like usual. *You* ain't no Douglass."

"Didn't say I was. I was just clarifying. Frankincense and myrrh, they's gifts. Famous gifts."

"Yeah, from two thousand years ago. To Jesus. From some wise men. This boy ain't no Jesus. Douglass ain't no Jesus. And they gift is from God."

"You the one said one time that Douglass was a savior."

"You's a damn lie! I ain't never said no such stupid thing. I said he was like a Moses, the way he freed his people. That's what I said. Don't go missaying my words." Otis tugged at Traquair's coat sleeve and then whispered, "You can see why I done nicknamed him Nat Turner. He

like to revolt, too. It's a good instinct. But this Nat ain't no more successful than the other one." Traquair suppressed his laughter, but his
face was lit with amusement. "Come on with us, Willie, around the
way here to the little spot. You can get a little taste of something to
warm you up. So you really friends with that wayward ass Johnnie . . ."

As Traquair followed Otis and Nat, they talked about John, who,
Otis admitted (and Nat confirmed), wasn't so much wayward as he was
"out of his way." Otis asked, "What the hell is he doing shining shoes
in Philadelphia? A nigger can do that anywhere. And if he's out there
looking for love, it ain't none of my business, but he might want to start
looking right here at home. . . ." "Kinda lost" was the way Nat put it,
which made Traquair a little sad; he had failed to detect any disqui-
etude in John. When Otis asked, Traquair explained the nature of his
travels, but the men seemed little interested in this topic. The steadiness of their steps indicated that they were eager to reach "the little
spot."

Finally, they came to a narrow road that bore no markings. Near the
end of this street, hidden by a thick cluster of trees, stood what
appeared to be a small house, outside of which lingered a few men asking for coins. Inside, the place was something more than a house. Lit
by only a few candles, the dark room they entered held about twenty
men who stood around drinking, smoking, and talking loudly in groups
of three and four. There was a small table at a back corner where a
woman poured drinks of whiskey in glasses the size of inkwells and collected money. To this woman's left there was a door that apparently led
to other areas within the house. After Traquair's vision gained lucidity,
he noticed that one group of men in the room consisted of three well-
dressed white gentlemen. The odd reality of their presence in a social
setting seemingly arranged for and dominated by Negroes shifted his
mood from mere curiosity to wonder, and he understood that he had
been guided into an uncharted cove where anything could happen. An
agitation of his blood warmed him, and he was about to reach up to
touch the side of his face with his hand when Otis shoved him roughly
through the crowd to the table where the woman with the whiskey sat
on a high stool. "Hey, Mae!" Otis yelled. "Give us three."

"I don't give nothing away," said Mae, pouring their drinks. "You
know that, O Tee."

"You know what I mean, Mae," Otis said. Then he elbowed

Traquair. "That's a lil joke between me and Mae. Give her some change, Willie, before she stops smiling."

"Hmph," Nat grunted. "O Tee, you know damn well Mae ain't smiled since befo the war." Mae looked sharply at Nat, but then she let out a little laugh.

Traquair asked, "How much?"

"Seventy-five cents," said Mae, sharing a quick blink with Otis that Traquair couldn't help noting, but he dropped the money into Mae's outstretched palm without comment or hesitation. They picked up their drinks, and Otis led the way to an area against the wall to their right.

"It's a small crowd today," Otis said, after sipping his drink. "Tuesdays is the slowest day in here, and it's still early. You showed up on a good day, Willie. Some days you can't even get in here. Right, Nat?" Nat nodded but did not speak.

"What is the name of this club?" Traquair asked.

"It ain't got no name, and you sure can't call it no club," Otis smirked.

"Yeah," Nat spoke up. "Mae won't allow you to call it Mae's. She says it's just a house."

"That's right," Otis said. "It's just a house, Willie. You understand?"

"Yes, a house but not a home," Traquair said, finding something to say, but not truly understanding. Then the door to the back of the house opened and two young, disheveled men came out. The depths of the hallway or room out of which they appeared were too dark for him to see into, but a feminine hand with a lacy wrist extended out into the comparatively well-lit front room and waved good-bye to the boys. In the brief time it took for the hand to grip the doorknob and pull the door closed, Traquair, with regard to the true nature of this "house," gained an architectural clarity, much as one would, quickly, in the right light, be able to distinguish a cute cottage from a shanty or a shack. He had heard about such buildings, such establishments, but he had not been in one until now.

"Walter!" Mae shouted, and a tall, balding Negro approached her, slid his hand into hers, and then went through the back door. Traquair watched Mae dip her fingers into the crevice of her bosom and then serve a skinny man in a black derby and bright yellow tie one of her glass-thimble specials.

"Drink up, Willie!" Traquair heard Otis shout to him from what seemed a great distance. He obliged his new friend's command, but the whiskey barely impressed his sense of taste. Perhaps the potency of the liquor was questionable, but more likely he had suffered a momentary diminution of all his faculties. This happened to him whenever he was faced with startling new circumstances or when he was concentrating on solving even the simplest mathematical problem—either of which could have been the cause of this present numbing, for Traquair had become absorbed in the shocking atmosphere of this seemingly non-descript, nameless house, even as he had consciously begun to move his strained gaze from man to man, customer to customer, counting his turn.

Otis and Nat, he soon realized, were in the house merely for the liquor and the scent of sin, which, if this room gave fair indication, was a decidedly quaint yet predictably intoxicating aroma, a soft mingling of various tobaccos and overripe but still edible fruit. Otis spared Traquair the difficulty of answering the question of whether he wanted to make full use of the services of the house and arranged with Mae— not nearly indiscreetly enough for Traquair's sensibilities (Otis had grown more and more expressive with each drink, and his talk with Mae had come after his third)—for Traquair to be placed on the wait-ing list to enter the back rooms. When Mae yelled, "Willie!" Traquair did not respond immediately, but Nat and Otis both nudged him, promising to wait until he returned.

"From the look in your eye," Otis said, "I don't think we gon be waiting too long! Huh, Natty!"

"I done struck matches I knew would last longer!" Nat joked, and Otis slapped his arm, letting out a wheezing snicker. By now, under the whiskey's influence, even Otis was laughing at what Nat had to say.

Following Otis's instructions, Traquair went to Mae to deposit what he felt certain was a rate reserved for the wealthy and the gullible, but he didn't care; when he rubbed hands with her, his fingers opened like petals in spring. Then, noticing a mole near the right side of her upper lip, he half heard, half lip-read Mae say, tossing her head toward the back door, "Charlotte." He slowly walked away and, as he'd seen the other men do, slipped through the entrance into the darkness.

On the other side of the door Traquair knew a sudden calm, the equanimity that was his normal disposition. Perhaps if his chastity had been all along more of a nuisance, if his struggle to maintain it had been more demanding, he might have developed an association with his virginity that would have made it impossible for him to dispense with it so impulsively. But such had not been the case. His celibacy had been silent, painless, and comfortable, as if it were his natural state. Lust had been foreign to him. Sure, he had known an occasional swelling of both body and spirit, but those instances had had no instigation that he had sensed other than a general strike from nature. Sometimes things had burst; sometimes not. Either way, actual lust had certainly played little or no part at all. His desire had known no point of departure, no direction, no destination. Yet the moment he had become aware of exactly where he was—"The Land of Lace," he called it to himself now, remembering the wrist of the girl whose hand he had seen close the door earlier—the compass of his heart had found its north. He had immediately understood lust: it was the primordial desire to leave something of oneself in a special place to which one fears one might never return. Taking one light step and then a second one, slightly heavier, he understood that the adventurous, daring spirit (he thought of men, yes, men, of course; youths; Susan B. Anthony, not *just* men; oh, yes, Oscar Wilde and his aesthetic comrades; slaves and runaway slaves, to be sure, who must have relinquished some capacity for carnality upon the occasion of their manumission and their subsequent settlement in lands less hostile; Americans in the West; Americans)—the spirit who at nature's urging or at the bidding of circumstance was driven to set out for and explore many more special places, both literal and figurative, than most—yes, the adventurous, daring spirit was inevitably a more lustful one.

"Charlotte," Traquair said, more firmly than he had intended, a solid six steps down the hallway.

A female voice near him said, "All the way down."

"Thank you," he said.

"Thank *her*," the voice said, as if its owner believed there was only one thing for which one should express gratitude.

Traquair took several more steps into the darkness and then called again, "Charlotte," this time in more of a whisper. A candle appeared at the end of the hall. Into the outer edge of its circular light—itself a beacon—a beckoning hand fluttered. He strode more quickly now toward her. Whatever had been the shield, the eclipse, the improbable dusk of his eroticism was lost along the way. Aurora, he thought as he walked toward the girl. Not Charlotte. And like sunlight and other things less grand, he and his, he knew, would burst.

As soon as he reentered the main room, Traquair, beginning to worry about the time, wanted to leave the house. But Otis and Nat coaxed him into buying another round of drinks. He had to wait for them because by now it would be dark outside and, without their assistance, he would never be able to find his way back to the Arlington. They finally left Mae's at about seven-thirty. On the way back, a drunk Otis ranted about the presidential murder trial of Charles Guiteau, whose verdict was due tomorrow. "Guiteau is as good as dead. Even if you crazy and got a good sense of humor, you can't git away with killing no president—not even Garfield."

When they reached the corner where Traquair had met them, they said their farewells. Nat, who had an arm around Otis's waist to support him, reminded Traquair of the way back to the hotel. "Thank you," Traquair said. "Take care of our Otis."

"He don't deserve me," Nat said. "He deserve Lou-Ella, and that's just who gon git him. Don't git lost, Willie. And next time you in Washington, be sure to stop by. You know how to treat a nigger right." They exchanged smiles, handshakes, and, finally, waves good-bye.

Traquair trotted back to the hotel, bearing the weight of his guilt at having been away from Oscar for so long. Today of all days! But then, only on a day like today would he have had cause for allowing himself to be delayed. When he entered the suite, he found the rooms in complete darkness. Oscar had demanded candles in place of the Arlington's gas lighting, but not a flame was burning. Traquair tiptoed to the desk in the front room and lit a candle there. When he peeked into Oscar's bedroom, he was surprised not to find him in bed. He went into his own room, and there he found Oscar sleeping in *his* bed, right where he'd left him hours ago. Could Oscar have been asleep the entire time he had been out? Traquair hoped so. He didn't want Oscar to know about his extended absence—to feel abandoned—so he didn't wake him. Choosing to go to bed early as well (he and Oscar would wake up tomorrow refreshed, rejuvenated), he decided he would sleep on the sofa. He undressed himself and put out the candle.

As he laid down on the sofa near the window, fatigue overtook him. He felt a comfort at not having to sleep in his own bed (Oscar's presence there seemed a blessing), for the day's experiences had left Traquair yearning for a new way of resting, a rest that welcomed, as part of its peace, restlessness.

At some point in the night, he was awakened by Oscar's voice, "Tra . . ."

"Yes," he answered from his reclined position, but Oscar did not continue. "Do you need something, Oscar?" Still there was no response. Oscar must have been talking in his sleep again, as he had done on that drunken night in Philadelphia.

Later, he was awakened once more. This time he heard only the sound of Oscar crying softly. Traquair did not say anything, hoping that Oscar would read his silence not as abandonment but as privacy, and this brief moment of privacy as some thin slice of precious obscurity.

BOSTON

WHILE Oscar was out being feted by Boston's art-conscious elite, Traquair lounged on the sofa in their suite in the Vendome Hotel reading, without permission, the manuscript of Oscar's play *Vera*, which Oscar was eager to see produced. He had become more accustomed to these late-night vigils, inventing ways of amusing himself, and he no longer indulged in dozing while awaiting Oscar's return. Traquair thought *Vera* no worse than many of the contemporary plays he had seen, but he found that it lacked the refinement of Oscar's originality and wit. Shouldn't a man's art approximate the quality of his being? If, as his writing *Vera* implied, he was leaving poetry for the dramatic form, might not his own manner, which itself was a form of theater, be the perfect model? *Vera* was essentially a tragedy about Russian aristocracy with uneven comic undertones. Why would a man with such a gift for humor conceive as his first attempt at theater a tragedy instead of the form more appropriate to his natural talent, the comedy? And Oscar, Traquair had noted time and time again, was a man who would just as soon speak a witty but false epigram as he would tell the truth. Why had he written *Vera*—whose title character's name even undermined its author's commitment to evasiveness? What had drawn him to tragedy, a *political* tragedy, no less? (Why, just this morning, bored with having to sign a book that Colonel Morse, who had been called in to coax efficiency out of Vail, was insisting he autograph for an Albany politician, Oscar had said to Traquair, " 'Politics'! So unnecessarily plural, the word fairly announces its own superfluity.") Was there something less visible in Oscar's nature that would explain this affinity to tragedy? Traquair thought of the sunflower, which Oscar insisted was an example of perfect form. How bright and playful and joyous was the corona of pointed yellow petals. Those petals created a ring of magical light so blazing as to blind one to the obvious wide, dense circle of ebonic intensity—was it brown or black or both?—that lay at the flower's core. Was there some similar darkness that lay dormant in Oscar's heart, something that, if one squinted past the glow of his personality, one might discover? Was Oscar aware of this possibility? Traquair recalled his own recent unexpected awakening at Mae's place in Washington, and he knew how completely the heart could conceal its true character from its host.

Still musing about *Vera* and what the play implied about its author, he heard Oscar's key in the door. As he was sitting in the front room, there was no time to return the manuscript to its proper place, atop the desk in Oscar's bedroom. Panicking and thinking only "Away!" he tossed it to the cushion at the far end of the sofa. Luckily a throw pillow fell upon the manuscript, almost completely shielding it from view.

Oscar entered in cheerful spirits, and Traquair rose to take his coat. "Tra, you have no idea how many young men I met tonight who introduced themselves to me as aspiring artists. I truly pitied them. Artists don't aspire; they simply are. Those who consider themselves aspiring artists toss their souls upon the heap of hopelessness. Yet, they were so young and so full of energy that they seemed capable of surviving even the great disappointment of failed aspiration. Can you imagine such youth, such passion? Of course you can. You are the embodiment of these things as well. They are American attributes, I believe. Not the attributes themselves, I suppose, but the completeness with which they envelop you. No one in all of England, all of Europe, for that matter, seems so girded against disappointment. It's probably for this reason that America will achieve so much, especially since the things that Americans seem to desire far more than art—money and machinery—are well within the means of aspiration."

"I think most people just want to be happy, one way or another, don't you think?" Traquair asked as they moved into Oscar's room.

"Perhaps. But happiness is a ruse. One must have something to fall back on. Wealth or love or a horrible vice—none of which is true happiness, but each of which is capable of performing an acceptable impersonation."

"Do you mean to personify happiness?" Traquair wondered playfully, removing Oscar's tie.

"No. I mean to personify wealth, love, and horrible vice," Oscar said with laughter. "The person who can represent all three of these—doubtful though his existence may be—is probably some sort of a god, admittedly a dangerous one, but one, nevertheless, who, once unearthed, should be worthy of eternal worship. Do you believe in God, Traquair?"

"That's a difficult question to answer."

"Not a particularly pleasant one to ask, either. I think you owe my effort the courtesy of a reply."

"Well, let me say that I don't believe that gods are so much to be believed in as they are to be beloved."

"And is it possible to love that in which one does not believe?" asked Oscar, tossing back his hair.

"I do not believe in my dreams, but I would be lost without them," said Traquair. "I adore my dreams. Don't you adore your dreams?"

"We've moved so quickly from love to adoration. Yes, I do adore my dreams. But then, of course, I also *believe* in them." Oscar sat on the edge of his bed. "How cleverly you've deflected my question, Tra. For this I adore *you*. I, too, prefer to keep the mystery of God alive. The only way to demystify God is to deny Him; the only way to surrender to Him is to deny oneself. Of course, denial has its place, which is not in the court of public opinion regarding the question of God, but in the courts of men on any of humanity's charges. That murderous Guiteau, even though he assassinated a president, had the right idea in standing his ground. Killing presidents seems to have caught on in America. It's a rather odd enterprise to flourish here, as it offers no profit that I can think of."

"It brings notoriety," Traquair said.

"Yes, but with the dire side effect of death, which tends to subdue one's capacity for enjoying one's success."

"I disagree."

"With death, Tra? To disagree with death is to prolong a lost debate."

"What I mean to say is that presidential assassins and the murderers of all great men do, through their notoriety, gain some measure of immortality."

"Immortality!" Oscar's voice was charged with disapproval. "A few lines in badly written history books? That's not eternal life. That's eternal damnation!"

Traquair held out a silk robe of a paisley print and assisted Oscar's luxurious but swift turn into it. He watched Oscar tie the belt around his waist. "I've noticed how much you admire this robe, Tra. When I leave for England, I shall hand it over to you."

"I didn't mean to stare," Traquair said. "But it is a fine cloth. I'd be less than honest to say that it had not caught my eye."

"I'm sure the spider who spun this fabric would be proud to have so ensnared you. Are you ready for bed? Do say no. I'd like to continue our discussion by the fire, if you're up to it."

"Of course."

They moved back into the cozy area where Traquair had been reading earlier. Oscar sat on the sofa, and Traquair hoped he would not move the pillow and reveal the copy of *Vera*. Traquair sat in one of the large, comfortable chairs and put his feet up on the ottoman. Oscar did not hesitate to speak. "Here's what I'm thinking—forgive me, Tra, but this night of Harvard intellectuals, an impressive lot, and the performance we saw of *Oedipus Rex* have understandably set me off. I'm thinking that presidents and monarchs, even, are not necessarily great men—or great women, for that matter. They may be great, but greatness is not a prerequisite. This fact is of no real matter. What is important to note is that they are not really men at all. They are *symbols*, symbols of the republic, of the monarchy—and as such they serve a definite, artistic purpose. People who assassinate them, as with your Mr. Booth and your Mr. Guiteau, do not simply kill men; they kill symbols. Their murderous acts are a rather drastic form of art criticism. Lucky for America that the method of replacing the symbol is so firmly institutionalized."

"*Constitutionalized*." Traquair used a word he'd never heard. "That is, if you mean that, in the event of an assassination, the vice president becomes president."

"Yes. How perfectly and puritanically American—you really shouldn't so readily accept all of England's bad habits—to take away a man's vice and call it a promotion. Now I've lost my point."

"You were saying we are lucky that our Constitution allows for the succession of the president by the vice president. How are we lucky?"

"That is the point—yes. You are lucky because, generally, when the symbol, such as your Mr. Lincoln, is killed, or when it dies of poor medical attention as Mr. Guiteau would have had us believe of President Garfield, or even when it dies of natural causes, or of heartache, of grief—whenever the symbol dies, the thing that it symbolizes dies as well. Even a second-rate symbol, say, a vice president or an immature prince, is better than no symbol at all, or so it would seem."

"Perhaps," said Traquair, "assassins are envious of the symbol they set out to destroy. Usually they claim to be killing in the name of a cause, but that can't be the whole of it. I think they must have *aspirations* of becoming symbols themselves, if I may return to your key word from earlier."

"Yes, that's it! They are aspiring artists, and I shall tell you how. Listen closely. The act of creating art is an act of violence—it is the willful destruction of nothingness. All true art is violence. Are all acts of violence art? No. Of course not. *Some* acts of violence are. But for the inartistic, the creation of violence is a crude substitute for the creation of art. Violence is usually not art because it merely destroys one form of nothingness and replaces it with another. True art always fills the void.

"Murder is not truly poetic; it only seems so because it causes death, and death—especially tragic death—is so poetic, so romantic."

"Ah, yes," Traquair said. "I suppose we've Homer and Shakespeare to blame for this impression."

"They, and anyone who breaks your heart. Make no mistake, murderers, as creators of death, think themselves great artists, and some of them are. But that John Wilkes Booth character was not artistic. He thought that by killing President Lincoln in the proximity of a stage he would appear dramatic but, in the end, he was merely theatrical."

"Oh, Oscar, how I do agree with you there. I've always thought Booth's act a sad confirmation of just how little art there is in contemporary theater."

"Yes, yes," Oscar said, smiling as brightly as Traquair had ever seen. "Both his style and his setting for the crime are aesthetically poor choices—only a real genius could have got art out of his scheme—and his entire venture is discredited upon the simplest analysis. But this Guiteau chap had a bit more substance than Booth. His act had real comedy. He shot Garfield in the ladies' waiting room at a railroad station, and his performance at his trial was outrageous, entertaining, even uplifting. It is not surprising that hundreds wanted his signature. He's convinced me that comedy may save theater. My own *Vera* is ill-fated, I fear. The epigrams are funny enough, but goodness, in the end the woman stabs herself. Still, Guiteau was a violent man who killed the president, however artfully. Not that I presume for one moment to deny Guiteau's talent simply because his chosen art form led to his eventual conviction and almost certain execution as a murderer. It is always a mistake to judge a man's art by the man. One should judge the man by his art.

"Man wants to create art. For some, as I've stated, violence serves as an alternative. So any place where one finds a dearth of art, one will surely find a wealth of actual physical violence. In America, a young country that I'm sure you will admit has yet to create her own art, your assassinations are obviously illustrative of this fact. Only the discovery of art, Tra, only the discovery of art can save America from her own inalienable will to create."

Traquair, having listened to these words with rapt interest, stared at Oscar with wonder. He cleared his throat. "Then your mission here is of a far more serious nature than you've publicly admitted."

"I suppose it is, and I'm trusting that this confession to you will remain a private matter—*juste entre nous*. It is essential that I be considered an impostor and that I be ridiculed in some circles, while in the drawing rooms, at the dinner tables, and in the presence of the more professional members of the press, I elicit a different kind of laughter. Wit is truth's most palatable and most potent pill. Let's get them all laughing, and perhaps they'll swallow the truth, their bitter elixir, without even knowing it. What a paradox is laughter! It is at once both infectious and medicinal.

"No—I cannot even hint at the severity of my mission in America or, I tell you, Tra, I should be as doomed as my poor *Vera*."

Traquair's eyes shot to the end of the sofa, where Oscar's manuscript of the play, but for the inch of an edge, lay hidden. One never knew—or did one?—what unobserved presence might occupy the very corner of the room where one reclined. Traquair had the distinct impression that a queer clairvoyance lurked within Oscar's being, hiding there like *Vera* beneath the pillow or like the secret importance of his mission or like the dark thing, as obvious as a sunflower's burnt center, in Oscar's heart.

II

"You are young. No hungry generations tread
you down. . . . The past does not mock you with
the ruins of a beauty the secret of whose
creation you have lost. . . ."

—OSCAR WILDE

NEW YORK

O SCAR had lectured in Brooklyn last night and Traquair, after several weeks on the road, was happy to be able to spend two nights at home in his own room before the tour headed upstate for a few stops, then to Chicago, the Midwest, and the far West. Baxter's absence lessened the joy of his return, but he was delighted to find a letter from London on his writing table.

25 January 1882

Dear Billy,

Whatever you do, don't let Oscar Wilde read this letter—it's about him! I hope you're not on a train sitting next to him or in the same hotel room as Wilde, if your father has forwarded this to you, because this is strictly for your eyes only.

As you know, I'm traveling with George Lefford. The day after we arrived in London he met a young actor named Graves, who eventually got us invited to a Saturday-afternoon salon at the Chelsea home of someone whom you'd never guess: Lady Wilde. Yes. Oscar Wilde's mother! The poet who calls herself Speranza. She is quite the character here in London. Outspoken, outrageously dressed, and irrepressibly sociable. In this way, she's not very different from what one hears of her popular son. Of course, she is quite proud of her Oscar, goes on and on about his fame in London and now in America. Did you know that he has a brother they call Willie? She goes on less about him. I get the impression that he is something of a disappointment on the whole. Lady Wilde, who is a rebel of sorts, an

Irish nationalist, took a real liking to me when I told her that my grandmother was Irish. Discreetly, she took me into her second drawing room and showed me some of her family's pictures. She laughed as she showed me a photograph of a two-year-old Oscar with curls in his hair, wearing a dress with lace about its edges. Mercifully, her laughter camouflaged my own. Evidently it is something of a custom here to dress boys as girls during childhood. Still, Lady Wilde admitted to me, "I had already had Willie, and I'd caught a glimpse of the limitations of boys. So when I realized that I was to have a second child I so wanted a girl. But I figured out very early on that Oscar would suffice nicely." She did later have a daughter, Isola, who died from a fever at the age of nine. Oscar, says Lady Wilde, was especially shaken by his sister's death, the only tragedy of his life. Oscar, twelve years old when Isola died, went often to visit her grave, and he wrote notes for a poem about her death. Lady Wilde shared this much with me.

> Tread lightly, she is near
>   Under the snow,
> Speak gently, she can hear
>   The lilies grow.
>
> Lily-like, white as snow,
>   She hardly knew
> She was a woman, so
>   Sweetly she grew.
>
> Peace, Peace, she cannot hear
>   Lyre or sonnet,
> All my life's buried here,
>   Heap earth upon it.

How awfully sad. It's amazing that he's the witty charmer that he is. He somehow let go of the sadness he expresses here and kept only his fondness for the lily. This poem must represent his first documented fascination with the beauty of that flower. Does Aestheticism, then, have its origins in grief? How unknowingly cruel his detractors are on the issue of his love of the lily. It would seem lilies represent not only the Aesthetic Movement and its commitment to beautiful physical forms but also, quite sincerely for Wilde, innocence and life itself. I wonder if even Wilde has acknowledged this fact to himself. If he has, how generous of him to lend so willfully this very personal symbol to such a public movement. How painful it must be for him to witness it succumb to such mockery.

With Lady Wilde having been so forthcoming about the loss of her Isola and its effects on her family, I felt an immediate closeness to her and shared with her my own sadness of having lost Mother when I was such a young boy. It was only as I said to Lady Wilde, "I miss her," that I realized the extent to which, in fact, I do. Mother's smell, jasmine; her brightness, the way her approach lit my room; her hair, which had the silky texture of fine wrapping ribbon and which fell around my face when she would bend down to embrace and lift me, as if I were her gift to herself. I described these things to Lady Wilde, who listened intently, and when I was done, she gathered me warmly into her arms. I must admit that I felt quite like a babe. Childish of me, at any rate, to have traveled all this way only to be pitied. I thought I'd come here to put the final few brushstrokes on a picture of myself as a man, when evidently I've quite a ways to go. Alas, it seems this letter is not only about Oscar Wilde but also about me.

By the way, I told Lady Wilde all about you. You have an open invitation to her salons, whenever you find your way across the Atlantic. She has invited me and George back on Wednesday, but I think we'll be off to the country by then.

Ever yours,
Bax

P.S. You've always had the haberdasher's eye, as have I, though I can't recall Father's blue tie with white dots.

As was his habit, Traquair read the letter twice. (Letters, magazine articles, books—he was fascinated with reviewing passages, as if doing so were a way of recapturing his own experience, which, in a way, it was—his experience of having read the passage in the first place—or as if it were a way of maintaining the present, fending off the future, dodging whatever came next. Was this tendency, he had asked himself on more than one occasion, merely the instinct of a nostalgic heart or,

more seriously, of one desperately fearful of its own mortality?) Poor
Baxter, he thought, peering at the words "I miss her." Traquair had
always assumed that Baxter, like himself, had little or no recollection
of Mrs. Gable—they had been only three or four when she had died
and never talked about her—but it was plain to him now that Baxter
remembered enough to have preserved an acute sense of loss. Had
Baxter known any real consolation before sharing reminiscences with
Lady Wilde, tales to evoke mutual mourning? Maybe not. Traquair
questioned his own insensitivity to Baxter's motherless fate. A tremor
flexed the muscles of his hand that held the letter. Guilt? The ghost of
Mrs. Gable? Traquair's eyes drifted back up to "fondness for the lily,"
and he thought about how Oscar, too, if Baxter's assessment was correct, was in need of consolation. Oscar claimed an affection for the lily
based purely on the applicability of its design to the decorative arts,
but now Baxter had revealed the possibility of a deeper meaning. Was
Oscar even aware of the significance of this flower to his own past or
was he oblivious to the lily's secret power over him? Baxter's observation about the lily struck Traquair as remarkably similar to his own
recent thoughts about Oscar's obsession with the sunflower. But then,
he and Baxter had always been of like minds.

That evening Traquair had supper with his mother and father at
the kitchen table, as he always did when he was home. With Baxter's
confession regarding Mrs. Gable fresh in Traquair's mind, his mother
achieved a renewed vitality in her son's suddenly more appreciative
eyes, and he gratefully watched her serve a meal of potatoes and baked
fowl, with squash and the flour-dusted rolls he loved and, whenever
away, craved. Gloria Traquair was a strangely demure woman. As best
Traquair could surmise, she had none of her husband's verbal agility,
nor his ability for managing difficult social situations. She lavished
affection upon Traquair, but with gestures, not with words. His father
had told him many times, usually after a few drinks, "Son, I love you,"
but his mother had never uttered the phrase. He knew that she loved
him, but her silence on the issue had left him wanting; their relationship was an elliptical attachment. What passed between his mother
and father seemed also, to Traquair at least, ill-defined. Despite his
father's professed admiration for his mother, he had never seen his parents kiss. He had seen them hold hands, though only at church, where
that touch might have had a spiritual as opposed to an amorous mean-

ing. The truth was that he thought his parents an odd match. They did possess somewhat strikingly similar facial features, as if they had somehow grown into each other, but that simply added to Traquair's sense that they were unusual mates. Whereas his father was a tall man of methodical, graceful movement, his mother was a short woman who shuffled quickly when she walked. And she had a habit of dropping things, as she had done just now. Rising from retrieving a silver serving spoon she'd been about to use to replenish Mr. Traquair's plate with potatoes, she said, "Excuse me."

"That's quite all right, dear," Mr. Traquair said. "I've had enough anyway. What about you, son?"

"It was delicious, Mother. The hotel food I've been eating has none of the flavor yours does. I have not been this satisfied in a month's time." His mother nodded her appreciation.

"Gloria, William and I are going into my study for a talk about his travels. Will you fetch us some tea?"

"Of course," she said. "As soon as I've cleared these things away. The kettle is already on."

The two men went into Mr. Traquair's private room, which could be entered from the kitchen, and Mr. Traquair, sinking into the wideback chair behind his desk, let out a deep moan in accompaniment to his being enveloped in comfort. Traquair claimed his usual spot: leather chair, desk-right. His father lit a cigar and offered one to his son. "You do smoke now and then, don't you?"

"It's not a habit I've acquired."

"Try a cigarette at least," Mr. Traquair said, lifting the lid of a large cherry-wood box on the corner of his desk. Traquair removed a cigarette, and his father lit it from the fire of his cigar and handed it back to his son. "What have you been doing while you've been away, if not acquiring bad habits?"

"I didn't say I haven't taken on *any* new habits." Traquair brought the cigarette to his lips and inhaled. Loose flecks of tobacco pleasantly peppered the tip of his tongue. His body throbbed with the creep of sensuality, and he thought of Charlotte, whom he'd called Aurora, and several other girls like her he'd met since.

"For instance?" From Mr. Traquair's playful tone and his heavy-lidded gaze, he seemed the satisfied recipient of a dose of his own private stimulation.

"For instance . . . I sleep late."

"Like all of the best bad habits, sleeping late is a sin and a sign of weakness," Mr. Traquair said with a relaxed smile.

"Yes," Traquair agreed. "And if one must display weakness, it's much less embarrassing if one does so while one is unconscious."

"Perhaps. But if you are to commit a sin and it is to be held against you, you should at least be awake to enjoy it."

"Well, Father, not all of my most recent sins have been committed while asleep, though some have been committed while in bed."

Upon hearing this, Mr. Traquair, who was in the middle of a long draw upon his cigar, began coughing uncontrollably. At this same moment, Mrs. Traquair arrived with the tea. She put down the tray and went over and slapped her husband's back a couple of times before he motioned that he was all right. Traquair was smiling at his father, who, once he gathered himself, nodded to his son. Mrs. Traquair stood next to her husband and observed the situation. Though there was nothing about the scene to inform her of the nature of the revelation he had just made, Traquair thought he detected a knowing glint in her eye. Her entrance had been abrupt, but he doubted that she'd been listening at the door. Maybe he, having finally let someone in on his secret, was himself simply displaying some indication of his newfound manhood, a confidence or a glow. Presently, after his father's eruption had subsided, Mrs. Traquair quietly exited the room, closing the door gently behind her.

Mr. Traquair tapped out his cigar. "You may have the tea if you like, but under the circumstances, I'll be having something stronger."

Traquair poured himself a cup of tea as he watched his father move to the corner where he kept his liquor. "I didn't mean to surprise you so completely, Father. You must admit that you were challenging me with your talk of sin. I had an ace, so I played it."

"This is merely a discussion between a father and a son, not a poker match."

"All conversation, I've learned of late, is a battle of wits," Traquair said. "Or at least it is in its most enjoyable moments."

"And you take pleasure in winning such a battle against your poor father?"

"A battle of wits has but one aim—the overthrow of the awful tyrant called Ignorance, who, despite our efforts, continues to govern us all."

"All of which is very prettily put but none of which is an answer to my question. Do you take pleasure in winning such a battle with your poor father?"

"If the battle enlightens my father, who, by the way, is hardly poor, I answer yes. It seems that where I take my pleasure is not only a part of your question but the very substance of my revelation—which I can't believe you've ignored with this chatter about the aggressiveness of my disclosure. Could it be, Father, that you are not prepared to discuss this matter with me?"

"Preparation is of no relevance here; appropriateness is. I'm not sure what is to be gained by my probing into your private affairs. What are the right questions anyway? 'Who was she?' 'Were you kind to her?' 'Were you, in the end, expressive enough of your gratitude?' 'How much do such arrangements cost young men these days?'" Traquair's head turned quickly toward his father with the utterance of this last speculative question, because all of his encounters with women had been of the paid variety (three more since Washington, for, as it had turned out, John Everest's friends, Traquair's guides, had been an adventurous, carousing bunch, as fun-loving and persuasive as Otis and Nat). "You're a man, William. If you wish to inform me of the who, when, where on this thing, I shall listen attentively, even more so now that I have this very good drink at my assistance. You are a man, son, just as you were before you tasted of the one sweet dark habit which sustains all of mankind." Mr. Traquair, as if in a toast to this habit, swallowed a large wave of alcohol. "You did say it was for you a habit?" he asked, brows arching severely, resembling two symbols of the interrogative statement. His face gave literal meaning to the phrase "quizzical look," Traquair thought, nodding a response.

"Which is to say you've done it more than once?" his father asked shyly.

"Yes. Twice." His father greeted this response with another gulp from his glass. After a moment, Traquair said, "More than twice. A few times, really. First in Washington. Then Albany. And twice in Boston."

"My goodness. I must say you've made the most of your travels. Has your personal itinerary left any time for sight-seeing? I should think not."

"Less than I would have hoped." Traquair laughed. "But my personal itinerary, as you so delicately phrase it—sight-seeing in the dark, shall we say—has provided me literally breathtaking vistas of myself."

"Oh!" Mr. Traquair's face deserted the curves of quizzicality for the straighter lines of exclamatory outrage. "Pardon my dismay, young man, but it strikes me as rather arrogant to have seen some of the great cities of the New World and to proclaim oneself, in comparison, more interesting."

"To travel inward, Father, is the first step to becoming 'worldly.' And, really, I'd be less than honest if I didn't confess that I believe I've at least twice the charm of Baltimore. Trust me—I've been there." They both began to laugh. "Now Philadelphia, on the other hand . . . Philadelphia . . ." Traquair's voice lightened into a pause as he remembered something John had said. He sipped his tea and let a moment pass before saying, "Father. I met a friend in Philadelphia, a young man named—well, I suppose his name is of no importance—but it was John Everest. I must call him a friend. He assisted me with handling some of my duties with Mr. Wilde at a time when I really needed help, and it is he who has led me to other welcoming people in various cities. During a brief but disturbing exchange, John quite innocently asked me a very simple question, 'Who are your people?' I'm not sure of the phrasing, but that was the gist of it. 'Who are your people?' And, to my great consternation, I found I could not answer him."

"How ridiculous. Did you forget so quickly the existence of your mother and father? Are we not people, *your* people?"

"Well, of course, I mentioned the two of you. But he was dissatisfied with that answer, and, to my own surprise, so was I. You see, I'm traveling all over now, and it seems such a waste of an opportunity, perhaps a once-in-a-lifetime opportunity, to meet relatives, however close or distant. Have we any? In jest I've spoken to you of my gaining knowledge of myself through relations with strangers. But I'm wondering now in earnest if there's a chance, through some knowledge you might give me now, of my turning strangers into relations. It seems to me that you said something once about having a brother. Will you tell me about him? Where does he live?"

Mr. Traquair was visibly agitated by his son's inquiry. "If I mentioned my brother once, then I mentioned him too often."

"That remark strikes me as peculiarly callous," Traquair said to his father.

"A trait worn as well by the man of whom we speak, or am I to have my way, of whom we do *not* speak."

"Very well. If you refuse to provide me with any help, I shall simply go to Mother."

"No!" his father yelled. "The scoundrel is *my* brother. Your mother doesn't know half as much about him as I do."

"Then you will tell me about him?"

There was no answer to this question. Instead, Mr. Traquair poured himself another glass of scotch. Then he did an unprecedented thing. He got up from his chair, walked around his desk, and sat down heavily in the chair next to Traquair. In all of the years of meetings between Traquair and his father in this room, the large desk had always rested solidly, immovably, divisively between them—serving at various stages in Traquair's development as a candy-store counter, a judge's station, and, lately, a battlefield's front line. Whether it was for a half-remembered discussion about biscuits when he was six or seven years old (he recalled only that his position was that he liked biscuits very much, upon the assertion of which his father had revealed one and offered it to him), a later admonishment about the need to improve his poor penmanship, or a more recent dispute about politics, his father had always sat or stood behind the desk. Mr. Traquair's presence beside him now was no small concession. Whatever his father was going to say to him, Traquair knew that it would amount to his being handed the keys to the candy store, being surrendered the spoils of war. How passive and inevitable this victory was. Its ease embarrassed Traquair.

"Son." Mr. Traquair sighed. "You do have people. I mean, *we* do. Everyone does, or did. I have—or had—a brother, just as you say I once mentioned. His name is Moses. My brother and I were orphans together many, many years ago in South Carolina."

"South Carolina!" Traquair had no knowledge of his father's life that predated his own consciousness, and this information about his father's boyhood home, so inconsistent with what he did know, surprised him and to some degree made him apprehensive as to what he was about to hear. His father a boy in South Carolina? How old was his father? Fifty. South Carolina? he thought again. Fort Sumter? What year? Eighteen sixty-one. It was now 1882. His body twitched with anxiety as his mind began subtracting its way into the not-so-distant past and into a mathematical certainty.

"Yes. South Carolina. What do I remember about it? Not much, not much at all. I do know that the world was a different place then. Larger, meaner . . . less refined. Moses and I often dreamed about heading northward somehow. Oh, we made an infinite number of impractical plans. He was always more passionate, more ambitious about such things than I. We came close to initiating these plans on two or three occasions, but something always impeded our progress. We were, after all, only children. We remained in South Carolina until one day we were selected, adopted you might say, by a man named Martin Traquair, who had come visiting from New Jersey. It seems to me that he was related to the man who owned the place where we were living. This is only a vague impression of mine. Moses and I were twelve and eleven at the time. He is the elder.

"We lived in New Jersey with several others like ourselves whom Mr. Traquair had adopted, including some who came from South Carolina with us, whom we knew to be our cousins from what some of the older folks told us. And we looked very much alike. I must say we had a great time growing up together in this way at Mr. Traquair's. We were essentially a large family. Moses and I remained very close for a time, but as we grew, serious differences developed. By the time we were in our late teens it was clear how like opposites we were. And whereas in boyhood our differences had drawn us together, in young adulthood they forced a separation. For years I had excelled at the studies Mr. Traquair made available to us. We had great teachers. This is how I first met Mr. Gable, whose father was a good friend of our Mr. Traquair. Mr. Gable, who was still in college at the time, came twice a month to teach us a strange combination of business and etiquette. Moses did well in his studies also, but he had been more enthusiastic about the work Mr. Traquair had found for him with a local construction company. And Moses was simply wilder than I was. He always talked about wanting to set out on his own, out west, he always said, speaking with the same passion and yearning he had when we had made our idealistic plans back in South Carolina.

"Well, one day Moses did set out on his own, which one might admire, were it not for the manner in which he did so. What he did forever turned my heart against him. Before running off to wherever he ran off to, Moses stole a very large sum of money from Mr. Traquair. Such betrayal!

"For the first time in my life, I was glad that my brother and I did not have a true name of our own, for if we had, his crime would have brought great dishonor to it. A small consolation to a rootless existence. As it was, I alone, his closest kin, his only brother, was left to suffer the indignity of his transgression. Why he did it, I'll never truly know. If he had asked Mr. Traquair for the money, he probably would have given it to him. But Moses preferred to steal it. His crime had something to do with his wildness, I suppose. It was as if he resented what Mr. Traquair had done for us. As if Mr. Traquair, in adopting us, had robbed us of our chance to be fugitives, our opportunity to know what it feels like to escape something. I know from our old South Carolina days that Moses very much wanted that experience of being on the run. He wanted that thrill of suddenly acquiring, of his own will, his freedom. Captivity had bred that desire within him. For so long, to contemplate our freedom was to contemplate a crime. Perhaps even his criminality had been bred within him. Maybe the crime itself, his thievery, was necessary for him to have a real sense of being free. Maybe that was why he did what he did." Mr. Traquair waited a moment before going on. His speech had slowed as he had struggled with trying to explain his brother's actions. Then he said quickly, "My theory makes him an interesting man, a complex man, maybe even a tragic man—but not a noble one. No, I cannot forgive his selfishness. I cannot forgive him.

"And this is the man upon whom you wish to waste your time, time which, as far as I'm concerned, might be much better spent cavorting with whores, a habit you incidentally share with your uncle. He left two children unattended in New Jersey. No doubt others are out there somewhere. You have, I suppose, cousins or whatever the kinship would be—if you care to claim them as such—though I cannot pretend to know where they are. Just as I do not know precisely where he is. As I say, he was headed out west. He wrote me once or twice from San Francisco. I threw the letters away without reading them, and I have not heard from him in ten years.

"Who are your people? If this question posed by your friend John cannot be answered simply and sufficiently with your two loving parents as the response, then you might search for my brother. In him, I'm sure you'll find a more elaborate, though, I assure you, more sordid reply."

Traquair said nothing in response to his father's narrative. He simply sniffed and sipped his tea. His father relit his cigar and relaxed
again in his chair. Traquair said nothing because his father's mono-
logue had left him in something of a daze. Despite the carefully chosen
words, Traquair surmised, *knew,* for the first time that his father had
been born and lived most of his childhood as a slave. The shock he felt
at learning this had less to do with the fact itself than with his own
ignorance of it. How could he not have known something so fundamental? It was as if he had just discovered, at his advanced age, the
verb "to be." Why hadn't his father been more forthcoming before
now? Did he not understand that what the world does not know about
itself, what a man does not know about himself, changes everything?
We define ourselves by what we know or think we know, and others
define us by what they know or think they know about us. Didn't his
father know that knowledge is identity? Had the man no concept of
the significance of history? Hadn't history been among those studies at
which he claimed to have excelled? Sure, history was filled with lies
and half-truths (he knew now, with his father's revelation searching
madly within him for a place to rest, that even unrecorded history is
filled with lies), but the future seemed irrelevant without it. Finally he
said simply, "Father—history!"

Mr. Traquair must have understood because he shook his head
slowly and said, "History . . . hurts. It is wild and dangerous. That's why
we each make of it what we will. We each tame time to our liking, for
our own safety and comfort. That's what history is—time tamed. For
my part, I considered the wild, wild world I had survived, and I was
determined to deny that legacy access to your civilized heart. I really
see no reason to let my past interfere with your sense of who you are.
History has caused every war, son. Most people think that wars are
what history is *made* of, and this is superficially true. But it's more accurate to say that wars are the *result* of history. If men could forget the
past, they might love each other."

Traquair countered, "Tell that to your brother. Besides, history has
a great deal more future in it, Father, than it does past."

"Sometimes I feel that the years of my youth were lived by another
person entirely, someone whose very kinship to me, much less to my
brother, I question. You make your future of my past if you care to. As
for me, I'm done with it. And I won't be drawn into another verbal

confrontation with you, about this or any other matter. I'm done with that as well."

He would honor his father's wish not to argue. The heat of his frustration had already distilled this essence out of what his father had just revealed: History, the past, is far more unpredictable than the future.

CHICAGO

OSCAR had upset the entire city of Chicago last night by criticizing the city's beloved water tower during his new lecture, "The Decorative Arts." He had called the tower "a castellated monstrosity with pepper boxes stuck all over it." Traquair watched the reporters, who had come early to the Grand Pacific Hotel suite, as they tried to corner Oscar with their questions about what he had said.

"Do you have a problem with water towers?" one asked.

"Only when they don't look like water towers. When they look like castles, I hope that the castles are made of sand."

"Is it castles you have a problem with then?"

"Why does my simple plea for an appropriate structure necessarily imply that I am disenchanted with castles? Indeed, I am rather fond of castles. In fact, I should like very much to be in a castle right now."

"But there aren't any true castles in America, Mr. Wilde," a different reporter said.

"The fact of which I am entirely aware," Oscar tossed back. "Please forgive my defensive posture," he added. "But what do you expect from a man lying upon fur?" Which was precisely what he was doing. Whenever reporters were expected, Traquair lined the sofa with one of Oscar's long fur coats and a few other provocative throws that formed a luxurious pallet. The furs and fabrics served both to impart an aesthetic air and, less explicitly, to accentuate Oscar's languidness, which, Traquair had come to understand, was something of a disguise for a small but definite anxiety. Reporters were always too curious about the outrageous presentation to notice any tension in Oscar. (Although none of them asked Oscar directly about the scene on the sofa, their published stories almost always mentioned it.) Traquair looked into the room from his position near the door that led to the bedrooms of the suite. Glancing at the newspapermen, he smiled, thinking about how little they would learn about Oscar with their probing but pointless questions. The Oscar Wilde they were discerning, the Wilde they would report about in tomorrow's papers, would not be the man Traquair knew. Their Oscar Wilde would be either too earnest or not quite as clever as he really was. Granted, the man Oscar showed to them was different from the private Oscar Wilde, but they would fail to capture even that fiction. For instance, no one would report what he had said about wanting to be in a castle instead of in the Grand Pacific Hotel. Did the reporters even understand that Oscar was saying that rather than endure this Chicago Inquisition, he'd prefer to be in another city, another country, altogether? A moment ago, Traquair had seen the waning of color from Oscar's face, not an uncommon transformation of his visage during these interviews. Reporters often mentioned the extreme fairness of Oscar's skin, implying that he looked somehow abnormal or unhealthy. ("Wilde's face had the look of a ghost, less an apostle for the arts than an apparition for the arts" was one recent quip.) They had no insight into the role they played in determining the face they would describe as Oscar's; they owned that face as much as, if not more than, he did. *In a world so filled with possessive personalities, it's odd that no one knows what to do with the apostrophe,* Oscar had said once to Traquair. The apostrophe "s" in the phrase "Wilde's face" belonged to its authors.

When, after a few more questions, Traquair quietly entered the room, a few of the reporters started, as if, in appearing from the darkness of the doorway, he had surprised them. He had thought they were at least subconsciously aware of his presence, but their reactions proved otherwise. He went casually to Oscar and whispered, "This is your cue to announce that you have other obligations, if you are ready to break off with these proceedings. If so, a quick glance at your watch right now would be a nice touch." Oscar reached into his pocket and removed the watch he used for occasions such as this and for little else.

"Gentlemen, I'd love to continue this session, but I have just been informed that I'm in danger of missing another appointment. Do excuse my rushing you in this way. Traquair . . ."

"This way, gentlemen," Traquair said, herding the reporters toward the door. They left slowly, a couple stopping to ask for Oscar's autograph.

ST. LOUIS

WHO IS this saint called Louis, and could he not have inspired a city of less moody inhabitants?" Oscar was continuing his diatribe against the unruly St. Louis audience to which he had just delivered his lecture. Traquair was leading the way down the dark backstage corridor at Mercantile Library Hall, heading for the dressing room where Oscar would rest before taking his carriage to a press club reception. Vail was trailing Oscar at a safe distance. "He probably wasn't a saint at all," added Oscar.

"I think the city is named for one of the kings," Vail said.

"Of course. The ninth Louis. That explains the problem," said Oscar. "Royalty and sainthood are incompatible. Someone should discuss this matter with the saint makers. Such mistakes can be avoided. And here, six hundred years later, a perfectly innocent American city is victim to this curse."

"It is innocence that makes the perfect victim, is it not?" Traquair asked as he opened the door to the dressing room. Oscar paused briefly as he passed Traquair, looked directly into his eyes, and said, "Yes."

Oscar tossed the leather folio that held his lecture papers onto the table, and as he sat down said, "Victimization is the curse borne by the innocent—which explains the destiny of Adam and Eve, and the plight of this city, but not my own misfortune here tonight. What is the curse of the experienced?" He paused for a moment and then looked up at Traquair and Vail. "Did I hear one of you whisper 'arrogance'?"

"Listen, Wilde, tonight's audience is of no real concern," said Vail in an upbeat tone. In the weeks since the Washington debacle and

Oscar's letter to D'Oyly Carte, Vail had become a much more astute manager. Colonel Morse's visit to impart professional guidance had been successful, and Vail's assistance to Oscar and even to Traquair had changed the relationship among the three of them. Vail was not as close to either Oscar or Traquair as they were to each other, but his opinion was now valued in most situations. Oscar gave him his attention, and Vail continued, "Tonight is not the norm. It should not reflect upon the momentum of the tour. We've done well in Detroit, Cleveland, Indianapolis—well, all right, best not to think about Indianapolis—but even Cincinnati was a triumph. I think it's the weather here. The rain and mud have frazzled the nerves of everyone in this town."

"Yes," said Traquair. "As you've said, Oscar, climate forecasts temperament." Traquair, who in his effort to assist in lightening the mood had slipped and used Oscar's familiar name, noticed Vail's quick look in his direction.

"I suppose you're right—I mean I suppose *I'm* right," Oscar said. Sitting at the dressing table, he tossed back his long dark hair and sighed. "What time are we due at the reception?"

"Whenever we get there," Vail said calmly.

"I take it you like this informality, Vail."

"Well, the press club invitations say nine-thirty, but I negotiated with the secretary for a less rigid time for our expected arrival. I thought it would please you not to have to rush after the lecture."

"Of course, it does please me. I was commenting on *your* new appreciation for languor. You used to be so beholden to that watch of yours—to no avail, I might add. What's become of it?"

"I still have it. It's been fixed. Only now, I seem to use it less."

"It's your vengeance upon time. I'm so proud of you. One should ignore time hourly. There is tremendous pleasure in watching the hands of a clock while one is resigned to doing absolutely nothing. Clock makers imprisoned leisure. How subversive that their invention should also document its release!"

"That's the way," said Vail with a broad smile.

Traquair joined in the sudden merriment by clapping his hands twice. Oscar's pithy words had cleared this little room of its stuffy air, and the three men all seemed to breathe with greater ease. There were two soft knocks at the door. Traquair, who stood near the entrance, turned in response. When he opened the door he found two young women with red cheeks and wide smiles, both in cream-colored gowns of slightly different shades, looking up at him.

"We've come—" the slightly taller, evidently bolder of the two began, stopping abruptly, unable to complete her sentence or, perhaps, Traquair considered, based upon the sudden detached look in her eyes, unable to complete her *thought*. Had his appearance, he wondered, frightened her or simply charmed her into confusion? He thought he saw in her eyes the flash of admiration that got him good service in restaurants or that generally preceded his being flattered with some synonym for "handsome."

"To greet Mr. Wilde's autograph," the second woman finished her friend's sentence nonsensically.

Traquair smiled at their comical nervousness and said, "If you'll first greet Mr. Wilde himself, you might persuade him to introduce you to his autograph." The women blushed even more upon hearing these words. The one who had said "to greet Mr. Wilde's autograph" opened her mouth as if to scream in laughter, but she released no sound. The lashes of the other woman—the one Traquair thought he might have accidentally beguiled—beat out steady rhythms whose fervor initiated an unusual fluctuation in the beating of his heart. The few beats that were now pounding so loudly and irregularly in his ears, to the exclusion of all other sound, reminded Traquair of an odd moment of deafness that had shot through him once at a symphony concert as he had sat in the audience paralyzed in anticipation of an overture. He had watched a man in the percussion section bring his mallets up and down in furious movements to start the performance. But Traquair had heard nothing; he had only felt a rumble of music. Involuntarily, he had held his breath, unable to breathe or hear again until the trumpets, several bars into the composition, had pierced the balloon of silence like pins, releasing air as both substance and sound. The one woman's unvocalized laughter and the other's fluttering lashes played like tension and silent timpani before him now. Was their overture for Oscar Wilde, who the women must have known was just on the other side of Traquair's high and wide shoulders? Or had he, Traquair, wooed out of them a music that for the moment only he could feel? He hoped the latter to be the case because—it was clear to him now—he wanted very much to kiss the woman with the lashes. And if the other one would have closed her mouth just a bit, he might have wanted to kiss her, too.

In unison, the two women handed him their cards. Traquair turned to see Oscar nodding his permission for the guests to enter. Looking at the cards, Traquair announced the women: "Miss Augusta Wilson Grant and Miss Theda Trenton." *Miss Theda Trenton . . .* Traquair stepped aside and waved the two misses into the room. The width of their dresses reduced the room to one-third its size, creating a coziness that Traquair, pushing in from the doorway, found exciting. He couldn't see the girls' faces as they nodded and spoke their hellos to Oscar. Nor could he see Oscar, whose voice floated up magically, the way it had on the first day Traquair had gone to meet him at the Grand Hotel in New York, the way it always did. Traquair had recently tried to describe Oscar's voice to Baxter in a letter: *"It has a quality that belongs generally to men who are destined to become professors or judges, but he, if pressed, I suspect would reject both teaching and judgment. A born mentor (or is it merely my own inclination to apprenticeship that makes him seem so?), he would rather praise his own intellectual fathers—at least for now. Ruskin. Pater. Gifted with a sense of what is just, he makes both right and wrong seem one and the same. The voice is filled with the brutality of truth, but its most common attribute is a resounding intonation of mercy. Yesterday, Baxy, I overheard a man say to Oscar that he hated his father-in-law, indeed that he was thinking of hating everyone. (People, I've found, with little or no provocation whatsoever, have an odd habit of revealing the most intimate parts of themselves to famous strangers.) Oscar, speaking with that tone I'm telling you of, responded to the gentleman by saying, 'Misanthropy is ill-advised. Hatred is too pure an emotion to be wasted upon men. Love men. Hate the gods—who are both far more worthy and far more willing to forgive the sin that is hatred.' "*

What was it that Oscar had just said to the women? Something to make them laugh. Vail had raised his hand with delight at the remark. Traquair had heard enough of it to piece together the overall meaning, but he had been unable to process Oscar's comment, distracted as he was by the slight tilt of Miss Theda Trenton's head to the right. When she had moved that way, the small, rounded edge of her chin had come into his line of vision. He wanted to be on the other side of the room with Oscar and Vail, so that he might see her more clearly and that she might see him. The idea that Miss Trenton—the one with the lashes, the kissable one—was now looking at Vail ruined his heart. That tilt of her head had been in response to Vail's attention-seeking hand going up in accompaniment to his loud laughter, so that she was indeed at this moment staring in his direction. He had witnessed Vail's desperation with ladies in the past; it had something to do with his deficient height, Traquair mused bitterly. He moved as close to the group as he could manage, the toes of his shoes all but touching the wide, lace-topped hems at the backs of the ladies' dresses.

"But surely you don't intend to spend all of your lives in St. Louis," Oscar was saying now.

"I'm only visiting from the North," Miss Trenton said. "It is my poor cousin here who is doomed."

"St. Louis is hardly as bad as all that, Theda," Miss Grant said. "Don't encourage Mr. Wilde in his harsh assessment of our fair city."

"I'm sure Mr. Wilde needs little encouragement after that rather *unfair* reception from the people of St. Louis."

"Miss Trenton is right, Miss Grant. I need no encouragement. Indeed, nothing so discourages one as to be encouraged. Tell me *not* to speak disparagingly of St. Louis, and I shall. Command me to speak, and I shall remain mute."

There was a pause, and then the women, followed quickly by Vail, began to laugh.

"What a man of contradiction you are, Mr. Wilde," said Miss Trenton.

"One man's contradiction is another's consolation," said Oscar.

"One *woman's* contradiction," Miss Trenton tried to correct him.

"Really?" he said quickly. "It was *my* contradiction. It's the consolation that is yours, Miss Trenton, should you choose to accept it." Oscar's words sounded unusually stern. Perhaps, Traquair considered, some of his irritation with the lecture audience had reentered his disposition, darkening his remark and his intonation.

"How true," Miss Trenton said with a softness in her voice, but Traquair couldn't determine precisely how much Oscar's comment might have hurt her. Relegated to the outer rim of the social circle, more by the lavishness of female sartorial fashion than by any other force, Traquair had only their voices to explore for clues of personality and bearing. Still, that sudden gentleness in her voice reminded him of the demure quality—a tone of feminine surrender—that was the most

salient feature of his own mother's voice whenever she addressed his
father. He would have liked to have heard Miss Trenton speak to him in
that way, to say to him, "How true, Traquair. How clever," even if in fact
he'd just obviously lied to her and quite without cleverness. But this
submissiveness in Miss Trenton's voice, tinged as it was with discomfort
or displeasure, impressed Traquair as uncharacteristic: her voice had
flowed far more gaily and naturally when pronouncing "one *woman's*
contradiction" than it had while sounding the conciliatory "how true."

"Mr. Wilde," Traquair now heard Miss Trenton say in a more natural tone, "have you been enjoying your travels here in America?"

"Quite," Oscar said. "Travel moves me." Both Miss Trenton and
Miss Grant laughed at this, which pleased Traquair immensely. He had
thought Oscar asleep when he had uttered this phrase, but here he was
repeating it. Was Oscar aware that Traquair had spoken the pun first or
had he made an unconscious note of it that night in Philadelphia and
now thought it his own? Traquair did not care which was the case. He
was simply pleased to hear Miss Trenton's laughter. He knew that it
was the work of his own spirit, aided by Oscar's supreme delivery, that
had touched her. In the future when he longingly thought of her, as he
was certain he would, maybe he could sustain himself on that.

In the space between the heads of the women, Traquair saw Vail
looking at his watch. Oscar, still not in Traquair's view, must have
noticed as well. "Now Miss Grant and Miss Trenton, Mr. Vail here is
about to insist that I press on to other engagements with the rest of St.
Louis. I'll be happy to sign your books now."

The women handed their autograph books to Vail, who put one on
the table for Oscar to sign. When Oscar had finished, Vail placed the
other one before him. Traquair was watching these motions from, at
most, a distance of ten feet, but he felt miles away. The task Vail was
performing was minor, but it was, nevertheless, the type of work that
Traquair had grown accustomed to doing. More and more these days he
was becoming strictly the valet. Even though he and Oscar remained
close, Vail's reconciliation with Oscar had affected Traquair's role.
Traquair understood the situation, but he couldn't help but feel saddened, when, as was the case now, his new, less demanding position left
him out of the round of conversation, out of Oscar's view, without a
peek at the faces, and, always, closest to the door.

After signing the autographs, Oscar stood up and said good-bye to

Miss Grant and Miss Trenton. Traquair opened the door and moved into the hall to make a wider passageway for the women and their dresses. Miss Trenton said to Traquair with a wave of her signed book, "You were right. He did introduce us to his autograph."

Yes, Traquair thought as he watched the two women walk away from him, but he did not introduce you to me.

Hadn't Miss Trenton smiled at him when she had waved her autograph book his way back at Mercantile Library Hall? What about all of that fluttering of her lashes? And then the toes of his shoes had touched the lacy hem of her dress. Or had they? Still, hadn't he and she made some connection? Traquair was riding in the cab Vail had arranged to take him back to the hotel for another lonely night of waiting up for Oscar. Thinking of Miss Trenton brought him pleasure. Holding her card in his hand, he saw that her address was 23 East Fourth Street, New York City, a simple walk fifteen blocks downtown from his own house. They had something in common. How ironic they should meet in St. Louis. But then, they hadn't really met. No, they had not met. The notion that they should struck him, in this moment of loneliness and longing, as not only reasonable but necessary. Why shouldn't they meet? After all, she had smiled at him. She had fluttered her lashes at him. Hadn't they touched? Traquair reached into the breast pocket of his jacket and removed Miss Grant's card. As he had hoped, her address was there.

"Driver!" he called. The man, who was moving the open cab at a slow pace, turned his head and grunted. "Mr. Wilde has asked that I leave a message at the address of Seventy-four Jefferson Road. I do hope it is not very far out of the way."

"It ain't far, but it ain't what that fella told me and it ain't what he paid me for. This cab is going to the New Southern Hotel."

"Assuredly. But Mr. Vail, the gentleman who paid you, was unaware that Mr. Wilde wanted me to attend to this errand."

The driver brought the carriage to a stop. "What you up to, nigger?" he asked with a gravelly and faintly humorous voice.

Traquair, determined to see Miss Trenton again, merely used the remark to deflect the man's attention from the scent of deception he so obviously and accurately smelled. "I suppose I am up to pleasing the man whom I serve, the man who pays me to perform certain duties without question." With this he took fifty cents from his pocket and offered it to the driver.

The man hesitated. Then he took the money and laughed. He turned and gave the horse a little slap. "Seventy-four Jefferson Road," he said.

Traquair scratched the tip of his nose with his index finger. While pleased with his handling of the driver, he had no idea what he was going to do when he arrived at Jefferson Road. He only knew that he wanted to see Miss Trenton and to say to her, "I am William Traquair." That would be enough. She could respond to him by saying, "And what of it?" or "And I am in love with you." Either way he would have accomplished what he set out to do: make her know him. Out of anxiety, he tapped his foot on the floor of the cab and composed a melody so odd that he knew that if, many years later, he tried to recall it to make the memory of this ride to see Miss Trenton more complete, he would be unable to do so.

As the cab slowed down in front of a large red house of nondescript appearance (Oscar would have hated it), Traquair saw a carriage driving toward the house from the opposite direction and veer toward the edge of the road.

"Here we are," the driver said. "I'll take the message to the house if you like."

"No," Traquair said quickly. "I mean to say that it is not a written message." He was distracted, hoping that the carriage contained Miss Grant and, of course, Miss Trenton, returning from the lecture. It would be easier to call out to them, less messy than knocking unannounced at the door of these people, who were, after all, strangers to him. He stalled for a moment. Oscar's leather folio, which he was taking back to the hotel, was lying on the seat next to him, so he picked it up, saying to the driver, "Oh, just a minute," implying that perhaps a written note did exist, or that he was going to write one, or that he needed to remind himself of the message by referring to whatever document lay encased within the folio. He opened the leather covers, and the papers from Oscar's "Decorative Arts" lecture shuffled before him. A few sheets slipped into his lap, but he ignored them, as his eyes peeked over the upper edge of the leather case at the other carriage, whose driver was now descending from his seat. Traquair felt the stare of his own driver, so he glanced down to pretend he was continuing his search for the imaginary message. His eyes fell upon a fragment of Oscar's words: *The human hand is the most beautiful and delicate piece of mechanism in the world. . . .* Then, pretending to have failed to find what he was looking for on the current page, he turned it, sneaking another look in the direction of the carriage. The driver was opening the door for his rider or riders.

"Well, did you find what you were looking for or not?" Traquair's impatient man asked.

"Oh, uh, yes," Traquair said. "Here it is, I believe." Nervously, he looked down at the papers and scanned more of what he had heard Oscar tell St. Louis this evening: *Let it be for you to create an art that is made with the hands of the people, for the joy of the people, too, an art that will be an expression of your delight in life. There is nothing in common life too mean, in common things too trivial to be ennobled by your touch; nothing in life that art cannot sanctify.*

When Traquair looked up he saw Miss Grant and Miss Trenton, with the aid of their driver, descending from the carriage. His heart, which had felt so ravaged at the idea of Vail's stealing Miss Trenton's attention, was at once fully healed. The rest of his body seemed unprepared for the extraordinary force of this rapid rejuvenation, and it responded with extreme self-consciousness and embarrassing growth. The lightning blow he had come to know and crave from his recent encounters with women struck, and he knew why so many people confused love and lust. Virtual opposites—one, as it desired only to feel itself, represented supreme emotion; the other, always desirous of feeling something else, represented supreme physicality—they each nevertheless depended so vitally upon the figurative (love) and the literal, blood-pumping (lust) workings of the heart. Surely he did not love Miss Trenton (he didn't even know her), but, just as surely, he desired her. Impassioned, he tossed the folio on the seat beside him and hopped down from the cab. "Careful there," he heard his cabbie say. "And don't be long about your business."

Business, Traquair thought. Business. Yes! That was it. He was here on business. He attempted to clear his head and settle his body. The driver's words had helped him again.

He took slow steps along the road toward the women, who had begun walking arm in arm, heading for the front door of the house.

Their driver was busy attending to his horse. All of the light in the area was radiating from a lamppost just to the right of the walkway to the house. As not to startle the women, Traquair made his way into the direct beam of the light before speaking. Then, he raised his right hand and said, "Miss Trenton . . ."

Both women looked up in unison. After a brief pause that resulted in what Traquair thought was vague recognition, Miss Trenton said, "Hello."

"Mr. Wilde has sent me," he said to her.

"Yes!" she said, now obviously remembering who he was.

"He has asked me to bring you a message. May I have a word with you?"

"Of course," she responded. She and Miss Grant exchanged whispers, while raising their eyebrows and expressing general delight. Miss Trenton handed her autograph book to Miss Grant and then began walking down the path to the lit spot on the road where Traquair stood. Watching her advance, Traquair did battle with himself: on the one side his impetuous, impractical passion, his heart; on the other, his powers of reason and imagination necessary for the success of this subterfuge, his head. Miss Grant, Traquair saw blurrily and peripherally behind Miss Trenton, walked to the front door and now stood there watching him and her cousin beneath the lamppost.

"Is there a note, a letter?" Miss Trenton asked, her eyes moving busily, almost tactilely over him, searching for the answer to her own question.

"No," Traquair said. He was silent for an awkward moment. Miss Trenton's probing eyes, into which he was staring most intensely, begged that he continue. It was his desire to please those eyes that told him what to say. "Mr. Wilde felt there was not time to compose a proper letter, so he has sent me instead."

"Not time?" she said, letting her eyes drift away from Traquair with a glance to Miss Grant standing back at the house in the distance. He might have been saddened at the sudden loss of contact, at the break with intimacy, but he knew her eyes would return to him. And, yes, here they were, as she continued, "I can't imagine what could have inspired such a sense of urgency, and I must admit that I am beside myself with curiosity." Her hands were encased in elegant white gloves dotted with tiny pearls, and she interlocked her fingers firmly, raising the doubled fist up to her chest.

"Mr. Wilde has sent me to extend his apology for one of the remarks he made to you earlier this evening."

Miss Trenton looked perplexed. "One of his remarks?"

"Mr. Wilde, upon reflection, thought, with regards to his response to your phrase 'one woman's contradiction,' well, that his comment was, indeed, a bit hard, cold, and more than a little unkind."

"Why, I'm not even sure that I remember just what he said," Miss Trenton replied. "Something about my consolation. And—oh, yes, 'one *man's* contradiction,' meaning his own, I suppose."

"Yes," said Traquair, remembering the concession Miss Trenton's voice had made to Oscar. "Mr. Wilde wanted you to know that the tone of those words was somewhat out of character for him."

"I was, indeed, mildly annoyed with his remark. But I hope I did not impart that displeasure in any discernible way. I am careful about such things. I was, after all, a mere uninvited guest into his small chamber of solitude. He needn't have bothered with us at all. Even so, if he's reflected upon it—and now he's sent you all this way—he must have noticed something. He must somehow have divined my ever-so-mild disappointment. What an impressive, delicate sensibility must have the man who would sense such a thing as that."

Overcome with a surreptitious pride, Traquair said, "You can understand that he wanted to put the matter straight immediately."

"Of course," Miss Trenton said with deep concern.

"Mr. Wilde hoped that you would accept his sincerest apology."

"Of course, of course. I shall write a note this evening doing just that and have it delivered to him first thing in the morning. You're at the New Southern, are you not?"

"Oh, no!" said Traquair, flustered at the idea of Oscar's receiving such a note.

"But the papers said that you were."

"Yes, of course we are. What I mean is that no letter is necessary in response to my visit. Mr. Wilde depends upon my ability in these matters."

"As well he might. Your delivery has been splendid," Miss Trenton said. "Sending you here instead of a letter was a wonderful stroke on his part. One does tire of receiving letters all the time. It is, of course, delightful to know that someone has thought of one. But what is a letter but, literally, a scrap of paper? Certainly, the words are the main thing, but even the best-written letter lacks the warmth of a human being. How typical of Mr. Wilde to understand that. By sending you, he has sent both his words and a flesh-and-blood representative of himself. There's more than a hint of personification about the tactic. How poetic, how *artful*. Don't you think, or have I been too thoroughly influenced by Mr. Wilde's lecture this evening?"

"I do not think it possible to be *too* thoroughly influenced by Mr. Wilde."

"I do like the sound of that," Miss Trenton said, laughing. "With your permission, I shall repeat it."

"Please do."

"And to whom shall I attribute the words?"

Without any coercion on his part, in fact as a result of his only truthful statement in this exchange with Miss Trenton, Traquair's moment of introduction had arrived. Softly, he cleared his throat and said, "William Traquair."

"William Traquair, Wilde's man. Thank you, William."

Traquair smiled widely at the sound of his name spoken by Miss Trenton's most natural and genuine voice. And when she had addressed him, she had said, "William." What bittersweet irony—that her superior station should grant her the use of his given name, which was strangely indicative of both social distance and personal intimacy. He was thinking mostly about the latter, the sweeter part of the irony, when Miss Trenton asked, "Is there something more?"

"Actually—Mr. Wilde did have one small request."

"A request?"

"Yes. What you've said about a letter being impersonal and inadequate is most appropriate. A letter could not possibly accomplish Mr. Wilde's plan—he always has a plan—and it helps that you understand that I am here, as you've said, as Mr. Wilde's representative."

"Yes, I do," she said, tossing to him, *finally*, that tilt of the head and the attention that Vail had stolen earlier.

"Mr. Wilde asked that you allow me, Miss Trenton, to take your hand."

"He did?" Miss Trenton asked, her right hand already beginning to lift before the silence had finished caressing her words into an interrogative.

"Yes," Traquair said. He noticed the glove on her hand. "Ungloved," he added. Without remark, Miss Trenton removed her glove and again raised her hand. Traquair accepted the hand into his large, coupled, upturned palms, saying, "Mr. Wilde asked that I take your hand and deliver to you this . . ." and here he bent his head and pressed his lips, for a moment, to Miss Trenton's bare hand, the likes of which, he knew, had inspired the word "exquisite," then rose, looked upon her freshly rouged face and into her lash-fluttering eyes, and said, ". . . kiss."

Her lips parted to say, "Mr. Wilde . . . ?"

"Yes?" Traquair said, as if Miss Trenton had just addressed him, as opposed to her having uttered an incomplete but decipherable question. "I mean, *yes*. Mr. Wilde asked that I deliver that to you."

"But why?"

"He said he hoped it would remind you of what he said in this evening's lecture about the human hand and that it might inspire you to create art whenever and wherever you can."

"It will," Miss Trenton said. "Please assure him that it will."

"I shall. Good evening, Miss Trenton."

"Good evening, Mr.—I mean, William."

Traquair watched Miss Trenton walk slowly back up the path to the house, where he saw Miss Grant standing with her hands covering her mouth, which he imagined was in its usual, unkissably open pose. Then he walked back to the cab.

"That's some *message* you delivered, boy," his driver said.

"Yes," Traquair responded. "Haven't you heard? Mr. Wilde is most articulate."

"Does that mean he can tell stretchers as good as you?"

"Stretchers?" asked Traquair.

"Lies, nigger."

"Oh," said Traquair, sitting back in his seat. "Yes, that is precisely what it means."

UTAH TERRITORY

W AS NORTH America, her vastness working against her, the Atlantic Ocean of continents? Traquair pondered this question as his country (at present, some undistinguished stretch of it, a dull patch of Utah) glided disappointingly past the window of his first-class berth. He had been anticipating the train ride, all one hundred hours of it, thinking it would provide him with a panoramic and enlightening view of parts of the country that most Americans had not yet seen. But after more than two days of slow travel, he was becoming disenchanted. Blank, dusty Utah, it seemed, had little to offer him. On the contrary, she seemed to be asking for something from *him*. That was the nature of emptiness, to demand substance from all that wandered into its vacuum, to usurp, or, with the thirst of a dry sponge or a desert, to absorb identity. In a less self-obsessed state, he might have donated something of himself to Utah, but not today.

At the last stop—before they reached San Francisco they would have made 230 such respites—in a little shanty of a restaurant, the woman who had served him, Oscar, and Vail a meal of potatoes, roasted antelope, and peas had been friendly and smiled at Traquair with a flirtatiousness that he normally would have responded to with some gesture that she could have taken home with her that evening, a wink of his eye that would have lifted her when she arrived at her house and found that her multiwived Mormon husband had chosen one of the others for the evening. Was that who she was? Probably not. She probably wasn't even a Mormon. The Mormons stuck to themselves; they were self-sufficient. She was more likely a free-spirited woman who had somehow made her way to this new territory. He had invented this fantasy to try to stimulate himself into reacting to her; it hadn't worked. Instead he had ignored the waitress and just picked over his cold antelope. Even when she was clearing their table of the plates and she had said to him, obviously flirting, "A big fella like yourself might do better to eat a bit more if he's aiming to stay a big fella," he had said nothing. And when she had offered him, at no extra charge, buckwheat hot cakes for dessert—"with enough syrup to paint a smile into the corners of your mouth"—he had declined, despite knowing that doing so was a small insult. The waitress had shrugged and sulked away from their table. Traquair had watched her sad departure, finding only slight pleasure in the plump, lower portion of her rear, which he knew deep down was worthy of far greater admiration than his current mood was allowing him to muster. No, he wanted to leave nothing of himself in Utah, mainly because, at the moment, he wasn't sure what he had to give, what he could spare. Right now he felt the way all of the West looked—empty, in search of itself.

Oscar and Vail sat side by side, facing Traquair. They were each reading: Vail, *Harper's Weekly*; Oscar, a French novel. Traquair decided to join them and removed from his jacket pocket Baxter's latest letter, which had been waiting for him when they had arrived in Omaha. They had rested there a few days after Oscar's lecture at Boyd's Opera House, before beginning this torturous ride to the West Coast. Baxter's letter, as richly and shockingly informative as it was, couldn't possibly surprise him the way it had at the first reading, but it promised entertainment enough to beat back the aggressive nothingness that sucked at the train-car window.

2 March 1882

Dear Billy,

    Lady Wilde has fairly adopted me. I should be in Paris right now, but I've postponed all that. George has gone on without me. Instead of making a public nuisance of myself in the cafés Elysées, I'm making a private one of myself at Lady Wilde's salons every Wednesday and Saturday. Whenever she introduces me to her guests she calls me her American boy. Can you imagine? To the painter James McNeill Whistler, who stopped by her den just last week, she

*introduced me that way. Her American boy. If Mr. Whistler had
painted my portrait at that moment he'd have been justified in
applying an inordinate amount of rouge to my countenance.*

*"Speranza!" Whistler exclaimed to her. "And I thought Oscar
had told me all of your secrets." It was an awfully naughty quip,
prompting Lady Wilde to redden head to bosom and to snort, "Don't
be absurd, Jimmy!" With that she lifted her chin and walked away to
visit with other guests.*

*"She's right to be offended." Mr. Whistler, smirking, turned to
me. A short man, he motioned for me to bend down that he might
whisper into my ear. "It was Oscar's father who made an art of
creating bastards." I started a bit because of his message and maybe
more so because his mustache was tickling the side of my face. His
frankness was foreign but his accent reminded me of the Boston boys
I knew at Harvard, and I've since learned that indeed he hails from
Massachusetts. The curious silver curlicue sprouting at the top of his
head caught my eye, and I recoiled in part to see it better but also to
remove myself from any implied collusion with his mischief. He went
on, "But then the Wildes insist on making art of everything, don't
they, even their mistakes. For instance, that dress Speranza is
wearing. Even in the intentional and merciful dimness of this room
we can't escape her talent for the art of tragedy. Sarah Bernhardt in
Macbeth chills one less."*

*Out of loyalty to Lady Wilde I avoided Mr. Whistler the rest of
the afternoon, though not before promising to visit his studio
sometime soon. You know how I want to draw a few decent pictures
while I'm here; it's a rare opportunity to watch a master at work.
And I must admit there is something strangely alluring about the
man.*

*After everyone else had left, including Willie, who I suppose was
either in his room or out for the evening, a less than sober Lady Wilde
voluntarily clarified Whistler's gossip, as if she'd somehow intuited
what he'd said to me. As there are no secrets between you and me,
Billy, I'll divulge to you that Lady Wilde admitted to me that Sir
William Wilde indeed did father three illegitimate children, all,
according to her, before their marriage. Oscar and Willie know all too
well of these siblings of sorts—one boy, two girls—as many years ago
they all used to summer together near Dublin before Sir William died*

and the Wildes moved to England. The two girls suffered wretched deaths eleven years ago. "They were dancing too near a fire," Lady Wilde said. Apparently their dresses ignited and the flames consumed them before they could be saved. Lady Wilde shed tears as she confided these matters to me. Me, her American boy. I hugged her, and we shared the most tender of moments, the kind I might have shared with my own mother had she lived to be a part of my life and had she ever felt the inclination to confess a family secret, the kind I suppose you're fortunate enough to be able to share with Gloria. I'll leave you with this image of me snuggling with the poet's mother. It would appear that if you are Oscar Wilde's secret secretary, I am his secret sibling—yet another!

Ever yours,
Baxter

The end of Baxter's letter made Traquair think of his father's "secret sibling," Moses. Traquair had already sent a telegram to the Palace Hotel in San Francisco asking that they secure the address of a Mr. Moses Traquair. If his uncle had indeed settled in Northern California, he would make every effort to find him.

Feeling somewhat unfairly informed of the indiscretions of Oscar's family, Traquair gently folded the letter and carefully replaced it in its envelope. He thought pleasingly of Baxter's deepening relationship with Lady Wilde; Baxter clearly had a need for maternal affection, the fact of which Traquair, heretofore, had not been aware. Serious emotions accompanied his friend's growing attachment to this woman who called herself Speranza, but a lightness in Baxter's tone, a playfulness, made Traquair think that Baxter had not fully explored the nature of his relationship with Oscar's mother.

As the train jerked along, Traquair stole a guilty glance at Oscar, whose droopy eyes were scanning the pages of the book in his lap. Vail had dozed off; his *Harper's* was but a mile or so of bumpy westward progression from completing its slow slide down his leg to the floor of the car. Traquair rescued the magazine, which he had no interest in reading. What he planned to read next, for the hundredth time, it seemed, was a newspaper article that had appeared in the *Sioux City Daily* on March 21. He reached into his pocket and removed the clipping that surely had added to his moody lack of interest in Utah, his fear of it, even, a melancholy dread that the big nothing outside the window might actually be a geographic articulation of himself, for the article, line by line, had siphoned the vitality out of him. He unfolded the square piece of newsprint into a rectangle formed of disturbing quadrants, and he read the opening of the article, the only part that really mattered to him:

AN AESTHETE IN UNDRESS.

Oscar Wilde as He Is When Off the Lecture Platform—Views and Raiment of the Apostle of the Beautiful.

The aesthetic-minded reporter called around yesterday forenoon to pay his respects to Oscar Wilde. On applying to the clerk at the Hubbard house he was told that Mr. Wilde's servant would take up his card. The servant indicated sat by the office stove, and was a likely-looking young man with just a tinge of the warm color of the tropics on his intelligent face. So this point is settled that the aesthetic thing in body servants is the light mixed liver. Ere long the servant returned. Mr. Wilde would see the gentleman, he said, and the reporter followed to the floor above, and was ushered into the presence . . .

Liver!

Traquair was infuriated. "Liver." Since he had first seen the word in print as a description of himself, he had yet to recover fully from the insult. He knew that probably only the people of Sioux City would see it, but the inaccurate application of the word angered him nevertheless. He was not the color of liver, the secretor of bile! One wanted it nowhere near the palette that would paint one's portrait. Most of the narrative drew a picture of him that had some truth and some delicacy, and then—slap!—"liver." It was as though the artist of his handsome portrait had suddenly splattered the painting with blood.

Yes, the liver, an essential organ of the body, was of important internal use, beneficial in its processes, but what could be gained by tossing the word "liver" around so sloppily to convey visual detail? The liver did have a distinctive color, but how likely was it that its actual tone would find true duplication upon human skin? He was, of course, aware of some of the other figurative uses of "liver," such as "liverless," "white-livered," and "lily-livered," but those were all negative, meaning cowardly. Understanding that these terms implied something positive about having a liver and, indeed, about the fortitude and vigor inherent in the natural, health-signifying, reddish-brown color of liver was of no consolation to Traquair. He simply could not tolerate the use of the noun or any of its adjective hybrids in reference to his skin— which, ironically, thanks to Oscar, he had been attending to with more vigilance than he had at any point in his entire life. Nowadays Traquair actually took pride in the tone of his skin. His private but vehement protest against the article was rooted in vanity, he knew, but he recalled Oscar's remark about the altruism inherent in vanity, and he decided that his self-indulgence was something other than self-indulgence. Washing vigorously and applying Oscar's cream regularly had buffed a glow upon his face. Liver did not glow. It had an odd, slippery-looking sheen, but it did not glow.

His all-consuming disappointment with "liver" had incited a complete reevaluation of the Sioux City newspaper story. He had expended irrational amounts of time and thought upon analyzing every detail of the article, growing more suspicious and more mercilessly critical with each subsequent review. For instance, the headline, which he had originally considered clever, he now thought simply vulgar. AN AESTHETE IN UNDRESS. What a desperate plea to gain attention, what a public spectacle the phrase made of itself in its desire to be looked upon, to be read, titillatingly promising a depiction of Oscar wearing little or no clothing. Surely that was what the title suggested. The lengthy subheading offered some clarification, but still kept the idea of wardrobe alive with the word "raiment," and the strong implication from the main heading that a defrocked Oscar would appear in the lines below. The headline was the chief raiment, the cover—the top hat, waistcoat, and trousers—of any newspaper story. How ironically naked this transparently lascivious headline left the body of its own story. At this observation, Traquair bounced his eyebrows with vengeful pleasure.

And, originally, he had thought the tone the reporter employed in the opening sentence cheery and self-effacing. "The aesthetic-minded reporter called around yesterday forenoon to pay his respects to Oscar

Wilde." But now he saw only the early indications of the insults to come. There was an obvious, haughty, mocking element to the compound adjective "aesthetic-minded." Why hadn't he noticed that in his initial reading! (One should always read everything more than once, he thought, asserting the validity of his long-standing habit. One could never astutely assess the written word upon one viewing. True meaning was inevitably masked by the hard, stony stillness of the visual presentation. Written lies were far more difficult to discern than spoken lies. With spoken lies some shakiness in the sound of the prevaricator's voice almost always exposed the existence of a trembling truth in hiding. But to detect the written lie, one had to be willing to distrust one's own eyes. One had to believe in what one could not see, the ghost of truth.) In the third sentence, the reporter called him "a likely-looking young man." Traquair had noticed the way the reporter had looked at him when they had met; it was the way people looked at him when they were about to compliment his appearance. But the reporter had not flattered him in person. That would have been too kind a thing to do. Or was it merely unnecessary to say to "Mr. Wilde's servant" the thing he had so palpably observed? He had held his tongue and scribbled a few words (one of whose identity Traquair was now woefully certain) and chosen to reserve his comments on Traquair's youthfulness and his beauty for the *Sioux City Daily.* Clearly he had been impressed, or why would he have bothered to describe Traquair at all? And why "likely-looking"—which had a vague meaning of good-looking? Why not say what he meant: "handsome"? He supposed the journalist had satisfied some poetic aspiration with the use of the more alliterative term—as if anyone, Traquair recalled Oscar's complaint, could *aspire* to be poetic. ". . . with just a tinge of the warm color of the tropics on his intelligent face." "Tinge" in this context, Traquair felt, was uncomfortably close to the insult of "dingy." The rest of the phrase he now understood was but a setup for the belly punch of the next sentence. "So this point," the sentence began. Yes, the reporter was out to make a point; that fact probably explained why he had bothered at all to describe Mr. Wilde's servant in such detail. "So this point is settled that the aesthetic thing—" There was yet another use of "aesthetic" or one of its variants, a good sign that a slur of some sort was impending. "So this point is settled that the aesthetic thing in body servants—" A nasty term, "body servants," with naughty implications, given the prurient suggestiveness of the headline. "So this point is settled that the aesthetic thing in body servants is the light mixed—" Here it came. No matter how slowly Traquair read it, it would come: "the . . . light . . . mixed . . ." Indeed, this slowing-down tactic served only to heighten the shock of what followed. Was there anything more potentially frightening than what might lie at the end of an ellipsis? Yes—what one *knew* lay at the end. No matter how many times he read it, he could not stop the word from coming: "liver."

Liver, liver, liver. He glared down at the word, focusing on it to the exclusion of its cueing neighbors. And in its sudden isolation, bereft of context, the word lost its meaning, or rather it took on a different meaning, took on a new identity, even, for the word "liver" did have such an ability, and he read it anew. "Liver": *one who lives.*

The entire piece was much longer, but Traquair had saved only the part about himself. He had saved it despite the effrontery of its language, and now he knew why. It was because reading about himself, something he had never had the privilege of doing, had somehow validated his very existence; he was alive. Surely, this stroke to his ego had contributed to his drive to read the story over and over again. The reporter, a Mr. C. Lionel Wycliffe, had written the opening with such narrative flair that during his repeated readings, Traquair had begun to think of himself as a minor character on the opening page of a short story or a novel called "An Aesthete in Undress." There he was being "indicated" by the Hubbard clerk, there he was sitting by the stove, there he was all young and handsome with just a *hint* of the warm color of the tropics on his intelligent face, there he was earning the title of "the aesthetic thing in body servants," there he was returning, there he was—albeit reduced to implication by the invisibility-inducing passive voice—leading the reporter upstairs and bringing him into the presence of Oscar Wilde. The description of his color was unfortunate. But its inaccuracy only added to the notion that he was a character, that the young man in the story was not the real him. In the story (yes, newspaper articles were stories, how appropriate to call them such), there was an element of fiction about him that opened his life up to greater possibilities, to embellishment. The important thing was that "his" story was in print. He would have to accept it as it was. Would no story at all have been better than this one? No. A fictional him, he decided, was better than no him at all. He was on record, as it were. Was Hamlet not more real than *any* undocumented dead man? Yes. Thanks to the article, Traquair was alive. Not nothing, but something. He was a liver.

His altered perspective of the story gave Traquair a new, brighter outlook. He gently folded the newspaper clipping and tucked it into his inside breast pocket and settled back into his seat. Oscar and Vail still sat tranquilly across from him; Vail still asleep, Oscar still engaged in his reading. Traquair let his eyes drift to the window again, and he watched Utah with a sense of longing. As a passionate liver, he had something to give to this emptiness. When they traced their way back eastward, he hoped he would see the waitress he had ignored at the last stop. He would eat all the free buckwheat cakes she offered. And he would say things to her that would make her blush. ("I *am* a big fella," he'd say. "Sometimes I eat everything in sight," he'd add, as he brought his large pinky finger, coated with syrup from the plate, to the tip of his tongue, with a smile.) He would give her something to remember. When he left her, she would think he had held her close to him and whispered something he shouldn't have; indeed, she would think, as she listened less sadly than usual to her husband pleasuring the other wife in the other bedroom down the hall that evening, that she could still feel Traquair's daring hand pressing its widespread fingers upon the best part of her behind. He would say something, only one word, perhaps, that would make her feel like a different kind of woman.

SAN FRANCISCO

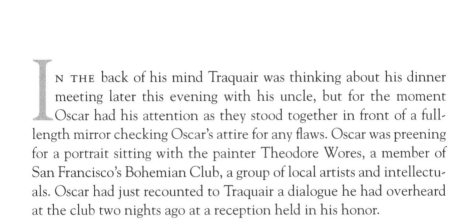

IN THE back of his mind Traquair was thinking about his dinner meeting later this evening with his uncle, but for the moment Oscar had his attention as they stood together in front of a full-length mirror checking Oscar's attire for any flaws. Oscar was preening for a portrait sitting with the painter Theodore Wores, a member of San Francisco's Bohemian Club, a group of local artists and intellectuals. Oscar had just recounted to Traquair a dialogue he had overheard at the club two nights ago at a reception held in his honor.

"He might be better off a girl," the first young man had said.

"I suppose—were it not for his face," said the other.

"Is an unattractive girl less desirable than an unnatural one?"

"What is unnatural? Nature has such a persistent way of producing the unnatural that one must question her reliability."

"My dear fellow, surely you don't rely on nature. It is the most unpredictable thing in the world."

"I rely only on art, which draws little distinction between the natural and the unnatural, or haven't you been paying attention to what our guest has been saying?"

"Are you mocking Wilde or defending him?"

"I'd like to think I'm clever enough to do both."

"The man is a Miss Nancy, plain and simple."

"If he is a Miss Nancy, he's not a plain and simple one; he's an extraordinary and complex Miss Nancy."

"There's your defense of him. Where's your clever accompanying mockery?"

"Surely, to be called an extraordinary and complex Miss Nancy is to be extremely mocked."

"You're more clever, Vee, than you've ever let on."

"Thanks, Cy."

Oscar had actually enjoyed the banter between the two men, or so he told Traquair. Not only had he gotten a chuckle out of it, but more important, it had put him on guard for what was to follow later that night. Some members of the Bohemian Club, including Vee and Cy, had tried to embarrass Oscar by serving him more to drink than was advisable for a cowboy, much less a Miss Nancy. But with Oscar's advance warning of their mild hostility toward him and his own capacity for holding his liquor, the young men had succeeded only in embarrassing themselves. Oscar had played along, telling them slyly during a round of poker, "Games are such important diversions. They allow us to forget momentarily that pleasure is a very serious business."

They had kept the drinks coming, Oscar reported to Traquair. "By the end of the evening they lay unconscious at my feet like so many cut flowers, no less beautiful, though substantially less thirsty. And I thought, 'Twelve lilies in a vase command the same respect as these twelve youths at my feet. Each group retains its beauty for a similar duration—roughly, a day.' It was this thought that kept me from disrobing them all and leaving them to awaken entangled in each other's naked limbs and caught in a marvelous panic about the tragic course of their lives. The clamorous approach of sobriety, I considered, would be painful enough."

After that night, of course, the Bohemian Club, in keeping with the rest of San Francisco, found itself under the spell of Oscar Wilde (they planned to hang the Wores portrait prominently in their library). The little trick at the club had been the only small resistance Oscar had encountered. By popular demand, he had delivered four lectures, including a specially prepared one on Irish poets. All of his appearances had been well received. Traquair had not seen Oscar this happy during all of their three months of travel.

Oscar was smiling now when he asked, "Do I love San Francisco so because she loves me, or does she love me so because I love her?" They were still standing in front of the mirror fine-tuning his appearance.

"I don't know," Traquair said. "But only sincere mutual affection could give rise to such a question."

"Have you ever known such mutual affection, Traquair?"

"I don't believe I have."

"You don't believe? Do you understand, Tra, that I am asking you if you have ever been in love?"

"No."

"Well, that *is* what I'm asking you."

"And I just answered you, Oscar."

"I see," said Oscar, glancing up at Traquair's reflection in the mirror.

"Have *you* . . . ?" Traquair let the question linger, there for Oscar either to answer or to let disintegrate like fog upon the glass before them.

"Briefly," answered Oscar.

"Could it have been love if it was brief?"

"That love is eternal is a myth. Brevity is one of love's truest indicators. True love explodes, rather like a bomb. What remains are ruins. The two agents, should they survive, are left to pick themselves up, dust off their tattered bodies, and move on. The love that lasts . . . is not love. It is something else."

Traquair, who had been brushing Oscar's hair, stopped his movements. Burdened by the weight of Oscar's wisdom, he let the hand holding the brush drop to his side. Oscar waved a thick strand of hair back behind his left ear. Attempting recovery, Traquair said, "Yes, but today you have the affection of San Francisco."

"Yes . . ." Oscar faced the mirror and opened his arms dramatically. Traquair, standing just behind him, saw his own face peeking over Oscar's shoulder. "Saint Francis and me . . . don't we make quite the couple?"

"Yes," said Traquair. "Now let's get you down to your carriage."

"Yes, let's," Oscar said.

They left the room, which was on the seventh floor of the opulent Palace Hotel, and took the elevator to the lobby. During the ride down, Oscar asked, "What are you to do today, Tra?"

"I have had good luck in locating a relative here. I have plans to visit him today."

"Is it one of those poor relations one hears so much about?"

"Not from the address I've been given."

"Splendid. If he is truly rich, you should persuade him to help the poor ones. Poverty poses questions to which only the rich have answers."

They exited the elevator, and Traquair guided Oscar through a wave of admirers. This group was one of "the crude hordes" that Baxter had cynically warned him against joining, though today they really were not crude at all. Most of them were satisfied simply to catch a glimpse of Oscar, or, if lucky, to make eye contact and exchange nods. Even those seeking autographs had a civility about them. Someone in the crowd asked Oscar the usual question: "What do you think of America, Mr. Wilde?"

Oscar replied, "America leaves one breathless—the smoke from the industry, I believe." There was a round of laughter. "But, really, I have detected in the San Francisco air something more conducive to effortless breathing than anything else in the world—real freedom."

Traquair heard applause as he assisted Oscar into his carriage.

Traquair was nervous about the encounter with his uncle. The only information he had about the man's character was what his father had told him. It certainly seemed possible that his father's animosity toward his uncle had unfairly darkened that description. But maybe his uncle really was the seriously flawed man his father claimed. He had detected nothing sinister in the note he had received from his uncle yesterday inviting him for a visit today. Moses Traquair owned a stonecutting and building supply company. A billboard for the company had caught Traquair's eye during the ride from the Pacific Union depot to the Palace Hotel. *Traquair's Quarry*, the advertisement had read, in letters formed from broken bits of stone that a large fist, illustrated above the company's name, had evidently crushed from a single boulder. The sign gave the company's address and noted its proprietor's name. When Traquair had arrived at the hotel, he had also found a note answering the telegraphed message he had sent requesting information on Moses Traquair, confirming his sighting of the billboard. That afternoon he had written a letter for special delivery introducing himself to his uncle, and the next day he had received his uncle's return note, written in a rough hand but on fine paper: "William, I would like to see you at my home, address above, on Thursday evening for dinner. Seven o'clock." That was all it said. From the wording, Traquair could deduce no essence of the man's reaction to having heard from the son of his long-estranged brother. The tone was curious, but not, Traquair decided, damning.

At the door to his uncle's large, bayside home, Traquair's anxiety slowed and softened his knock. Presently, a Chinese woman appeared with a smile and said, "Hello. Please come in." Traquair walked into a large entranceway and waited for the woman to close the door. His eyes were soothed by the dark blue walls. Two small, opposing sconces were flickering, and he could see additional soft light in the distance angling into the foyer from another room. A lush carpet of blue, red, and orange stretched out before him.

"Follow me," the woman said. Traquair thought it odd that she had not asked him for his name or a card or any verification of who he was. She walked ahead of him with the firmness of step only a diminutive person can truly assume. With her as his guide, he suddenly felt less gangly. He shortened his own normal stride, and some of his apprehension dissipated with the arrival of this new, mostly vicarious control of himself. She turned into the room whence the light was coming into the hall, and he trailed her closely.

A long table occupied most of the space in the dining room. Fourteen well-spaced chairs surrounded the table, on top of which rested three candelabras. For a moment Traquair wondered if others had been invited for dinner, until he realized that only two places had been set. His eyes were focused on the place settings at the end of the table to his left, when some slight motion in one of the candle flames tossed light a few feet farther out into the room, in the way that an inch of movement of a flame is accompanied by an exponentially greater movement of its aureole of light. The candle settled down, its tip burning straight up, but its motion had revealed a man standing a few feet from the table. The woman must have noticed that Traquair had seen the man because she smiled, taking this development as her cue to leave. Traquair turned to see her go. With each of her steps away from him, he felt the gradual retreat of his newfound fortitude.

"Come . . . in," the man said, in a voice whose slightly declining tremble Traquair thought conveyed its own loss of stability at the woman's departure. "Summer will be back soon."

Traquair considered these mystical words of uninspired prophecy and thought, Yes, in about two months summer would return, but why was this the first thing his uncle would say to him? Was he fond of summer? When Traquair turned to face his uncle, his countenance must have betrayed his confusion because his uncle added in an explanatory tone, "With the food."

With the food? Of course. The Chinese woman was named Summer.

He walked toward his uncle, who stepped closer to the table, into the brighter light, revealing a man of astonishing resemblance to his father, and therefore to himself. Now Traquair understood why Summer had invited him into the house without questioning his identity. His uncle was about six feet tall with dark skin and short black and gray hair. His hairline was receding slightly, much in the way Traquair's father's was; apparently Traquair could anticipate that fate as well. His uncle had an intense look in his eyes, and Traquair sensed emanating from the man an anxiety that matched his own. When they were within arm's reach of each other, his uncle extended his hand. Traquair joined him for what began as one firm shake. But before Traquair, in his nervousness, could withdraw his hand, his uncle was emphatically jerking his entire arm in an exuberant up-and-down motion. The man had a physical power that Traquair's own father lacked, and yet Traquair understood that the impetus of this rigorous exertion of his strength—a tendency toward the sudden display of emotion—was something his two elder kinsmen shared. His uncle smiled widely now and emitted a hearty laugh. Small wrinkles formed around the outer edges of his eyes, and Traquair watched these dry little furrows, when his uncle blinked, instantaneously become rivulets. Were these lines the natural markings of age or had they been trickled into existence? Traquair wondered. The man's emotion affected him deeply, and he thought, My people.

"Come," his uncle said, guiding him to the table, setting a heavy palm upon Traquair's back. "Sit down." They sat together, and Traquair watched sadness come over his uncle, who immediately produced a handkerchief from the breast pocket of his jacket and dabbed his eyes dry. Traquair looked away to give him a private moment to gather himself. "You must think I'm a damned fool," his uncle said.

"Certainly not," Traquair said, looking quickly back at his uncle, hoping to correct the man's mistaken assessment of his demure glance away.

"Well," his uncle responded, "that's only because you don't know me very well yet." They both laughed at this self-effacing remark, which had the effect of cutting the emotional gap between them roughly in half.

Remembering the words of John Everest on the subject at hand, Traquair said, "I have no fear of fools. A friend told me once that fools are underrated and, by and large, quite likable."

"If I were you I'd be wary of such a friend. The man is likely a fool himself."

"Perhaps," said Traquair. "But if so, then it is largely the counsel of a fool, that very same fool, in fact, that has set me here before you today—thereby, I must hasten to emphasize, proving his point exactly."

"If a fool has brought you to me, then may the world be filled with foolishness."

"Let my presence at your table assure you that it is."

At this statement, the two men again shared a hearty laugh. "You're too clever for your uncle, William. What is this odd banter you've brought into my home?"

"Merely words of playful exploration," Traquair said.

Moses Traquair raised his eyebrows for a moment, then let them settle. "My days of exploring are done, I'm afraid to say. The seafaring wanderer in me perished long ago, and now he haunts me like a ghost."

"What killed him?"

"Time," Moses said flatly.

"Ah. The Great Assassin." As he said this Traquair rested his elbow on the table and touched the knuckles of his right hand to the side of his face, a pose he had seen Oscar assume so frequently.

"Yes." The older man looked squarely and deeply into his nephew's eyes. "You're wiser than you need be. Go easy on me. My education, like my wandering, ended a long time ago as well. You've obviously been to a university."

"Yes, sir. But I think I've learned more in the past few months than I did during all of my college years. Something new every day."

"How young you are." Moses relaxed and sat back in his chair. "That eagerness in your eyes reminds me of my own brashness so many years ago. That's the thing that I've lost. I once had that passion to go on quests for the unknown, to learn things about the world and about myself. It is what brought me here, all the way across the continent. But that thirst for knowledge, it dies, you know, like everything else. Not easily, but soon enough it is quenched. Oh, it returns now and then, like some phantom of the past, but mostly to mock what you've become, to remind you of all you haven't learned or haven't done and what you are no longer capable of doing. Some days I walk to the bay, look out and imagine the ocean, and I wonder why I stopped here. With a little more drive and courage, I might have crossed the Pacific. I'm not even sure I ever wanted to do that when I was a young man. But I wanted to do it twelve years ago when I was just thirty-nine, and it was already too late for me. So I never made it to the Orient. Maybe that's one of the reasons I married my beautiful Summer, even though I had vowed never to marry. Summer does not want to go back home, not even for a visit—for the same reasons, I suppose, I won't go back to the East Coast. Too much history. Promise me that you will attend to that thing I see in your eyes, young William, while it lives within you."

"I promise," Traquair said quickly. As he listened to his uncle, he sensed something amateurish about his fatherly tone. It was as though Moses Traquair had wanted to say these things to someone for a long time, but he had had no one to say them to. Traquair wondered aloud, "Do you have any—"

His uncle's attention shifted to a place over Traquair's left shoulder. Traquair turned to see Summer enter the room rolling a serving cart of food and beverages. As he watched her casual approach with the meal, Traquair welcomed the return of her sturdy demeanor and poise, though he felt he had begun to gain a steadiness of his own while alone with his uncle. He noted how lovingly his uncle observed Summer's presentation of the plates of duck, beans, and dark-colored rice. Traquair thought his uncle's alert eyes, as they fell upon Summer, spoke of a more tender version of the very eagerness their owner had just disavowed possessing.

"Summer, our nephew here is not only just as handsome as his uncle, but he is even more intelligent."

Without stopping her work or even sneaking a glance at Traquair, she said with a smile, "*More* handsome."

"Who?" Moses asked.

"*Him*," she said.

Moses playfully tapped his wife's hip and winked at Traquair. When Summer had finished serving the food and placing wine and water on the table, she left without saying a word.

"Are you hungry?" Moses asked.

"I am *now*." The food smelled dark, mysterious, and inviting, with none of the faked richness of the meals he, Oscar, and Vail had eaten at any of the thirteen dining rooms they had visited at the Palace Hotel over the last few days. "I was so worried about coming to see you that I wasn't sure I would be able to eat at all."

"Worried?" His uncle picked up his fork and motioned a gesture of encouragement for Traquair to begin his meal as well. "Had your father warned you about his monster of a brother?"

"You've guessed it exactly."

"Hardly a guess. Even though I haven't see him in all these years, I know my brother well. Is he still working for the man in New York? Gates, our former teacher?"

"Gable," Traquair corrected him.

"Yes, Gable."

"He is indeed."

"I tracked him down there many years ago. We hadn't seen each other in more than ten years. I wrote him, but he never answered my letters. Maybe he never read them."

"How did you find Father after being separated from him for so long?"

"I had contacted Mr. Traquair, our benefactor in New Jersey. He was the gentleman who saved our lives by taking us, purchasing us, I suppose, from the misguided man in Charleston who thought he owned us. Mr. Traquair raised us, as your father has no doubt explained to you. As your father and I grew, our differences became obvious. We discovered that we really didn't like each other very much. He hated my philandering, as he called it, and I hated the way he was always so willing to serve. Even now . . . He was the thinker; I was the doer. We banged heads over just about everything. Anyway, one day I saw the chance to leave, to strike out on my own, and I did. It was not under the most ideal circumstances. I admit that. I did some things that years later, looking back, I understood were wrong. I suppose I knew all along that they were wrong."

"So you came to San Francisco," Traquair said.

"Not at first. I stayed back east for a few years. New York, Boston, and Washington."

"What were you doing?"

"I had money that I had borrowed, without permission, as it were, from Mr. Traquair—but that I've since repaid—so I worked a little . . .

and philandered a lot. I was a young man. About the age you are now. Maybe just a bit older, but still in my twenties."

"Did you have any children?" Traquair asked, completing the question that Summer's entrance had truncated.

"As a result of the philandering? I am aware of two. I had a daughter in Boston with whom I corresponded until she died two years ago. And I have a son, I believe, in Washington."

"You're not sure?" Traquair asked.

"I'm not sure of many things. He may not still be alive, either. I don't even know whether the child I saw was a boy or a girl, though I've a sense he was a boy. I was too flustered by the situation to ask. His mother was bitter when she gave me the news, as if it was all my fault. She screamed at me, 'Go away!' So I did, in quite a state of confusion. This was after the child was born, and I was just passing through Washington again. I caught a glimpse of him before she ran me off. She was a professional girl, if you understand me, which makes me only one in a large pool of paternal candidates. Why she insisted that I was the father, I'll never know. And I don't know where the child is. It was that last encounter with her that convinced me I needed to move far away and start over again. I kept hearing her crying, 'Go away!' That's when I came to San Francisco. After I became settled here and successful in my business, I tried to reach her but I had no luck. The whole world has changed in the twenty-two or twenty-three years since I've seen Mae, and someplace in it, I *believe*, I have a son."

Traquair savored his third or fourth forkful of the perfectly cooked, nutty-tasting rice. The rest of the meal was equally delicious, the best he had had since he was last at home. The duck had a lemony tang that was smoothed by a spice he didn't recognize; there were small, tender bits of onion in the peas; the wine was sweet, but its contrast to the rest of the sensations was interesting. The flavors of the meal had insulated him from the full impact of his uncle's words. He sipped the wine, which cleared his head for a second. "Wait a minute. Did you say . . . ?"

His uncle looked up at him. He waited not a minute, but a few seconds, during which time Traquair was unable to complete his question, the wine, just as suddenly as it had cleared his head, muddling his thoughts. Then his uncle waved away the lost thought, saying, "It's just as well. That's more than enough talk about me. Tell me about yourself . . . and tell me about my brother."

Traquair drank again from his wineglass before saying, "You look like my father."

"Looks can be deceiving," his uncle said.

"Yes, I know. But deception itself is sometimes the mask not of a truth but of a lie."

"That may be so, but it is also confusing and, really, is it relevant?"

"Only in that it reveals the probability of something I've surmised— which is that you and Father resemble one another in ways that neither of you want to admit."

"There you are again, William, with that talk that rattles around in my head and makes me dizzy."

"Are you sure it isn't the wine?" Traquair asked.

"I'm no genius, but I know the difference between wine and wit."

"As do I, though at the moment I can't think of a single advantage to the possession of such knowledge. Intoxication, I've surmised during my rare encounters with the state, asks not for recognition but for submission."

"I dare say you are in the midst of surmising such a fact at this very instant."

"I fear that I am," Traquair said, laughing.

His uncle reached across the table and tapped the rim of Traquair's glass. "Then this shall be your last."

"That is something my father would say."

"That is something *any* father would say."

Traquair nodded affirmatively. "Your brother has a way with words. I am sure that I have inherited this trait from him, as my mother is a quiet woman. Sometimes, I think that Mother may have something to say, but she can't quite bring herself to say it. And it is not saying that thing that keeps her from saying very much else." Traquair paused, his mind analyzing what he had just said, because it was the first time he had actually been consciously aware that he felt this way about his mother's silence. He was remembering a private moment he had shared with her right before going off to college. She had called him into the kitchen at an odd hour of the day, and they had sat at the table for about fifteen minutes. At first she had held his hand and almost cried. Traquair had told her, "Everything is all right, Mother. I will be fine." "No," she had said. "There's so much you don't know." "That's why I'm going to college," he had said. His mother had relaxed her shoulders when he said that. And then his father and Mr. Gable had come into the kitchen, each smoking a cigar. The day must have been a Sunday, because they smoked and drank together only on Sundays. Traquair's mother had risen quickly, as if she had been discovered doing something illicit, and went to the stove. When she returned to the table with biscuits, Mr. Traquair and Mr. Gable had already left the room. Traquair had eaten a biscuit while his mother watched him in silence.

Traquair said to his uncle, "And your brother likes to smoke cigars."

"Wretched habit!" his uncle yelled.

"Do you never smoke, Uncle?"

"Of course. Regularly. Summer is mildly disturbed when I do, which I think thrills her a little. I know it does me, her being disturbed, I mean. Is this a little perverse of us?"

"A little perversion is probably fine, though a lot might be better."

His uncle chuckled with curiosity. "Is that something you've learned to believe during the last few months?"

"That is something I've learned to *say* in the last few months. To believe it shall require a bit more resolve. To live it, less."

"As a statement or a belief, what you say might have some humor and even the blush of plausibility. But to live a life dedicated to perversity a man must surely die."

"Yes, but in *that* sleep of death what *dreams* may come."

Moses Traquair looked upon his nephew with confusion and awe. "Are you making fun of your uncle?"

"Certainly not. I'm merely making fun of myself."

"Oh," his uncle said, clearing away his consternation with the wave of a hand. "So long as one of us is entertained. Now tell me what brings you to San Francisco. Your address at the Palace Hotel left me very curious."

Traquair had purposely avoided discussing this matter. His uncle had already mentioned his displeasure with the idea of servitude, and being too specific about his position with Oscar would certainly disappoint this self-made businessman. "I'm the traveling companion and personal assistant to a touring lecturer. Oscar Wilde is his name. You may have read about him in the papers."

"Yes, of course. He talks a lot about art and is an odd dresser. Is he the one you mean?"

"Yes. In recent months we've been all over the Northeast. From here we'll be slowly working our way back home and then to the South. Maybe to Canada."

"I see," Traquair's uncle said. "So it is your traveling that has given you a new way of looking at the world."

"Traveling from coast to coast is a sure way to broaden one's horizons."

"Having done so myself, I must agree."

Summer returned with coffee and blackberry pie. "Summer," his uncle said, "I must now report that our nephew is as strange as he is intelligent."

"The strange and the intelligent—inseparable mates," she said.

"Like you and me," Moses Traquair flirted.

"That would make *you* strange," his wife said quickly, with one stroke both stating and proving an implicit claim to her own superior intellect. Traquair laughed.

"William, do you see what I live with? Consider yourself warned: never marry."

Traquair said, "Dear uncle, young men read caveats not as reasonable warnings against danger but as irresistible invitations to it. Or have you forgotten your own youth?"

"That is one of the few things I remember. Then I say: marry! Let that be my advice to you, and may your youthful infatuation with recalcitrance save you."

Summer shook her head at their remarks and then left them alone again. The pie was more tart than sweet, which Traquair found slightly disappointing. Still, he left only crumbs and a thin glaze of purple on his white plate. He and his uncle each drank two cups of coffee as they discussed Traquair's future. "I'll probably teach," Traquair said. Watching Oscar stand up before needy audiences and deliver wise, clever speeches had sparked within him a desire to be similarly generous. To give of oneself in that way, he thought, required courage, and he had begun to see the challenge teaching presented. The war against ignorance, as he had told his father, was one worth fighting.

"Why do you say 'probably'?" his uncle asked him. "If you want to teach, determine to do it."

"I'm enjoying the thrill of equivocation for the moment. Someone said to me recently, 'Once a man discovers his true calling, he may as well retire.'"

"Was it that same fool you were discussing earlier, or some other one?" Moses Traquair asked.

"Some other one."

Soon the conversation turned back to Traquair's father.

"Tell him to let your mother speak," Moses Traquair told his nephew. "What is her name?"

"Gloria."

"You tell him to let . . . Gloria speak." He cleared his throat before continuing, "You haven't said he's the problem for her, but I know he is. He never wanted me to speak out, either. Strange, a man so gifted with language should feel so threatened by the expression of others. There's a weakness in such a man. What is his fear? That someone will challenge him? Or that someone will tell his secrets? A father's secrets are part of a son's inheritance."

"Not those secrets that go uncovered."

"No," Moses Traquair agreed.

"Those," said Traquair, "are more often silent *rivals* for the son's inheritance."

Traquair and his uncle laughed at this remark for a moment, paused, and then laughed again, this time uncontrollably. Summer appeared at the doorway with concern on her face, or so it seemed to Traquair when he turned and looked at her through teary eyes. She came over to them and said, "I thought I heard crying, but it is only laughing."

"Sometimes," Moses Traquair said, reaching for the handkerchief he had used earlier to dry his eyes after first meeting his nephew, "the two occur simultaneously. Tears are confusing."

"Only to men," Summer said.

Moses Traquair looked at his wife with the mock perturbation Traquair had come to understand as a part of their relationship. "*Women* are confusing."

"Only to men," she repeated.

"Must you be determined to answer everything I say?"

"To answer you does not require determination."

"You know—" Moses Traquair stopped himself before completing his thought. "I surrender."

"That is the wisest thing you have said today," she said, winking at Traquair, who felt strangely at home with this couple. They were con-

tent, balanced. His presence seemed not to disrupt their skillful inter-
play, so in tune were they. Domesticity, as he had witnessed it practiced
by his own parents, was something in whose presence he had always felt
uncomfortable. Its polished finish had frightened him. The glint it
flashed promised to settle somewhere over his shoulder in a corner of
the house, allowing him to look deep into the shiny thing itself and see
himself reflected there. But this promise had gone unfulfilled. With his
parents, he had always found himself squinting. In contrast, his aunt
and uncle were lovely together, flirting in the soft candlelight of their
pleasant dining room, their dust-shifting exchanges chasing away the
lies of lint and gently exposing small but solid verities that meant something to them and, quite incidentally, to him. He adored them for
themselves. He freed them from the parental burden of being an example to him. And yet, in the role he assigned to them—happy, loving
mates of casual perfection—they so excelled that he could not help but
see them as a paradigm, if not for himself, then for his parents and for
the rest of the coupling world.

Moses Traquair insisted on driving his nephew back to the Palace
Hotel. As they rode along in the cool night air, Traquair relaxed in the
cradle of the San Francisco evening. Low clouds shielded the stars and
moon from view, but a glow filled the sky.

"Tell me, William," his uncle said. "Is your mother a woman of a
rich brown complexion?"

"Brown?"

"Yes. A bit darker than me and your father."

"I suppose that would be accurate."

"And would she be a woman roughly two or three inches taller
than Summer?"

"I suppose that would be correct as well. How do you know this,
Uncle?"

"I know who your mother is. Your father married our cousin Gloria."

Traquair could not confirm this fact, but his uncle's description and
the certainty in his voice gave him no reason to doubt it. "You know
her?" he asked.

"Yes. Well, I knew her. She was another charge of Mr. Traquair's.
Your father was always taken with her, though he pretended not to be.
I guess the truth of his heart must have persuaded him in the end."

"And was she in love with him?" Traquair asked hungrily, seizing this opportunity to inquire about matters he had never discussed with his parents and that he feared he never would. His uncle started to say something and then retreated, saying, "I suppose you'll have to ask her that question."

Traquair let his disappointment pass and then, thinking of his conversation this morning with Oscar, laughed and said, "It's odd. Just today, for the first time, someone asked me a similar question, if I had ever been in love."

"And how did you respond?"

"In the way I thought he'd expect me to."

"And, that is to say, not truthfully?" Moses Traquair asked.

"That is to say I gave no as an answer when, in actuality, what sane twenty-two-year-old is not in love with himself?"

"Love is to be shared, William."

"I have my moments of generosity. Not unlike you in your youth, I—" Traquair, in recalling his moments of "generosity," suddenly remembered something.

"What is it?" his uncle asked.

"During dinner, there was something I wanted to tell you, but I forgot, because of the wine, I guess. But in my travels, I have mimicked you and your youthful philandering. And I have been to Washington, to a place there that catered to the desires of young men and the desires of old men nostalgic for their youth, and I met the owner of the establishment, a woman named Mae."

"Surely not," Moses Traquair said incredulously.

"I surely did meet a woman named Mae. Whether or not she was the woman you mentioned to me, the one you knew, I can't say. But she was situated in Washington, and her name was definitely Mae. I remember her distinctly because she overcharged me for drinks . . . and services."

"That fact alone gives me strong reason to consider her as possibly being my Mae. She always drove a hard bargain."

Traquair searched his memory of Mae and then added, "She had a mole right here." He pointed to the right upper corner of his mouth.

"Mae!" Moses Traquair exclaimed. "She did always talk to me, in what I thought irrational terms, about wanting her own business. She had ambition. We shared that quality. That was one of the things I fancied most about her. It sounds as though she got what she wanted.

Do you remember her address? I would like very much to communicate with her somehow."

"I'm afraid not. Don't you remember how difficult it is to find such places?"

"I always went straight to a brothel without any trouble. It was only when I headed for home that I realized I was lost."

The carriage pulled up to the hotel, and Traquair and his uncle embraced. "You must come for a long visit someday, William, when you are done with your travels. Summer and I will welcome you into our home."

"I should like that very much."

"Tell your father and mother—" Moses Traquair looked away.

"I shall," Traquair said, touching his uncle's arm. "I shall tell them almost everything." Traquair stepped out of the carriage. His uncle did not look back at him. When Traquair saw his uncle's back start to tremble, he turned and walked away.

Oscar returned to the hotel late that night, bringing Traquair a slice of chocolate cake. "I thought this might cheer you up. Nothing like an evening with the relatives to depress one with the notion of what is actually coursing through one's veins."

"But I don't need cheering up," Traquair said. "I'm perfectly happy."

"How impractical of you, Tra. If I am ever perfectly happy, I hope someone puts a stop to it immediately."

SALT LAKE CITY

TRAQUAIR, Oscar, and Vail were laughing at the Tabernacle. The three of them had completed a tour of the great Mormon place of worship and were in a carriage on their way back to the hotel. Oscar had just pronounced the Tabernacle a soup kettle. Traquair knew it was the kind of remark Oscar would likely repeat, and some of his own laughter was due to his understanding that the world would someday soon hear this scathing critique of the building's outrageous appearance.

Oscar was going on, "Surely a man as creative as Brigham Young, a man of great religious ingenuity if not originality, did not intend this. If one's church is a kettle, then God is a cook; man is meat; life, a stew. While not entirely inaccurate, the metaphor is grotesquely inartistic."

Soon the laughter subsided, and the mood in the cab changed. Oscar's countenance had suddenly lost the tight perkiness of the comedian and had taken on the relaxed pallor of the serious essayist finding a new thesis. While Vail was still humming away his last few lingering moans of amusement, unaware of the new environment—that indeed the weather had changed from clear and sunny to somewhat cloudy, the terrain from flat to ever-so-slightly bumpy—Traquair was already tingling in anticipation of what Oscar was about to say. Yes, Oscar was about to say something. Traquair remembered again the first day he had met Oscar, when, before he had even seen him, he had heard the voice of the genius clarifying the meaning of "genius." And he remembered that moment when Oscar had stood up and swayed back the crowd of reporters, who were all awaiting his definition of a rose. Since that first day, whenever he had caught sight of the face Oscar had presented at that moment, Traquair had been aware of the sensation of imminent enlightenment. He could recognize this feeling with Oscar as surely as he could recognize a similar feeling when in the presence of anything that promised great pleasure: imminent enlightenment from Oscar on the one hand, the thrill of the Land of the Lace on the other. Traquair admitted to himself now that the presence of Oscar and the walk down the hall toward the girl he had named Aurora had something in common. (Theda Trenton's walk to meet him under the lamppost back in St. Louis, while undeniably laced, as it were, with pleasure, was to him somehow a different matter.) Each produced in him an irresistible desire *to know*—one in the real sense, the other in a figurative, biblical sense whose root meaning he had not really understood until now. There was something sensuous about Oscar's velvety, truth-ridden language, just as there was something to be learned from physical pleasure. For the moment, his infatuation with Oscar's brilliance was confusing his sense of what knowledge really was. (Meeting Miss Trenton was different, he surmised now, in that she had induced in him a strong desire not to know but *to be known*. Had he stumbled on yet another definition of "lust"? Was it the desire to know? If so, did that mean that "love" was the desire to be known? What did these possible meanings say of his feelings for Theda Trenton? Nothing, he protested. After all, he didn't really even . . . know her.) Traquair's strange—he considered it strange—comparison of Oscar's seductive, overpowering wisdom to the physical delights of the girls he had been with pushed forth this thought: Genius corrupts.

"And yet," Oscar began now in a serious tone, "and yet—the artistic failure of the Tabernacle is not man's, not the architect's, not Brigham Young's. It all must come back to God Himself—the Christian God, whom I have so often pitied. Yes, as a fellow artist, I have great sympathy for this God. Great sympathy, indeed. That what was to be one's crowning artistic achievement—the creation of man—should fail so immediately, so disastrously, so completely is surely, daily, a heartbreaking reality to witness. To blunder so stupendously in the act of creation is every artist's nightmare. To be the one who set in motion the perpetuation of this error is to suffer a truly cruel fate. To have made a mistake so colossal as to require the sacrifice of one's only son, one's sole physical incarnation, to correct the fundamental defect is unbearably poignant. The creation of man is without doubt the single greatest artistic tragedy. God set the standard for artistic imperfection. One cannot dispute that we are made in His image. It is not so much our lives that prove this fact as it is our art. Witness that disastrous Tabernacle there behind us.

"And this is why men so love the Christian God. Christianity reduces Him to our level. Yes, He can speak loudly, yell at us, call us names for being disobedient, promise us punishment—but the thing of it is: He made us. Man is the craft of an imperfect hand. Our error is His. Our badness is His."

"Perhaps that explains God's silence," Traquair said.

"Maybe He simply doesn't exist," said Vail. "Maybe *that* explains His silence."

Oscar relaxed his wide shoulders and smiled. And from this smile—which, like a large wave approaching the shore, seemed to have the entire force of an ocean behind it—Traquair knew immediately that the mood would shift again. Oscar said, "God's silence toward man proves only that He is a discriminating conversationalist."

The carriage was again filled with laughter. Traquair loved moments like this one with Oscar and Vail, the camaraderie among them. His entire body seemed to levitate with energy of an unknown variety. He wondered if the others felt the same way, that they were part of something unusual and powerful. To Traquair's mind, they formed an odd celestial phenomenon, he and Vail as two planets orbiting Oscar's sun. Traquair had often marveled at the thoughts that grew within him when the three of them consorted in this way, and the scene became aglow with the Wildean light. For instance, as the carriage moved along now and as this most recent revolution into and now out of the light ended, his thoughts began torquing inward. He found himself thinking about Oscar's professed sympathy for God, and his own sympathy for the unknowable force emerged.

Unknown, but all-knowing. It was God's omniscience that broke Traquair's heart. Omniscience was a curse. If one knows everything, Traquair thought, there is a paradoxical thing that one can never know: the thrill that comes of *not* knowing. No—the *thrills*, for there were many. Traquair pitied God that. God would never know the pleasure of suddenly understanding the answer to a riddle; He already knew all of the answers to all of the riddles, including, one could only presume, the riddle of Himself. God would never know the satisfaction of the surprising resolution of a mystery. He would never know the terror of a great secret just revealed. He could not get lost in a maze and know the joy and relief of finding His way out. He would never feel the sense of accomplishment that comes with inserting the last piece of the puzzle and finally seeing the picture whole and clear; all was already clear to Him. For God there were no adventures, no undiscovered continents. He could do what man could not do, travel the entire universe, and yet He would never know the thrill of discovery. Omniscience was the highest and loneliest plateau.

But what of His omnipotence? mused Traquair. Mightn't He use His limitless powers to counter the drudgery of knowing everything? Well, His troubles in creating man, if Oscar's reasoning was to be taken seriously, might have shaken His confidence in His powers; perhaps they were not without limit. But shouldn't He, in His omniscience, have *foreseen* His error? Was His knowledge also somehow incomplete? Or did God, fully aware of the fatal mistake He was making with man, go through with the act, which seen in this light could be viewed only as an act of masochism toward Himself and sadism toward His creation? Or could it be that God cherished man because man presented Him with the constant reminder of the one great and tragic discovery He would ever make: the discovery of His own fallibility? Was man God's lone, cherished souvenir from the moment of His fall?

Traquair let these questions spin his head around and around. He had no real answers, and he suspected there weren't any. Not knowing, he surmised, was the centrifugal force of thought. The omniscient God, then—the one who knew everything—could feel but, in all probability, could not think. Traquair wanted to say this aloud, "God does not think," but he did not. In this moment of deep contemplation he was sharing with the others, he felt that he already had an idea of what Oscar's response would be: "You are correct, Traquair. God does not think. But it is His particular genius that, despite this affliction, occasionally He manages to be thoughtful."

LEADVILLE

A CHILLED Traquair stood at the bottom of the Number Three shaft of the famous Matchless Mine, looking upward with his arms stretched out, awaiting Oscar. Strapped into the same ore bucket the other twelve or thirteen men already in the mine had used, dangling from the same rope, Oscar was slowly descending. It was two-thirty in the morning, and the frosty Rocky Mountain air had Traquair's eyes tearing and his ears tingling.

"Tra!" Oscar shouted down to him.

"I'm here," Traquair yelled, his voice cracking in the cold. "Hold on tightly, and you'll be fine."

"We rode up all those miles above sea level only to be tempted to plunge back down even more intimately into the womb of the earth." Oscar's voice had a quiver in it. Was it from fear, Traquair wondered, or had it been caused by the jaunty motions of the bucket as it was being lowered? Oscar had certainly shown no fear in deciding to go through with this adventure into the mine. People in Denver had warned that while Leadville was the richest city in America, it was also the country's and quite possibly the world's gun-toting roughest. "This inclination to descend into, to sink oneself into dark places has surely got something to do with the male predicament." Oscar sounded to Traquair as if he was trying to calm himself by casually initiating one of their typical rounds of repartee. "And then, too, while mountaintops, from a distance, are beautiful, they somehow lose their charm once one has conquered them. The man who hugs the peak knows the ultimate in loneliness. I suppose once one has reached such heights, one is forced to admit that the dark underground is the only real repository of the world's true treasures."

A particularly dirty miner elbowed Traquair. "We ain't found no true treasures down in this hole. Only false ones."

Traquair whispered a response: "I sometimes think it's the false ones Mr. Wilde prefers."

The man smiled along with Traquair, but confusion creased the corners of his eyes. "Huh?" he grunted. "The false ones? Well, even them is scarce." The man nudged Traquair again and whispered, "So according to old Piss-on, your boss man's supposed to look like Laffite and talk like Lincoln. We figured we ought to know a sad scoundrel like that, a feller you can just look at and see something about him ain't quite right, a joker who talks so much he gon git hisself shot down."

Traquair raised his eyebrows and said, "I should think Mr. *Pishon* meant to describe Mr. Wilde as dashing, daring, and diplomatic. But I suppose if Mr. Wilde were ever counted among the pirates, he should be the president of their lot. And do beware. If you are not careful he just may steal your mind and emancipate your heart." The miner's dirty face brightened with perplexity, and it occurred to Traquair, who was moving quickly to assist Oscar from his chariot onto the floor of the shaft, that bewilderment could be cleansing.

Oscar reached for his arm, asking, "Whose idea was this?"

"Yours, of course." Traquair pointed to the rubberized, underground outfit Oscar had borrowed for this occasion, which he wore beneath his overcoat. "You thought it would be fun to wear that suit."

Oscar looked at his strange attire and remarked, "First my knee breeches cause a scandal, and now this suit leads me to the bottom of the earth. I may be the only man of my generation consistently shamed by his desire to put clothes *on*."

"Desire of any sort has a way of complicating things," Traquair tossed out playfully, attempting to assist Oscar in creating, in this alien atmosphere, a more comfortable environment. A man from a London newspaper named McDonald was accompanying them, along with Mr. Charles Pishon, assistant to the wealthy owner of the mine, Mr. H.A.W. Tabor. Vail had remained in Denver, to which they would return after this stop. Traquair hoped his comment would help inspire Oscar's wit. He was searching for the verbal equivalent of the fur coat and the scarves he always laid on the sofas in the hotel rooms where

Oscar, in a setting conducive to his languidly linguistic performances, regularly entertained guests.

Oscar took the cue: "Desire does not complicate things, Tra, it simplifies things. It's marvelous in that way. It forces one to focus one's energies. It is not want itself but rather the particular thing that man wants that complicates matters. The woman. The world."

"What a man desires most is to be wanted," Traquair countered, as if casually placing a green velvet throw over an unattractive footstool. He was thinking of Miss Trenton and how he wanted her to want him.

"Perhaps," Oscar said. "But, oh, how quickly a wanted man will renounce desire."

"Except those wanted men who desire no longer to be wanted," Traquair said. "They simply surrender."

"Yes, and I suppose there's nothing quick about surrender. The moment of surrender is eternal. Napoléon never really left Waterloo, did he? And Robert E. Lee is still signing all of those papers at Appomattox."

Their dialogue was interrupted by a faceless voice. "I was once wanted in four states."

"Oh, yeah?" a man up front holding a shovel said. "Ain't one of them the state of insanity, Dalton?" Some of the other men laughed. "I hear you own a few acres o' land there. Any truth to it?"

The professed wanted man was pushing his way up front now. At first, in silhouette, he appeared tall and heavy to Traquair. But as he, Dalton, moved closer to the lamplight, his form gained definition. His neck was particularly muscular, and his large, dark face was rough and menacing. His eyes, squinting now, appeared trained to track offense, and the lower edge of his chin had, faintly, the soft lines of a blunt weapon. Instead of being merely big and heavy, Traquair could see that the man was in fact powerful. Dalton stood facing his adversary and said only, "Hush up, Winky."

Oscar, as if wishing to distract Dalton, asked, "What do you mean that you were *once* wanted in four states? Are you no longer wanted?"

"Well, my mama wrote me a letter a while back and she said they don't want me no more in Missouri or Illinois. So that leaves me being wanted in just one state, the way I figure it."

Winky couldn't resist. "The way you figure it is gonna wind you up a citizen in the state of incarceration."

"What? That don't add up to the right number?" Dalton asked.

"It adds up to a number across your chest," Winky said. And the men laughed until Dalton gave Winky a hard shove on the arm. Winky winced and smirked at once.

Oscar again interceded. This time he moved to a spot between the two men and touched Dalton's shoulder lightly. "Not to worry, my friend," he said. "Men who know too much about numbers cannot be counted on to know the score."

Traquair thought of his friend John from Philadelphia. John knew numbers, and he seemed always to know the score; you could count on him. Oscar was right in a way—but he was also wrong. Was the ability to be both at the same time a gift or a curse? Traquair hoped the former to be true, as he had acquired this ability himself over the past four months of listening to and sparring with Oscar. Maybe he hadn't really acquired it. Maybe it had always been a part of him waiting to be exposed. Maybe it was a part of everyone, he thought. Was Oscar's ostentatious use of paradox just a way of insisting upon being frank about his—and everyone's—dual nature? Traquair was bothered by the obvious generality of his own question. He cornered himself: If Oscar has a dual nature, what is it? If *I* have a dual nature, what is it? There. That's what I want to know. *To know,* Traquair thought, returning to a proposition he had considered recently (Where? he asked himself, the trail of cities starting to trick his memory. San Jose, Leavenworth?), to know was the dangerous thing he desired.

The talk had continued around him, the bottles of whiskey circulating miner-style. Each man who had a bottle opened it, took a taste, and passed it along to the next man. Traquair's cold body welcomed his first swallow of alcohol. It was becoming obvious that the impetuous notion to join the miners for "dinner" would leave the guests hungry. But the liquor promised to make them all forget about the limitations of underground hospitality. Traquair made a note to himself to stay alert enough to make arrangements for an early breakfast as soon as they returned to the hotel.

A man with a dusty, full beard said, "Mr. Wilde, since you got so much to say about wanted men, I'm wonderin what you think o' the way they got ole Jesse James week before last."

Oscar's eyes brightened. "Oh, we were on a train—weren't we, Traquair?—heading from San Francisco to Stockton when we learned of the terrible news of the murder of Jesse James. Yes, I remember it distinctly. The beautiful little details of his catastrophic life as the newspaper quite thoroughly reported them." Oscar paused and appeared deep in thought for a moment before going on. "Things that happen on trains seem to have a more devastating quality, an almost theatrical impact. That fact must account, in part, for the way the Jesse James story moved me. It may be that a train's physical motion is a powerful metaphor—excuse me, a strong symbol of dramatic action. There is a sense in which the moving train is drama given physical form. Drama that appears to be escaping. It is no wonder that men want to possess it."

"Men like Jesse!" the bearded man yelled.

"Precisely," said Oscar.

"They say he robbed more than five hundred trains," another miner said.

"Five hundred—that don't make no sense," said Winky. Then he added quietly, sarcastically, "How many you reckon, Dalton?"

Oscar instinctively raised his right arm, stopping a blow from Dalton, who had taken aim at Winky's face. Dalton looked at Oscar, and he quickly settled down. He said, "Hush with that teasin, Winky. You know better'n to keep on with me."

Mr. Pishon stepped forward and said, "Both of you, be quiet."

"Go on, Mr. Wilde," a man said, stepping over to Oscar and handing him a bottle. Oscar took a long draft as the men looked on, many of them taking advantage of this moment to turn up a bottle of their own.

"All men want drama," Oscar said. "They want it more than anything else."

"I want me a woman!" said the man who had just handed Oscar the bottle and was already reaching for its return.

"What is a woman if not drama personified?" Oscar responded.

"I want me some gold!" another man howled.

"What is gold but drama crystallized, an alloy of action and dreams?" Oscar said. "No, all men want drama. Drama is the enactment of all emotion. There is no emotion that cannot be dramatized and therein made more real and certainly more accessible. We return to Shakespeare again and again, some of us, because one passage promises us joy, another sadness, yet another the shock of love, as if the emotions were our own. Men want drama more than they want love because drama *is* love and every other emotion, only with a perfection and a power that even love does not possess. This fact explains the irresistible attraction of fairy tales, the power of parables, the lust for scandal, the thrill of tragedy."

The man leaning on his shovel looked up quizzically and wondered aloud, "But that don't say nothing about Jesse James."

"It says everything about Jesse James."

"How do you mean?"

"Well, imagine for the moment that you *are* Jesse James." Then Oscar made a motion of inclusion to everyone. "Each of you. Imagine that you *are* Jesse James." The men, almost in unison, raised their bottles, as if putting their imaginations to work required refueling. Oscar and Traquair were handed bottles, as were Mr. Pishon and McDonald, the reporter. Every man drank. Some of them found clear patches of ground or small boulders to sit on, and the gathering, it seemed to Traquair, suddenly had the intimacy of a neighborhood saloon . . . or a chapel.

"Let yourself become the beloved outlaw," Oscar went on. "That bullet hole in your head, just placed there by Bob Ford, a member of your gang, as his cowardly brother Charles looked on, is about to bring you crashing to the sitting-room floor of your house in St. Joseph, Missouri. You stagger. You worry about the future of your wife, your two lovely children, Mary and Jesse, and your poor, dear wounded mother, who lost her arm years before when Pinkerton agents were trying to capture you. All of these loved ones live with you in your little white house with green shutters. And Frank! Your only brother, Frank! Would the Ford boys kill him, too, before someone could stop them? No, Frank would be all right. It was you they wanted. You were the one everyone wanted.

"Why were you so special? you ask yourself, as a line of blood begins to trickle down your forehead. You remember the early days when you were only sixteen and Frank was only eighteen and you enlisted in the Confederate cavalry. Your job is to stir up as much trouble as possible along the Missouri and Kansas border. You are to maraud and pillage. You have been commanded to break the law in all the ways that war allows, which is every way imaginable. In these endeavors you are accorded tremendous freedom. One day as you and Frank, with the help of three brothers named Younger, are pillaging a small store of cash and ammunition, you catch a glimpse of yourself in a mirror behind the counter and you are surprised to see the great expression of pleasure that resides upon your face. And you notice something dexterous and perfect in your own movements. All around you the other fellows are plundering with a grace similar to, though not quite as distinctly beautiful as, your own. As you reach behind the counter and into the glass display case to gather a handful of gold watches, you think, 'Oh, why can't it be like this forever! Just me and the boys, our wits working, our Colts cocked.' You wind one of the watches and stare at it as it does its work, acknowledging that in its small, seemingly silent and steady motion lay your ultimate ruin and decay. As clearly as you have just seen the beauty of your face in the mirror, you now see your ruin upon the face of the watch. You don't think of any of these things in quite this way, but the watch inspires a sweet, poignant admission of your own powerlessness against the forces of nature. And yet, in the next breath, you make a strange vow: never to die. Like most vows, it is unreasonable. Instinctively, you decide to keep this watch for yourself, and you place it in your pocket.

"As time, indeed, would have it, the war ends. It's back home to Clay County, Missouri. There you must face angry Union supporters, who are interested in something more than an explanation for your wartime actions. And though you want to be good, you know all too well the pleasure that comes of being bad."

Several of the miners laughed knowingly at this remark. "Hush," someone said. "We's about to start really robbin now."

"Yes, you and Frank leave home and, with the able assistance of the Youngers and a few qualified others collected along the way, you begin to rob banks and loot other establishments in Missouri, and Minnesota and Texas and Kentucky."

"Don't forget Nebraska," a man with a red cotton scarf tied around his neck said. "We make it up to Nebraska."

"Yes, Nebraska," said Oscar.

"And Iowa," another man said.

"Yes. You seem insatiable in your hunger for things that belong to others. Occasionally you question your right to dispossess men of their property, but you always think that it simply wouldn't be fair to the others you've already plundered to stop now. Those unfortunates would already be asking themselves, 'Why has Jesse struck me?' If you stop now, your randomness will seem ungodly. You owe it to your circle of victims to continue. With every announcement that you have robbed someone else, their grief is diminished, their faith is increased. The larger their number, the smaller the individual share of pain. To continue your scourge is to comfort the scourged.

"Then one day—a fine summer day—after a marginally profitable excursion, you, Frank, and your gang are relaxing under the shade of an immense tree somewhere in Iowa. You are sitting with your back up against the trunk of the tree. You've taken off your hat and placed it on the ground next to you, and the back of your bare head is tapping gently against the rough bark. It's a cooling sensation, aided by the crown of sweat your tight-fitting hat has generated. You reach up and tousle your hair, which is thick and long. You've removed your boots and stretched out your legs, and the breeze blows over your feet, relieving you. Your men are sleeping nearby. You hear faint snoring off to your left and recognize it as your brother's. Nothing is more reassuring to you than Frank's steady breathing. You are strangely alert in your reverie, but the rhythm of Frank's inhaling and exhaling lulls your head downward. Next to your hat you notice a small patch of wild, red roses. The flash of color, so unexpected, jars you out of the throes of slumber. In appreciation, you pick a flower and bring it to your nose. The soft scent reminds you of a woman. You think of your cousin Zerelda and remember how one day her beauty had surprised you, the way this rose has just done, awakening a man's heart from the repose of childhood.

"As you concentrate upon the rose, you become aware of a faint sound, a sound other than your brother's breathy moans. It, too, is rhythmic, even more so. With romance momentarily on your mind, you fantasize for a second that it is the sound of your heart. But soon you discover that the sound, muffled and metallic, is emanating from your vest pocket. Yes, it is your watch. You remove it from your pocket and look at it. Ah, that magical day of more than ten years past when you had acquired it. Ten years! you think. Has it been that long? No, more than ten years, because the war has been over for eight years. All of that time has gone by. You had thought back then that all you wanted was to be out living hard and strong with your gang. You've made that happen. But here time is moving on, literally slipping through your fingers, as you sit under a tree yearning for a woman. Zerelda. Where is the great feeling of excitement and action you witnessed in the mirror during the robbery all those years ago? Have you failed to be true to the spirit of that fine moment? What can you do to right that wrong? Where is the drama you beheld in that mirror? You find the persistent ticking of the watch unbearable.

"And then, off in the distance, you see the train, slowly approaching from the west. It is small at first, like the seed of the idea that your renewed sense of ambition has suddenly produced and is nurturing. The approach of the train and the development of the idea are linked in a mutual rapidity of advancement. With each second, the image of the train grows larger and larger, the idea closer to reality. Like consciousness coming, the pace of the train appears to quicken as it nears. The thick cloud at its head comes to life, a surging stream of confetti— a fanfare, dusty and dark. The hum of the train becomes a rumble, and the sound of the watch is rendered inaudible. Forgotten, the ticking instrument slides from your hand. You still clutch the rose in your other hand, but the blossoming of your idea renders it devoid of significance and soon it, too, falls to the ground. All that you want is cast into the vision of the train. There's nothing left but you and the train—nothing left but a man and his raw desire. How simple. But you want *the train*. How complex. If you could hug the train and wrestle it gently from its rails, you would. But, alas, some things cannot be hugged into submission. Some things, to be possessed, beg the invention of a new mode of conquest. Only a great artist could take possession of something so free as a moving train without the assistance of violence, indeed with something as loving as an embrace. Only a very great artist. But to conquer the moving train through force would require merely a great *man*. You, Jesse James, are that great man! And suddenly, in this moment, you know it!

"Impassioned by your vision, filled with the knowledge of what glory lay before you in the years to come as you make the world see the grace with which things, evil things, can be done—many of these deeds already accomplished in your heart—you rise up from your seat on the ground and remove the two Colt revolvers from their holsters at your side. You raise them high above your head, and with the private abandon of a man who has discovered a new way to love, indeed, with the sparks of your feelings for Zerelda in part igniting your joy, you fire your weapons at will. Sometimes simultaneously, sometimes alternating the shots. You are celebrating your invention, your love, and your own greatness. And you shout, *I am Jesse James! I am Jesse James!*"

With these words, a loud clamor of gunfire erupted in the Number Three shaft of the Matchless Mine. Blasts of fire and sparks spewed from the barrels of revolvers upward toward the distant starry sky, splattering the darkness like bright yellow, red, and orange paint being smeared against a black wall. Through the din, Traquair heard shouts of "I am Jesse James!" and "Bring on the trains!" and "Wake up, Frankie!" As the shooting had commenced, Oscar had immediately drawn up his coat for cover. Now Traquair put his hands up to protect his ears. His muffling of the noise sharpened his vision, and various bits of the pandemonium came into focus. In the splotchy brightness, he saw the miners jumping and kicking up dust in strange, photographic poses. Next to Oscar, Dalton was shooting his large revolver, and Traquair read his lips as they mouthed—in typical Dalton fashion, one syllable short—"Zelda, I love you!" McDonald, the reporter, demonstrated himself to be unexpectedly lithesome in his swift retreat to a nearby wall. Mr. Pishon, too, was forced to call upon a dexterity of his own, clasping his left hand over his ear and hunching his opposite shoulder up over his other ear, all the while furiously motioning, with a manic window-washer's waving of the free right hand and a wing-style flapping of the bent left elbow, for the men to calm down and stop firing their weapons.

The explosion seemed to last for several minutes, but it was probably less than sixty seconds in duration, ending finally when the cocking and the trigger squeezing began to produce only impotent clicks. Traquair watched as each man wasted a few gestures, before lowering his hands from his ears. Some of the men let out yells of rebel joy, the purest and most eloquent of which was "Got-dayum!" A couple of men laughed with wonder at their own behavior, and then for a moment everything was still and quiet. Mr. Pishon seemed stunned and embarrassed. McDonald wrote nothing on his reporter's pad.

Oscar lowered the collar of his coat, unveiling his surprisingly composed self. He looked around and assessed the aftermath. Then he merely sighed.

"Jesus Christ, mister," the miner in the red handkerchief said to Oscar, "you oughtn'ta go gettin a bunch of fellers so riled up."

"It's a free country," said Dalton, still huffing from his exertions. "He can rile a feller up if he likes."

"You're right, Dalton," said Winky, with none of his earlier sarcasm toward his coworker. "Certainly he can."

"Don't come kissin up to me, Winky. I ain't forgot how you was houndin me."

"I . . ." Winky—sincere, it had seemed to Traquair, in the apologetic tone he had used with Dalton—didn't finish what he was about to say. Rebuffed and possibly hurt, he just looked away.

Mr. Pishon had gathered himself by this time and stepped forward. "Mr. Wilde, please accept my apology for this unfortunate display. Mr. Tabor will be most distressed to learn what has happened. And I can assure you there will be repercussions."

"Come on, Mr. Pishon," one of the miners pleaded. "Ain't no harm done."

"Yeah," another man said. "Mr. Wilde don't seem upset none, Mr. Pishon."

"I believe that's Piss-on!" someone from the back of the shaft called out.

"Who said that!" Pishon looked around with a sudden rage.

An amused Oscar said, "Mr. Pishon, there is no reason to disturb Mr. Tabor with the news of what has happened down here tonight. And for that matter, Mr. McDonald, I do not think you need to terrify the world with such incendiary news from the underground. Besides, no one, save my mother, would believe you. I should think you would be denigrated as an inventor of fairy tales, and I cannot condone anyone other than myself being so honored." Mr. Pishon nodded his acquiescence, and McDonald put up his hands in surrender.

"Listen up, you son-of-a-bitches!" shouted Dalton. "Nobody can't talk about what we just did. That's the way Mr. Wilde wants it. So that's the way it will be. Word gets out, and somebody will have to answer to me."

"We got no problem with the pact, Dalton," someone said.

"Fine." Dalton added a grunt for emphasis. "Now Mr. Wilde can get on with the story."

"The story?" Oscar asked.

"Yeah, you left poor Jesse staggerin round in his living room with that bullet hole in his head. Remember? And then he started thinking bout the good ole war days and the good ole train-robbin days. But he was still back at his house bleedin and carryin on. What happens next?"

A roar of laughter, almost with the intensity of their gunfire, blasted forth from the men, but this time Dalton did not appear to be fazed by the derision of the other miners.

"Jesse *dies*, Dalton," said one man, whose face appeared to be in pain as he tried not to laugh at his friend's naivete.

"Well, course he dies," said Dalton with confidence. "But Mr. Wilde's the only one can kill im off right and proper."

"Do not acquiesce so quickly, Dalton, to the provincial proclamations of your colleagues." Oscar touched Dalton's shoulder lightly and then addressed the entire group. "It is a popular misconception that Jesse James died. A misconception that has its roots in a coroner's literalness, a wife's suffocating loneliness, a mother's blinding grief, a nation's lack of imagination. But what you men proved unequivocally with your spontaneous outburst of emotion just moments ago is that Jesse James *lives!*"

III

"Indeed, so far from being humorous, the male
American is the most abnormally serious creature
who ever existed. . . . It is only fair to admit that he
can exaggerate, but even his exaggeration has a rational
basis. It is not founded on wit or fancy; it does not
spring from any poetic imagination. . . ."

—Oscar Wilde

NEW YORK

T RAQUAIR sat on a stool at the kitchen table watching his
mother slowly smooth thick white icing over a round, two-
tiered, buttery-looking cake. Her efforts were in preparation
for an appearance at the house by Oscar Wilde, who, at Vail's suggestion, would have drinks and dessert this evening with Mr. Gable. Mrs.
Traquair lifted the bowl she was using and spooned together one last
scoop of icing and dolloped it onto the cake. Then she placed the bowl
on the table and slid it down to her son. Traquair rubbed the bowl with
a fingertip, gathering a rich, creamy ball, which he licked with delight.

"I hope your Mr. Wilde likes that as much as you do," she said.

"As it turns out, he and I have remarkably similar tastes," said
Traquair, his speech slurred by the sweet, sticky icing. "Our obvious
differences are misleading."

"Obvious differences?" His mother's question was casual. She was
clearly more interested in her cake. She was always more talkative
while cooking and baking, he had noticed, but nothing ever truly distracted her from her work.

"Yes," he said. "Appearances, the sounds of our voices."

Mrs. Traquair glanced up at her son and then looked back at the
cake. "I hear something different in your voice these days."

"Really?" he asked, genuinely surprised at her observation.

"Mm-hmm. You sound a little bit like a foreigner. Might it be the
influence of Mr. Wilde?"

"I suppose so. But it might be the traveling. Leaving home is one of
two sure ways to achieve alienation. Remaining at home is the other."

"There's no sin in a son staying home."

"Which is precisely why sons leave home, Mother."

"Mmm. Now that sounds more like the influence of Moses Traquair."

Traquair was about to taste another fingertip of icing but stopped abruptly, as he was shocked to hear his mother speak his uncle's name. He'd never heard her refer to him in any way. "Did Father show you the letter I sent him about my delightful meeting with my uncle?" he asked excitedly.

"Oh, yes. We talked about it in great detail."

"And is he prepared now to admit that Uncle Moses is a man and not a monster?" Traquair heard footsteps and turned to see his father entering the room.

"I never questioned my brother's manhood," Mr. Traquair said. "I questioned his manliness."

Traquair was glad his father had shown up, but he wished he had been able to find out more information from his mother first. Ignorant of his father's assessment of his visit with his uncle, Traquair would need to be alert in this confrontation. He could feel a surge of energy from the sugar paste, which would help, but he lamented having to spend it all in yet another duel with his father.

"Did my letter alter your opinion of Uncle Moses at all?" Traquair asked.

"First, let me compliment you on your letter-writing skills. They are much improved. There is a decidedly poetic lilt to your words."

"Yes, poetic!" his mother exclaimed. "That's the difference I meant earlier when I said 'foreign.' "

"Poetry *is* a foreign tongue, Mother," Traquair said, in part to distract his father.

"Yes," agreed Mr. Traquair. "Which makes it so very difficult to know if a poet is telling lies."

"Or telling truths," Traquair said emphatically, wanting to counter his father's implication that his letter somehow lacked credibility, that it hid something about his uncle or somehow embellished him. He thought his father's veiled accusation about his letter, which had reported in great detail his uncle's success (his business, the bayside home, Summer), might owe to envy. Then, just to confuse his father— the battle was on—he added, "But don't be deceived by the truth, because some lies must be believed. Besides, it's not so much *what* a man says that makes him a poet; it's *how* he says it."

"No self-respecting poet would intentionally tell lies," Mr. Traquair ah-hahed him.

"There is no such thing as a poet with self-respect," Traquair began, without knowing exactly where he was headed. "Poets who dote on themselves are prosaic. Poets respect *others*, and prove it by constantly giving them lavishly beautiful things. And all poets tell lies. It is practically the first requirement. What is a metaphor if not a lie, calling something that which it is not? Is life really but a walking shadow, Father, as Mr. Shakespeare would have it? I should think not. Poets lie or they fail."

Mr. Traquair grimaced before saying, "To tell the truth is to be set free."

He's retreating to the Bible, thought Traquair. Now I've got him. "If that were true it would certainly help explain why poets, the best liars among us, seem always in danger of being imprisoned. But it can't be true because if truth were the way to freedom, then we, every one of us, liars that we are, would all be in chains."

"Is it your thinking that we are not?" Mrs. Traquair said quickly, but with a detachment that obscured the seriousness of the remark. Both Traquair and his father turned their heads sharply toward her. Ignoring their stares, she carefully picked up the cake from the table and carried it over to the counter. Father and son looked at each other, a sudden soberness in their eyes.

Traquair said finally, "It is my thinking that my father is practicing his usual evasive methods, this time in an attempt to conceal his misjudgment of Uncle Moses."

"You have your judgment of him. I have mine. On this matter, I am not afraid of a lasting disagreement."

"Neither am I." Traquair looked at his father out of the corners of his eyes and added, "A family that has nothing to disagree about simply isn't communicating."

His father slapped him on the back and then took him by the arm. "Come. Help me prepare the parlor for your Mr. Wilde," he said. As they walked toward the front of the house, Mr. Traquair whispered, "Is his wife *really* a Chinawoman?"

❀　　❀　　❀

Traquair retired to his room to read the latest news from Baxter.

26 April

Dear Billy,

Still in London, living a dream, or reveling in some reality other than the one we normally call "life." J. Whistler invited me again to his studio today for "a lesson," as he termed it. He had offered to allow me to watch him work and to make a few sketches of my own if I chose. Upon my arrival at his place, I was startled when the door was opened not by a servant or by JW himself, but by one of the most beautiful women I've ever seen. "Baxter!" she said to me with an impossible familiarity. Imagine, Billy, a beautiful woman unexpectedly calling out one's name. You should know that pleasure! "This way, dear boy," she said, taking me by the arm and leading me down a short dark entrance hall. "You must tell me all about America, the real America, not what one hears from the jaded and jealous Englishmen who make the journey and survive to tell about it. Even the letters Oscar sends strike me as calculated for effect." We entered the bright light of the studio, and the pungent odor of the paints stung my novice nose. I sneezed, and JW's bespectacled face angled out from behind the large canvas he was dappling as it rested on an easel, and he said to me, "Bless you."

The beauty looked toward the artist and said playfully, "Something in your tone, Jimmy, when you say that, begs us to consider your powers of grace, not God's."

"Me? Beg?" Whistler's voice was sharp and brittle, disembodied, too, as he had darted his head back behind the canvas. "My dear Mrs. Langtry, I do believe you are hearing things. Not surprising for one about whom so many things are heard."

Mrs. Langtry—yes, it was the famous beauty herself, Lillie Langtry—went suddenly sad at Mr. Whistler's remark, and her hands, I note even now with a sadness of my own, fell from my arm. She recovered, however, saying to me, "Now his tone turns bitter. Envy, perhaps, as I'm the one who's to tour your America next, Baxter. Not him. First our Oscar. Now Lillie. Poor Jimmy."

"I've no need to tour America. I am America. In me, my Massachusetts father and North Carolina mother bred one uniquely continental. There are those among us, as you well know, Mrs.

Langtry, who are unsuccessful at being even merely continent." JW
peeked from behind the canvas and looked at Lillie Langtry after he
said the latter, and I understood that he was quite plainly accusing her
of some indiscretion. The sparkly flecks of violets and blues in her
eyes dissolved into the more dominant gray. "I was born free, Mrs.
Langtry, of your slavish desire to possess the symbol of freedom.
Young Baxter here is your opposite. He is drawn here by the need to
indulge himself in our country's rather morbid fascination with its
great symbol of tyranny, England. After all, I should know. So I've
brought the two of you together to commiserate, for at some point you
shall each require consolation. To desire a symbol is to court disaster.
Draw the symbol or write it and one arrests desire, captures its
object, freeing oneself forever."

Mrs. Langtry had no response this time. Gliding across the room,
she came to a stop in the dimmest part of the studio, the same spot
where, evidently, she'd been posing before my arrival. "But then,"
Whistler said, resuming in earnest his work on the portrait, "perhaps
our Mrs. Langtry has already suffered enough." I took a seat on the
floor not too far from JW and watched him paint, sometimes
forsaking his brush in favor of his fingers, for more than two hours.
His performance moved me more than the picture, which, he told me
when I had summoned the spirit to ask, is called "Arrangement in
Yellow," after his other "arrangements," such as the gray and black
one of his mother.

After her sitting, Mrs. Langtry left abruptly without speaking to
me or JW at all, slamming the door behind her. Mr. Whistler became
immediately more direct about his insinuations. Smoothing out a
brown and yellow patch of paint into an ochre line with his thumb, he
murmured down to me (I was still sitting on the floor, the abject pupil
that I was), "She might have employed such swiftness in evacuating
the room of the man—not her husband—who, just last year, seduced
her into motherhood, that illusion of immortality. I want to seduce
her into sitting still long enough to allow me to create my own illusion
of her, a true immortality. If I thought she'd listen, if I thought she
could hear me, that is the thing for which I'd actually beg."

We both stared at the painting for a while, and he never quite got
around to my lesson, or perhaps he had done so without my realizing,
only it was a very different lesson from any I might have imagined.

*By the by, JW's "Mother" will be shown in New York soon. Look
for it. Seems odd that such a great talent has yet to be acknowledged
in his homeland. But then he is, as am I, so very far away: he for
more than fifteen years, I for slightly better than fifteen fortnights.
Already, for me, things seem so distant and begin, a bit, to fade. I
suppose one cannot fault the forgotten for forgetting. But I
shamelessly beg, dear Billy, do not to me what America has done to
JW. Write soon!*

Ever yours,
Baxter

That evening during the dessert gathering, Traquair performed the
duties expected of him. He poured Oscar drink after drink and lit his
cigarettes, tasks he had performed hundreds of times before, but never
in this setting, one of the parlors in his own home. Growing up, he had
always managed to avoid having any domestic duties assigned to him,
though his father had made several early attempts at recruiting him into
the corps. He had had to study his lessons, more often than he wanted,
in the seclusion of his room, in order to remain out of his father's sight.
Baxter had been a big help. Their close friendship had made Traquair's
abduction into his father's way of life more difficult. Sometimes Baxter
and Traquair had simply been too busy just being boys, and Mr. Traquair
seemed to respect that. At other times, if Mr. Traquair had come around
calling for him with too much authority in his voice, Baxter would hide
Traquair in his room and lie about not knowing where he was: "No,
Henry, I haven't seen him. Have you tried his room?" Even Mr. Gable
had lied for him once. His father, having publicly threatened to teach
him the proper way to polish belt buckles, thought he had found
Traquair in the upstairs hall, only to find Mr. Gable standing there with
his back to the seven-foot-long table that lined the wall. "Haven't seen
him" had been his response to Mr. Traquair's question, when in actuality Traquair, along with Baxter, had been hiding under the table behind
Mr. Gable, tugging at his pants legs.

Over the past five months, Traquair had gotten used to attending
to Oscar—Mr. Wilde, for the evening—but being reduced to a servant
here at 141 East Nineteenth Street, after years of having dodged such
a fate, felt like some final defeat at the hands of his father.

Henry Traquair, on the other hand, appeared as jovial and confident as ever waiting on Mr. Gable and Vail, whom he was serving on the other side of the small sitting room. "More cake, sir?" he asked Vail, who waved him away. Mr. Traquair's response, an eyebrow-raised downward look with more than a little disdain, amused Traquair. Vail was starting to take another sip of his drink, but hesitated. "Wait there, Henry," he said. "I think I'll have a second piece after all." His father had a gift for quietly leaving an impression. He's *good*, Traquair thought, concluding that with enough style and dedication a man could overcome the most unfortunate of circumstances, could triumph despite the incredible odds against him, and influence the proceedings. Was this the lesson of his father? Traquair knew that, in his own seemingly insignificant role as Oscar's valet, he had had numerous opportunities to influence and guide Oscar and those around him. Oscar regularly wore the scarves that Traquair selected, and he even quoted some of the things Traquair had said to him. And Traquair had winked, nodded, tipped, and generally charmed his way through months of cities, hotels, train stations, strangers. He had had the advantage of traveling with a celebrity, but he gave himself—and his father, whose skills, he was now acutely aware, he had acquired or inherited—much of the credit for his success. He remembered fondly the way he had handled the delicate situation with the driver in St. Louis who wanted to take him directly back to the hotel, when he had wanted to find Miss Trenton and coax from her lips the enunciation of his name. How magically he had done that. (A beautiful woman *had* spoken his name, he would love to inform Baxter. Not Lillie Langtry, but a very beautiful woman nonetheless.) He remembered, too—he would remember it forever—the way he had finessed the kissing of Miss Trenton's bare hand. That had been scandalous! The memory of his conquest lifted his mood. (Miss Trenton . . . She had been in St. Louis on a short visit. Shouldn't she be back in New York by now? Did he still have her card?)

Suddenly, with an enthusiasm that only a moment ago he would have reserved for venues less jarringly familiar, for hotel rooms and the provinces, he offered Oscar more wine.

"Mr. Wilde, it seems that you've seduced a nation," Mr. Gable was saying.

"Yes, and I must say that it has been quite tiring." Oscar did look a little fatigued, Traquair thought, the sound of Oscar's voice drawing him out of his Theda Trenton trance. But then he'd never seen Oscar relaxing in a private home in this way. Traquair remembered the secret seriousness with which Oscar took his mission to inspire an appreciation of art in America, and he thought that what appeared to be Oscar's weariness might actually be a calculated nonchalance, part of his subtle method, along with humor, of delivering his message. "Seducing a nation," Oscar went on, "requires much more effort, I'm quite certain, than the seduction of actual individuals—and with none of the ultimate benefits. The seducer of a woman needs merely patience and private property. The seducer of a man, somewhat less patience . . . and a private room."

There was laughter at this. Vail coughed a piece of cake onto the carpet, and Traquair winced as his father bent down and, with a napkin, scooped it up.

Mr. Gable asked, "And what were the more exhausting requirements for your seduction of an entire country?"

"Gilbert and Sullivan's *Patience* . . ." Oscar said.

"And?" Mr. Gable prompted him.

"The opposite of privacy," said Oscar, pausing to draw upon his cigarette elegantly. "Publicity," he concluded, releasing the cigarette smoke in concert with the various forces of the four syllables of the word. Everyone was amused for a moment, especially Mr. Gable, who was moved to laughter, an infrequent occurrence, to Traquair's recollection. "So clever," Mr. Gable said. "So terribly, terribly clever."

Then Oscar added, "But really, I don't think Americans are at all interested in being seduced by foreigners. They are too busy seducing one another. Haven't you found this to be true, William?"

Traquair didn't answer. His mind, confirming Oscar's statement, had drifted back to Miss Trenton.

"William," Mr. Gable said, "can you confirm Mr. Wilde's assertion?"

Traquair looked at his father, who tilted his head upward, aiming his eyes at the ceiling.

"I believe there is some truth to what Mr. Wilde is saying," he finally said. "I must admit that I have sensed a certain sensuousness wherever we have traveled." Traquair felt his father's disapproving eyes upon him.

"Nonsense!" Gable countered. "That is the infatuation of young men. No doubt Baxter would say the same thing about England." Traquair thought about Baxter's letters, and he couldn't remember any comment that would indicate this to be true. "At any rate, something has seduced him. London, it seems, will not let him go." Then Mr. Gable turned to Oscar and asked, "Is it all sensuousness, really?"

"No," Oscar said. "Certainly not. There is also a great deal of love here. The country is very much in love with itself as well."

"Hmph," said Mr. Gable. "You wouldn't have said that twenty years ago."

"The war?" Oscar said. "Oh, the war, like every war, was all about love."

Mr. Gable moved his cigar away from his face. The trail of blue smoke served to accentuate his look of horror. "Excuse me, Mr. Wilde, but do you speak of the *Civil* War?"

"Indeed. It is really quite remarkable to me the way that love goes about constantly masquerading as anger or hatred or, less violently but no less tragically, as mere disinterest, or worse still, as friendliness. Actually, anger and hatred are two of the more obvious disguises. Here in America, the North and the South failed to come to terms with their love for one another, not their hatred. Everything we know about the attraction of opposites supports my theory. The North and the South, their longing for each other is a universal law." Traquair looked at Oscar and, for the first time since their initial meeting, found himself staring at Oscar's blue and gray eyes; their blended color would go unnoticed by the other members of this party, but they lent Oscar's words a subliminal sincerity and force.

"Your ideas completely ignore certain social realities, Mr. Wilde."

"Do they? Is love not the greatest social reality?"

"Well," said Mr. Gable, "the *economic* realities."

"Love knows no economy."

"You force me to say it—slavery." Mr. Gable turned to look over his shoulder at Mr. Traquair. "Sorry, Henry." Mr. Traquair, face softening with gratitude, raised his eyebrows.

"Slavery," said Oscar. "Another subject altogether, but also about the brutality of love. Slavery, at least in its American variety, with its black and white dynamic, was about opposites at war with their mutual attraction. Only the peculiar institution of love could have devised so passionate, so prolonged, so cruel a kiss."

Mr. Gable was visibly disturbed by these words. He gripped the arms of his chair and slid himself forward. "Mr. Wilde, for the South to have wanted to keep slavery so badly—it was merely a salve, you know, a cure for her disastrous economic predicament—that she would send her own sons to death is truly indefensible."

"The kiss that cures, addicts," said Oscar.

Mr. Gable sat back in his chair. "I believe we are speaking about two entirely different things, Mr. Wilde. The Civil War that I speak of was a terrible, bloody, and, thank God, successful campaign to save a nation, and in so doing, to save lives and to emancipate slaves, to free men. You speak in metaphors. I heard and appreciated your lecture at Chickering Hall in January. A poetic imagination, such as yours, produces lovely and admirable effects when applied to the subject of art, but it cannot save lives. It cannot free men."

"To the contrary," Oscar said. "The poetic imagination is the only thing that can save lives. It can even resurrect them. Your Civil War might have been prevented entirely with just a tiny bit more of it. President Lincoln understood this, in part, though not well enough. The South's leaders did not understand it at all. And the poetic imagination is certainly the only thing that can *free* men—but the freeing of men is quite a different endeavor from the emancipation of slaves."

Later that night, after a frantic twenty-minute search through his satchel and his still unpacked bags, Traquair found Miss Trenton's card in the right front pocket of the jacket he had been wearing in St. Louis on the night he met her. He couldn't believe he'd been so careless with such an important memento. Even if he had never ultimately needed it for the vital information it held, he should have tucked it into the special book of fliers, hotel cards, and newspaper clippings he was saving. Still breathing heavily from his rummaging and from the anxiety that he might not be able to locate the prize he was now pinching between his right thumb and index finger, he sat on the edge of his bed staring at the card, reading her address with relief and anticipation: 23 East Fourth Street. Yes, he remembered now. She was right there, just fifteen blocks away.

Falling back on his bed, sinking into the soft mattress, he stretched his arm straight out, up, and beheld the card against the backdrop of the high ceiling. Looking at the lofty little symbol of Theda, so clearly within his grasp, yet somehow just out of reach, charged his desire. As his emotion and its manly manifestations swelled, he seemed almost to levitate with longing, but still he knew that, if he were truly to attain her or a symbol of her more meaningful than this paper rectangle, some greater force within him, not just his nature, would have to rise.

A knock at the door arrested his thoughts of ascension. "Come in," he said, sitting up and tucking the card under one of his pillows. His mother peeked in and said, "Mr. Gable has asked to see you. Did something happen tonight? Did the company mind the cake? Did Mr. Gable?"

"No, Mother, he did not mind the cake, but I suspect he minded the company."

"Oh, dear. And is that what has your father so upset as well? He's down there waiting for you, too."

"Of course. Philosophically he and Mr. Gable are as close as kin. No doubt what has offended one has offended the other. They seem more like brothers than Father and Uncle Moses."

His mother hummed lightly in agreement and said, "You and I did not complete our discussion about Moses. Another time, I suppose, as they are waiting. But . . ." She looked away, as if unsure of whether to continue. Traquair stood and went over to her quickly.

"What is it, Mother?" Not wanting to risk her fading into her usual silence, he arched his inquiry into a plea.

Mrs. Traquair slowly leaned back against the door, shutting it completely. "Well," she began tentatively, "I feel something of a traitor . . . in revealing this to you."

"A traitor? To whom? In revealing what?" Riled by curiosity and impatience, he fired the questions in rapid succession.

"Well, I make no accusation, so you mustn't, either. But more than two weeks ago I placed a letter from Moses on your desk."

"There was no letter from my uncle waiting for me."

"Yes, I know. It disappeared two days before your arrival."

"What! Do you really think . . . I mean, would Father really do such a thing?"

"I should like to think not. But to protect you he'd do worse than that. You know what he thinks of Moses. After all these years he still feels wounded by him. And he doesn't trust him, which I suppose I can understand. In Henry's defense, I think he fears your corruption at the hands of Moses. You must admit that your note to your father indicated an instant rapport between you and Moses. And I think he fears, as irrational as it may seem, that his brother will somehow take you away from him. And, too, I sense an element of jealousy on Henry's part. If he took your letter, these are among the reasons."

"But it's thievery!" Traquair waved both his hands. "It is the same crime for which he refuses to forgive Uncle Moses! Thievery!"

"Is it thievery if you steal to keep your possessions from being stolen?"

"Father doesn't *own* me."

"No. But you own his heart. If he loses you, he loses that. Do remember what I'm saying to you."

Traquair had never seen this side of his mother before. Why was she defending his father? "Then why did you bother to tell me at all?"

"Because Moses may think you've adopted your father's attitude about him if you do not keep in touch with him, which would not be fair—to either of you."

"But what should I do about the letter?"

"Say nothing," his mother offered. "Write to Moses. Have him respond to you in one of the cities you are scheduled to visit. Your father doesn't have to know anything. Just keep it from him. That's the thing to do. Look at what his knowing has done to him—made him a lesser man. Just don't tell him." She took Traquair by the shoulders and shook him in a gentle gesture of persuasion. Her touch relaxed him, and he said, "I suppose I can keep my future relations with my uncle to myself, just as Father for so long kept his past from me. Knowing him, he would probably condone our conspiracy. It is, after all, his way."

Turning the doorknob with the hand behind her back, Mrs. Traquair said, "They're waiting." As they walked down the staircase, Traquair, following her lead, said, "And what about you, Mother? Are you, too, to remain true to that most Traquairian of traits, the habit of hiding the truth? Father has told me the story of his youth in Charleston, the circumstance of which I know was yours as well. These may be difficult matters to discuss, but I believe you owe me at least—"

"Owe you?" She stopped suddenly on the stairs and Traquair

bumped into her back. "A person's past is his own—or her own, for that matter." She started her descent again and Traquair, walking closely behind her, peered vacantly but sharply downward over her shoulder. "You'll find, my son, as you experience the full gamut of emotions, that the most poignant episodes of your life are, if decency and mercy prevail, private. That my greatest insult—or what the world thinks my greatest insult—should be considered a matter of public record does not endear to me the act of disclosure. Nor would publication of my greatest moment of joy, which is also quite personal, bring me any additional pleasure. Think about your own experiences. Would you want your single greatest moment of tragedy publicized? Would you want to tell the world the intimate details of the kiss that changed your life forever? Would you want to tell anyone? Would you even want to tell me?" Traquair couldn't answer. Not because he wasn't sure, but because his life was bereft of tragedy, and he was still in search of that kiss. "No," she answered for him. They had reached the bottom of the stairs. "No." With that denial, a proclamation of concealment as creed, of distance as doctrine, she turned and embraced him, and, quite unexpectedly, quite ironically, Traquair realized he had never felt closer to his mother, never known more about who she was, and never more assuredly felt her love.

"*There* you are!" the voice of Henry Traquair boomed forth, and Traquair and his mother drew apart. "Mr. Gable would like you to join us in his study." She released his hand and walked away, disappearing down the hall leading toward the kitchen. Traquair had wanted to add some slight trill to their separation—a wink, a whispered "I love you"—but his father's manner (Traquair whiffed the evidence of one drink too many) had a demanding edge to it. As he turned to follow his father, Mr. Traquair whistled a few notes of a tune Traquair didn't recognize, and he watched his father open the door to Mr. Gable's office with a move of casual choreography inspired by his own accompaniment.

"Come in, William," Mr. Gable said with a smile. He was leaning against the front edge of his desk smoking a cigar. Mr. Traquair picked up a cigar as well and assumed a similar stance next to Mr. Gable. An audience with the two masters; he thought: They're up to something. "Have a seat, have a seat. A smoke? A scotch? Henry, please—"

"No, nothing, thank you," Traquair said. He sat down, casually crossing his legs. With an idle glare he searched his father's face for guilt about the letter, but the wince that had a glimmer of remorse proved merely the result of a misdirected inhalation, the prelude to a cough.

"William, Henry and I are really heartbroken over tonight's proceedings. Aren't we, Henry?"

"Heartbroken?" Mr. Traquair said, angling his head upward theatrically. "Perhaps. *Outraged* might be more accurate." Here he dotted the air once forcefully with the hot point of his cigar.

"Yes, William, your father and I are both heartbroken and outraged. Equal parts, each. Right, Henry?"

"Equal parts? Hardly. More outraged." More exaggerated cigar play, Traquair observed.

"Yes, William. Henry would be more outraged. I would be more heartbroken. What percentages, I can't really say."

They were both drunk. Traquair could not suppress a faint snort. Drunk—and, apparently, heartbroken and outraged.

"The point is, William. We're simply opposed at this point to your continued association with this Oscar Wilde."

The point . . . at this point. At what point? The point of inebriation? Traquair could feel his cheeks getting hotter, that ever reliable measure of his frustration. Oh, he had seen Henry Traquair and Charles Gable like this before. Usually they just drifted through the house bumping tables, chuckling about things Traquair couldn't imagine. Eyed from two parlors away, they were just two harmless, domesticated lushes, quaint and mildly amusing. But in the same room with them, listening to them calculate the course of your life, they weren't amusing; they were laughable. He would let them prattle on and then tell them; he was going forward with the tour, staying with Oscar. ". . . Wilde's trivialization of tragedy," he heard a snippet of something Mr. Gable was saying and thought, Why should Oscar's comments on the war and slavery be reduced to that? To his ears, Oscar had heightened the power and the significance of those tragedies by comparing them to love, the ultimate emotion. Perhaps it was, at present, an imperfect analogy, but it was a worthy one nevertheless, one ripe for further exploration. "Son," he heard his father saying, "we've decided there's no need for you to suffer such insults." Insults? Was it an insult to note, as Oscar might be said to have done, that to free a mind is an endeavor as noble as to free a man? Traquair did not think so.

"William, Wilde is a foreigner," Mr. Gable said flatly.

"Yes!" his father agreed loudly, slapping the desk with his hand, startling Traquair.

"A foreigner in the extreme, I might add," Mr. Gable continued. "Do not be fooled by his language. Just because you can understand his words does not mean that he is one of us. Who can understand his words, anyway?"

"Who cares, Gable? What he says is irrelevant! For no matter what he utters, Wilde is the one who cannot understand *us*! He cannot understand what we've been through."

"Precisely, Henry, precisely! Don't yell at me. *I* understand." Mr. Traquair nodded, and he and Mr. Gable, with a glance, reconciled. Traquair, disenchanted with the scene, wished now that he had accepted the drink. Calmly, more soberly, even, Mr. Gable said, "William, simply put, we've raised you to be an American. We will not hear of your being corrupted."

More corruption, Traquair thought. First his uncle, now Oscar. His father had stolen his uncle's letter. What crime would they commit to keep him away from Oscar?

"Now, it's clear to us that you are enjoying your travels. We wouldn't want you to forgo the pleasure that comes of seeing new lands or, for that matter, to deny you the kinds of thrills to which you've become accustomed. Ample thrills, if rumors are reliable." Mr. Gable's rakish smile and sideways look at Mr. Traquair were met with a disappointing smirk. Dear God, thought Traquair, so this was the kind of thing that made them giggle while they roamed about the house intoxicated! His father, stingy with the details of his own life, was a gossip about the intimacies of others, or at least the intimacies of Traquair. Mr. Gable, with a clearing of his throat, recovered. "Indeed, we're thinking, why not broaden the scope of your travels? We're proposing that you leave behind this Oscar Wilde, with all of his silliness, his peculiar, pointless flamboyance, his, his . . ."

"Eloquent disrespect!" Mr. Traquair finished the phrase.

"Yes!" Mr. Gable agreed loudly, slapping the desk with his hand, startling Traquair. "Leave him behind. And, next week . . . next week you set sail for Europe!"

"Europe?" Traquair asked with a mixture of wonder and devastation, his entire face aflame. Europe! How could they offer him Europe?

Now. Months and months too late. His father knew how much he had suffered over not going to Europe with Baxter, and if his father knew, then Mr. Gable knew as well. *They knew.* Yet to induce him to quit Oscar, to exercise their will, they would appeal to what seemed to him at this moment an ancient yearning. Only now, now with it dangling on a string before him, did he realize, with much delight, that he no longer wanted it.

"You'd meet Baxter in London, and the two of you could set out from there! Oh, won't it be grand?"

"Yes, son. Grand!"

Their attempt to lure him in this way felt like emotional extortion. That was the crime. A stolen letter, now this use of Europe and Baxter. All this corruption in the name of averting corruption. But even though he thought their plot a misguided misdemeanor, Traquair was nevertheless touched by it. He thought he owed them something for their minor sacrifice. If someone was willing to sully even some tiny sliver of his soul for you, the least you could say was . . .

"Thank you. I'm truly moved by this proposal. Europe. Well, both of you know, I'm sure, just what that meant, I mean, *means* to me. And, of course, I'd love to see Baxter. But I must say that I'm quite comfortable with my current situation. I'm not afraid of Oscar Wilde. To the contrary, I'm very fond of him. He's not a tyrant. He's my friend. And believe me when I say that if I've been corrupted in any way, he's not been the cause. I take you very seriously, Mr. Gable, Father, when you say that you've raised me to be an American, and such being the case, I know that you will not stand in the way of my freedom to choose for myself which way to go. Between Europe and home, I must choose home."

Propped up at the desk side by side, Mr. Gable and Mr. Traquair, cigars puffed to stubs, looked at each other and shook their heads in defeat. Traquair stood up and said, "Now if you'll excuse me, I have a busy day in the city tomorrow. People to see and . . . thrills to seek." This final remark incited another squabble, he heard, as he closed the door behind him. But it would end, he knew, as surely as the others had, with the Gable-Traquair alliance intact. Subversively, Traquair found himself painting the men with Oscar's metaphor. All of their skirmishes, their little battles and wars, would forever end in affectionate truces, so strangely yet so plainly were they armed against each other with love.

✳   ✳   ✳

Not merely out of mischievous intent had he spoken of people to see
and thrills to seek. What he intended, more seriously, was to know the
thrill of Theda Trenton.

So the next morning, with an impetuousness he was not compelled
to harness, he made his way downtown. It was such a short walk that
it did not allow him enough time to gather his thoughts. Just as in
St. Louis, he was off to see her without an invitation and without
knowing quite what he was going to say. He felt guilty about the lies he
had told Miss Trenton when he first met her, and he wondered now if
he should tell her about how deceitful he had been. Would she be merciful if he confessed? She did seem to have a certain worldly quality that
would indicate an awareness of what men were. If he confessed to her
his fraudulence, she would probably be able to understand and forgive
him. Besides, weren't the claims he had made about being a kissing
messenger preposterous? Some part of Miss Trenton must have looked
upon Traquair with disbelief. Yet she had offered up her hand with no
hesitation, with eagerness, even. Perhaps the same part of Miss Trenton
that knew Oscar had not sent him to kiss her hand wanted to be kissed
by Traquair. Maybe, on some level, she wanted him. Did he need to tell
her the truth or should he perpetuate the lie? "To tell the truth is to be
set free," his father had said yesterday. But Oscar had countered with
"The poetic imagination is the only thing that can free men." Was
there room for both points of view? Perhaps. But it was not freedom
that concerned him now. Striding inexorably and irrationally toward
Miss Trenton's house, he realized that the moment he had taken her
hand into his and pressed his lips to it, he had forsaken his liberty. *The
kiss that cures, addicts*, Oscar had said to Mr. Gable last night. As if
he were a fiend, as if the effects of opium or absinthe were to be felt in
the presence of Miss Trenton, Traquair walked on, following the lead
of an impractical obsession.

As he rounded the corner and turned onto her block, his body
twitched—for there she was. Serendipity, he told himself, was to be a
part of their relationship. She was wearing a ruffled white summer
dress and carrying a lacy parasol. The vision of her flushed Traquair.
All matters philosophical and poetic were momentarily blotted out
with blood. How she had the gift of making him instantly aware of his

corporeality! He wanted only to be closer to her—she was strolling alone—and that was easily accomplished. Suddenly, he began to take long, playful strides toward her, bending his knees and lifting them high in a sort of prance. She was not looking in his direction at first, but his exaggerated walk must have drawn her attention. She stopped abruptly, resting the stick of her parasol against her shoulder and lightly touching her hand to her face. Traquair, sporting an uncontrollable smile, was only a few feet from her when she said with surprise, "William!"

"Yes!" he said. "Miss Trenton!"

"Yes!" she said. "You remember me?"

"Entirely. I was only hoping that you would not have forgotten *me*."

"One meets so many people that forgetting most of them is quite necessary," she said. "I cannot bear remembering people from one season to the next. It seems so forward. But I could not forget you, William. I've read that Mr. Wilde is back in town briefly, and I wondered if you would still be with him."

"Yes, of course. We are inseparable until the tour is done, which I can only hope will be . . . I'll confess it—I hope it will never end."

"An innocent enough confession, I'll assure you."

"Yes, I suppose."

Miss Trenton took a step, and Traquair thought it an indication that she was bringing the meeting to an abrupt close. "Shall we?" she said, inviting him to join her. "I was just off on my morning promenade. It's a bit of a scandal in the neighborhood that I go it alone. They say it is good for the lungs. The walk, not the scandal or the loneliness." Traquair walked beside her in a familiar daze of pleasure, ignoring thoughts of scandal and loneliness (two pertinent concepts, he knew, under the circumstances, as one or the other seemed the likely outcome of these relations between himself and Miss Trenton), submitting instead to the intoxicating effects of her companionship, just as he'd done in St. Louis. "I think I shall make a confession of my own to you, William, though it be far less innocent than yours."

"I am disinclined toward innocence, Miss Trenton." He sneaked a sideways glance at her, wondering if she'd be repulsed by the quiet candor of his remark.

"Yes, all the world is," she said. "It makes life as a woman these days almost thrilling." She was fearless, he rejoiced, like Susan B. Anthony.

"And your confession?" he asked, a lilt in his voice, for hope, rhythmically speaking, has a lilt.

"Yes. Well, it has to do with our encounter in front of Cousin Augusta's house." She paused.

"At the risk of seeming impertinent, I remember its every detail," he said.

"That . . . encounter," she went on, "was simply—how shall I put it?—well, poetic. I know I said that before, but I must say it again. That moment when together we discovered the artfulness with which Mr. Wilde had dispatched you in his stead, you in preference to a cold and impersonal letter, was only the most lyrical experience I've ever had. The personification of an apology, the personification of 'I'm sorry'—two of the kindest words we know—why, it was the invention of a poetry that puts not language first but humanity. That gesture was the work of a man who would make his mark not in art so much as in life. One can preach art, but one must live life.

"I am not ashamed to say, though perhaps I should be—and here is my confession, William—I am not ashamed to say that I have not been quite the same since that meeting. For one thing, I never write letters anymore! They seem so shallow to me now. Why, even just before you appeared here I was thinking of what happened between you and me in St. Louis. That would account for the startled look you must have seen on my face. Imagine my dismay at thinking about you one moment and then suddenly seeing you dancing in my direction the next. I must tell you it felt like something other than reality. I have examined our encounter over and over again, as one might an exquisite flower or a sonnet or a painting—not some Old Master, something fresh—looking for clues to its origins, luxuriating in its sensuousness, concerned with its hidden meaning. And yet, one does not want to know all there is to know about it. Some of the mystery of it must be preserved."

"I agree with that," said Traquair, who was reeling from Miss Trenton's honesty. "And I am even honored that you remember me as an apology, as an 'I'm sorry.' One can never appear regretful enough, I'm afraid." He hoped he had managed to inject an ample amount of personal penitence into his voice, in the process, he imagined, earning the thing he was longing for, a liar's absolution.

He must have succeeded, because Miss Trenton said, "If that is another confession, William, albeit a rather veiled one, I should argue for your immediate acquittal. A man who has once played so master-fully the role of 'I'm sorry' merits mercy."

"Thank you, Miss Trenton. I can only hope that my performance has prepared me for other, greater roles."

"Greater roles?"

"Oh, such tidings as 'I love you' and such inquiries as 'Will you marry me?'" Traquair flinched as he spoke these words. After all, Miss Trenton couldn't see the quotation marks that caressed his words into innocent states of objectivity.

"Yes, you are right, William. I think men would be considered much kinder if in fact they did dispatch specially trained envoys to do that type of work, work for which they themselves are so ill-suited."

Traquair laughed and said, "Surely you are not so cynical about men, Miss Trenton."

"Occasionally I am," she said. "When a woman says 'I love you,' she means it. When a man says 'I love you,' very often it is a *means*."

"Are you saying that men lie about love?"

"Men lie about everything—and that is the most interesting thing about them. Women know this fact, and yet we live. That is the most interesting thing about us."

"But isn't this lying a most destructive trait when it comes to something as delicate as love?"

"Love can survive many monstrous lies," she said. "But one tiny truth can kill it."

Traquair was thunderstruck by how much like Oscar she sounded. Here was the combination of the laciness and enlightenment all embodied in one warm, wise being: Theda Trenton. Overwhelmed, he felt the mind-numbing blood-rush surge through him again, and he had to tense his ears to hear, ever so faintly, Miss Trenton say, "Generally, women are better than men. Naturally, men detest generalizations." He only *heard* the words; they held no meaning for him.

"William," she said, raising her voice a bit. "Did you hear my final insult to your entire sex?"

"Yes," he said, delighted to note that Miss Trenton was no longer seeing him for what he metaphorically represented but for the thing that he was: a man. Then he repeated her conclusion about men to himself until it gained significance. "Miss Trenton, I do believe you are trying somehow to provoke me."

"Oh, just like a man. Men always think that of women. If I am trying to provoke anyone it is myself. I want to inspire myself somehow to be daring enough to recapture that sense of wonder I felt with you in St. Louis."

"I want that, too," he said. "I want that more than anything. Is it possible to recapture that?"

"I felt it just now when you spoke of love and marriage." Did she intend to disarm "love" and "marriage," he wondered desperately, with quotation marks of her own? He had no way of knowing. "Did you not feel it?" she asked.

"I did, but I didn't dare think that you felt it too," he said. "I thought the mere utterance of the words might strike you as vulgar."

"No. Hypothetical expressions of love are never vulgar. But it's amazing how often actual ones are. And all proposals of marriage are hypothetical and, of course, vulgar."

He had played along with her evasions long enough. "Yes, Miss Trenton, but what is to be done about the rather strange hypothetical of you and me?"

"Well, first of all, we are hardly a hypothetical, William. We are all too real. Pity, as things are so much more manageable when they are not real. Even memories, which are not real, can be manipulated. I would blush to tell you what in my mind has become of our meeting in St. Louis." She had kept up a girlish tone. Traquair began to think it strained and secretive.

But now she stopped walking and let her parasol drop back against her shoulder again. Intimacy engulfed them. The smell of her. Her eyes—oh, how her lashes still fluttered the way they had in St. Louis. His shadow fell upon her face, shielding her, in part, from the sun. Seeing his own form cast upon her made him dizzy. The silhouette of his nose contoured and sniffed the curve of her perfumed forehead. The partial outline of his lips kissed the edge of her cheek. Her soft nose and warm mouth (he was close enough to divine texture and temperature without touch) could not resist the safe, cool, shady projection of his wide, dark neck. Then the lashes stopped moving, and she looked into his eyes. Her voice deepened and saddened. "But reality . . . reality is cold and unromantic."

"I shall find a way to make of this reality something romantic," Traquair said firmly.

"It is a sweet thing to say," she said, turning her head casually to the side. "But some things are impossible or at least forbidden."

"I don't care!" he said loudly.

She quickly turned to him and said gravely, "And I do." Then she tried to assume her earlier attitude of detachment, saying, "Yet another point upon which the sexes regularly and vehemently differ. The point of caring."

Traquair refused to return to the lighter mood. "Miss Trenton, I cannot leave without some concession."

"Some concession? All right, William. I'll give you this. We shall meet once more."

"Once?"

"Yes. At a time of your choosing."

Traquair thought for a few seconds. "After the tour," he said. "We have Canada and the South, and I don't know what damned else!"

"Whenever it is. You write to me. And somehow I will come to you."

"And then what will happen?"

"To answer that question would be to deny any hope for romance."

"Yes," he said. "You are right."

She sighed, and they started walking again, almost as if they had not just engaged in a serious exchange. "I should tell you, William, that I've been quoting your remark about it being impossible to be overly influenced by Mr. Wilde."

"Yes?"

"I must report that it meets with mixed response."

"Oh, Mr. Wilde would be pleased," Traquair said distantly. "That is his favorite kind of response."

"And what about you, William? It is *your* remark. Are you pleased?"

"No, Miss Trenton," Traquair said quietly, flatly, with something less than a lilt. "I am not pleased. A mixed response is not my favorite kind. But I suppose, for now, it will have to do."

CANADA

25 May 1882

Dear Baxter,

While back at home earlier this month I read your latest with great interest. Oscar was delighted to hear the news that Whistler is painting Mrs. Langtry's portrait and said to me, "I am confident Jimmy will be the one who finally captures Lillie's true beauty. No other living artist is as willing to tell the lies necessary to achieve a truth of such magnitude."

I must say that your tales of the frighteningly entertaining Mr. Whistler and the London life you're establishing lead me to think your claim to loneliness somewhat disingenuous. But at least one of us has found stability. I still light from port to port, all of my anchorings hopelessly temporary, in a succession seemingly endless.

Today I am in Toronto, as you have no doubt gleaned from the face of this letter's envelope, and I thought of you there in London because here in Canada the celebration of Victoria Day is going on about me in all manner of joyousness. I cannot help but think that such frank acknowledgment of a queen's birthday is somehow death to the myth of monarchy. Where is the claim to divine superiority in such a common beginning? She might more grandly claim to have descended from the heavens. Even the nonbelievers would appreciate the effort at eccentricity. But as she has determined that her one eccentricity will be the demand of a conformity whose intensity is rare even among monarchs, we shall have to content ourselves with the queerness of that obstinacy. I am even writing to you from a humble haven named, by someone with a propensity for overstatement, the Queen's Hotel.

Oscar is out with several gentlemen in the midst of the excitement. He's particularly energetic due to the wonderful reception Canada has given him so far. I, too, have not failed to gain some notoriety here. I have recently been dubbed "The Ethiopian Lily" in one place and "Cetewayo"—yes, as in the famed Zulu warrior!—in another. I'm not sure that I can live up to either of these extremes, but Oscar has encouraged me to let nothing stop me from trying. (Every would-be insult seems a challenge to Oscar.) If I am truly to be successful, however, I am sure I will need to know a great deal more about Africa than these Canadian observers—misled, dear innocents, by the cleverness of my disguise—give me credit for knowing. If they were aware of the challenges posed to me by this continent alone, they might not be so quick to ship me off, in jest or otherwise, to lands even more distant and far less familiar. I refer not to the physical demands of cross-continental pilgrimage but to the emotionally exhausting demands of discovering oneself. An unsuspected rigor is required to traverse that terrain. Several large traveling trunks do not budge the scales when measured opposite the burdensome weight of even the smallest personal truth.

To learn, as have I over the last months, that one is susceptible to the everyday temptations of ordinary men, that one's heart is vulnerable to the charms of the world, that one is subject to the laws of nature, that one is prey to the secrets of one's father's past, his history, is to realize that we are all born, beyond our control, into the ranks of the commonplace. What a shock to learn that one is not even the monarch of oneself!

But then all travel, all exploration, is a meeting with history of some sort—a journey into the past. I know this now. My father has advised me to avoid history. "History hurts," he warned me. I thought he was speaking of his personal injuries—he has them, you know—and maybe he was. But the thing about history that my father doesn't understand is that it is unavoidable. It permeates everything, including us. The only way to avoid history is to become it. Even then it has its way with one's remains. Like oxygen, its lone rival as the thing most relentlessly, yet most surreptitiously present, history carves mountains, rusts metal, and fans flames. It hurts. But, I

wonder, does history possess any of the favorable properties of the
precious air? For instance, can history heal? That is what I would like
to know. I suppose only the future can answer that for me.

All of this chatter, it would seem, because Canadians have called
me an Ethiopian Lily and Cetewayo. I have such intense reactions
when the world confronts me. How Victorian of me, in the end, to
demand the world conform to my image of myself! How royally
ridiculous I am! For, really, to be thought—even in a mocking
tone—a lily, a thing pure in form, to be thought a warrior, a thing
pure in character, is to have imposed oneself upon the minds of
others. One cannot hope, in life, for much more than that. Well, of
course, one can, really. One can hope to touch another's heart. But I
have learned just lately of the serious complications that accompany
that particular pursuit.

Oscar Wilde came to the house to spend time with your father
before we left New York. Of course, they disagreed about everything
imaginable, even about imagination. The best was when Oscar told
him that the Civil War was about love. Master Gable nearly
swallowed his cigar on that one. The incident prompted him and
Master Traquair to summon me to a conference that evening, the
details of which are too delicious to impart without the benefit of
pantomime. I shall reserve the full telling until we next meet.
However I must note that the next afternoon your father called me
back to his study, where he spoke to me in the most sentimental of
manners, divulging to me certain memories he had of watching you
and me grow up in the house together, sharing things I don't recall
and that you probably don't recall either. For instance, he told me
something that happened on the day the war ended. He said he had
decided to pay you a visit that day to try to explain the meaning of it
all to you, his little five-year-old boy, but when he opened the door to
your room he had found the two of us crawling around on the floor
playing some game, oblivious to the momentous thing that had just
occurred. He even remembered what we were wearing: white shirts,
blue shorts with suspenders, and black leather shoes with laces.
Because we were the same age and about the same size, we were
often dressed alike, he said. How queer! Do you remember that? He
said he did not interrupt our play. He just watched us, he said, and
thought about how he was glad we had been children during the war

and not subject to any of its awfulness. We looked to him like the not-too-distant future of the country. He was proud, he said to me, that his house had always had the face of the nation. It had remained unmarred by the ugliness and, yes, the hatred—he called it that, I believe, to emphasize what he considered Oscar's unforgivable use of the word "love"—of the war.

Before he excused me he insisted that I take another ten dollars per week for the "torture" of having to endure a few more months of Oscar Wilde.

And endure I shall, and in grander style. Will you really not be home until Christmas? I feel we've grown so far apart. The letters are wonderful, but they can explain only so much. I miss from you the pleasures of the immediate retort. There is no substitute for the actual person—except, of course, another person. (I have personal evidence that this trick has been known to succeed.) But there is no substitute for you, Baxy. And—well, there are riddles to be solved.

Ever yours,
William

When Oscar returned he was in a boisterous mood. "Tra!" he said as he bounded into the hotel suite. Traquair quickly put aside his pen and writing papers and turned to face him. "Oscar!" he said, mimicking the gleefulness of his friend's greeting.

Oscar whipped off the large-brimmed black hat he was wearing and tossed it to Traquair. "I've just witnessed the brilliant game of lacrosse. Do you know it?" He flung his cape onto a sofa and approached Traquair, who remained seated.

"No, is it some sort of Christian-informed version of cricket?" he answered, toying with the sound of the game's name.

Oscar considered this and let down the corners of his mouth, feigning sadness. "Now you've ruined it for me. Your invention sounds like a great deal more fun. Why has no one thought to combine religion with sport? And Rome has such a great legacy in the area of entertainment. It leaves one rather disappointed in the Catholics."

"Tell me about your game of lacrosse," Traquair said.

"I'm told that it is a creation of the Indians, so I suppose the game is actually quite pagan. I am certain this accounts for its superior physical aspects. Civilization discourages the body. Thus, croquet. In today's match it was the Toronto team against a group of full-blooded Indians from a nearby reservation. The Indians were sharper in certain ways. But the Torontos have a masterful defenseman named Ross MacKenzie. I shall remember his play always. And in the end the Indians were literally beaten at their own game. If the natives held any hope in their hearts for subtle advancement of their cause or for the comfort of a small moral victory, today's defeat on Victoria Day must feel an unnecessarily cruel play of Providence. The Indians made gestures and spoke a language that intrigued me, but of course I could not decipher it. It may be that there is something about defeat that renders one unintelligible."

"Yes," said Traquair. "I believe you are right. At any rate, the conquered always feel misunderstood."

"Oh, just ask any one of my fellow Irishmen, and he will tell you that he *is* misunderstood—and in a prose or poetry that shines so brightly with his own patriotism as to obscure his meaning. *And* eliminate your interest. It will be interesting, however, to see what we find in the coming weeks as we travel to the South, home of the recently defeated. What twisted tongue, I wonder, awaits our arrival?"

MEMPHIS

MR. TRACY—" said Oscar, addressing the man supervising his Memphis lecture, as the two of them, along with Traquair, rode in a covered carriage en route from the train to Gaston's Hotel. Tracy and Traquair sat side by side, with Oscar sitting across from them.

"Gen'ral," Tracy corrected Oscar in a casual but proud drawl.

"I beg your pardon," Oscar gently apologized.

"Oh, it's but a remnant of the war," Tracy demurred, blinking a glare in Traquair's direction. "But then, isn't everything?" Traquair felt upon his face a wave of Tracy's nostalgic breath, which, despite the heat of resentment that he guessed had sent it forth, had the effect of cooling him like a sudden summer gust. Tracy's disapproval of him, if that's what it was, evinced a quiet, wounded civility, a timidity that rendered it tolerable. Yes, on the whole, Traquair, who had been somewhat apprehensive about heading south, felt relief at Tracy's wistful reaction to his presence. If this response was an accurate forecast of the tenor of antipathy to come, Traquair felt he would manage nicely, somehow turning things to his advantage, as he had succeeded in doing in difficult situations of late, and he understood right now that one man's disillusioned sigh was another man's breeze.

"General," Oscar said, "I must commend you for thinking of this ingenious method of transportation." Previously Vail had arranged for open carriages, showing Oscar off in the streets as a sort of live advertisement for the lecture. But with Tracy in charge here, Vail had gone ahead to New Orleans to prepare for Oscar's arrival. Traquair watched

Oscar explore the lush interior of the carriage, fingering the frilly gold edges of the green velvet curtain that was pulled back from the window.

"Why, it's just smart business," General Tracy said. "If I paraded you around in the wide-open world, half the town would see you without our benefiting in any way from their satisfaction. Why, even a whore knows better than to do something that stupid. The only thing dumber would be to let everybody in free *tonight*. The main reason people are willing to pay for tonight's show is to get a good look at you."

Oscar released his own disillusioned sigh. "Have they no interest whatever in hearing what I have to say?"

"Well, you could say that they want to hear you, yes. They want to hear the sound of your voice. But, then, that is not quite the same thing as wanting to hear what you have to say. You see, they've been reading about your message for weeks. Basically, they know what you're about: art, remember art, don't forget about art, keep art in the home, keep art in your heart, and the like. Be nice. They know all that. And to the extent that folks can find time for all that, to the extent that it doesn't cost them too much money, they don't mind going along with you. But what they really want right about now is to get a good look at you. Why, I don't think we would have many requests for refunds if all you did when you took the stage tonight was recite the text from the front page of this evening's *Memphis Daily Avalanche*."

"Thank you, but I've no gift for minor tragedy," Oscar said. Traquair, suppressing laughter, leaned forward to look out the carriage window. The sun lit his smile as he looked out at downtown Memphis and listened to the sound of Oscar's voice.

"I've been called a circus attraction for so long now that I suppose it was my destiny to become just that. I am the sideshow that happens to be the main attraction as well. Believe me, I know too well the trauma of the ridiculous. Remember that 'Wild Man of Borneo' drawing in the *Washington Post*, Traquair?" Traquair nodded without leaving his position at the window. "How awful," Oscar continued. Then he laughed softly and said, "I know how remarkably small the giant feels when all those eyes of the normal look down upon him. And I know the gargantuan ache of the dwarf. It is never affirmed, never even considered, that genius, too, is deformity."

Now Traquair glanced back over his shoulder. He was planning, with a mere wink or a raised eyebrow, to tickle more laughter from Oscar, but he was distracted by the strange mixture of shock and fear that had registered upon General Tracy's face. Tracy pressed himself back against the seat, as if trying to move as far away from Oscar as possible. "Perhaps," Tracy said finally, with some difficulty, "perhaps it's just your pants." He motioned toward Oscar's infamous knee breeches. That comment brought back the laughter, and Traquair chuckled along.

"It may be the pants, General," said Oscar. "But everything that I am chose these pants. If they are a spectacle, then I am as well. A man doesn't choose his particular genius. It chooses him. And it comes with certain undetachable accoutrements. If I were wearing a linen suit, I should be someone else. And a decidedly average someone else at that."

General Tracy seemed unnecessarily alarmed. "I hope you did not think for one minute that I was suggesting that you change! I believe I am contracted for the pants."

"Contracts that forbid change are the genesis of all insurrection."

"I am afraid that as a businessman I must insist that you adhere to the terms of our agreement."

"General, I have no interest in interfering with your business."

"I should say you don't, because, of course, my business is also your business," said General Tracy, calmer now. "Seats at the Leubrie's Theater have sold very well. I've priced tickets invitingly at one dollar for the main house and fifty cents for the gallery. More than six hundred should show up to see you. If you look out that way you will see the theater shortly." General Tracy pointed Oscar toward the side of the carriage where Traquair had been looking out the window. Traquair and Oscar touched shoulders, making room for each other within the confines of the small, horizontally dominant, rectangular window. Their heads were tightly framed there, outer ears slightly cropped, and they bobbed gently with the jerky movements of the slowly advancing carriage, Oscar's long hair occasionally swiping Traquair's cheek and chin. Two couples were walking together about ten feet away, and one of the women recognized Oscar. She pointed him out to the others in her party, and they all waved. Both Oscar and Traquair smiled a greeting in response. As the vehicle neared the Leubrie's Theater, their heads and eyes rose in unison toward the direction of the marquee, which read, *Oscar Wilde on "Decorative Art" 8 o'clock tonight.* About twenty people were in line to buy tickets, and a few of them recognized Oscar as well. They saw the two faces in the window and witnessed the gestures of a brief exchange, though, of course, they didn't hear Oscar whisper to Traquair, "What do you think?"

Nor did they hear Traquair's instinctively specific response to this most vague of questions: "The black velvet jacket."

"Yes. It will be warm, but it is perfect. The lace ruffles?"

"A must. Along with the green silk scarf."

"All in all, a worthy setting."

Oscar and Traquair sat back in their seats. General Tracy was wearing another look of dismay.

"Oh—and the pants," Oscar added, evidently trying to assuage whatever worries lay beneath the general's frown. Oscar's words did have some effect, Traquair noticed, though he couldn't help but sense that the general's face begged for some other response, some explanation. Neither, however, was forthcoming.

Traquair's fingers pinched into place the second lacy cuff of Oscar's fresh white shirt, which he thought looked a bit too stiff, so he stood in front of Oscar and fluffed the sleeves by tugging on each one a couple of times. Then he walked behind Oscar and loosened the body of the shirt by fanning its sides near Oscar's waistline. Oscar raised his arms to accommodate Traquair's movements.

"Is that better?" he asked Oscar.

"You know it is," Oscar replied. He stood still as Traquair dressed him.

Traquair almost ignored the remark, but he responded casually, "I suppose I do." Then he walked over to the bed, where he had laid out Oscar's scarf, vest, and jacket for a couple of afternoon interviews and, later, the lecture. These were the nicest things available among the clean wardrobe, and Traquair was planning to have all of the shirts laundered and the suits pressed when they went back to New Orleans. As he was bending down to pick up the scarf and the vest, he heard Oscar say, "Tra, if you know that what you do for me makes things better for me, then why must you ask, 'Is that better?' "

Traquair did not know how to answer this question. A quiver of anxiety went through him as he folded the vest over his left arm. He picked up the dark green scarf, and the feel of the silk soothed him. He replied, honestly enough, "I don't know." Then he walked over to Oscar and began to tie the scarf loosely around the collar of the shirt. "Maybe it was merely a rhetorical question."

"Have we come to that? Mere rhetoric."

"What do you mean, Oscar?" He held the vest open for Oscar's entrance.

"I mean I think you're bored with me," Oscar said, inserting one arm and then the next into the vest as Traquair moved around him to make the dressing easier. "I think you're bored with this whole enterprise."

Traquair stood in front of Oscar again, buttoning the vest and adjusting the scarf beneath the top button. "And I think you know that is not true."

"Does it surprise you that I should say something I know is not true?"

"Now look who's asking rhetorical questions." Traquair inspected Oscar's appearance. "Look at your hair," he said. "Have a seat at the mirror, and I'll unpack the brushes." Oscar did as he was told, and Traquair found the case with combs, brushes, and various colognes and brought it over to the vanity table. He removed Oscar's favorite silver-handled, soft-bristled brush and began to stroke the dishevelment away.

"All right, perhaps you're not bored," Oscar said. "But I've begun to sense lately that you are preoccupied with your own thoughts."

Traquair considered this accusation; he knew what Oscar meant. He frequently drifted into reveries about his travels, not about Oscar, but about John, Otis and Nat, Mae, his uncle, a letter from whom he was eager to read as soon as he finished dressing Oscar and sent him downstairs for his first interview. And Theda Trenton rarely left his mind. Thoughts of her, more than anyone or anything else, had diminished his infatuation with Oscar. If the visit to Mae's had been the final act of his youth (and he'd come to think of it as such), then his spontaneously orchestrated duet with Miss Trenton in St. Louis had been his first mature act. He was still haunted as well by the intimacy of their stirring, utterly adult encounter on the streets of New York. All memory is self-indulgence, it occurred to him. Finally he said to Oscar with an unintentional but telling dreaminess, "Everyone is preoccupied with his own thoughts."

"Yes. But you used to be more preoccupied with mine. Or so you pretended. I liked that. I liked that very much. But now you've drifted. I can sense it." Their eyes met in the mirror. Traquair felt an odd twinge of guilt. He took in a quick breath to say something, but Oscar cut him off, "No need to argue. I've lost you to your own thoughts—or whatever. If you've drifted, I suppose it's really my own fault. I've given you nothing new to preoccupy yourself with of late. No new thoughts. I need to give you something new. If you are neglecting me, it is because I am neglecting you."

"You are making too much of a simple question about your well-being, too much of one comment."

"If the whole world can be changed by one comment—and it can—why shouldn't a man's mood be just as susceptible?" Oscar said. Traquair put down the brush and dusted a few strands of hair from Oscar's shoulders. "But I shall not so easily allow you to return to yourself, Tra. I shall seek to regain your attentiveness. I shall give you something new. Maybe not today—but soon. Don't you give up on me just yet. Keep listening. And I shall find a way to win you back."

25 May 1882

Dearest nephew,

I'm writing to tell you that your visit in March has changed my life.

Before you arrived I was content to have forgotten all that had happened to me back there in the East. I do not believe I owe anyone any apologies for having done so, having forgotten, that is, or really for anything else, unless they are apologies to myself. No, this claim is not entirely true. I can think of two apologies that, for me, would matter. The letter I sent to you, the letter that you say was misplaced, contained one of them. It contained that and little else—but its loss may be for the best.

On some level, the happiness I have achieved here with Summer, our home, and my work is enough of an answer to any questions I might have about my own methods. Yet, after meeting with you, I became infatuated with the idea that there was something about myself that I did not know, something that I was not allowing myself to know—but that I needed to know. I suppose it was my dissatisfaction with my long estrangement from my brother, of which you so obviously reminded me, that was behind my shift in mood. Your appearance forced me to confront that tragedy. Since your father has never responded to my overtures of reconciliation, I resolved to come to terms with other parts of my past, wherever and however those parts might allow, or, should I be so fortunate, welcome such an intrusion.

I went on a search for Mae. You will remember my admitting to having fathered a child by her. I hired a private investigator in Washington, who took six weeks to locate her. He delivered a message from me asking about her well-being and about the child. The investigator noted that at first Mae was very mysterious with him, which he assumed was because of the nature of her business and a fear that he might be a policeman or some federal authority. But eventually he convinced her that he meant no harm. Mae sent back word that she was fine and that she would only divulge such information if I traveled to Washington to meet with her in person. When I discussed the matter with Summer she said, "I do not believe you are asking me if you should go. I believe you are asking yourself. And if you need to ask yourself, then you should go." As usual, she was right. And so, despite my vow never to return to the East, I leave tomorrow on a trip to Washington. By the time you read this, I may already be back in San Francisco. Know that I will write to you to share the results of my visit to Mae, since you are in no small way responsible for setting me into motion and since, of course, we are family and whatever I discover will be of interest to you.

Do you remember how I confessed to you when you were here that whatever fire I once had in me for adventure had long since died? Well, now, on the eve of my journey, I feel that it's been rekindled. Thank you for the inspiration, William.

Your loving uncle,
Moses Traquair

The letter provoked within Traquair a cautious pride. Though his uncle credited Traquair with influencing him to undertake a cross-country journey, Traquair had not intended to spur him in any way. He even regretted having upset the happy equilibrium of the Traquair West household. It occurred to him that a person might, simply by one's presence, have a much stronger effect than one realized, that a person, quite unintentionally, could change another's life. Existence carried with it this passive power and, as one had no real control over its use, it was, he realized even as he vicariously rejoiced in his uncle's impetuous charge to recover his past, quite dangerous.

That night during the lecture a six-year-old girl briefly interrupted the proceedings by approaching the stage to present Oscar with a basket of flowers. Traquair, who often avoided the lectures these days, had made a point of accompanying Oscar in Vail's absence. The girl's small stature accentuated Oscar's size. From his position just offstage standing next to an animated and joyful General Tracy, Traquair poked his head around the gathered curtain to glimpse the audience. Their eyes were fixed upon the visiting monster as he met one of the most delicate of their own. There was a trace of fear in the quiet but palpable anticipation that accompanied the little girl's brief, bold march toward the strange stranger. Oscar Wilde was a thing unknown to the crowd, unknowable. Traquair watched the tiny girl ascend the steps to the stage and offer up her tribute, and he marveled at how, even in this mode of acceptance, Oscar created the distinct impression of being a giant performing an act of extreme generosity.

NEW ORLEANS

Nᴇᴡ Oʀʟᴇᴀɴꜱ was hot. Traquair had moved a chaise longue to a spot near an open window in the bedroom of their St. Charles Hotel suite, and he was relaxing there, smoking a cigarette, hoping another breeze would blow over him soon, as had happened a few times already. He had escorted three reporters into the front room, where they were interviewing Oscar and, as it would be a while before he would have to show them to the door, Traquair had stretched his legs out and crossed them at the ankles. The cigarette had a cooling effect of its own as he listened to Oscar tirelessly entertain the inquisitive visitors.

"I love the heat," Oscar was saying. "Look there at the lovely, slow movements of the people." Traquair clasped his left hand behind his head and angled his vision out over the edge of his elbow into the next room. He saw Oscar there, arm extended dramatically, pointing toward the windows. "They can barely make their next steps. Heat induces a sort of perpetual reverie, a certain listlessness. And languor, I believe, has an important relationship to the creation of fine literature. I'm designing my career based on this premise. Without heat in its figurative manifestations—passion, ardor—there is no such thing as art. Is it possible that the more sultry corners of the world incite within their inhabitants the metaphorical equivalents of their climates and therefore more and better art as well? Quite. Think of Italy, and you will begin to know what I mean. Had Shakespeare the blood of Romans he might have invented the novel. Richard Wagner must retire to the jungles of Africa if he is to compose the *Gesamtkunstwerk* of his dreams. The South, too, has a genuine superiority in this regard, and an obligation, I think, to lead your country in its artistic advancement. New Orleans, specifically, has an enormous advantage in that she, as near as I can perceive, has no rival in all of America for the sheer romantic quality of setting, a quality conducive to the production of art. The great river that winds through the town inspiring your ironwork artisans to show the river what winding is really all about. The great church that has scented the air with the aroma of God. Even without the steady ringing of the bells, one would know that the church has a strong presence here. God is here because he loves the sun, his own first significant creation, as you have doubtless heard.

"New Orleans and the South—though they have yet to make any important use of it—have yet another artistic resource that places them ahead of the rest of the country: the Negro." There was a pause into which Traquair, removing the cigarette from his lips, exhaled visibly, and he watched the smoky evidence of his existence rise. He closed his eyes before it dissipated and listened as Oscar continued this lecture that even Traquair had never heard. "Yes, I know. Those expressions you gentlemen are sharing with me match my feeling exactly. I, too, am astounded that none of your artists has seen the obvious merits of the Negro as a great artistic theme. Your fine novelist Mr. Cable has made overtures. His descriptions of the voodoo dance ceremony led me to witness one of those fascinating and inexplicably enchanting rituals just last night—where I heard new sounds and sensed new possibilities for spirituality. But Mr. Cable's work is only a faint hint at what could be accomplished. Why, the physical attributes of the Negro alone offer an unthinkably rich and bright model for any true artist. The movements of the people belong to the realm of art. Where is the great sculptor or the great choreographer who will acknowledge this? And a simple but careful study of the variety of hues that distinguish the American Negro would introduce new colors to canvas. New reds, new yellows, new blues. The painter who would discover this would reshape the world of portraiture, indeed the world of art. The colors of the American Negro—I have studied this carefully and up close, I do not speak flippantly—oftentimes vary even upon the same individual from season to season, a little-known fact. In the Southern heat, I have been distracted by the beauty of the Negro more so than any place else. Not only because Negroes are more plentiful in the South, but the light is different here, and the Negro obviously has a more intimate and more mutually loving relationship with God's sun. Yes, Adam was a Negro. How clear it is to me now. His face has seen and been kissed by every sun since Eden. Only a man who once reveled in the nearly infinite pleasures of paradise could so incite such rumors of sensuality, of an inclination to leisure, and of an insatiable desire for an odd and luscious fruit."

"But, Mr. Wilde, they really do love watermelon," said one of the reporters with a laugh.

Oscar made a sound that registered to Traquair as a laughing hum or a series of melodic grunts, and then continued, "In a land like the South, like New Orleans, a land that features such a plenitude of reconfigured Adams, Adams of those same new colors that a true painter might discover, must discover, those colors could be used to fashion an entirely new art for America. You look at me as if the things I describe are unreal. Well, I assure you that the only thing in the natural world worth discussing and worth reproducing is that which is unreal. Your artists—your poets and novelists, your dramatists, your musicians—should not look so hungrily to Europe for an image of what to create. A new world deserves a new art. I would not guarantee that this new art would be an altogether pleasing invention as even great, newly imagined art has *some* of its own world in it.

"If your painters hear me, they will create a fantastic, patchwork portraiture. If your new art is a literature, it will be some form of decomposed poetry. But, as America is the noisiest country in the world, I predict a new music, and your noise will, of course, be in the music. And should your new art in fact be a *great* music, it will be the sound of art dying."

"And will the Negro *be* in the music?" asked one of the reporters.

"No," said Oscar.

"I didn't think so," said one of the other reporters.

But Oscar added quickly, "The Negro will be the music."

And a current wafted through Traquair's open window, rushing over his face and body, brightening the glow at the tip of his nearly spent cigarette, and he breathed in its rhythms.

BEAUVOIR

FTER a brief tour of Beauvoir, Jefferson Davis's charming raised home, aptly named for its magnificent view of the Mississippi coastline, Oscar Wilde sat outside on the great gallery that faced the Gulf of Mexico talking with the former president of the Confederate States of America. Standing on the front porch after a walk through the house, Mrs. Davis had invited Oscar into the second parlor, "a more intimate space," she had said. But Oscar had insisted upon remaining out in the open air: "Intimacy is for those who know either everything or nothing about one another. Your husband and I have just enough knowledge of each other as to give us hope for something more lasting than intimacy, actual friendship."

Mr. Davis sat in a rocker and Oscar on a mattress-covered bench in front of one of the four grand windows on the face of the house. The shutters and the window were open behind him. Traquair, who had earlier escorted Oscar into the house, was now standing at the bottom of the wide stairs that led up to the porch. Robert Brown, Mr. Davis's servant, stood beside him. Traquair looked up and saw Oscar's long hair blowing in the breeze as he chatted with Mr. Davis. From Traquair's position the two men were separated by one of the squared columns. He moved his head from side to side trying to frame Oscar and Mr. Davis together without the intrusion of the pillar, but he realized that only by moving farther back from the house and much more to the left or right side of the stairs could he have achieved that perspective. He thought the two men posing together would make an important picture, the young rebel meeting the old, but there was no photographer here to document it. No reporters had followed them from New Orleans, despite their knowing about the trip to Beauvoir. (Vail had gotten the word out, but there was no interest in covering the visit. So with no entourage planning to accompany Oscar, Vail had gone ahead to Mobile to prepare for tomorrow's lecture.) Traquair wanted to know what Oscar and Mr. Davis were discussing, but he was too far away to hear their voices. That this moment, which was certainly of historical significance, would go unrecorded saddened him. He thought about his conversation with his father on the subject of history. Learning about his father's secret past had forced him to defend the necessity of history, to argue for its relevance. But now he wondered about history's true value, when so many incidents went undocumented. Its accuracy, and therefore, perhaps, its real worth, was always in question. Someone would inevitably come along later— historians and other less formal fabulists—and try to make something out of nothing. Yes, *nothing*. The past, like ghosts and God, was an abstract concept based on rumors and hunches and a faith whose strength was directly related to the individual's ability and willingness to conjure. Every moment expired into myth. All of the past was but fodder for a Bulfinch.

Robert was tapping him on the shoulder. "I said, *hey*, William!" Traquair turned from his fixation on the porch sitters to look at Robert, whose perfectly round face with symmetrical features wore a calm plea upon it. Traquair was several inches taller than Robert, so he leaned his head down now to assure Robert that he was paying attention.

Robert said, "We don't have to wait here if you don't want to. They'll be up there for hours. That's how he is. He can talk with the best of them."

"That's precisely what he is doing."

"Come on thisaway," urged Robert, tugging at the sleeve of Traquair's jacket and pulling him along the right side of the house. They walked in the shade of a huge oak tree. "Let's go around back."

"What's there?"

"Where I live, and the kitchen. Y'all came on a good day. It's Miss Winnie's birthday. My wife is baking the cakes. And whenever Isabel starts to baking, she always makes me something special. That's the kind of woman I got. You married, William?"

"No, not yet."

"Got a girl, though," Robert said in a tone so presumptuous that it willed his conjecture into fact.

"A few," Traquair lied, in an attempt to accommodate Robert. No, he did not actually *have* them now, meaning those girls he'd known in Washington, Boston, Chicago, New York, and a few other places; he had *had* them. It was a bad response. "But I love only one," he flippantly amended the comment, knowing that these words would better fulfill Robert's imperative. He had never made such a statement to anyone, not even to himself. It, too, felt like a lie, but he was instantly aware that it was in fact the entire truth.

"Where is she?"

"Back home. New York."

"Well, you better go on and marry her before somebody else does. A woman won't wait around forever, you know. Let the rest of em go. Just let em go."

"I assure you I already have." And this, too, was the truth. Since the tour had headed south, Traquair had not contacted any of the people whose names John had given to him back in Philadelphia. He had avoided socializing at all, not because he thought he would be tempted, but because of Theda Trenton. And now here he was admitting to himself and to a stranger why: *he loved her.* Who would document that myth? he wondered. If he failed to capture her lasting affection, as circumstances predicted, would the legend of his love be lost, even to himself?

As he and Robert were about to turn to go toward the back of the house, Traquair noticed a little white cottage about one hundred feet up ahead and to the right. The building had a pointed roof that draped down dramatically to meet its support, a series of columns that were diminutive versions of the ones on the main house. Centered beneath this cover was a small, boxlike structure that gave form to an even smaller interior room. Green shutters, open on the side Traquair could see best, guarded the entrances, doors made of framed windows. The entire little house was surrounded by a four-foot-deep porch and rested much lower to the ground than the main house. Its isolation appealed to Traquair. "What's that building?" he asked Robert.

"That's the library. It's where Mr. Davis does his writing and his important thinking." Traquair had stopped walking, intrigued by the building and its uses. He felt his companion's stare. "You want to take a look inside?" Robert asked. Traquair nodded once emphatically. "Come on thisaway." Robert guided Traquair a few steps away from the back of the cottage before moving forward. It was a simple but unnecessary movement, and something about it suggested furtiveness.

"Are you sure we should?" Traquair's voice instinctively reduced itself to a whisper.

"It's all right." Robert spoke softer than before as well. "I go in there all the time." He glanced back over his shoulder at Traquair, but then also beyond Traquair up to where Oscar and Mr. Davis were. "Many's the time that Mr. Davis be working up there in the big house and, when he needs a book or something, he'll send me out here for it. Look. I have my own key." He removed from his pants pocket a set of several keys all gathered by a knot of red ribbon, and he jingled them near Traquair's troubled face. "Don't worry. Just follow me." They continued around to the back of the library, climbed the five steps up to the porch, and walked quietly along the side of the cottage that was not visible from the main house. All the while, Robert's movements, in opposition to his assertions of authority to enter the building, exhibited the meticulously improvised rhythm of stealth. Before turning the corner onto the front porch, the side facing the Gulf, Robert paused to sneak a peek around the edge of the building. Then he said, "Come on." They turned, took four very quick steps—Traquair followed Robert's lead—and arrived at the front door.

Robert put his key into the lock and fidgeted with the knob for a moment. "Hurry up!" Traquair whispered emphatically, acknowledging, as Robert would not, that what they were up to was, if not forbidden, at least mischievous. They both turned their heads together back toward the house. "No," said Traquair. "You watch what you're doing. I'll keep a lookout." Traquair pressed himself into Robert's back with the idea that if they blended themselves together, the two of them would become less visible, but he could not see the house too well from this position. Holding on to Robert's shoulders to balance himself, he leaned his head back for a better view. From this distance and this angle, he could see Oscar and Jefferson Davis gesturing to each other, no longer divided by the column as before. "My key is stuck," Robert said. "That don't never happen." Traquair leaned forward again. As Robert struggled with the key, his right elbow was jabbing Traquair's ribs. Ignoring the bumps, Traquair looked through the large windowpanes of the door and into the little library. He saw shelves of books lining the walls nearly from floor to ceiling. A plain, light-colored desk, along with its armchair, occupied the center of the room. Two other desks with chairs, a small table, a fireplace, and, propped against some shelves and resting on the floor, a framed portrait of a woman who might have been a younger Mrs. Davis filled up the space. As Traquair was pressing harder into Robert's back to get a better look at a hidden corner of the room, the lock finally ceded its conceit, and the door flew open into the room. The combined weight of Robert Brown and William Traquair lent significant force to the entrance, and the two men tumbled wildly into the cottage. Robert, who some-how managed to keep his hand on the knob and stop the door before it banged against the inner wall, landed on his butt and slid quietly to the right side of the room. But Traquair was thrown about three feet into the air, performing a complete, involuntary, and inelegant somer-sault before crashing to the floor, first onto his backside and then over onto his heels. His momentum continued to roll him forward, thrust-ing his head into one of the bottom rows of books. The impact of his landing or one of his flailing limbs displaced a few books from the upper shelves as well, and some of these flapped their pages around his head, buzzing like mosquitoes before a sting, while others remained closed and heavy, thudding into his body like lead. When the pelting stopped, Traquair lay still for a moment. He groaned as he slowly uncovered himself, resting on his back, propped up on his elbows, and saw Robert on the other side of the room through the legs of the desk. Robert was staring back at him. There was a moment of absolute still-ness and silence, and then they both began to laugh, softly at first, but gradually more loudly and more deeply. In midlaugh, Robert closed the door and crawled over to the side window that offered a view of the house. He poked his head up and looked out. Then he turned to Traquair, exhaled loudly, and said, "We made it."

Traquair gathered himself. "I thought you said he wouldn't mind," he said.

"Of course he would mind. Don't nobody want nobody meddling in their private business. Specially him."

"I suppose you're right." Traquair picked up the books he had knocked from the shelves. "What should I do with these? I'm not sure where they belong."

"I'll take em," said Robert, rising and walking over to retrieve the books. Without looking at the actual titles, he placed them on various shelves in the area where Traquair had fallen. Traquair shuffled around the room, fingering some of the other books that rested undisturbed in their proper places; there were hundreds. Among those he touched were *The Writings of John Adams*; *Debates on the Federal Constitution*; *Life and Letters of George Cabot* by H. C. Lodge; the Comte de Paris's *History of the Civil War*; *The American Conflict* by Horace Greeley; *The Confederate First and Second Missouri Brigades* by Bevier; *The Record of Fort Sumter* by W. A. Harris; and *The Prison Life of Jefferson Davis* by Dr. John Cravin. He was tempted to pluck one or two of these volumes from their places in line, but he didn't want the bother of trying to find the right spot in which to replace them when he was done. He turned and faced the room itself, and his eyes moved to the desk in the middle of the floor, which sat as isolated as the cottage itself. He waved his hand toward it and asked, "Is this where he does his writing?"

Robert carelessly propped on a high shelf the last of the books he was handling and turned toward Traquair. "Yes. That's where he wrote most of his book. Some days he would have me bring the desk out on the porch and he would work out there. But most days he would just sit in here researching with Major Walthall or dictating to Miss Dorsey. She was the one used to own this whole place—was something between the two of them if you ask me. Or some days he would dictate to Mrs. Davis, or he might just be writing some of it out on his own. But then sometimes he would just sit there and think. He do that more and more these days. Just sit and think."

Traquair walked over to the desk. He gripped the back of the armchair there and rested his weight on it. "Go ahead," Robert said. "Sit down."

Traquair sat down in Jefferson Davis's chair. He didn't find it very comfortable—he was too tall for it—but he liked the fact that it swiveled. As he slowly drew the chair forward, he relaxed into its care. A small brass lamp and five books shared space on the desktop, but it was mostly vacant. Traquair rubbed his opened palms over the smooth black leather that was stretched out before him. He noticed that two of the books, each about two inches thick, stacked together on their sides, were actually volumes one and two of Mr. Davis's own *The Rise*

and Fall of the Confederate Government. He picked up the heavy volume one and dropped it onto the desk directly in front of him. He said,
"Have you ever read this book, Robert?"

"Which book?"

"Mr. Davis's book."

"I would rather do fieldwork than read that much of any book. You
read it?"

"Yes. Well, most of it. Mr. Wilde shared his copy with me when he
was done preparing for this visit." Traquair picked up the book and
thumbed through it. In the margins of several pages, he noticed hand-
written notes. Mr. Davis, he guessed, was in the process of making cor-
rections for a future edition. Traquair turned to the preface and then
glanced at Robert, who was moving to take a seat at one of the other
desks. "Listen to this," Traquair said. "He tells us at the beginning what
he set out to do in writing the book: 'The object of this work has been
from historical data to show that the Southern States had rightfully
the power to withdraw from a Union into which they had, as sovereign
communities, voluntarily entered; that the denial of that right was a
violation of the letter and spirit of the compact between the States;
and that the war waged by the Federal Government against the seced-
ing States was in disregard of the limitations of the Constitution, and
destructive of the principles of the Declaration of Independence.' "

Traquair stopped and looked up at Robert, who said, "Read that
one more time—slower." And Traquair did so.

"That's what he try to prove in that book?" Robert asked.

"Yes."

"And do he prove any of it?"

"Without a doubt, he proves all of it."

"Well," Robert said nonchalantly, "he usually do what he say he
gon do."

Traquair flipped a hundred pages or so of the book, when something—a word, a name—caught his eye. He read the entire passage to
himself first. Then he smiled and said to Robert, "Listen again. Now
he's talking about the Constitution, disputing what someone else said
about the individual states not even being named in the document,
which actually they are. He writes: 'Leave out all mention of the
States—I make no mere verbal point or quibble, but mean the States
in their separate, several, distinct capacity—and what would remain

would be of less account than the play of the Prince of Denmark with the part of Hamlet omitted.' "

"Denmark! What the hell he talking bout now?"

"He means that the Constitution of the United States of America is a drama, or at least the outline of a drama, about the *individual* states, that the states are the stars of the show."

"Like on the flag."

"Precisely."

"But the Constitution and the Declaration of Independence is supposed to say what the country stand for and how it work. If they say the whole operation is set up a certain way, then how could President Lincoln and the Republicans go rearranging all of that?"

"You ask a good question. Union forces would argue that the existence of slavery in the South presented the North with a license and even a moral *obligation* to take up arms."

"Oh, yeah," Robert said sadly, almost apologizing for having asked. He closed his eyes and pinched the bridge of his nose as if he were lost in some painful personal memory. Then he opened his eyes wide, fixed an intense glare upon Traquair, and said, "But . . . but what gave them the *right*?"

"Constitutionally, nothing did. Technically, Mr. Davis argues convincingly, the North was wrong to fight the South's secession. Legally, they had no right."

"Well, I'll be damned," said Robert.

"The North sinned on the soul of the Union . . . to save the soul of the Union," Traquair heard himself conclude.

"Whoa—I guess sometimes two wrongs really do make a right." Robert paused and then asked, "Is that in Mr. Davis's book?"

Traquair shook his head and smiled. "Not quite."

"In all them pages—how many pages?"

Traquair fanned the books quickly. "In both volumes . . . about fifteen hundred."

Robert warbled the downward-spiraling whistle of enchanted disbelief. "You'd think he would have got right on down to the root of it in all them pages: Sometimes two wrongs really do make a right. I like the sound of that."

"So do I." Traquair put the books down and reclined in the chair, clasping his hands behind his head. He remained in a state of meditation until Robert said, "You want to stay here a while more or do you want to go get some cake?" It was the return of that polite way he had of guiding Traquair in the direction he desired. Traquair was about to succumb to Robert's will and answer him by rising to leave when the front door slowly began to open. He had noticed Robert's face first, his eyes suddenly focusing on a point beyond Traquair's left shoulder. Then the widening wedge of light invading the library from floor to ceiling drew his attention. Out of the corner of his eye, he saw a trembling Robert stand. Traquair swiveled his chair around to face the door. He wanted to stand, too, but something, fear, weighted him to the seat. The door finally opened to the silhouette of a woman. The sunlight behind her left Traquair squinting to see her more clearly. She spoke softly. "Who are you?"

Traquair stood now to greet her. Behind him he heard Robert bump into a table as he tried to move forward. "Miss Winnie," Robert said, taking a place beside Traquair. "This here is William . . ." Robert's hand bounced three times on Traquair's shoulder.

"William Traquair," Traquair completed the phrase for Robert.

"Hello, William Traquair," she said. "I'm Varina Davis. I'm called, among other things, Winnie—or Miss Winnie, as the case may be—because Mother is also named Varina, you know. I suppose it keeps confusion to a minimum. No girl should ever be mistaken for her mother. It somewhat restricts the possibility of any future engagements—presuming, of course, her mother is married." She took a step into the room, and Traquair's view of her was no longer hampered by the sunlight. He saw, disappearing at the corners of her mouth, what must have been, a second before, something of a smirk. Winnie had dark, curly hair that was gathered around the front of her head like a tiara. Her face had a softness about it despite its prominent, somewhat masculine nose. The pink dress she was wearing looked brand-new, probably made especially for her birthday, Traquair considered. The bejeweled belt wrapped tightly around her waist would have been too much adornment for everyday attire. Yes, she was dressed up for the occasion. Traquair noticed that she was in fact the girl in the painting that was propped against the bookshelves to his left. Glancing down at it now, he read the two lines engraved into the brass plate at the bottom of the portrait's frame: *Varina Anne Jefferson Davis, "The Daughter of the Confederacy."* He looked back at Winnie. Caught between the real girl and her painted image, he found himself thinking that there was something peculiarly artistic in Winnie's manner.

"What are you doing here?" she asked him.

Traquair and Robert looked guiltily at each other. "Well," said Robert, "I just wanted William to see the library and to, you know—"

"No," Winnie said. "I mean, William, what are you doing at Beauvoir?"

"Oh," said Traquair, "I'm accompanying Mr. Wilde."

"I thought that might be the case," she said. "Where is Mr. Wilde now?"

"I believe he and Mr. Davis are still up on the front gallery," said Traquair.

Winnie looked out the side window. "Father will wear him out before I've had a chance to talk to him." She pouted a little.

"It's not easy to wear down Mr. Wilde," Traquair said.

"Miss Winnie, didn't you hear your mama calling for you when they first got here?" Robert asked. "She was trying to tell you to come on and meet Oscar Wilde. That's when you missed your chance to get ahold of him before your papa started in on wearing him out. Why didn't you answer your mama? She hollered like a hound."

"I *heard* her, Robert. I simply was not yet ready to meet Mr. Wilde. I'm still not ready."

"Why aren't you ready?" asked Traquair.

"Why?" Winnie looked directly at Traquair and started to say something more—but, with a blink, her eyes shifted to Robert and she halted whatever words she had been about to utter. Her face relaxed a little, and she let her arms dangle playfully. Then she said, "Robert, why don't you go to the kitchen and check on Isabel and the cakes. Come back soon and let us know how things are coming along."

Robert hesitated awkwardly but said, "Of course, Miss Winnie." He started out the door and with a touch of sadness said, "See ya, William." Winnie closed the door behind him and waited until Robert's footsteps stopped sounding on the porch.

"He and Father talk about everything," she said.

"Really?" said Traquair, wondering with slight concern whether or not Robert would speak to Jefferson Davis about their conversation regarding his book.

"Yes," Winnie said. "But some things are private."

"Have you many secrets from your father?"

"Yes. But I've made it well known that I am secretive." They laughed together at her jest.

Traquair thought he detected some mild perfume scenting the air. Undecided about its actual existence, he didn't dwell on the question, freeing his mind to ask something else.

"Tell me," he said, pointing at the painting of Winnie, "why are you called 'The Daughter of the Confederacy'?"

"Because I was born in 1864 in the Confederate mansion in Richmond when my father was president. I have a sister, Margaret—but she was born too soon to be considered the daughter of anything except our parents. She's in Memphis, married."

"Do you have any brothers?"

"Not anymore." She twisted a strand of her hair like the ingenue she was, or perhaps sadly and a bit nostalgically, like the little girl she wasn't.

"So Robert tells me it's your birthday!" Traquair said brightly, seeking to emphasize the more hopeful present.

"My eighteenth! And in my family that is an achievement."

"Surely you have higher goals than that," he said. "Complacency's lone act is the slaying of ambition."

"I have great ambition. I want more than my eighteenth birthday." She paused and lifted her chin with a touch of arrogance. "And I want something more than marriage, too . . . something other than Memphis. That concerns what I wanted to ask your advice about."

"My advice?"

"Yes. And, really, it's what I would like to speak to Mr. Wilde about that I don't want my father to hear." Winnie waved her hand from Traquair toward the chair at her father's desk, and he took a step back and sat down again. Moving quickly about the room, she slid one of the other chairs close to Traquair. She sat, put her left hand on her hip, leaned even closer to him—mmm, so it *was* an actual perfume he had sniffed earlier and not merely the scent of laughter—and she asked, "How well are you acquainted with Mr. Wilde, William?"

Traquair said quickly, "Probably about as well as Robert is acquainted with your father."

"Yes! That is what I was hoping. You can help me. You see, my great ambition is to become an artist. A writer, in fact. No one else is aware of this fantasy of mine, least of all my parents. The appearance of Mr. Wilde here today—on my eighteenth birthday—I take to be a sign that I am right to pursue the life of an artist. I want to talk to Mr. Wilde about just that, about being an artist. So, William, if you tell me now that Mr. Wilde would be open to such a discussion and if I can summon the nerve and have a moment alone with him later, I should like to speak to him seriously about this matter. I know, I know, it seems obvious from the stories that are printed about him that he *would* avail himself to someone like me. But I know all too well from my father's situation that one can't really judge a man by what one reads about him. So tell me, William, as one who is close to the man, as one who really knows him, is Mr. Wilde the sort of man who is open to giving an audience to an aspiring artist such as myself?"

"Very definitely," Traquair said. "So long as she does not present herself as an aspiring artist. When you speak to him alone—yes, such a thing can be arranged—you must not call yourself an *aspiring* artist."

"What should I call myself?"

"An artist."

"But that is a lie. I only *hope* to be an artist."

"If in the future you become an artist, you will always have been one. If in calling yourself an artist today you are in fact lying, then there is no hope of your ever becoming one."

Winnie squinted and said, "Well, even if it is true, it would be immodest of me to proclaim myself an artist."

"To modesty, Mr. Wilde prefers truth." Winnie smiled at this remark. Traquair felt that her smile—which reminded him of that coda to a smirk he had glimpsed when he first met her—admitted to something personal, perhaps that her instinct was not toward modesty at all. She sat back in her chair and appeared to be considering another thought.

"Is there something more?" He felt sure that there was.

"I must admit, William, that I am somewhat afraid of Mr. Wilde. Again, I know only what I have read. But—I'll be frank. I believe there may be something wicked about Oscar Wilde."

"Wicked?" Traquair asked, remembering Mr. Gable's warning that he should not be corrupted by Oscar. "Whatever do you mean?"

"He's a great man. All great men are somehow wicked."

"What about your father? Is he wicked?"

"Father was spared the curse of greatness. Instead, he's merely good—which has its own dark side, I suppose."

"I believe a man can be both great *and* good."

"Only one man has managed that trick, William, and rumor has it that he was not really a man at all. The Son of God. Now there's a title of birth more conspicuous than my own. Yes, he was great and good—but look what happened to him. The world treated him as if he were wicked anyway. What did you say to Robert when you were reading from Father's book? Yes, I overheard what you were saying. Something about sinning to save a soul? Christ's sin, as the world saw it, was that he *refused* to sin. It seems that it is somehow the duty of a great man to be wicked. Do you understand?"

"You are almost correct," Traquair said. "Really, it is the great duty of all men to be wicked. You see, without wickedness, Christ's dying would have been in vain."

"That is a cruel thought. How do you know it to be true?"

Traquair said with confidence, "I sense it."

Winnie sighed. "But what becomes of forgiveness in a world of institutionalized evil? I don't think I could live in a world that was not forgiving. I—I wouldn't want my father to live, to have lived in such a world."

"Forgiveness does not belong only to the saintly. Evil is quite compatible with forgiveness. Indeed, forgiveness itself is inherently sinful. Yes, there is about forgiveness at least some small sense of betrayal of the original offended principle. Forgiving the thief requires some acceptance of thievery. Forgiving the murderer, some acquiescence to murder. Forgiving any of the brutal acts of man, some acknowledgment of and admittance to the rights of evil. Thus forgiving—the holiest act—is ever so slightly unholy. The very act of purification is itself impure. To forgive is to sin. Yet *not* to forgive is the only thing that is truly unforgivable. We must choose to sin. We must sin to save our souls. That's what I was speaking to Robert about."

Winnie glared at Traquair, her naughty grin sprouting. "William—you're as wicked as Wilde."

"One of the hazards of standing in the shadows of greatness," said Traquair.

"And what awaits one like me, one who has been raised in the shade of goodness?"

Strangely, Traquair knew the answer. But because you cannot tell an eighteen-year-old that her destiny contains something tragic, he said with a vagueness that could be read as optimism, "Something other than Memphis."

There was a knock at the door, and they stood up. "Miss Winnie? William?" It was Robert.

"We'll be right out," Winnie said. Her face wore a look of frustration.

"Don't worry," Traquair said softly. "I shall see to it that you have your private audience with Mr. Wilde."

Winnie nodded quickly, saying, "Thank you, William." Traquair opened the door, and they greeted Robert as they exited the library. Mumbling a good-bye, Winnie stepped off the porch, heading east, away from the house. Robert locked the door, and he and Traquair walked to the building behind the big house. Isabel greeted Traquair politely, but she was busy baking. When Robert asked, she gave him and Traquair each two pieces of cake, before sending them out of the kitchen. They strolled the grounds, and Robert showed Traquair the orange grove and the vineyard.

Finally Traquair said, "I think we should make our way back to Mr. Wilde and Mr. Davis." Robert agreed, and they walked toward the house. Instead of following the same course they had taken around the outside of the house, Robert began to ascend the back stairs leading up to the main level. To reach the front of the house, they would have to go through the long inner hallway. Traquair, sensing that Robert was overstepping his bounds again, said, as before, "Are you sure we should?" Robert just motioned the way with his head. Here we go again, thought Traquair. Robert eased open the back door, which, of course, creaked. They proceeded into the house anyway and had made it roughly halfway down the hall, when—

"Robert, is that you?" It was Mrs. Davis's voice, coming from another room. The two intruders stopped abruptly. "Y-yes, Miss Varina, it's me."

"Does Mr. Davis want something?"

"No, ma'am. I mean, that's just what I was about to ask him."

"Well, let me know if he does," she said.

"Yes, ma'am."

"I'm not sure what to make of that Oscar Wilde," she said in a whisper. This comment had not been solicited nor did it seem to warrant a response.

Robert and Traquair walked out onto the front porch. "Excuse me, sir," Robert said to Mr. Davis. "Miss Varina sent me out here to find out if you need anything."

"No, Robert. I'm fine. Mr. Wilde, do you need anything?"

"A century that will understand me," Oscar replied.

"I should like one of those myself," Mr. Davis said through a ripple of laughter. "Nothing now," he told Robert, who just shrugged, then whispered to Traquair, "I'm going back for some more cake. Coming?" Traquair shook his head no. Robert went back into the house, as Traquair walked softly on the porch, moving a good distance away from Oscar and Mr. Davis, though careful to stay close enough to hear their voices. He leaned his shoulder against one of the columns, looked out at the Gulf, and listened.

"Oh, that's enough about my book," Mr. Davis said. "Tell me, do you foresee yourself documenting your Aesthetic Movement in any way?"

"Daily," Oscar said. "I foresee my life itself being the documentation of my movement. If my biographer is adequate, he will note this fact. But biographers, in their enthusiasm to re-create life, bear a great resemblance to Mary Shelley's Frankenstein, and their creations are just as monstrous. And I don't think a talent so rich as mine should be wasted on the tediousness of writing an autobiography—an endeavor which, of course, modesty precludes."

"You might change your mind about that point should you live as long as I," Mr. Davis said. "One might think that when an old man lies down upon his bed at the end of one of his many long days, all he would want to do is rest. But what you will learn is that at some point simply to rest becomes too much like death. In the relentless retreat that is old age, an old man looks for pauses. He spends entire mornings and entire afternoons and evenings searching his mind for remote islands of memory, for familiar but exotic distractions. He reflects incessantly upon a past illustrious or inglorious. One way or another he writes his autobiography. That is what I do now over there in my little library when the mood strikes me, which is often. I must admit that there is a temptation to grant oneself perhaps more importance than one is due, to lend to oneself a representative quality, to attempt to take on all the meaning of one's people. This may be my personal predicament only, but I'm not so sure. I would wager that a poor, destitute soul who dies a lonely death in a dark hole someplace feels bearing upon his spirit the weight of the entire Confederacy of the Wretched."

Traquair glanced over and saw Oscar staring out at the water. "There is something else, young man, something else that may be of much greater value to you someday." Mr. Davis stopped the motion of his rocker. "I want you to understand this, so listen carefully." Oscar turned to face him. "I have watched your advances here as the great apostle of art. And today I can see from your tremendous confidence that you have the right attitude about handling your successes and your failures, all of the challenges that have beset you and that will continue to do so. You are wise, shrewd, and diplomatic. You will go far. But what you must be aware of is that in accepting your position as the leader of a controversial movement, you have placed yourself in grave danger. I do not wish to alarm you unduly, but there it is. I was imprisoned for two years, you know. Two horrible years . . . for crimes unnamed, unknown." Traquair watched closely. He wanted to remember forever the intensity with which Oscar's eyes were staring upon Mr. Davis. "When they came for me, I ran. I ran, only to be caught . . . *embarrassingly*. The great mess of running and being caught. Remember this: *Never run! They always catch you!*" His face grew red as he continued: "And then later, the charges were dropped. What charges! What charges! What law exists that justly denies rebellion against tyranny? Is prison really the proper place for those with whom one has moral and philosophical differences? Where is the crime in following the lead of one's heart? I must warn you that society and the revolutionary hold very different opinions on these matters." He paused, took a deep breath, and then began to rock again. Finally, he said to Oscar, "As your movement develops, you may one day find yourself in a position similar to my own. Be careful, I tell you." Shaking his head from side to side, he repeated softly, "Be careful."

Mr. Davis turned away from Oscar and looked out at the Gulf of Mexico. Oscar struck a pensive pose as well, and Traquair followed suit.

It was into this silence and stillness that Winnie Davis appeared at the center of the bottom of the stairs leading up to the porch. Traquair watched her begin a slow ascension of the wide steps. Determined in her upward advance, she blushed in the rosiness of her dress against the gray background of the Gulf. How Traquair admired Winnie, how he marveled at the approach of this birthday girl who had the bravery of all who dared to carry on beyond the grace of youth—an eighteen-year-old just leaving it all behind her. Earlier, in their conversation in her father's library, her inexperience had forced wisdom out of him, and his session with Robert had thrust him into the role of instructor. Both incidents, Traquair understood, had pressed him to assume mature and, for him at least, unusual poses, professor to an uninformed pupil, big brother to a little sister. With Winnie rising up the stairs faster now, moving toward him with the inexorability of time, Traquair felt old for the first time in his life, and he thought: The only thing that gets younger as one ages is youth.

ATLANTA

2 June 1882

Dear Billy,

I regret to report that your friend Oscar and my friend Speranza have, respectively, a brother and a son called Willie who is rather a ruder version of a Wilde. Yesterday, completely unannounced and with a brittleness I shall herein describe, he showed up at the door of my new apartment here in Chelsea. I've given up on hotel living as it looks as though I'll not be leaving London anytime soon. I've let a place—two upper rooms, one with light—very near Mr. Whistler's, which is where I spend my days, watching him work. No lessons yet, as I'm too afraid to allow him to see my sketches. I work some here alone, though not nearly enough. I was, however, penciling an ever so ragged bouquet of peonies yesterday sometime after two in the afternoon when Mr. Willie Wilde came knocking.

Despite my relationship with Lady Wilde, Willie and I had only spent a few moments together, and I'd formed no opinion of him except that he seemed destined to live in Oscar's shadow. The seclusion of shade, either Oscar's or anyone else's, would have been the proper place for the man who visited me yesterday. Upon opening my door, I was immediately taken aback by his appearance. Large and heaving, he crouched before me bearded and potently breathy, his fuming exhalations some mix of the exertion of climbing two flights of stairs and early afternoon imbibition. In his state he struck me as a stupendously less successful version of Oscar, and I couldn't help but feel sorry for him, as one must feel when in the presence of the *obvious lesser of two siblings. It makes one wish that brothers were ever equals. But, alas, Nature knows not democracy. And, yet, looking upon Willie, I felt a certain warmth for this pitiable stranger owing to my growing affection for Lady Wilde and, I am sure, hers for me. That filial feeling I've known in her presence inclined me to receive her true son, however unappealing his presentation, with a fraternal heart. I choose my words with care here, for I must if I am to convey to you the shock of what was to follow.*

First, I extended my hand to greet Willie, but he demurred to offer his in return. He grunted instead, and I whiffed again the scent of his indulgence. Withdrawing my hand, I awkwardly invited him into my rooms. He declined, saying, "I should think not—as I have come to ask that you return the favor."

"The favor? What favor?" I asked, confused by his words and made anxious by their tone. He looked over my shoulder into my first room.

"Nice place," he said. "Nice place, indeed. You should be pretty comfortable here. No real need after all to seek so frequently the comfort of the households of others. Wednesday after Wednesday. Saturday after Saturday. Sometimes sneaking tea in between." I tried to speak, but he raised his voice. "Listen, boy! I'll have no more of this pretense. You are not my mother's son. Nor are you my father's son! Are you?" Stunned, I could not speak. He said firmly, "Shake your head no, as I shall require confirmation of the latter." I acquiesced, moving my head from side to side. "Right!" he said.

"Did Lady Wilde—" He interrupted me. "Of course not. She's infatuated. Everyone, it seems, is infatuated with something or other nowadays. Oscar with art. Mother with you. Well, art my arse, I say. And you . . . well, the same. I've been put down twice already: by Father for his beloved bastard Henry—may he rest in peace—and by Mother for Oscar—may he simply rest! Am I now to see you, a Yankee, become my equal, or worse, my superior? Am I to suffer such indignity, and in my own house? I think not, old boy." He pinched the whiskers at his chin, assuming a pose of ersatz gentility, but nothing, I tell you, could elevate his position above its abject puerility.

Then he said, "But I am not heartless. I'd approve your coming round once more, say in a week or so to see Mama one last time. She *really is quite fond of you. To her, you're the embodiment of her absent Oscar. Were you a little paler and a little less handsome, you might actually pass for him, at least in Mother's lowly lit parlors. She thinks that, oh, Oscar's there in America but, oh, wonder of wonders, an American has mysteriously been sent to her in his place. I can tell you this trick appeals to her fairy-tale mentality. Lovely old woman. Oscar won her from me years ago. Silly that brothers should battle each other for a mother's affection, should fight over love. Yes, she looks at you and sees Oscar. And so do I. But for me you are a much darker vision, don't you see, representing as you do the shadow of my greatest defeat."*

And those wistful words, while not providing complete justification for his behavior toward me, did provoke in me an empathy for his keen emotional response to my very presence. There was something poignant about his crisis. I was on the verge of forgiving his initial rudeness when he said, "Come once more. But after that, you're no longer welcome at one-four-six Oakley Street." And with that Willie Wilde abruptly left me alone, brooding and feeling fairly ill.

As you might guess, it was my worst day in London. Possibly the worst day of my life. I don't know that I've met with any real disappointment until now. Please don't tell anyone about this, Billy. Of course not Oscar, just as I can never tell Lady Wilde. It's so embarrassing to be cast off in this way, without just cause. You can't know. You can't know. The one consolation is that the incident occurred in a private setting. I should have fainted from humiliation had Willie carried out his repudiation of me in a more public forum. Today I feel better, but I am nowhere near recovered. The entire episode has left me wondering about my place here.

Ever yours,
Baxter

❈   ❈   ❈

4 July 1882

Dear Baxter,

Your letter from the depths of despair has reached me at the heights of happiness. All about me the sounds of celebration are ringing. The shouts and cries of joyous children oblivious to the reason for their revelry are rising up to me through an open window. Firecrackers burst loudly, occasionally with such force that my room trembles. In the distance I can still hear the brass band that marched by nearly an hour ago. Nature may not know democracy, but Atlanta certainly does! Against this backdrop of American cheer, I've just read of your disenchantment there in England, and, oh, how I wish you were here at home, safe from the rejection of disapproving strangers.

I've just heard Oscar say to the reporter who's interviewing him in the next room that the gaiety outside is too loud, too raucous for a celebration of something as fine and noble as the Declaration of Independence. "Oh, the patriots, the patriots!" Oscar has just yelled out, referring to the thousands of people in the streets, Negroes, mostly, whose merriment does indeed expose the wilder, more boisterous side of freedom, the side that implies, by its youthful vigor, freedom's recent birth. I suspect, based upon personal reflection and an arrogant conclusion, that such celebrants should require the privileges I've known if they are to display the Jeffersonian restraint and eloquence that would suit Oscar's taste. (Speaking of Jeffersons, you must remind me to tell you all about my visit last week to the home of Jefferson Davis. It occurs to me now as I sit here watching this Independence Day festival that Mr. Davis's nation, as reliant as it was upon a faith in freedom's foil, made at its creation a stranger declaration, a Declaration of Dependence, as it were. Oh, the expatriates, the expatriates!) Sadly, your self-imposed expatriation has left you vulnerable to the likes of Willie Wilde and his personal brand of bigotry, the backlash of his wounded pride. I hope you'll hurry home before any other insults of this sort are inflicted upon you. If you were here with me today you'd be witnessing this spectacle, your heart teeming with a fully intact pride of its own, succumbing to this rush of romance. I can feel my face, more manly I'm sure than you remember, burning with the same childish wonder and jollity wafting up to me from the youngsters frolicking below. Were I staring into a mirror right now I'm certain I'd see reflected *there upon my skin a rutilant luster I've had occasion to deny. And now, as I bring my hand to my face in idle test of this theory, a warmth conducts from cheek to palm, reminding me of lesser flushes I've felt, pressing forth a confession. My shame soothed into irrelevance by the sensuousness of my mood, I'll utter a secret you've probably already guessed.*

I can admit to you now that once, not so long ago, I envied you your trip abroad. Petty, but true. Just as earlier—I'll admit this, too—I had envied your acceptance into the college of our choice. There. I've said it. I've envied you. Yes, it would seem that not unlike your new nemesis, Willie Wilde, Willie Traquair harbored toward you a resentment rank in its puerility. Forgive your friend, dear Baxter, as these transgressions were the sins of an unrefined or, if you will, an unaesthetic soul. But since you and I parted, or more accurately, since I began my apprenticeship with Oscar Wilde, I've embarked upon a journey not only through the heartland of our country but also through the land of my heart. Neither tour is complete, but today, at this writing, on this occasion that henceforth shall always inspire within me an assessment of just how far I've traveled, I thrill to the elegant pageant of retrospection, remembering where I've been, determining what I feel, defining who I am.

"Travel moves me," I once said to Oscar, and he has since repeated that comment. He had told me to feel, and it was the first thing, with any spirited articulation, that I felt, but I had no notion, none whatsoever, that hidden in those words were the language and the tone for a poetic interpretation of myself. Now I am abundantly aware that there were. Oh, the power of the poetic imagination! Did you know that a blind man stumbling through the streets of Washington can find his way to light? Did you know that a man— one as dead in spirit as you were in writing your most recent letter— while riding across a lonesome stretch of Utah, can suddenly know life? Such things are true. And if in Biloxi, Mississippi, I knew faintly but completely the sweet cooling scent of Jefferson Davis's daughter's perfume as it shielded her against and mingled with the humid June air of the Gulf of Mexico—and I did—then I know that I've within me a tropical element that warms my soul in defiance of history's chill. And if in San Francisco there resides a man whose home has a view of the Bay at which he looks out with a sadness symbolic of all the

unconsummated things in his past—and there is such a man, one I call uncle—then I've reconciled myself to the existence of an oceanic expanse of desire for a future (in the form of the loveliest of ladies, called Theda) likely to remain unconsummated. Indeed, Baxter, are you aware that at a voodoo ritual in New Orleans, you can hear drums that sound as if they were being beaten by hands that speak a foreign language? I am, just as I know that the rhythm of Oscar Wilde's voice has a musical power that affects me like magic or like religion.

Oh, Baxter! So much of it—this rapture—is about love. About Theda—whom I've mentioned but demur to describe for fear of breaking the fragile reality of her existence. When I lose the war with the realities of love—as I'm wise enough to know I shall—and the memory of her becomes, as Willie Wilde might say, "the shadow of my greatest defeat," I don't want to remember her so well as to feel forever the ache of a broken heart. Love, that other "peculiar institution," Oscar has correctly called it. How it breaks us in two! Oh, yes, the heart in love is a rebel, forcing its secession from oneself. Sooner or later the warmer half of yourself dons the gray suit of desertion and leaves the other half behind feeling blue. The body, equipped to heed the heart's call to arms, embraces the mission, forsaking the mind's cool reason. We're all born, it would seem, with this Confederate instinct. Isn't "I love you" the most abject yet the most beautiful Declaration of Dependence? Yes, I'm sure it is. I'm sure it is! "I love you," we say, professing the highest of principles. Oh, the shame: that we should feign such purity when all we really want is the right to possess another! Peculiar institution indeed.

I hesitate to recruit you, my friend, into this perverse, almost certainly futile campaign, but like a zealot I'm compelled. It's your destiny anyway, so I'll say to you: become a rebel, Baxter. Enlist in the war of love and forsake the antebellum actuality that is loneliness.

The reporter interviewing Oscar is from a newspaper called, appropriately enough, The Constitution. *Such a wonderful name for a newspaper, such a noble and ambitious promise it makes to document judiciously the ongoing revival of this town that fewer than twenty years ago suffered the blistering fury of war. The newspaper's name has in it the implicit acceptance of and commitment to the greater plan. The reporter is to follow us all day, from here at the*

Markham Hotel to De Give's Opera House for the lecture, and still later to the train station, when we depart for Savannah in the last hour of this most glorious of days. Will the reporter get it right, the wonder of the day? Certainly not for me. He's documenting Oscar's perspective, not mine. But I'll look forward to reading his version nevertheless, for it will be an account, at least, of the time when I established a true understanding of myself. I'm perfectly happy. I once said those words to Oscar, to which he replied, "If I'm ever perfectly happy, I hope someone puts a stop to it immediately." Spoken like a man who has never truly been happy. What I know, speaking from this lofty perch, is that the fall from here is not to be desired, even in jest. To survive such a plunge—what shall I call its bottom, supreme sorrow?—would require something reminiscent of a resurrection. I'm so glad that reporter from The Constitution is here to capture the highlights of this day. All the rest of my life, I'll gladly, hopefully read whatever he writes, and when I do, I'll experience these emotions again, relive this moment in which my spirit has been defined and in which, manifest in the sentimental ecstasies of this missive, all my passions converge.

   You ended your letter by questioning your place there. I'll end mine by saying that if in time you discover you've no place there at all, you'll find upon your return that you, as do I, have every place here, and that this Willie, unlike my counterpart there, holds you dear, and we'll exult together in the unique brotherhood that is our own.

Love,
William

CHARLESTON

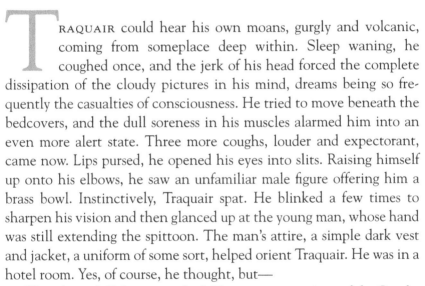

TRAQUAIR could hear his own moans, gurgly and volcanic, coming from someplace deep within. Sleep waning, he coughed once, and the jerk of his head forced the complete dissipation of the cloudy pictures in his mind, dreams being so frequently the casualties of consciousness. He tried to move beneath the bedcovers, and the dull soreness in his muscles alarmed him into an even more alert state. Three more coughs, louder and expectorant, came now. Lips pursed, he opened his eyes into slits. Raising himself up onto his elbows, he saw an unfamiliar male figure offering him a brass bowl. Instinctively, Traquair spat. He blinked a few times to sharpen his vision and then glanced up at the young man, whose hand was still extending the spittoon. The man's attire, a simple dark vest and jacket, a uniform of some sort, helped orient Traquair. He was in a hotel room. Yes, of course, he thought, but—

"You through?" the man asked. His accent, a variant of the Southern cadences Traquair had gotten used to hearing during the past two months, assisted his memory even more. Traquair nodded his head and made a sound, and the man pulled back the bowl, placing it on the floor. Then he sat down in a chair at the foot of the bed and relaxed there, dangling one arm over the metal bed frame, patting the mattress with his hand.

"Where am I?" asked Traquair in a hoarse voice. He cleared his throat, hoping that the next time he spoke he would sound more like himself.

"The St. Charles Hotel." The man's expression was a mix of curiosity and concern.

"Oh." Traquair was still confused. "In New Orleans?"

"No . . ." A head scratch and a half smile filled the young man's pause before he said, "Charleston."

"Oh." Traquair couldn't remember how he had wound up in this bed. His face must have begged his attendant for an explanation, because the man, fully lit by a broad smile now, said, "You got sick on the train ride from Augusta."

"I did?" Traquair rolled his eyes in a halfhearted attempt at recapturing the memory.

"Mm-hmm. They brung you here when they checked in and put you to bed. I heard em talkin bout it. They had to explain it cuz Mr. Fields, who run the hotel, was afraid you coulda had somethin the other guests could ketch, but your people said, no, you didn't. They said you was just feelin bad. Your face had got red, they said, or it was like somethin was red, or somethin you read. I don't know. That main man, the big one, the famous one with the long hair, he was in the lobby talkin all loud and people was lookin at him, but I couldn't understand a word he was sayin. The other one was makin a whole lot more sense. Anyway, I do know that some kinda way you went and fainted on em. Don't you remember nothin? You had a fever. You been sleep for a while."

"Where are they?" Traquair asked through a tremor of illness or humiliation.

"The big man and that other lil redheaded fella?"

"Yes."

"They went to the Academy for the show. They told me to wait here with you until they get back." The man paused, and then he asked, "Which one of em is going to pay me?"

Traquair was about to say that he would pay the man, but he had no idea where his wallet or any of his other belongings were. "Don't worry. I assure you that you will be well compensated." He coughed again.

"Water?" the man asked, already rising and moving toward a table next to Traquair's bed where a silver pitcher and two glasses rested. He filled a glass and handed it to Traquair, who emptied it quickly. The man took the glass, asking, "More?"

"No. Thank you." Traquair tried to sit up, and the man came over to assist him, propping up the pillows behind his neck and shoulders. Traquair thanked him again, laughing a little.

"What?" asked the man, resuming his casual pose at the edge of the bed.

"I was just thinking about how ironic life is."

"I-ronic?" Traquair heard the question as a double interrogative: What about this moment made Traquair feel that life was ironic—and what did "ironic" mean?

"Well, of the places that we have left to visit—a bit more of the South, parts of New York, a few stops in New England and Canada— Charleston was the one place that I was most looking forward to exploring."

"You never been here before?"

"No. And now I'm trapped in this bed, and we leave tomorrow. Instead of taking a stroll through the town square or maybe taking a ride along the coast, catching a glimpse of Sumter—is it still there?"

The man shrugged and said, "I guess so."

Ever since hearing about his father's early years here with Moses, Traquair had been anticipating this stop on the tour; he had fantasized about encountering an important part of his family's past. In his mind, he had already begun the letters to his father and his uncle describing the feel and the smell of the land that they had, in their childhood, dreamed of escaping. Surely they must have wondered from time to time what had happened to this, what had happened to that, where is she, where is he? Surely they must wonder what had become of the thing they had survived. He could understand, of course, if they could never return; his father could barely even speak of South Carolina. All the more reason for Traquair to be their eyes and ears and bestow upon them a less painful revisitation to their dark cradle. Traquair's description of Charleston could have stirred his father somehow. Something in a phrase inspired by this place might have struck a nostalgic chord, perhaps in his father or in his uncle—or *both*. Yes, that was what he had wanted to find here: some small thing he could offer them that would re-ignite the warm feelings that had marked their childhood relationship. In Charleston, Traquair had secretly hoped—he admitted this to himself now with great embarrassment—to stumble upon the key to his family's reconciliation. As if one could do such a ridiculous thing as that, he thought with self-deprecation. "Instead of a stroll through the city, a ride in a park, a good look at the old fort, instead of any of that," he said to the young man, "I'm stuck here."

"Well," his caretaker said, "at least you woke up." They caught each other's eye and began to laugh at this comment, and through their laughter they heard a door open. Oscar came rushing into the bedroom with an armful of lilies, with Vail trailing behind him holding more flowers.

"You're better!" Oscar said, coming to the bed. Rather carelessly, he put the lilies into the water pitcher on the table and sat on the edge of the bed. Traquair heard Vail's voice behind Oscar saying, "Much better, much better."

"We brought you flowers and Vail ordered tea downstairs. Didn't you, Vail?"

"Certainly."

"I'm fine, really," Traquair said, the attention making him feel small and helpless, but, somehow, indeed better. The lecture must have been a success because he could sense, beneath the thick layer of solicitude, that Oscar was happy, which made him feel better as well. "How did things go tonight?" he asked, trying to smile.

"No, no," Oscar said. "Let us concern ourselves with *your* suffering, not my own."

"He's only joking," said Vail. "The audience was as delightful as any I can remember, even if not as large as one might have liked."

"Vail, how entirely callous of you even to have noticed the mood of all those strangers while our dear boy was laid out here, all ill and unconscious. And that you bothered to count their number is the height of insensitivity. My respect for you grows daily."

"Why!" Vail said, flustered. "William, I feel pressed to acknowledge that the flowers were *my* idea."

Oscar said, "A man who proclaims that the flowers were his idea has lost all sense of reality. Vail, I think I love you."

Vail had crowded into the little space between the table and the bed, and he, Oscar, and Traquair huddled together in a state of amusement. They were interrupted when the young man who had been sitting with Traquair made a coughing sound. "Oh," said Vail, and he started to move away. Traquair tugged his sleeve and whispered, "He was very helpful." Vail nodded and reached into his pocket as he went over to the man.

"I don't remember what happened to me on the train," Traquair said to Oscar.

"Nothing remotely shameful," Oscar said, with something like regret in his voice. "You fainted, from whatever it is that causes one to faint—the burdens of tomorrow . . . the yoke of yesterday."

"I had a fever, didn't I?"

"You and I were walking toward the dining car. You were slowly leading the way. Then you came nearly to a stop. And—well, I caught you as you were falling."

"You did?"

"Yes. We pressed the train staff to allow you to utilize my sleeping space, and when we arrived here in Charleston, Vail and I transported you off the train and into a carriage. You staggered a bit on your own, but you were not well." Traquair felt a sudden chill and shivered visibly. "And still you're not." A look of concern came over Oscar. He glanced sharply at Vail, who had just returned, and said sternly, "Where's that tea?"

"I'll check on it."

Oscar turned back to Traquair, who began to slide under the covers, and helped adjust the pillows. "We'll have a little tea, and then you'll get some more rest."

"I'll be fine," Traquair said, closing his eyes, trying to remember his dreams.

Traquair awoke late that night to the sound of Oscar's soft laughter. "Oscar," he said.

"I'm sorry," Oscar replied. Enough light was spilling into the bedroom from the other rooms of the suite to allow Traquair to see an outline of Oscar sitting in the chair where the young hotel worker had sat earlier. He held a cigarette, whose smoke Traquair could faintly smell. "Did I wake you?"

"I heard you laughing. Why aren't you asleep?"

"I was happy sitting here thinking."

"What were you thinking?"

"I was thinking of a story."

"A story? Oh, tell me the story." Traquair pushed himself up a bit.

"Are you sure you wouldn't rather be dreaming?"

"A story and a dream have everything in common."

"Not everything," Oscar said. "Strictly speaking, one is made up of words, the other of pictures. I will admit that the best stories are dreamlike and that the best dreams tell a story. But that is all."

"Do you object to the superstition that dreams have hidden meanings?"

"Dear boy, to object to any superstition is to align oneself too closely with reality. And reality, by its very nature, is superficial. The meaning of life is hidden beneath the mask of life. This fact is the best argument for the existence of God. Because life, reality, offers no support whatsoever of His existence, indeed, with its brutality and its ugliness and shameful meanness, does all that it can to cover up beauty and goodness, one begins to suspect His existence. The missionary might be more effective by admitting that reality utterly fails to support his case, by admitting that his is the ultimate superstition. It is the same superstition that insists that stories have morals. It is why, in fact, they do. This is what the Bible gets right. All good books end with revelations."

"Does the story you were thinking of end that way? With revelations?"

"Oh, my story. Yes. And now that I have properly introduced it . . ." Oscar stood and slid his chair much closer to Traquair. He was still wearing the same wrinkled gray jacket he had worn to the lecture; his movements belied his fatigue. Maybe it was not just tonight and Traquair's illness but the cumulative weight of the long, arduous tour that was beginning to take its toll on Oscar. Still, Traquair felt a twinge of guilt at being incapacitated, unable to perform his duties. But when Oscar sat in the chair and faced him, he saw in Oscar's eyes a great contentment. Oscar took another pull on his cigarette, and then began to tell Traquair the story.

"Heaven was in decline." He paused a moment for effect, then continued. "With the fall of the Great Angel rumors persisted of the development of a powerful and interesting netherworld. God appeared not to be worried, but many of His closest advisors warned that He should not ignore the potential danger.

" 'Really, sir, the Fallen One is quite devious,' said the angel called Peter at the monthly council meeting. 'Just as I closed the gates to him, he offered me a splendid position in his organization.' God merely nodded. Of course, He knew all of that already.

"Another angel said, 'Oh, he promised me a third more of everything I have here and a shiny new halo. He showed me a prototype. Really, it was quite lovely, Lord. A lesser angel would have succumbed to his charms. We must retaliate quickly.'

"'I agree,' said another. 'It is not enough merely to provide streets of gold and endless soft white clouds and splendorous light. Nowadays, angels are looking for adventure. Have we anything more to offer, Father?'

"And God spoke: 'Silence! I have heard enough! Do you think I have not analyzed these rumbles of discontent? Do you think I cannot see where this inquietude will lead? The ones who today walk proudly upon the shiny streets of gold will soon bore of the magnificence that is luster. And they, in turn, will bore me, and I shall come to call them 'lackluster.' And the cloud-spinners will weave their dissatisfaction into their work and when we experience a cloudy day we shall feel their gloom. Even the grandeur of Heaven's brightness will come to connote monotony, and the masses will crave the Nameless One's darkness.'

"Yes! said the others, but only to themselves, for they never interrupted God when He was preaching. Yes! God understands, they thought. And they felt better because truly they had begun to worry that His attitude was quite—what was the word He had promised to coin in the future?—lackluster. But, no, God understood the situation. Still, what was He prepared to do about this unrest within the angelic community?

"And God spoke again: 'Silence!' He said, halting the noisy, mildly disrespectful thinking of the inner circle of angels. 'I have an idea.'

"And there was even greater joy amongst the angels. Their confidence was immediately renewed, for God always had such marvelous ideas. The oldest members of the group remembered the day when, not so long ago, God had decided to expand the heavens. The renovation had been built partly by angels, but in actuality had required only a simple gesture, a wave of His hand, and Heaven had become immensely more comfortable, acquiring a luxuriousness worthy of its legend, which the angels had read about in the historical accounts of Heaven to be found in both the fiction wing of the great library and in some of the more serious scholarly journals in the periodicals section. Now, with the Fallen One and his dazzling recruitment skills, what was to be the use of all the vast new spaces of Heaven? They were glad God had an idea. It was good to know that the bad angel, who had broken His heart, hadn't broken His creative spirit.

"And God spoke: 'There is a place, a very special place known only to Me and the Nameless One.'

"'Known only to You and the Nameless One?' asked Peter, who felt slightly betrayed by the fact that God had secrets from him. But he knew that he and God had secrets from the others, his every thought, and that each of the other angels shared similar secrets with God. Peter calmed himself and listened to God. 'The Nameless One has managed things very poorly in this place, mostly to his own advantage. Attending to Heaven's concerns in this admittedly lower world might be, I believe, the type of challenge that some of the angels are wanting. It is not as low a place as the Nameless One's new world, but it has a gravity all its own that gives its inhabitants the sense of existing at the bottom of something.'

"'Yes, that is what the angels are after,' said a council member. 'The opposite of up.'

"And God appointed ten angels to an ad hoc committee to create a plan for rescuing the foreign place. The committee decided that the first step would be to dispatch a thousand angels to assess the situation. Then a course of action would be determined. The committee knew that the prospect of meeting the disciples of the Nameless One—or possibly even the Fallen One himself—would be a great temptation to thrill seekers, so it put into place a rigid application process. Notices that participants were needed for the Mission were posted, and Heaven was filled with anticipation. The competition for the trip was great. Some exaggerated their experience on their applications. Peter, chief reviewer of the submissions, was touched by the little phrases he read: 'helped to pave the most recently developed fifty thousand acres of La Ville de la Ligne D'Horizon'; 'worked directly under Gabriel's supervision'; 'received the second highest score on the A3 exam.'

"His favorite, though, was from a young angel named Judas. Peter was particularly intrigued by this application because, with the exception of the angel's name, the form provided no information whatsoever. What kind of a boy, wondered Peter, would offer so empty a representation of himself? Was he truly devoid of all experience, of personality even, or did he have something to hide? His reticence hinted at a naivete or perhaps—and this was the possibility that most enthralled Peter regarding the blank pages before him—perhaps Judas was admitting to absolute innocence. Since the descent of the Nameless One into his own kingdom, innocence had rapidly fallen out of favor among the younger angel set. The popular stance now was to pretend that one had things to confess, that one had done and felt things that one shouldn't have. How refreshingly candid was Judas in his application, for the truth, as Peter well knew, was that all of the angels were innocent in every way.

"Peter met with Judas in his office on the following Wednesday. He had his secretary fill the usually empty vase on his desk with fresh lilies for the occasion. When Judas came into the office Peter took one look at him and said, 'You're perfect.' That is what he said, but what he meant was that Judas was beautiful, for to be perfect is to be ultimately beautiful. And without asking Judas any questions, Peter hired him for the Mission.

"One month later, after several training sessions, Judas and the other nine hundred and ninety-nine angels left Heaven for a place called Earth. As Judas flew swiftly downward with the others, he was humming to himself the simple final instructions: 'Be good, have fun, beware of the Fallen One.' It made a lovely chant that all of the angels took up, and as they advanced into Earth's atmosphere, the chant became a song. From a distance, Earth's clouds had appeared as fluffy as Heaven's, but now that he was in them, Judas found them to be thin and wispy. His wings waved through them as if they weren't there. He hoped that Earth itself would prove more challenging.

"The angels did as the council had instructed them. They made their camp in the clouds that crowned the highest mountain peak. Most of the angels had duties supporting the maintenance of the camp. But ten had drawn the coveted assignments of Earth Explorers. Judas, owing to the deep impression he had made upon Peter, was one of the chosen angels. His supervisor commanded him to assess the situation in the Midwestern Territory and to report back within five years' time. 'Remember,' said the Mission manager. 'Be good, have fun, but beware of the Fallen One.'

"Judas repeated the words to himself and set out to explore the Midwestern Territory. The descent to his first encounter with life was brief. On the way down, he met a hawk named Terius, who said, 'It's a lovely time for you to have arrived. Yesterday I had a cold, but today I feel fine and will show you around.' Terius introduced Judas to all of his bird friends, whom Judas liked very much. If their conversation was ultimately lacking in substance, it was at least melodious. Judas had known many angels whose talk had neither meaning nor melody. After two years Judas knew it was time for him to go farther downward, so he kissed his friend Terius good-bye and bestowed upon him eternal life. 'No more colds for Terius,' he said as he left.

"And he spent another two years in the trees with the monkeys and squirrels and lizards. A monkey named Simon introduced himself the first day Judas arrived and volunteered to be his guide. They spent hours jumping from tree to tree. Sometimes they made vines from branches and leaves, and they would go swinging from the trees together. It was great physical fun. One day they heard a tremendous commotion coming from below. 'What is that?' asked Judas. 'The cousins,' responded Simon. 'They roam and rule the bottom of Earth. Very often they lose control. Sometimes they throw sharp things at us. My friend David fell to them. It is good that you are up here with us.' And Simon's last words reminded Judas that he could not stay up in the trees with the animals, for it was his duty to continue his exploration. He said his good-byes and kissed Simon, bestowing upon him eternal life, so that no harm might come to him, as had come to his friend David, and he might play in the trees forever.

"Though his trip to the ground was short in distance, Judas struggled to complete it. Moving down, he felt the power of Earth's pull as he had not since arriving here, and something in him resisted. Gravity felt like two strong hands grasping his ankles. 'Beware of the Fallen One,' he said to himself, the phrase echoing in his head. As he was falling, it occurred to him that it was in the very physical nature of Earth to seduce. Gravity was the tug of temptation. Finally his feet touched the ground, and he thought, 'How unheavenly.' He saw the horror, all of the bad things: murder, wars, poverty, essays without transitions, poorly acted dramas, sloppily executed landscapes, all manner of unrefinement. And he was afraid. He stood still and looked around for someone who would be his friend and help him navigate the madness, but he could find no one. He decided he should report back to camp immediately, for surely the Nameless One had taken hold of the people of Earth. But when he tried to fly up away from the madness, he was unable to. He flapped his wings for several minutes, but to no avail. Just as he was beginning to think that his powers and God had forsaken him, a vine dropped before him. 'Up, up,' he heard Simon calling down to him. And Judas grabbed the green rope and climbed up to meet his friend. Safely back in the trees, he thanked Simon for his help. He rested for a moment before flying back up to the camp.

"Hundreds of angels greeted him with cheers when he arrived. His supervisor came to him and said, 'Judas, you are the only Earth Explorer to return. We have lost all of the others to the Nameless One. Peter and God have asked to see you in Heaven.'

" 'Me?' Judas asked.

" 'Yes. And there's no time to waste. Up, up!'

"And Judas flew up to Heaven and went straight to Peter's office. Peter's secretary sent him right in.

" 'Congratulations!' Peter said. 'You have made me very proud.'

" 'Thank you, sir,' Judas said. He looked around for God.

" 'God is with us,' Peter said to comfort Judas. 'He is too distressed to make an appearance. But He wants me to tell you that He has an important assignment for you. Soon a child will be born on Earth, and He will be the Son of God. And he shall save the Earth from its misery.'

" 'Oh, that is great news. The Earth knows great suffering, mainly in its lower regions.'

" 'Yes. And the Son of God shall save the Earth by dying a terrible death.'

" 'Oh, that is sad. Must it be so?'

" 'God feels it is the only way,' Peter said.

" 'Well, I suppose He should know,' said Judas, looking about the room uncomfortably. 'And what is my assignment, sir?'

" 'Yes. Well, it seems that you are to ensure that the death of the Son of God comes to pass.'

"And Judas was dismayed at what Peter had said to him. He could not speak.

" 'God—we feel that you are the perfect angel for the job. I knew it when I first laid eyes on you. And now you've been to Earth. You know your way around down there. And you're trustworthy. You were the only one to come back to us. Your purity is absolute. We know you will handle things.'

" 'But how?' said Judas, finally managing to respond.

" 'Oh, you have a way of making friends very easily. Get to know the Son somehow, and . . . well, we're sure you'll think of a way. You have about thirty-three Earth years to come up with something. You must complete this mission. Not only the fate of Earth is at stake, but, more importantly, the fate of Heaven. If you triumph you will show the angels that Heaven, too, offers the possibility of great adventure, and the stability of Heaven will be restored.'

"Judas left Peter's office feeling dejected but resigned to the awful task that lay ahead of him. He spent the next twenty years in the Earth camp preparing himself for the new mission. When the time was right, he went down to Earth, and he made Jesus his friend, taking his place among the disciples. And Jesus taught him how to be good and how to beware of the Fallen One. And when Jesus said, 'I am the resurrection, and the life: he that believeth in Me, though he were dead, yet shall he live: and whosoever liveth and believeth in Me shall never die,' Judas, better than any other disciple, knew every word Jesus spoke to be true. But he had a job to do. And when the time was right he made a bargain with the chief priests, taking the silver pieces so that they would believe he was committed to them. And Judas betrayed Christ with a kiss, because that was how he said good-bye to all of his friends when bestowing upon them eternal life.

"He returned the silver coins to the chief priests and prepared for the difficult endeavor of leaving Earth. He was relieved to find Simon's vine in the same spot as before. Weary from his work on Earth, he began to climb the green rope slowly. When he had reached a height on the vine only slightly greater than his body's measure, he lost his balance to the demands of his fatigue and became entangled in the thick twirls of leaves and twine. He struggled to release himself, but when his twisting calmed and the trembling of the green rope settled, Judas dangled against the insistence of Earth's gravity, with his feet just above the ground.

"His strange death martyred him. And when the angels heard of his amazing story, his heroic accomplishments, they were no longer fascinated by the tales of the Fallen One. And Heaven was saved."

Traquair watched Oscar's lips pinch his cigarette for one last meaningful draft and asked, "What is that story about?"

"A boy named Judas whom we must forgive. It's a story about forgiveness."

Traquair remembered what he had said to Winnie Davis about the dark side of forgiveness. "What kind of forgiveness?" he asked Oscar.

"All kinds. The forgiveness of evil, of course, as well as the all too infrequently practiced forgiveness of good."

"And why do you tell me this story?" Traquair asked.

"Because I thought you might profit from its moral," said Oscar. "But mostly because you asked me to. Isn't it obvious by now that I do just as you command?"

When Traquair awoke the next morning, he had almost completely recovered. Thirsty, he looked to the bedside table and saw that the pitcher was still serving as a vase. However, someone had placed a glass of water on the table and, angled against the glass, an envelope. "Ah," he said softly, rejoicing as he read his uncle's carefully drawn, distinguished handwriting. He heard Oscar and Vail moving about in the next room. Not wanting to alert them to his awakening, wanting to be alone, he gently sat up in the bed, which squeaked a little, and forgetting about his thirst for the time being, carefully opened the letter.

> 16 June 1882
> San Francisco
>
> Dear William,
>
> When I first received your itinerary with the instructions to send letters to you in the cities of my choice, I knew immediately that one day I'd post something to you there in Charleston. Writing to Charleston from San Francisco I knew would be an opportunity, no matter what I said, to articulate just how far I've traveled, how far I've come. I had no idea, dear nephew, how profound the content of this note would be, but perhaps I've intentionally timed my actions just so, for effect as it were, without letting myself in on my scheme. Whatever the true cause of the momentousness of this writing, be it luck or quiet calculation, recent events—the past twenty years by history's standard, the past twenty days by my own—insist that I write to you, William, and to Charleston with a flourish!
>
> At this moment, my son (yes, my very own son!) is resting peacefully in the room next to mine and Summer's, here in our home. Summer says your cousin reminds her of you, but I disagree.

Frankly, he does not have your polish or your bearing. How could he? After all, he was raised by Mae, who despite her many wonderful traits suffers the maternal disadvantage of being a whore. I say that without any bitterness or condescension, because if there are disadvantages to such an upbringing, I've learned that there is one important advantage, at least one that manifests itself in my son. He has wonderful entrepreneurial instincts, which shall suit him well as he joins me in my business. At the risk of inciting your jealousy, what I suspect Summer means when she compares my son to you is that he possesses a charm equal to your own. Suffice it to say we have fallen for him as quickly as we fell for you. I should tell you more about him now, but I want you to see him for yourself, which I believe will happen before the year is done, for reasons that will become clear in this letter.

How has it come to pass that I should be but moments away from my son instead of many miles? I shall tell you the little story as best I can, but in truth how does one document a miracle?

Of course it all hinges upon my meeting with my son's mother, Mae, which owes to you. Shortly after I wrote to you in Memphis, I made the trip east with a mix of hope and trepidation. True to her word, Mae met me in a small café not far, she said, from her place, which she didn't care to show me at that time, though I've been there since. We just stared for a while. It was the first time we'd seen each other in more than twenty years, since before the war. She was, I must say, shockingly large. But then I suppose she must have found me disturbingly gray. Her weight, however, was irrelevant—it was my heart that was heavy with the ache of remembrance. And my grayness, I could tell, ultimately mattered not to her, for in her eyes I saw my image reflected in a pure and angry blackness. Over coffee and sandwiches, we talked at first about nothing of any real importance. Then, gradually, matters of greater substance were introduced. She admitted how much she had missed me after I left— after she, in fact, had insisted that I leave, I reminded her. She remembered things differently, but I did not argue the point. She had traveled a bit, she told me, before settling in Washington. And she told me the story of how she had come to own her own establishment. Some extraordinarily pleased patron, she said, had bestowed upon her the gift of a large sum of money, part of which she had used to found her place. I had the distinct impression that she was embellishing the tale of this generous benefactor in a crude attempt at making me jealous. I cannot deny that she succeeded somewhat in this attempt. As a young man, I had loved her, deeply. She and Summer are the only two women I have ever truly loved. The only two. All of the others were either dalliances or great sins. But even with Summer, my precious Summer, it is not the same. Mae was the love of my youth. And the bright love-light of youth dooms the romance of an aging heart to a flame less luminous.

I was overjoyed when Mae finally asked me about myself. With excessive cheer, I told her all about my Summer, "the love and light of my life"—which was both the truth and a lie. Mae always brought out the rascal in me. I wanted to hurt her a little as well. She and I sat in the café smiling at each other's cruel stories, partly because each of us, in very different ways, even under difficult circumstances, is quite congenial, but mostly, I believe, because smiling is simply much less conspicuous than crying.

When I finally asked her about the child, her reason for wanting to see me in person became clear. She stated plainly that in exchange for information about my child, I would have to give her money. I should have anticipated this demand. Mae is a woman who makes her living by negotiating improper trades. It occurred to me that she might have extorted that money to start her brothel. It was an ugly thought on my part, but, in truth, I would not be surprised to learn that her grateful patron had been coerced into his unusual act of charity. At any rate, I knew immediately that there was no use challenging her about the money. And besides, years ago I had paid for her services, I had paid for her time, I had paid for her. Now I would have to pay for the child. There was a disturbing justice to it all. I must also admit that something in me wanted to pay. No, this urge was not rooted in a sense of guilt or in some feeling that I needed to do penance. My wanting to pay was of a far more selfish nature. I thought of the old days when your father and I were children held captive there in Charleston trying to devise a way to rescue ourselves. Buying our way out of the situation was one of the many schemes we returned to over and over again. At that time, of course, that was a popular method of liberation. Yes, what Mae was proposing was an unexpected but completely welcome chance at a long-lost form of heroism. The notion *of the exchange of money for my kin made me nostalgic for a gallantry that no longer exists. In considering what my response to her would be, confident in the knowledge that I could meet any price she would ask, never have I felt so successful and powerful and free. It must have been the sheer intensity of these feelings, my confusion, that led to my offering Mae the absurd amount of one hundred dollars. She smiled a little, and I could see that she was impressed. But she's a shrewd businesswoman and would not accept my first offer. "That ain't enough," she said. And then, with the pride of a salesman of fine merchandise, she said, "The child we're talking about is a son."*

What an instinct the woman has! She understood her customer. To me, a son was worth more. I doubled my offer to her, and we shook hands on the deal. The next day I brought her the money, and she told me where to find my son, which was, in fact, some distance from Washington. The following morning I made the journey to him by train.

Bear with me, William, as I try to recapture the wonder of meeting my son. First, let me say that, as odd as it may seem, our long-delayed introduction was not in the least bit awkward. We simply and completely charmed each other: I with my sincere, profuse apologies, he with an impossibly swift forgiveness, an absolution granted willfully. My appearance, he explained to me, was the answer to his prayers. I could not doubt him, William, for when we finally embraced (he initiated the act—I didn't dare presume his acceptance of me in this way), so rigorous was his hug, so intense his touch, that I sensed I was to him the ultimate intimate. I understood plainly that the countless seemingly insignificant grasps and greetings he had made heretofore were in preparation for this moment, in hope that one day he would deliver such greetings to me. And then, in a whisper, he said: "Papa." And with that single word he created a new me. I felt perfect, and, as such, a bit unreal.

"Papa." Can you imagine? The sound of it thrilled me like music. No, like poetry! "Papa" is poetry. I've never shared my brother's obsession with such trivialities. Henry was always reading sonnets and the like. But there in that instant as I embraced my son, I knew how a man could become so passionate about words as to be, in fact, seduced by them. "Papa." I was captive to its rhythm and its rhyme. I understood poetry. To be called "Papa" for the first time is to

become a little literary. What a word! Surely to be called such a thing as that is to have been written beautifully and indelibly into the heart of the speaker, by the speaker himself. Sheer poetry, William, so primal and so universal.

With those emotions stirring within me, I had a realization that I can only confess to you, my nephew, for I know you understand this way of thinking and that you can fathom the depths of my—what shall we call it?—my crime. As much joy as I felt upon hearing my son call me "Papa," I knew as well a great grief. And the tears that began to flow were mostly the result of this grief, not of the joy, for it was clear to me that if the word "Papa" was all I felt it to be, then in abandoning my son all those years ago and in not being there for him to call out to me in this way, I had denied him his birthright to innumerable instances of perfect expressions of love and other quieter but important emotions. I had muted his utterance of line after line of vital verse. I had robbed him of his personal legacy—does any other legacy really matter!—as a poet.

Bearing the weight of this transgression will not be easy, but bear it I must. I am counting on a second trip back to Washington to lighten substantially the load of my guilt. It seems that my son finds himself in the same predicament I was in all those years past with his mother. About a year and a half ago, a young woman bore him a son. Yes, I am a Grand Papa as well! The mother is actually one of Mae's girls. My son, alas, like you and me, has an eye for dark flowers. We made contact with the girl before we headed back, our scheme, of course, being somehow to convince her that the boy would be better off coming with us. She acknowledged that her living arrangements with Mae are not suitable to the upbringing of a young boy. And as she and my son have no emotional attachment whatsoever, her coming with us was not an option either party cared to discuss for long. And, too, Mae stepped in not long before we were leaving to say that she would be handling matters on the girl's behalf, so you can imagine where negotiations are headed. At any rate, if there is any way I can spare my son the tragic estrangement from his son that occurred between him and me, I shall.

When Summer first heard about the situation, she threatened to divorce me if I did not return with the grandchild. I sent the woman the longest telegram of my life from Washington, and she responded:

"No boy, no me!" She hasn't left yet—but she's placed me on notice. I have until Christmas, she says. Such is the will of my wife and the state of my household, a harmony masquerading as discord.

Sometime late this fall, I am hoping, we will make a trip back east to rescue my grandson. You should have returned home by then. (As you are leaving Charleston, do wave another good-bye for me. I never tire of reliving my moment of departure from her, even vicariously, it would seem.) We shall plan a stop in New York, where I shall introduce you to the son you helped me find, the cousin you never knew.

Your loving uncle,
Moses Traquair

NEWPORT

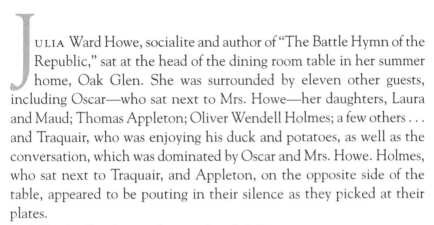

JULIA Ward Howe, socialite and author of "The Battle Hymn of the Republic," sat at the head of the dining room table in her summer home, Oak Glen. She was surrounded by eleven other guests, including Oscar—who sat next to Mrs. Howe—her daughters, Laura and Maud; Thomas Appleton; Oliver Wendell Holmes; a few others . . . and Traquair, who was enjoying his duck and potatoes, as well as the conversation, which was dominated by Oscar and Mrs. Howe. Holmes, who sat next to Traquair, and Appleton, on the opposite side of the table, appeared to be pouting in their silence as they picked at their plates.

"Oh, the South is really quite lovely," Oscar was saying in response to Mrs. Howe's question about his recent travels. "I can certainly understand why a war was fought to retain her riches. There is an artful aroma in the South. Surely, the war, on some level, was a fight for art."

Traquair smiled. What about the war being all about love? Didn't Oscar have any allegiance to his own pronouncements? Or were love and art interchangeable, maybe even the same thing to Oscar?

"What can art and war really have to do with one another?" Mrs. Howe asked. "Art is so peaceful and war is, well, war."

"War is but another mode of peace," said Oscar. "It is peace at peace." Traquair heard a faint gasp and looked up. Oscar continued, "And art is far more destructive than any war. It is the destruction of nothingness."

Several members of the party, hearing these words for the first time, nodded their heads. Traquair wondered just how many times Oscar might have repeated them since Traquair had first heard them many months ago back in Boston. Some of the guests, the men mostly, raised their eyebrows at Oscar's comments. Mrs. Howe, evidently aware of their skepticism, said, "Mr. Wilde, so much of what you say sounds like both the truth and a lie all at once. How do you answer your critics who question your persistent use of the paradox?"

Oscar hummed softly and said, "The only critics worth answering are those who don't pose any questions."

"There!" said Mrs. Howe. "That is precisely what I mean. Why do you keep up this flirtation with falsity?"

"If my relationship to falsity appears a mere flirtation, then I'm far less audacious than I intend." Oscar gently put down his fork and addressed everyone, especially, it seemed to Traquair, the men. "What the paradox always exposes is the vulnerability of the truth and the importance of the lie. Just as there is no meaning to life without death, there is no meaning to truth without lies. Not to equate life with truth, for that is an unlikely equation. Life is much more like a lie—playful, quixotic, ever dynamic—while truth has the finality of death. The less impressive the life, the less powerful, the less meaningful the death. Similarly, without lies, there is no drama in the moment of truth.

"Besides, very often, to tell the truth is to lie in one's heart. If a man is yearning to lie—for whatever reasons—but does not, when he tells the truth he is denying his true nature. In telling the truth to the world, he lies to himself. Sometimes there is tremendous comfort in telling a lie, so much so that one wonders whether in fact an honest man is an earnest man.

"And all great art is based on a lie, Mrs. Howe. Art's one great, inescapable obligation is not to tell the truth but to *reveal* the truth, just as life's one great, inescapable obligation is not to live but to die."

There was silence for a moment, and then Mrs. Howe said, "Does that mean that the greatest work of art is *Hamlet* because of Shakespeare's understanding that the great question in life is death? I saw Edwin Booth in the role early this year. Simply sublime."

"*Hamlet* is certainly not the greatest work of art," Oscar said. "As to what is, I know the answer, but I should be curious to hear what others have to say on the matter."

After another brief silence, Mrs. Howe raised her head proudly and put the question directly to her guests: "What is the greatest work of art known to man?"

Traquair heard four answers pass round the table: *Lear*, Dante's *Divine Comedy*, the Pyramids, the Holy Bible. Oscar responded only to the latter, saying, "God is a better sculptor than writer. But your answer is close."

"Man!" someone else shouted.

"Who said that?" Oscar asked, and a woman with long black hair draped strikingly against her white dress shyly leaned forward and raised her hand. "Mrs. Howe, please withhold Miss Breland's dessert." A round of giggling broke out among some of the women.

"All right, Mr. Wilde," said Mrs. Howe, "I'm dying to know the answer."

"The answer is Christ. Jesus Christ is the single greatest work of art. What makes Him even more impressive is that He created Himself. His instruments? The same as those of all great artists—love, faith, and a willingness to die for one's art. And I needn't articulate the lie that His great art is based upon."

"Mr. Wilde," said Appleton, speaking for the first time since he had sat down for dinner, "are you really speaking so highly of Christ and yet in the same breath professing a lack of faith in God?"

"Atheism may be the only redeeming quality of a man who truly loves Christ. To love Christ truly *and* to believe fully in God is to be out of touch with one's humanity."

Appleton laughed not with humor but with something akin to astonishment or fear. Mrs. Howe waved her hand and two servants began to clear the plates from the table, followed immediately by two others who distributed large saucers with slices of dessert cake and fruit. Traquair nodded to Maud, who was sitting to his right. He felt obligated to communicate with her somehow, though he had nothing of substance to say. The pressure built as he watched Mrs. Howe and Oscar whispering things back and forth and as the others began private conversations around the table. Finally, Maud said to him, "I heard Mr. Wilde tell Mother yesterday when you arrived that you are frail somehow. But you don't look frail at all. In what way did he mean?"

Frail? Traquair had no idea what Maud was talking about, nor did he know what Oscar might have meant by telling Mrs. Howe that he was frail. He was surprised that Oscar and Mrs. Howe should have discussed him at all. "I'm not sure," he said. Then he remembered Charleston. "Oh! I was sick a while back in South Carolina, but I've fully recovered."

"He said that it was on account of your frailty that you needed to have the full meals with us. One really can't believe a word Mr. Wilde says, can one?"

"I've found that his words are the only thing about him one *can* believe. It's the rest of him that courts incredulity." He meant no real harm by the remark; he had thought that Maud might be entertained by his ever so slightly duplicitous candor. Maud's mouth opened slightly, and she and Traquair lifted their eyes together and watched Oscar wave his hand daintily while he made some point to Mrs. Howe. They looked back at each other, and then began to laugh simultaneously. He had won her over. She laid her fork down and picked up a strawberry with her fingers. Playfully she bit its tip. "So," she said—and here she took on a disloyal tone of her own, one filled with mock grandeur, in obvious parody of her mother's voice—"what do *you* think is the greatest work of art known to man?"

Traquair put his hand to his face to hide his laughter. "Well—" He stopped and considered the question. He had not really thought about an answer when Mrs. Howe had posed the riddle earlier. He thought now about the answers the others had given, but none of them would do. Oscar's, of course, had been the best. It opened up entirely new possibilities for what might be considered art. But he couldn't repeat Oscar's choice; doing so would cause him to forfeit the slight advantage he had just gained with Maud. No—he needed another answer, something very different from what Oscar had said. Not a man, like Christ, but a thing. Not something small, but large. Not something old, but new. And he needed something that would deepen the genteel conspiracy against Oscar he had entered into with Maud, something that would draw the two of them closer together. (In his mind he saw pictures of himself, a series of sharply focused photographs, not unlike the publicity pictures that Napoleon Sarony had taken of Oscar when he first arrived in New York, pictures of himself in Philadelphia posing with John, in Washington clowning with Otis and Nat, in St. Louis kissing Theda's hand, at the window in Atlanta gleefully writing to Baxter as fireworks exploded in the sky outside, in all of the cities he had visited—even with Maud right here in Newport—but Oscar was not visible in any of the photographs.) Yes! He had it! Perhaps because he felt the guilt of betraying Oscar, his foreign friend (Oscar had predicted this moment in their very first conversation—*"I should hate to be attended by a* known *enemy—it so spoils the subsequent surprise of treachery"*), and maybe because he felt that in what he was going to utter he would somehow be committing the sin that is forgiveness (he was about to suggest elevating to the high, high status of art a thing unfinished and occasionally unholy, a thing very much unlike Christ), Traquair could just barely bring himself to whisper his answer—there really was something frail about him—and in the last moment he even softened his response into the form of an interrogative: "America?"

Maud's eyes opened wide. "Yes!" she said, resting her hand gently on Traquair's shoulder. "Mother!" she called out toward the other end of the table. "We've discovered another answer to your question. We've discovered a work of art!" Everyone paused now, waiting to hear what Maud meant. "William here did it." She tapped Traquair's shoulder twice and nodded her head to the others. "Go on," she said. "You tell them."

Traquair cleared his throat and said, "Well, I merely suggested, in the form of a question, I should add, that maybe we should consider . . . America a work of art."

A few ah's were sighed around the table. Mrs. Howe looked at Oscar and said, "We'll leave it to Mr. Wilde, whose friend has made a very interesting proposal. A very interesting proposal, indeed. America herself a work of art. Mr. Wilde? Any credence to this idea?"

Oscar looked at Traquair, and they exchanged smiles. Traquair felt redeemed for his earlier brush with treachery. "My friend and I have been traveling together for so long now that I suppose we've begun to think alike," Oscar said, "for his is an idea that I, too, have begun to explore of late."

"Well, give America the test," Mrs. Howe said. "If she is a great work of art, then she must be based on a lie. What would be the lie that America is based on?"

One of the guests spoke up now. "America is not based on a lie, Mrs. Howe, it is based on a truth. All men are created equal. The Declaration of Independence."

"And there you have it!" said Oscar. "There is your lie, for nothing is more self-evident than the opposite. All men are *not* created equal. That is the great truth that no loud declaration to the contrary can undo. To say otherwise is to state a wishful, sentimental lie. To say otherwise is to deny all that is exceptional in men, the extreme good, the extreme evil. To say otherwise is to disregard everything that is great and unique about any individual. The great artist is surely of a very different construction than the petty criminal—not that one man cannot be both. But imagine the tremendous delicacy of the artistic being, of the great being. Think of the short but persuasive list of Plato, Shakespeare, Julius Caesar—who bears that most brutal but persistent mark of greatness, the mark of betrayal—and, of course, Christ, who bears it as well. They and the other truly exceptional few are the blatant evidence of inequality. The more subtle evidence is as simple as the variances in the signatures that so elegantly line the lower margins of your Declaration of Independence. And if, in asserting that all men are created equal, Thomas Jefferson (another one of the exceptional whose magnificence disputes his own theory) meant that all of the *souls* of men are equal, he is again wrong; one need only consider the souls of those I've mentioned weighed against the soul of oneself to understand quickly the folly in the logic. One needn't conclude whose soul is of greater import or of better quality, only that the souls are not of the same import or of the same quality. If you do believe your soul is of a similar quality to these men's, either you suffer from severe egotism, which makes you my immediate kin, or you possess a most abysmal self-esteem.

"No—all men are not created equal. All men are *conceived* equally. That is the chief generalization that one can assert."

Then Oscar looked directly at Traquair and said, "The truth is, it is only when a man realizes the way in which he is *un*equal to others that he truly knows the meaning of liberty, and only then can he set out in pursuit of happiness—if indeed he has determined that happiness is to be a part of his destiny at all.

"I'm forced to conclude that with the great, seductive lie of equality at her core, America is in an unprecedented position to become a truly stunning work of art, something for the ages."

IV

"And, by the way, one of the most delightful things I find in America is meeting a people without prejudice— everywhere open to the truth."

—OSCAR WILDE

NEW YORK

THEY had finished the tour with a series of stops at various summer resorts in New York State and with another few lectures in New England and Canada. Upon their final return to New York City, Traquair and Vail had helped Oscar settle into rented rooms at 48 West Eleventh Street. They promised to visit each other frequently, but with the arrival of Lillie Langtry in late October, Oscar had become preoccupied with the actress, whose beauty he had helped to make famous back in England (and whose most scandalous secret Traquair had learned from Baxter). With the tour over, Traquair was right back where he had been nearly a year ago, at home trying to figure out what to do with the rest of his life. It seemed as though many years, as opposed to months, had passed since that day last winter when he had sat in his father's study feeling all depressed and hopeless, without any means of escaping the restrictions of the destiny into whose trappings he'd been born—before suddenly learning the news that he was about to be rescued by Oscar Wilde. That his liberation should have worn the guise of enslavement resonated with him poignantly as a personal paradox. Perhaps if he studied it carefully enough, it might someday help him sort out who he really was—although his recent experiences and his apprenticeship with Oscar had affected him significantly, he still didn't know quite who he was or, for that matter, who or what he was to become. With relief he noted that he no longer felt the pressure from his father to decide anything immediately; his having successfully performed his duties with Oscar had evidently given Mr. Traquair a respect for his son's willingness to work at something, a faith that Traquair could complete an adult assignment. Besides, Traquair had saved enough money from the tour to do whatever he liked for a while. He could even afford his own apartment if he wanted to move out of the house. He contemplated doing some traveling; maybe he would go to Europe, on his own terms, and spend some time with Baxter. According to a letter dated October 3, Baxter had rallied from his encounter with Willie Wilde and was not planning to come home anytime soon. And there was even more important news:

Dear Billy,

Her name is Constance. Constance Lloyd. The girl of my dreams, the one who, at your wicked advisement, I've allowed to incite a gray rebellion in my heart. And, just as you might predict, my moments away from her are the bluest of the blue.

I first saw her at Lady Wilde's salon, my last, three weeks ago. I'd gone to say good-bye to the grand dame and perhaps to England altogether. After the initial jolt of Willie Wilde's demand for my withdrawal from the scene, my spirit had rejuvenated itself, albeit slowly, thanks in no small part to the letter you sent from Atlanta. Your words made me realize how foolish I'd been to have truncated my travels. I came to understand that my posturing here in London was mere self-indulgence, whereas your movement across a continent had inspired you to transform self-indulgence into humanism. I began to consider returning to my original plan of exploring as much of Europe as my idle nature and my father's money might support— which, as you know better than anyone else, is no minor expanse of territory. Jimmy Whistler encouraged me in pursuing this plan, sharing with me his fond memories of his days in Paris as a young man. In contemplating all that I'd missed, I'd made up my mind to see Lady Wilde once more, and then move on.

So when I walked into the familiar, dark front parlor and kissed Lady Wilde hello on the cheek (it was really farewell), as ebullient as she ever was and unaware, I guessed, of my commanded betrayal, I almost cried. As I tried to pull back from the embrace, she pressed me to her bosom a moment longer than usual, and I gained the unmistakable knowledge that she knew of or at least suspected my imminent withdrawal from her circle. Overcome with emotion, Lady

Wilde pulled away from me quickly and retreated from the room. I stood alone looking around for Willie, secretly hoping he had observed his mother's display of affection for me and that he had been ever so slightly but eternally wounded by it (my accepting his edict did not resolve the bitterness I felt for him)—but he was not in sight. Instead, standing at the mantel, wearing all white, looking like one of those pale arrangements by my friend Mr. Whistler, was my Constance. I stared at her as if she were indeed a work of art. And what was even more fascinating was that, with a similar intensity, she was staring at me. The poetic Constance, not the prosaic Willie, was staring at me, and with wide welcoming violet eyes beneath a heavy brown crown of curls. Her pout, while plainly permanent, I chose to read as a sympathetic gesture, a mute maiden's condolences for whatever was troubling me. I sensed in Constance, whose very name would shock me moments later with its evocation of the sadness that belongs to all things perpetual (even hope and life, in their fantastic, eternal varieties, bear the wearying weight of the sin that is excess), I sensed in Constance, if not the full force of my emotions, a harmonic complement to them. The twinge of hatred I had reserved for Willie Wilde was subdued by the sudden emergence of that other emotion whose name, in distrust of the impetuosity of my tongue, I dare not speak. Was that vaunted sensation, I couldn't help wondering in this situation, merely two people's sudden shared aesthetic appreciation of one another? In response to my question, dear boy, I offer this: as I took my small, slow, methodical, inevitable steps toward Constance, instigated by our mutually artful gazes, I felt as if I were a wittier interpretation of, as if I were the very personification of that now famous phrase "Aesthetic Movement." This thought made me smile broadly, and I was laughing when I reached Constance—which induced her to chuckle along with me. "What are we laughing at?" she asked finally, her mouth retreating to a grin more grave. "Art," I said. "Art."

"Ah, yes," she said. "When contemplating something as serious as that, one is wise to seek the solace of laughter." "Solace," she said, William, as if she instinctively knew exactly what I needed. Our interaction continued in a manner so harmonic as to render accurate quotation of our dialogue beyond my capacity. I should require a musical aptitude far superior to my natural endowment to re-create

or even approximate with any emotional delicacy the things that passed between us.

We've had two subsequent meetings, one at the British Museum for tea (she's quite well studied in painting and is taking lessons herself) and the other just yesterday at one of Mr. Whistler's Sunday breakfasts. During our time together we've extended the overture of our introduction. At times we are tranquil, at times our exchanges are filled with the propulsive quality of elements heading toward a conclusion that is logical, inexorable, and beautiful. Suffice it to say, something symphonic is happening!

I'm to see Constance next week in the park for a picnic. Her brother, Otho, is ever near, but she's vowed that we shall sneak away from him for a private moment. If our scheme is successful, I plan to speak to her in the only language other than music that all the world comprehends: the language of love. There, I've said it. And I shall attempt to discover the harmony that happens when lovers' lips come together to make a music all their own.

So, I'm staying in London after all. As I write to you, this time from "the heights of happiness," I've a strange sense that if I take my time and look more closely, I might be able to see the entire world and the whole of myself from here.

Ever yours,
Baxter

So Baxter was in love. Both he and Baxter were in love, and Traquair's thoughts of visiting Europe dissolved as he considered Theda Trenton.

As soon as he had returned to New York, he had sent her a note to arrange the meeting she had promised him. The following day he had received a response, obviously written in haste, saying that she was on her way to Chicago for a month and that she would write to him to plan their rendezvous—that's what she called it, a "rendezvous," an encouraging term, he thought, each of the twenty or so times he read it—when she returned. He had no real illusions that anything would come of the meeting, but he hoped that somehow their strange friendship would become even stranger, if only through the experience of one more encounter, and he would find a way to live on that. He wanted another moment like the one in St. Louis, when he had moistened her hand with the phantom kiss of Oscar Wilde, or like the one on East Fourth Street, when they had stood together in the sun, his face projected onto hers, and he had watched with delight as his own shadowy lips had leapt out, beyond all of his control, to kiss her cheek. So no, it was not that he had *no* illusions about her; it was that he had *only* illusions about her. While he had been out finishing up the tour with Oscar, there had been enough distractions to occupy his mind with other matters, but now that he was home, in New York, his town, her town, with nothing better to do than wait to see her again, he became obsessed anew with Theda Trenton. For six weeks, everything he did was accompanied by her silent assistance. For instance, when he helped his mother in the kitchen these days, he felt that he assumed a more feminine air. Or when he sat in the big study with his father and Mr. Gable smoking and drinking after dinner, he felt out of place, uncomfortable with the conversation. On one occasion he had wanted to apologize to his imaginary companion for his implied complicity with the two elder men, whose opinions he felt certain she would despise. He didn't think the way they did. Really, he didn't. Was there any way for her to forgive him? And when he climbed into bed at night and opened a book, he nestled under the covers with a warm body—yes, hers—next to his. Together, they read parts of the Bible and all of *The Adventures of Tom Sawyer*. Miss Trenton's ghostlike presence was real to him. Oh, how he had learned to *feel* while on the tour, to imagine; of course, he had Oscar to thank for that.

About a week before Miss Trenton was due to return from Chicago, Traquair became extremely vigilant about any mail arriving by special messenger or even by regular post. His father, who handled all deliveries to the house, had appeared suspicious once when Traquair, who never answered the door, had actually greeted a messenger delivering an invitation to Mr. Gable. Traquair had handed the envelope to his father, who had come up behind him in the entrance hall as he closed the door. They had merely exchanged nods.

The next day, Traquair arrived at the door just after his father did. This time Mr. Traquair turned to his son and handed him a single envelope. "I suppose this is what you've been waiting for," he said with a disappointment that Traquair had not understood until he looked down and read the envelope. It was not a letter from Miss Trenton. It was a telegram from Washington from Moses Traquair. It said simply: *Grand Central. Noon tomorrow. Lunch. Surprise. Moses.*

Upon returning home from the final stop of the tour, after he had told his parents about the news his uncle had sent to him in Charleston, Henry Traquair had said, "See, William, I warned you that something sordid would be revealed if you insisted upon knowing the truth about Moses. A sordid tale indeed."

"What do you mean, Father? Something wonderful has come to pass."

"Wonderful? You've told me a story about a whore and a bastard, with the promise of a future installment about a bastard of this bastard. What fills me with wonder is your appreciation of these dealings! I'm frightened by this licentious streak of yours. You must fight it. Please, William, let us have no more talk of any of this."

Gloria Traquair had followed her husband's lead. Traquair had tried to corner her for a private discussion about his uncle, but she had hastily backed away from him, apparently disturbed, shaking her head in denial.

Clutching the telegram, Traquair sighed, watching his father walk away. After Charleston he had thought that maybe when his uncle came to New York, he would find a way to inspire his parents to consider participating in a day of reconciliation. How foolish, how naive he had been. That would never happen. Never. He accepted it now. It would forever fall to him to be the link between the two factions of his relatives, to embody the familial affection that, for whatever reasons, they had determined to deny themselves.

San Francisco might be fun, Traquair thought to himself as he sat on a bench at Grand Central Depot awaiting the next train from Washington, which was running more than an hour behind schedule, the clerk had informed him. Yes, going to San Francisco was a tempting idea. Maybe he should just take the train with his uncle, his cousin, and the baby boy (surely that was the surprise his uncle's telegram promised), and spend Christmas out west. He was smiling and laughing to himself, thinking about how plausible and absurd a notion it was (plausible because, yes, he really could do it if he wanted to, and absurd because he knew he had to stay here and have his heart broken by Theda Trenton—her note had arrived late yesterday asking to meet him tomorrow at the little park near her home at four o'clock), when he heard, "William!"

It was Vail. "Jimmy Vail!" Traquair said, genuinely happy to see him, suddenly flushed even more by the old sensation of needing to set out for someplace new. As he stood and shook his old traveling buddy's hand, he asked, "So, where are you off to *now?*"

"Nowhere today. Just purchasing a few tickets for tomorrow. Haven't you heard? I've hitched my wagon to the Lillie Langtry train. She needed help with the management of her tour, so I'm heading out on the road again, if you can believe it. Lillie tells me it was actually Oscar's idea that she hire me. I suppose I must have won him over in the end. I should have thought he might have mentioned my new position to you."

"No, no," said Traquair, too embarrassed to tell Vail that he hadn't seen Oscar since the day they had moved him into his apartment.

"Let's sit," Vail said. "How is old Oscar? I never see him. Really, it's quite odd that he's still here. No one seems to understand what's keeping him. Especially now that Lillie's tour is about to get under way in earnest. And extra especially since she's taken up with Freddie Gephardt. It's all quite scandalous. The papers are peppered with the silliest innuendo. They've no idea how close to the truth they really are. You'd blush to learn what I know—" Vail stopped abruptly, his own face suddenly flushed, and glanced shyly at Traquair. "Well, you understand what I mean. But, really, how is our boy Wilde? I read a bit in the paper lately about him. Only a little bit. Scarce, really, any real news about him. They're done with him. But what they want to know—did I say this already?—they want to know why he's still here. Something sad beneath it all, don't you think? You must know, you and he being so close. I swear sometimes I thought the two of you were teamed against me, that Oscar and William had it in for me."

"No," Traquair said flatly. There had never been any conspiracy against Vail, he could say with honesty, though he would have to admit that early on during the tour, there had almost certainly been a moment or two when he and Oscar, of separate minds and individual motivation, would have each shoved Vail out the window of a moving train. Perhaps they had been unfair to Vail, he considered.

"Oh, I'm not so sure," Vail said. "You know, if I hadn't come to know the two of you the way I did, I dare say I should have thought you the two biggest snobs in the world!"

"Snobs?" Traquair said, his contrition recoiling.

"Oh, now don't take it to heart. I know you're no such thing. Why, I've seen you with my very own eyes making acquaintances with persons far beneath you. I've witnessed you befriending beggars." Traquair looked quizzically at Vail, who countered with "I saw more than you think I saw." He hummed a light note then said, "And Oscar—a snob? All I need tell you is that he cried all the way to Savannah." Vail looked shyly at Traquair, who looked away. "Not to relive it, old boy. But after that incident with your train ticket in Atlanta, he just couldn't stop crying. It was quite a scene, I tell you. I helped him into his sleeping berth, but even then he was beyond all control. Someone sent for a porter, but Oscar was simply inconsolable. I've never seen anything quite like it. All the way to Savannah. I suppose snobs may cry, but not for *others*, and certainly not like that."

A silent moment passed. "And so I've talked, talked, talked, and without so much as inquiring where you are headed, William."

"Nowhere, really. Just meeting family. What time does that old watch of yours have?"

Vail pulled at his fob. "Nearly twelve-thirty, which of course makes me late for my next appointment." They stood and shook hands again. "Great to see you, William, really."

"And you, Vail."

Vail began walking away, but he yelled back to Traquair, "And if there's anything you can do to convince Oscar that his work here is done, please by all means do it!"

Traquair spent the next thirty or forty minutes reading newspapers. He was considering buying *Harper's* when he realized that the Washington train had pulled into the station without his having noticed it. Passengers were already disembarking. He left a trail of *Tribune*, *Herald*, and *World* in his wake as he began with some urgency a shoulder-bumping navigation of the rushing crowd. Standing nearly a full head above most of the other oncoming pedestrians, he saw Moses Traquair, eyes searching, toddler in tow. They waved and jostled their way to each other.

"William!"

"Uncle Moses! You did it! You did it! And before Christmas. Summer is saved!"

"Yes. Yes." His uncle was holding the baby's hand and extending it to Traquair. "Say hello to Cousin William, Johnny."

"Hello, little Johnny," said Traquair, who instinctively looked around for his older cousin.

"Oh, Big Johnny is getting the bags. We're running very late, it seems, and our next train is leaving shortly. Sorry, William, but we won't have time for lunch after all. Still—wait until you see him!" They looked together back down the platform toward the baggage car, and Traquair had only to scan the crowd for an instant before he spotted his cousin. Even from this distance the young man had a face as familiar as his own. Not only because it possessed a family resemblance, though it surely did, but also because it was a face Traquair had seen before. The hat and the clothes were new: a derby, like Traquair's; a tailored tweed suit that Traquair would have liked for his own wardrobe; a calf-length tan topcoat. How had he failed to notice the stark physical similarities between him and his cousin before now? How had he been unable to see beyond the young man's once shabby attire and his unrefined way of speaking? Indeed, had some snobbery on his part, as Vail might have said, blinded him to the possibility of their kinship? Yes, the garments were different now, but Traquair knew the man, and the man, who was smiling in his direction, knew him. Big Johnny, not little Johnny, was his uncle's surprise.

"Willie!" said John, setting down the two suitcases he had been carrying and putting his arms around Traquair.

"John!" Traquair said, reaching out to embrace his friend from Philadelphia, overwhelmed as his mind quickly retraced the trail from John to Otis and Nat to Mae to his uncle Moses to Henry Traquair back to himself, the whole shocking combination of genealogy, geography, and fate that had brought him to this moment at Grand Central Depot. Miraculously he had arrived at a new place, this time without ever having left home. It was as if he had made his way to the end of some secret line or all the way across a continent (he knew what that felt like and it very much resembled this sensation). Relief and inevitability choked him as he rejoiced at having completed a private journey without even knowing he had been a passenger—a trip, as it were, on the underground railroad to the manifest destiny of himself.

They held each other for some time. When they finally separated, Traquair, sniffing away his emotion, looked at John and said, "Nice suit. Nice coat."

John pulled his coat down, fitting it tautly onto his shoulders, and said, "Brooks Brothers."

A train whistled loudly, and Moses Traquair hurriedly came over and handed the baby to Traquair. Little Johnny stared at him and gnawed his own fist. Traquair, who had never held a child before, felt awkward and thought he would have been of better use carrying the bags, but his uncle and John, each with a suitcase, were already walking away at a brisk pace. "Come along, William," his uncle said. "We've no time to lose."

"Yes, come along, William," John said, looking back over his shoulder, approximating his father's manner and accent, winking at Traquair.

As he stood on the platform watching the figures of his uncle, John, and the baby recede from him and plunge into their future together, Traquair felt as lonely as ever. Circumstances, his loved ones leaving his presence, his being suddenly alone, tempted him to indulge himself with the notion that he was truly sad. If Vail had approached him now he might have reasonably asked, "What's wrong, William?" But then Traquair felt a wave of reality. That he was alone was the most obvious of lies, for there were people pulsing all around him: that woman there in a pink and gray wool cap and that marvelous smoke-colored fur coat, four boys and a girl trailing behind her; that striking young couple with matching herringbone overcoats and tan leather cases, such exceptional portmanteaus!; the old man with the speckled beard in the poorly blocked green fedora; that pretty blue-eyed girl with a ticket in her hand sneaking a glance at Traquair—the way such girls sometimes felt compelled to do—and then looking back at her ticket with the sadness of a traveler who has booked passage for the wrong destination; the policeman tapping a vagrant's hip with his club, "Move along there, fellow, move along." Traquair let the phantom melancholy pass, and he came into himself, for truly a rare happiness had set itself upon him. As he walked quickly through Grand Central, and then, as he jogged down and across Manhattan, heading homeward with a compulsion to tell his parents about his uncle's surprise, he smiled at strangers here and strangers there, as if they, too, were old acquaintances and not-so-distant cousins.

✳   ✳   ✳

Traquair rushed into the house in search of his parents. Though they should have been there to see Moses and John, he was actually thrilled that the news was his to tell. He called out for them, but there was no response. Mr. Gable, he knew, was in Boston on business, and the front part of the house appeared vacant. He dashed into the kitchen, where his mother would usually have been—she wasn't there. She might be upstairs in her sewing room, he thought, and maybe his father was upstairs taking a nap. He took a step in the direction of the stairs, then changed his mind and spun around to check his father's study first. Throwing the door open, he yelled, "Father!" only to find that Mr. Traquair wasn't in there either. He closed the door and decided to use the front stairs instead of those off the kitchen. This route took him past Mr. Gable's study, the door to which was closed. Normally, he would not have bothered to open it, but as he was passing the room, he heard his parents' voices. With the wild force of his enthusiasm, he swung the door open. "There you are!" he said. His parents looked up with the startled faces of cornered escapees. Traquair knew that Mr. Gable's study was not exactly the place his parents should have been at that moment, but their reaction to being discovered seemed extreme. Even if he had been Mr. Gable himself entering the room unexpectedly, nothing would have come of their being there. "I'm sorry," he said, responding to the tension in the room. "Am I interrupting something?"

His parents glanced at each other, and his father waved for him to enter. There was another brief silence before his father said, "So—how was your lunch with my brother?"

Traquair's excitement returned, and he said, "Oh, the train was late, so there was no time for lunch. But I have rather remarkable news! As I've told you, Uncle Moses has located his son."

His parents again looked at each other. His father's eyebrows lifted slowly and held themselves in suspension. He said, "His son—yes."

"Yes. Well, today I met my cousin—and to make things even more interesting, my cousin, by the most amazing twist of fate, has turned out to be John, my friend from Philadelphia. You remember John, Father. I told you about him."

"Really? Well, that's quite interesting, indeed. But, trust me, things get far more interesting than that," Mr. Traquair said. "Have a seat, William." Traquair saw that his father's words upset his mother a great deal. She raised a handkerchief to her mouth, and he heard her gasp into it. The gravity of the moment forced Traquair's descent into the nearest chair.

"What's happening here, Father?"

"I want to tell you something about your uncle's son."

"About John? You know him?"

"Of course not. But I know my brother. We both do. Your mother and I." His mother began crying when Mr. Traquair said this, and she rushed out of the room. Traquair stood up and said, "Mother!"

"Let her go!" his father yelled. "She's all right. She'll be all right. Sit back down." Confusion, fear, and fascination persuaded Traquair to do as his father commanded. Mr. Traquair, completely composed, lit a cigar and puffed it pleasurably. "This is all my fault, really. All my fault. I was the one who insisted that you take that job with your Mr. Wilde. That's what did it. You went out there traveling and meeting inquisitive people, like that clever John, whom you now call cousin, and all of a sudden you needed to know everything. Every journey intensifies the quest for knowledge. I know this from when my brother and I traveled up to the North from South Carolina all those years ago with Mr. Traquair. A lesser man might try to blame it on that damned tour you went on, maybe even on that Oscar Wilde. But, no, I'll take the blame. I'm good at that. That's really the problem—the way I always want to take the blame. I'm too damned noble. That's what you need to know. Too damned noble."

"How are you too noble, Father?"

"Well, I've told you about the time when Moses stole that money from Mr. Traquair and ran away. When he fled, he left me not only to suffer that shame but to cover up another. As I've tried to explain to you and as recent evidence supports, my brother was a wild young man. He was loved by many women. He had a way with them, a charm that I did not possess. His intentions with these women were never honorable. He only wanted to conquer them, as if he were Caesar or Napoléon and they were enemy territory. To put it plainly, he was lustful. There. It was lust." His father's metaphor made Traquair think of his own definition of lust: the primordial desire to leave something of oneself in a place to which one fears one might never return. He understood his uncle in a way that his father never would.

Mr. Traquair continued, "There was one woman on whom both he and I had our sights, but maybe he has told you that as well. Or maybe he did not really know that I liked her. I certainly never told him. Well, the long and the short of it is that, predictably, he was successful with the woman, and I was not. And when he left, she came to me wanting to talk about what losing him meant to her, but I was too depressed with the entire situation to listen to her. I pushed her away. A month after he had been gone, she came to me again, this time with the news that my brother had left her with child. Well, I was embarrassed for her and for my brother both. And I wanted somehow to correct the mistake. It was my nobility—" Mr. Traquair paused. "No," he said, his voice dropping, surrendering whatever had been falsetto in its tone and false in its content in favor of the deeper tenor of truth. "Not just that. No. To be completely candid, as finally I realize one must be, I also loved her. There was something about her that I found irresistible. Really, one cannot control such passion. It was her beauty, I suppose. That Lillie Langtry they're going on and on about in the papers is not the equal of the youthful Gloria, I assure you. Oh, quite desperately, I loved her, despite the fact that she loved Moses and not me. I loved her, and I saw a chance to win her, and I took it. I told her I would take care of her. The day after she told me of her condition, I proposed marriage to her. I would be her husband, and I would be the father to her child, my niece or nephew. She accepted. I knew she didn't love me, but what else could she do? We married, and shortly after that we left Mr. Traquair's farm and came here to work for the young Mr. Gable, our instructor, who had also just been married and whose aging father had become ill and needed special attention. Several months later our child was born . . . and we named him William."

They sat in silence for a while. Mr. Traquair smoked his cigar. Traquair let his thoughts sort themselves and settle, which he found remarkably easy, given the life-altering revelation he'd just heard. Some delicacy in his father's delivery had acted upon him as a sedative, an analgesic. His father—yes, the man sitting here across from him with the cigar in his hand and the slightly apprehensive look on his face was his father and always would be—had a distinctive way of telling a story. Even as he engaged the listener with his tale, he had a way of blessing one with a sense of safety and distance. If, in the telling, something shocking happened, in the event of something tragic being divulged, his method served to lessen the blow. Why, if you listened closely enough to his tone and to the subtle meanings of his words, you could feel yourself being healed, without even having to acknowledge that you had ever been wounded at all. Some artful instinct was required to achieve that feat. Maybe his father, Traquair proposed, had perfected this gentle strategy in the course of telling and retelling his own, painful story to himself all these years. And Traquair thought of the way he himself had already found softer phrases to describe the harsher incidents he had experienced during the past year. These considerations gave him the courage to admit that there must be immense poetry in his father after all (if there was not, then there was no poetry in Traquair), which confirmed, as irrefutably as anything, including blood, could, his own, close kinship to Henry Traquair.

"I have something that belongs to you," Mr. Traquair said, handing Traquair the letter he'd stolen. "Now that you know everything, maybe you can forgive me."

Traquair nodded and began to open the letter. "Papa," he said, without thinking, "I can forgive anything."

His uncle's card fell into his lap. The back of the card read: *Thank you! Give this to your mother.* He looked inside the envelope and withdrew a second sealed envelope, on the face of which his uncle had written in large letters: GLORIA. Traquair handed the envelope to his father, who read it, took a deep breath of resignation, and tapped the letter to his chin.

Then Traquair remembered the typically evasive way his father had introduced what he had just revealed to Traquair, and he asked, "What was it you were going to tell me about John?"

"Oh," Mr. Traquair said, drawing deeply upon his cigar. "What you've, no doubt, surmised by now—he's your brother."

The next day, as scheduled, nervously clutching the small bouquet of white lilies he had stopped to buy at a florist on Eighth Street, Traquair stood in the park waiting for Miss Trenton. He had arrived at the meeting place almost twenty minutes early, which meant that he would have to endure this period of anxiety about whether or not the meeting would prove in any way successful. He really had no idea what he would say to achieve the moment of unity all of his hours of daydreaming had designed, a new variation on something as simple as a kiss. Maybe instead of his inventing a way to kiss her, this time she would find a way to kiss him. That was an interesting possibility. He knew that she was bold, daring. Why, she took walks alone. She scheduled private meetings with men, like him, who had never met her family. If she had something to say, she said it. Twice she had had intimate conversations with him. She had not shied away from their curious encounters. She had a definite streak of dangerous independence in her. Yes, she was like him and Oscar and Moses and Mae. If Traquair could give her a reason to, Miss Trenton might kiss him. In his head, he heard parts of the kind of conversation he might use to entice her:

Miss Trenton: Flowers? For me? The last man who brought me flowers had bad things on his mind.

Traquair: Miss Trenton, I believe the mind should be reserved for the good. Bad things should be left to the body.

Miss Trenton: An interesting philosophy, especially for a man whose hand has just performed an act so delicate as giving a girl lilies. Does your apparent purity lie?

Traquair: The appearance of purity is always a lie. Purity is but another form of that unattainable thing we call perfection. The notion of purity is only possible because of the dullness of our senses. The blemish is always there; only, we are too insensate to see it. Our blindness makes us look at the laughing baby and say, "How perfectly charming"—when in fact a baby's first smile is its first act of deception. We look at the pristine virgin and say, "How lovely, how unstained"—when the truth is that she is covered with the soot of denial. The only real, lasting purity is impurity, which can never be defiled.

Miss Trenton: If I did not know better, William, I might think that you were negotiating for my chastity.

Traquair: Surely not! I would have nothing valuable enough to offer in exchange for something as precious as that.

Miss Trenton: Only a lifetime of the perfection that is impurity, the way you tell it.

Traquair: Miss Trenton, your suspicious nature, no doubt aggravated by the bad intentions of the last man to bring you flowers, has placed me in a damaging light. My motive—yes, I'll admit to having one—is far less demanding, far more quaint. All I am really seeking is something small and quite inconsequential. A kiss. I had no—

Miss Trenton: A kiss? Oh. Is that all?

Traquair was shaken from his daydream by a series of tugs at his sleeve. "Mister!" He looked down and saw a boy of about eight or nine years of age. "The lady said to give you this." The boy was handing Traquair an envelope, which he took as he looked around in search of Miss Trenton. "The lady?" he asked the boy, who just nodded in response and then walked away quickly, disappearing around the corner. At a glance, Traquair could see that the stationery was Miss Trenton's. She had written "William Traquair" on the front of the envelope. He moved over to a bench and sat down. Still clutching the lilies, he opened the letter and read:

9 December 1882

Dear William,

How interesting life is! Far more interesting than art. Not more beautiful, but more interesting. If life were more beautiful than art, I suppose I'd be with you there in the park, sharing another of those captivating moments that have so distinguished our previous encounters. Instead I am here and you are there, and my words are about to send us off to explore the next phases of our lives.

As you are aware, I spent several weeks in Chicago. I stayed longer than expected on account of my having met a simple, charming young man, Thaddeus Dodd, with whom I have a great deal in common, many mutual friends, a love of travel and books. He had even seen Oscar Wilde lecture there at the Central Music Hall in March. In fact, he won my heart at a party my sister gave when he came to Wilde's defense in a stirring fashion. In response to someone who was arguing that Wilde's infatuation with art was all wrong, my Mr. Dodd said, "You may question Mr. Wilde's tactics but not his infatuation. Art is never wrong. That is what makes it art. How can you begrudge a man his adoration of what is right?" At that moment Thaddeus became real for me in a way that he had not been before. I'll confess—and this was when I knew you and I could never really meet again—that I thought of you as I watched him champion the cause of Oscar Wilde. He had the same disciple's fervor that I've seen you demonstrate. I knew he would propose marriage, which he did. I knew I would accept, which I did.

So then why did I arrange the rendezvous if I knew I couldn't meet you? Why are you standing there—are you still standing, are you still there—reading this letter instead of talking to me? The only answer I can think of is that I wanted to keep the possibility of romance alive for you as long as I could. You're romantic, William, and, truthfully, so am I. Yes, you've a decidedly starry-eyed quality about you that it disappoints me so to disappoint. But if a man stares long enough at stars or even merely our sun, he may lose sight of some important things, things as essential, for instance, as color, which makes most beauty, including yours, possible, and many other things—including us—impossible.

I suppose I could have kept up our little illusion of romance a bit longer. This note could have said that I was unable to meet you today due to illness or because of some other fabricated reason, and that we should reschedule for another day, tomorrow, let's say. And from there I could have kept up the charade through the holidays, creating lovely, believable excuses for my repeated postponement of our reunion. But, alas, it would seem, I'm not quite that romantic.

It is without doubt this same shortcoming that is allowing me to break the rule of the surrogate that Wilde established for us when he sent you to me instead of an apologetic letter, the rule that you and I both admire. By that commandment, a lovely young woman (lovely, for she should be your equal), dispatched in my stead, ought to be saying these words to you. But please forgive me, as expediency and cowardice press me to whisper them here in this letter, in the most artless of manners: I'm sorry. It should soothe you to acknowledge that the hand that would craft such a pitiless prose as this is not worthy of the poetry of your kiss. Seek out the hand that is.

Ever yours,
Theda

TRAQUAIR

TRAQUAIR wasn't sure how he had arrived at 48 West Eleventh Street, at the door to Oscar's apartment, but that was where he stood now, looking around himself, feeling rather lost, like on that day in Washington when he had somehow found Otis and Nat and then meandered with them all the way to Mae's and to that fateful consummation of his curiosity. Today, in the absence of human guides, he had followed the lead of dejection and loneliness, and these escorts had steered him directly to Oscar.

Ah, yes, he remembered now. He remembered the rambling route he'd taken. When he had left the park—Miss Trenton's letter dangling daintily from his hand, like a handkerchief, a consoler of grief, as opposed to the heartbreaking sliver of cotton that it was—he had felt as if he had no place to go. Almost seven weeks had passed since the tour had ended, and now, even more than yesterday at Grand Central, with all hope of his desired destiny dashed, he missed the city-to-city certainty of a planned itinerary. After nearly a year of more than 150 predetermined moves, he saw finally that he had come to the end of the line, and he was face-to-face with a terrifying reality: he had no destination. Thoughtlessly, instinctively—he'd been reduced to all feeling—he had first walked east on Fourth Street, but at Broadway had turned north, heading homeward, to avoid having to pass Miss Trenton's house. At Tenth and Broadway, he had glanced to his left, and his drooping eyes had been drawn by the distant image of the clock tower rising skyward at the Jefferson Market Courthouse on Sixth Avenue. And so he had walked along Tenth Street toward the courthouse clock, thinking vaguely of time and justice, the moment and truth, and when he'd reached the ornate structure whose ticking facade and inner inquisitions might have symbolized his own predicament, he moved past the building without hesitation. Indeed, his pace had quickened as he had turned north and crossed Tenth, for he had become suddenly aware of his proximity to Oscar, the touchstone of the organized itinerancy whose steady rhythm tapped faintly in a nostalgic corner of Traquair's mind. And the image of Oscar, clearer than the courthouse tower, rose up before Traquair as if Oscar were the next scheduled stop on the tour, not only the next stop, but the final stop, the terminal terminus. Yes, he had a place to go, he had thought, and he was practically already there! Up one block, back across Sixth Avenue, and there he was: 48 West Eleventh. *Here* he was.

But the letter—where was it? He looked down at his hands to find only the bouquet of lilies. He started to search the pockets of his overcoat, but then he remembered having bumped into someone while walking across a busy intersection during his dazed trek to Oscar's; he must have dropped the letter in the middle of the street. In his mind he saw it being trampled by the dirty feet of a few hundred uncaring New Yorkers, which he thought a fitting burial for a document that had so willfully ruined romance.

The memory of the letter released within Traquair another surge of despair and longing, so much so that when he knocked on Oscar's door, he did so with an unintended fury and with the quake of unsated desire. Oscar opened the door with a look of terror at first, as if he thought Traquair's banging represented the return of all those pesky reporters who had once, though no longer, hounded his every move. But upon the sight of his former servant, Oscar's face brightened. "I knew if I waited long enough you would come to me!" The exclamatory registry of his voice bounced with a pronounced lilt.

"You sent for me?" Traquair asked, confused by Oscar's remark.

Oscar did not respond to this. He looked at Traquair's bouquet, which was dangling carelessly, and said, "Flowers? For me?"

Traquair lifted the lilies quickly and held them out to Oscar in a gesture of mock chivalry, accompanied by a strained smile, his wounded heart thumping distantly, *Theda . . . Theda . . . Theda . . .* Oscar took the flowers and stepped back into the apartment so that Traquair could enter. The room was warm, and it was scented softly with a fragrance Traquair did not recognize. He noticed that Oscar had done little decorating. Aside from the essential furnishings—a few chairs, a small table, and a sofa near the fireplace—the living room exhibited none of the decorative care Oscar had spent the past year telling the world it needed. The only accents Traquair saw were three parasols in red and black Japanese patterns hanging on the wall to the right. The uncharacteristic austerity made him think that Oscar might be lonely. He remembered Vail's gossip about Lillie Langtry's scandalous behavior, and he thought that the rumors about his friend's beloved beauty might be affecting Oscar, who did look paler than usual. Oscar quickly went over to the table and dropped the flowers gently into an empty vase.

"Take off your coat, and we'll sit over by the fire," he said. When Oscar turned to face him, it was immediately obvious to Traquair that the thing he had just mistaken for pallor was something else, something more like a glow. Before Traquair could begin to remove his coat, Oscar came over and said, "Here, let me help you." Oscar stood behind him and—with a dexterity that surprised Traquair, with an assurance of movement that matched Traquair's own in such service—gently gathered into his hands small sections from each side of the collar of Traquair's coat. Oscar's breath tickled the back of his neck and Traquair thought of all the times he had stood behind Oscar and removed Oscar's garments at such close proximity. Had his own exhalations ever inadvertently fanned the hairs on Oscar's neck? No, he guessed, for Oscar's long locks would not have left him vulnerable in this way, a conclusion that came as a relief to Traquair, who would have considered such a physical disturbance of Oscar's person, even an unintentional one, a professional breach. Oscar lifted, pulled, and slowly peeled the coat away from Traquair, who worked his arms out of the heavy sleeves. "There!" Oscar said as he tossed the garment onto the back of a chair near the table. He took Traquair by the arm and led him to the sofa, where they sat together in the warmth of the fire.

For a while neither of them said anything, with only the occasional minor explosion of sparks in the fire interrupting the silence. After weeks apart from Oscar, Traquair found it immensely comforting to be in his presence again, the place where he had spent most of his life over the past year, where he had gained such knowledge and been exposed to so much philosophical insight. He wondered if the things they had shared held the same significance for Oscar as they did for him. Not the same significance. Of course not the same. The tour had changed Traquair's life. But did the times they had shared hold any real meaning for Oscar, a worldly man, the most worldly man he knew and probably ever would know? Traquair looked at Oscar and smiled softly. The glow was still there.

"I—I suppose you'll be leaving soon," Traquair said.

"Yes. I'm afraid the journalists will have it no other way. They think I've run out of things to say, but the truth is I've decided that their quotation marks are no longer worthy of my wit. There is something sad about the man who makes a living by merely recording what other, greater men have said, all the while following his petty little rules of attribution. Somehow the plagiarist is more worthy of our respect."

"Does that mean that you will be retiring to a more private life?"

"Oh, I shall have a great private life, especially after the public has embraced me."

"Your plays, you mean? I know you have hopes for *Vera*."

Oscar raised his eyebrows, as if to dismiss his own play. "Oh, I mean much greater works than that," he said. "I shall create a new theater, for the acoustics of the old one do not flatter my voice. And I shall write untold stories that feel like allegories. I shall invent a philosophy based not upon thought but upon feeling. A philosophy of feeling."

"You are so lucky."

"Oh, no," Oscar said gravely. "No . . ."

"*Yes,*" Traquair insisted. "You are truly a liberated man, as you yourself have defined it. You remember? The kind of man you described when you were talking at the dinner party at Mrs. Howe's in Newport. You said that it is only when a man discovers the way in which he is unequal that he can finally know the true meaning of liberty. You have already discovered the way in which you are unequal, the *ways*, I should say. You are a free man. I, on the other hand, having not discovered myself at all, really, remain, well . . . something of a slave."

"Well, I confess that I do know what makes me special, but I am certain it is not what you think. You are probably thinking, 'Oh, Oscar is going to create great art. Oh, he will do great things, and he will be triumphant, and what's more he already knows it!' And, of course, you are right in thinking that. But that is only the glamorous part of it. You don't see what I see."

Oscar paused, then got up slowly from the sofa and stood directly in front of Traquair. He fell into silhouette there with the flames of the fire flickering behind him. Traquair looked up at him, impressed by the big, shadowy Oscar that had risen up before him, entranced by the reds and oranges and yellows that swirled behind the figure. "The truth is . . . I am destined for darkness," Oscar said. Then he began to pace as he spoke. "It was our visit to Beauvoir that set me off on the road to understanding this. Something Jefferson Davis said to me. You were on the porch at the time, but I suppose you weren't close enough to hear his voice. He warned me about the danger that attends a position such as the one I've been chosen to fill. He told me to be careful. He was speaking from his own experience, of course, but I believe he spoke a general truth. And, as real truth is eternal, the man who speaks it is not only a reliable chronicler of the past and the present—he is also a prophet. I was frightened by his prediction, and I fought against its implications until—until we were on the train heading out of Atlanta. It will seem strange to you, but what happened on the train, an event that was really your own personal crisis, was what showed me the way in which I am truly unequal.

"You remember it well, no doubt. It had been a long day. That reporter from the *Constitution* in the afternoon, the lecture that night. I, in particular, wanted to escape the mayhem of Atlanta's celebratory masses. We were all tired. We wanted to sleep. Vail, bless him, had purchased our sleeping-car tickets. But then there was that awful man insisting that you had no right to your ticket. Who was this man? What false law was he enforcing? I wondered. We were right, of course, to resist his authority. And then he brought in the Negro porter to describe the terror that awaited you in the next town should you not give up your berth in the sleeping car. Finally, we acquiesced. As they led you away, I thought of the celebration we had witnessed that day from the hotel windows, the Negro children running, screaming—too loudly, really—the fireworks, all of the Fourth of July, Independence Day clamor. What was happening to you on the train was not just tragedy—it was ironic tragedy. Like all true tragedy, it was also glorious. And it was beautiful. And—and I realized, quite clearly, that I wanted it. I wanted very badly that particular beauty, as you embodied it. I wanted it in every way. The way men want things they should not have, things that do not belong to them, things that probably *should* not belong to them. And, too, I wanted it the way men want women. And I wanted it the way the artist wants a metaphor.

"I say 'artist' and yet what became clear to me at that moment was that it was *not* the pursuit of art that would consume me in the future. How foolish and simpleminded I had been to have so loudly proclaimed to the world that art was the object of my desire! Art! No! Watching you being forced to leave me, *you,* for whom I felt such a strong attraction, such a great affection, such a great . . . dare I speak it"—and here Oscar, before continuing, drew one soft breath sharply and deeply into the back of his throat—"*love* . . . I knew I would spend the rest of my life in the pursuit of something grander than art, grander than happiness. Yes, I would spend my life in the pursuit of tragedy. And I knew, too, that for me somehow tragedy and love would forever be wed. It may be true for us all that there is no tragedy without love, and no love without tragedy.

"I know it may seem foolish that a man should need a muse to show him the way of his life, but that is the case more than we realize. No great life is possible without the inspiration of a muse. Just as no great art is possible without the breath of a man. How shallow of us to believe that a muse works solely in the realm of artistic creation. Traquair—my Melpomene."

Traquair's eyes had not left the fire. As Oscar had spoken, his figure had been that of an apparition to Traquair, occasionally floating through his line of vision. Oscar's words, seemingly coming from nowhere, had acquired a supernatural luster and power, and Traquair believed Oscar devoutly, the way he would have believed a ghost or a god. "Love?" he asked, not because he doubted Oscar's admission of loving him, but because he felt it was the question Oscar needed to answer. "But you never said anything to me about love."

Oscar came back over to the sofa now and sat down next to Traquair, who couldn't bring himself to look Oscar in the eyes. "In only a thousand different ways did I tell you," Oscar said. "In every way except in the exact words. Think back and you will know this to be true. Why, the very first thing I said about you was that you were beautiful."

Traquair thought back to their first meeting, and he recalled

Oscar's precise words. "No," he corrected Oscar. "You told Vail I was perfect."

"To be considered perfect is to be considered *ultimately* beautiful." Traquair looked at Oscar now and saw upon his face the look that usually accompanied more profound statements. "And when you said to me, in Philadelphia, 'Travel moves me,' what was my response?"

Traquair was surprised at how quickly he remembered what Oscar had said. "You said, 'Would that I were travel.' " Oscar nodded with satisfaction. "But you were half asleep when you said that."

"If you thought that then, you should have known better when you heard me repeat your remark in front of others. I made the point of doing so as a means of clarification for you. I repeated the comment, I believe, in conversation with those two women who made their way backstage in St. Louis. I remember because I was terribly rude to one of them, as I felt she had been flirting with you at the dressing room door. I said something unkind in as mean a tone as I could manage. I only wish I could have somehow apologized to that poor girl. She had no way of knowing she was interfering. Even you didn't know."

Traquair, stunned by Oscar's confession, clasped both of his hands over his forehead, the bottoms of his palms covering his eyes. "I didn't know," he said softly. "I didn't know."

"And where was I when you returned to the hotel in Washington after spending nearly the entire night out?"

"In my bed," Traquair said, his pulse quickening with the presentation of each new piece of Oscar's evidence of his love. It was as if Oscar were lifting layer after layer, turning page after page, toward the confirmation of an obvious truth.

"And when we stood in the mirror together in San Francisco just after you had dressed me to go out and have my picture painted, and I said, 'Don't we make quite the couple . . .' "

"I thought you meant you and San Francisco. You and Saint Francis—"

Oscar seemed not to hear him. He continued, talking over Traquair's comment, "When we were in New Orleans, when I knew you would be listening to me, I formulated beautiful, new, true things to say about you—just as, out of fear of losing your admiration, I had vowed to do. With my words, I turned you into art and history and religion. I turned you into Adam!"

Traquair took in a short breath through his mouth and pressed his hands harder to his eyes, his head tilting downward. His hands, cupped, intent upon fulfilling the purpose of the form they had assumed, coaxed sympathy for their mission from his eyes, and he felt drops tapping the bottoms of his palms.

"Once," Oscar said, "once, while we sat on a train with a reporter, I answered a question by concluding that England and America are not related as cousins or otherwise, but instead they are great, great lovers. I forsook my own beloved Ireland to profess, in poetic terms, my love for you.

"With you as inspiration, I have painted myself into a veritable portrait of love. I've brushed into the painting adoration, adulation, admiration, lust—and jealousy, pity, and sacrifice. There is but one stroke missing from the picture now. And it is this—"

Traquair heard, smelled, and felt Oscar moving and leaning toward him. He let his hands drop away from his eyes, but he kept his eyes closed. Overwhelmed with emotional and physical excitations, he felt that if he exposed one more sense to this moment he might just perish.

The kiss was calm, warm, and long. It was the kind of kiss one would expect from a man, one who had waited so long with seemingly little hope for consummation. It was the kind of kiss Traquair would have given Miss Trenton—a real kiss, putting an end to illusion. It was the kind of kiss that robbed mirrors and masks of their powers. This kiss, the pressing of lips, was a call for silence. It made the existence of secrets meaningless, as there was no means of telling them—even as it boldly created new secrets. The kiss killed language, asphyxiated the lie, strangled the truth. And yet, somehow, it spoke. First, Traquair heard only its hearty laugh at logic. Then he listened as it redefined reason as sensation, as taste and touch. The kiss was a long essay spoken by the lips of a philosopher of feeling, and it had a strange relationship to poetry, even as its chemistry dissolved rhyme. The poet who would follow the odd but swift rhythm of its meter would always create a literature ahead of its time.

That was some of what Traquair was reading now upon his lips. But this kiss, he would soon learn, had a full life. It would move, grow. The kiss told its own story; it was autobiographical. In its expressive present tense, it relayed a life of wild adventure and downward determination. It detailed its actions so skillfully and with such telling nuances of description that it assured its listener—Traquair—of its own ravishing individuality. Oh, the kiss knew how to hold the listener's attention, exhibiting a remarkable flair for self-effacing comedy, all the while generating a genuine sense of suspense. A couple of hours later, when the kiss, along with its story, was over, Traquair felt as if he knew all of the great joys and great sadnesses of that kiss: its yearnings and ambitions, which were numerous, its fears, which were few. And in the end, the very end, he instinctively let out a sound he had never uttered in his life, a sound he recognized as the same howl the miners in Leadville had let fly after Oscar had told them the story of Jesse James, part of the chorus of yelps that had accompanied the round of gunshots that had lit up the mine, the proud cry of the creative outlaw Oscar had described, the shout of the joyous rebel: "Got-dayum!" As Traquair lamented the death of the kiss, he would have cried, but again he heard himself mumbling something close to what one of the miners had said, "Oscar, you oughtn'ta go gettin a feller so riled up." Traquair was actually laughing out loud when he remembered to himself how the miner named Dalton had responded to that: "It's a free country. He can rile a feller up if he likes." Oscar could not have known what the laugh was about, but he joined Traquair with his own display of happiness.

As Traquair was readjusting and buttoning his shirt and trousers, he told Oscar about all that he had recently learned about his family. He wanted to hear Oscar's opinion about those revelations, because he knew Oscar's constructive cynicism would help him put it all into perspective. "Isn't it remarkable," he said, "that I should have met John, my own brother, while you and I were traveling?"

Oscar shrugged, seemingly unimpressed. "Actually, I'm sure such meetings are commonplace." Oscar's confident tone reminded Traquair of Oscar's own siblings by his father's mistresses. "It's probably difficult to walk out one's front door without bumping into an obscure cousin or two. What's genuinely shocking is how few true strangers there are left in the world. There are not nearly enough of those to go around."

"Yes, but my kinsmen are, in a sense, strangers," Traquair said. "I don't know what is what and who is who after what my father told me today."

"Only literally are your kinsmen strangers. And that particular alienation is to be cherished. Befriending relatives is risky. It often leads to all sorts of entanglements—legal disputes about money or, worse, proposals of marriage. And on the issue of who your father really is, the last person you should listen to is your father. A father's claim to parentage is rarely anything more than speculation. At best, it's an opinion; at worst, propaganda. Occasionally, it's merely a misunderstanding. And when a man takes the bold step of assigning parentage to another man, as your father did today, he is simply making a rather dubious claim to clairvoyance."

Traquair was exhausted when he got home. Since yesterday he had avoided his parents, but he knew that in the morning he would have to speak candidly with them—after he had had a night's rest and begun recovering from what had happened with Oscar and what had not happened with Miss Trenton. He went straight up to his room, where he found the lamp at his desk had been left on with a low light. Resting there was a letter from Baxter, which Traquair was disinclined to read tonight. If things had progressed for Baxter as his last letter had indicated they might, then the pages in the blue envelope with the familiar scrawl would probably announce Baxter's engagement to Constance Lloyd. Traquair didn't feel up to the challenge of receiving such news with the cheeriness becoming a best friend. Not tonight, he thought. Maybe tomorrow. If he read it tomorrow maybe he wouldn't be as susceptible to reverting back to his old ways of resenting Baxter's good fortune. Gently, he placed the letter on his desk and vowed that when he finally read it, he would do so with a heart capable of expressing, if necessary, genuinely felt felicitations.

Wearier still, he changed into his nightshirt and climbed into bed. As he slid under the blankets, he was overcome by tremendous waves of anxiety and loneliness. He rolled onto his back, propped himself up against the pillows, and pulled the covers up over his nose. He drew his hands together and warmed his knuckles with his own breath. There was comfort in that. But still he felt—

There was a soft knock at his door. Before he could speak, he heard his mother's voice say, "William."

He was both relieved and startled at hearing her. His loneliness dissipated but his anxiety intensified. "Yes. I'm awake. Come in."

His mother entered slowly, closing the door behind her. In the soft light from the desk lamp, Traquair was surprised to see that she was not yet dressed for bed. She walked over and sat down on the edge of his bed. He did not adjust his position; rather, he lowered his angle of vision in her direction. What he saw was the steady profile of his mother, who began to speak plainly. "You have had an interesting year, haven't you?"

Traquair laughed softly at this simply understated truth.

"A defining year, even."

"Exactly," he said, surprised now at the precision and the accuracy of his mother's words.

"I had a year like that once," she said, "oh, many years ago, before you were born."

"Really?"

"Your father—Henry—told me that he explained to you this after-noon some of what happened that very year. I'm sorry I was not able to stay and clarify things for you. I try not to get so emotional anymore, but it's not easy." Her voice broke, she took a breath, and then she said, "Thank you for my letter from Moses." She was crying, but she was controlled enough to speak. Traquair, not wanting to disturb her momentum, did not move.

"It's Henry I hate to see struggle with this matter. Really, after all of these years you would think the truth would be obvious, even to him. But I suppose things don't always work that way. It seems that some-times until even the most obvious truth is actually spoken, it remains a secret." Traquair thought of how he had never understood Oscar's intentions toward him until Oscar had directly informed him of them this evening, despite what, in retrospect, was an impressive amount of evidence of Oscar's affection. He nodded slowly, but his mother, still looking away from him, could not have seen his gesture of sympathy.

"Henry was always jealous of Moses and me," she said. "That's what has blinded him to the truth for so long. In the last year that the three of us were all together, 1859, it became clear that Moses was my favorite. He and I broke away somewhat from Henry, who, even as a young man, was as rigid as he is now, perhaps even more so. I knew Henry was in love with me. And I knew Moses had other women. But I preferred Moses. I loved him. And despite his flirtations with other girls, I believed he loved me, too. Over the course of that last year,

Moses and I had gradually plotted out how we would take the large sum of money that Mr. Traquair so often left in an unlocked drawer in his library and how we would run away and start a new life together way out west. This was before the war, so there would have been some danger involved, but we didn't care. Moses thrived on a sense of danger. That was one of the things I so liked about him. His daring nature would explain why he stayed here in the East during the war. I would love to talk to him someday about the adventures he had after he ran off alone, adventures that he and I were supposed to have shared. His letter contained only an apology. No details. There are many things I will never know.

"On the night that we were to leave together, we planned to meet at our special spot in the woods behind the two cabins where some of the others Mr. Traquair had rescued lived. It was a secluded little nook we had covered over with branches that no one else knew about. On that night I went to the spot and waited for Moses to show up. I waited and I waited. Gradually, it became clear, and then clearer still that I was waiting in vain. And yet—I waited even longer. You're still a young man, William, too young, I'm sure, to know what such a hopeless wait feels like, too young to know what it feels like to be left waiting for love, only to have it never show up. Such a crisis leaves one weary, but wanting still. Oh, I hope you'll never know such weariness, my son, and such wanting. And yet—it was such a moment of longing that was ultimately responsible for your very being. Oh, I know this confession will be difficult for you to understand, but it will mean everything to me, everything, for you to try.

"In the woods that night, while waiting for Moses, I eventually succumbed to sleep. I woke up in the morning hoping that he had changed his mind and that I would find him in the main house. I dusted myself off and rushed back to look for him. But when I got near the house, the first person I saw was Henry, and I could see that something was wrong. He was angry. Very angry. And he wouldn't speak to me. I gathered from the others that Moses was gone, and the money was missing. They had thought I had run off with Moses, but they were happy to see that I had not. I told them that I had been visiting my friend Elizabeth at Mr. Benjamin's. They believed me. They must have read my devastation at having been left behind as abject sincerity.

"Before lunch, I tried to approach Henry again. I needed his support; I was hurting so. After all, he was my closest friend other than Moses. We were all cousins, you know. We had all grown up together in South Carolina. But Henry still would not talk to me. I suppose he had his own embarrassment to deal with, his own pain, but I was so distraught I did not know which way to turn.

"And then after lunch, it was time for our lessons. When Mr. Gable arrived, Mr. Traquair informed him of what had happened and asked that we cancel lessons for the day.

"Mr. Gable—not the aging man you know now, but a young, handsome Mr. Gable—he must have known that I was particularly close to Moses. Everyone knew. I was walking around outside when I saw him coming out of the house. He always wore gray suits that looked a size too small, and I remember thinking—even in the midst of my depression—that I would love to alter his jacket to a proper fit. To this day, as you well know, I still tailor all of his suits. I must have been staring at his jacket as he walked over to where I was standing. I know I wasn't looking at his face when he asked me what was wrong. 'It's Moses, isn't it?' he said. When he said that, I knew I was about to cry, so I started to run away from him. I didn't want him to see me cry. I didn't want anyone to see me cry. As I've told you, such things are private matters. I ran as fast as I could into the woods, back to the special spot that only Moses and I knew about, sobbing all the way. I fell onto my knees, and I understood something I've never admitted to anyone, William. Always before when I had found myself weeping like a child, it had been at the harsh memory of what Henry, Moses, and I had endured as captives in Charleston, horrible memories of brutal, motherless childhoods. But that day, abandoned by my Moses, my great love, I was crying harder than I had ever cried before. And the tears were just for me, because I realized at that moment that my life had changed forever. Because of what Moses had done, I would now have to define myself in a different way. It came to me in a rush: the greatest tragedy of my life was not the way men had enslaved me . . . but the way one man had set me free."

Gloria Traquair began to tremble with the emotion of this admission, and Traquair moved to put his arm around her. She calmed herself somewhat and continued, "In my state, which was nothing short of delirium, I didn't even notice that Mr. Gable had followed me. He rushed over and held me. 'Gloria, Gloria,' he said to me, in a voice I mistook at first for simple compassion. But then he said, 'You have no idea how it pains me to see you so distraught.' I knew he was a kind man, but he was right—I had no idea that he could have cared about my feelings beyond the general sympathy of one human being caring distantly for another. But when I looked up into his eyes, it was clear to me that he meant something else. I experienced a moment of sheer terror, such as one feels only in the proximity of real danger and of love, but it was quickly crushed by the force of the embrace that followed. It was a powerful, mutual embrace. A long embrace of comfort and consolation—with consequences." She glanced quickly in Traquair's direction when she said this, and then turned back into profile.

"By the time it became obvious that I was with child, Henry had already become my friend again, and he assumed the child belonged to Moses. He really loved me, he said. He wanted to marry me. I saw no reason to absolve Moses, in Henry's eyes, of the sin he had committed against me; in that moment I, too, hated Moses. He *had* sinned against me, only not in the way Henry imagined." Mrs. Traquair's chin dropped a few inches now.

Traquair cleared his throat. "Does Mr. Gable have a full understanding of my relationship to him?"

"Yes, of course," his mother said. "Isn't it clear to you now? Think of all of the innumerable acts of kindness he has exhibited toward you. Think of all of the tender moments he has shared with you. I have witnessed many with my own eyes. Surely there are many that I know nothing of."

Indeed, Traquair was overcome with the memory of countless private moments between him and Charles Gable—the casual pats on the head, the vaguely covert delivery of a series of birthday books that had been a secret between the two of them, the careful handwriting lessons, his schooling, the money, the advice, all of which he had always thought of as incidental to their sharing the same household or as examples of Mr. Gable's unusual generosity to the son of his servants. And—oh—it had been Mr. Gable who had accepted the appointment to work with Oscar in his name! And the blue tie with the little white dots that Mr. Gable had worn to Oscar's lecture at Chickering Hall back in January, the one that Baxter couldn't remember—Traquair recalled now that he had given that tie to Mr. Gable, who, in wearing it, must have had Traquair, William, his secret son, in mind.

His mother looked at him and said, "That is why you have never wanted for anything, why *we* have never wanted for anything—and never will."

"And so Uncle Moses is not my uncle and John is not my brother. They're both my cousins."

"Yes, as Moses and Henry are my cousins. For the most part, you look like a slightly brighter version of the men in our family."

"And Baxter . . ." Traquair's eyes drifted toward the letter on his desk as if it were the man who had sent it "Baxter and I are brothers."

"Yes!" His mother's shout was explosive, releasing its affirmation of the truth that she had stifled all these years. "The two of you—so obviously brothers. Don't you feel the truth of it?"

"Yes. I suppose, on some level, I have always felt it." And Traquair, bringing his hands up to touch his face lightly, thought that his mother's disclosure also explained the hint of redness that annually, during the winter months, gained prominence in his complexion. The "slight tinge of the tropics" that the Sioux City newspaperman had reported to the world had nothing to do with the tropics at all. "Ah!" he said aloud, startling his mother. That clarification, a relatively slight one in the context of this dizzying day of revelations, made him sigh and smile broadly. He gave his mother a kiss on the cheek she had shown him as she had told her strange, inevitable story. "It's all right," he said. "I understand. I know more about love than you think I do." His mother smiled and kissed him. When she stood up to leave, the lamplight caught her eye, drawing attention to the unopened correspondence, and she said, "Did you see the letter from Baxter on your desk?" Without waiting for Traquair's response, she hummed a single soft note and left him alone in his room.

Bolstered by the knowledge of his true relationship to Baxter, Traquair decided to read the letter after all. He got up and went over to his desk. The envelope peeled open easily between his fingers, and a thick bundle of six or seven folded white papers slid out quickly, spine slapping into the palm of his hand, half-sheets fanning like the pages of a book. So what if Baxter was to marry Constance. So what if Baxter's good fortune made him jealous. Baxter was his brother, his *true* brother! Hadn't Cain's crime and subsequent punishment won all brothers the privilege of indulging in the fraternal pettiness of which Traquair was guilty? Unfolding the pages of his brother's letter, he understood now, finally, that his propensity to envy Baxter was not merely an incidental, unappealing trait; it was the entitlement, the commandment of his blood.

20 November 1882

Dear William,

Oh, the impermanence of Constance!

Oh, the impermanence of almost everything, I suppose. I say this with the knowing resignation of a man whose recently shattered heart has just begun to reshape itself into a thing that might once again instinctively and gracefully beat out the normal rhythms of life. I'm pleased to note in this reparative state that, mercifully, not even a broken heart, it would appear, lasts forever.

As I compose this letter in my little apartment, I'm forced to pause from time to time, to put down my pen in favor of my brush and rush across the room to dapple at the canvas that beckons to me. Mr. Whistler says that now that I've failed at love, at life essentially, I'm much more motivated to succeed at art. He claims my lines are straighter, my colors more purposeful, my palette, shall we say, more palatable. Yes, I've at last begun in earnest my lessons with the master, and I dare say I've learned more from him in the last month than I learned in nearly an entire year of socializing in the salons of London. And I'm as happy as I've ever been. When I work, either in Mr. Whistler's company or while alone, as now, that music I'd hoped to make with Constance I hum to myself in a lighter, more humble orchestration. My brush behaves as a conductor's baton when I think of her as I paint, which is often, informing the rhythm of my strokes, influencing the outcome of my effort. How did I lose her? you wonder. How am I left with only tremors of disappointment that my willing imagination transforms into lyrical lashes of artful invention? How? Look closely, my dear William, and you will discover that hidden in every "how" is a "who." So here's how. Here's who.

You will, no doubt, recall that I was due—oh, it seems ages past—to enjoy a very special rendezvous with Constance, a picnic where we were to sneak away from her brother and consummate our incipient love with a kiss, or rather, should I have had my way, with

kisses. I won't bore you with the secret thing I'd planned to whisper to
her, to ask of her, though I'm sure you've already guessed my
intentions. Well, on the morning of our scheduled meeting,
Constance sent me a short note. It read simply, if cryptically:
"Baxter, Cannot meet today. Cannot meet. Regrets, Constance."
The vague quality in her words left me disturbed. They seemed
purposely evasive, and an eerie finality echoed in the repeated phrase
"cannot meet." Curious, anxious, I sent a reply immediately begging
some explanation for her cancellation. I waited, but no response
came from Constance. Instead, I received a note the next day from
an unexpected correspondent—the who of my how: Lady Wilde.
"Baxter," she wrote. "Must see you to explain. Constance insists. I
shall expect you tomorrow at two. Willie is away." She signed the
note "Speranza," which seemed to me a superfluous use of her poet's
moniker, claiming as it did authorship to so prosaic a composition.
Knowing what I know now, I think I understand her use of the
pseudonym. She was placing a necessary obstruction between us. She
did not intend to face me as my friend; she could not do that. The
words she'd speak to me the next day could be spoken only from
behind the shield of a mask.

My return to her home that following afternoon released a
nostalgia in me, an ache for the warmth I'd felt from Lady Wilde
from the first time I'd met her, for the closeness she and I had
cultivated before Willie had undone our intimacy with his rough
reminder of just who I was, or rather was not. But Lady Wilde was
about to undo an altogether different intimacy with her own vision of
just who Constance was, or rather, was to become.

There were no formalities, no greetings, no tea. We sat in the first
parlor, and she did all the talking. "Oscar always has a plan," she
began, twirling between her fingers the thick rope of pearls that hung
about her neck. "Or should I say a plot. This is what I ask you to
understand. He is off in your homeland right now no doubt writing
and rewriting the lives of those around him to suit his own purposes,
to make him what he is meant to be. The greater part of his genius,
perhaps of all genius, is the art of manipulation. A genius seduces the
world into seeing things his way. As Oscar is essentially a poet, his
chief method is through the exploitation of words, which influences
emotions and actions. No one is safe from the dramatic twists

proposed by his tongue. No one is safe from his plotting, perhaps in the end not even he. But certainly not, in the present, I. Indeed as I began to contemplate the role I must play in recasting your romance with Constance, I considered that Oscar had set me in motion with words he'd uttered, in the tone of a prophet, only months before he sailed for America."

Lady Wilde sighed deeply and said, "They were first introduced— Oscar and Constance—last spring at the home of Mary Atkinson, Constance's grandmother." She paused here, as if to allow for the cultivation of anticipation within me or, if motivated by a more caring instinct, to grant my intuition a moment's grace in which to divine the truth, thereby softening the blow of destiny. Whatever Lady Wilde's intent, I was not truly afraid of what she was about to reveal, but I did feel a sense of dread, and I dare say I detected faintly the onset of grief. "Constance was as ravishing a vision the day he met her as when you met her, and Oscar was equally charmed by her. I won't pretend to know what the two of them spoke about to each other in the long private session they shared. You would know better than I, for in these matters your gender and your youth tie you closer to Oscar's nature than my blood does me. When Oscar left the girl's side, he remained strangely quiet for the remainder of the afternoon. The miracle of that silence should have alerted me that something momentous had occurred. As we departed the Atkinson home, Oscar took my hand and broke his silence with words that left me no choice but to alter the course of your courtship with Constance. 'By and by,' Oscar said to me, 'by and by, Mama, I think of marrying that girl.' They met on several other occasions before he left for his tour. That day you met her was not her first visit here. I've felt it my duty to maintain a familial attachment until Oscar returns and makes good on his prediction. As I've said, I realize that I've been manipulated into acting out my part of doting mother. After all, any mother would do her best to see her son's pronouncements come true, forcing upon the world but one conclusion—that her son is a prophet. When Oscar marries Constance, I'll know for myself what the world will eventually accept: my son is a prophet. And this is why I cannot let you have her."

In the stillness that followed, I glimpsed a prophecy of my own: a life without love. Lovelessness but, somehow, not loneliness.

*Something would save me from loneliness. My grief-stricken heart
lifted at this rising faith. As I fled Lady Wilde's, which I did with all
dispatch, bumping a table and destroying a vase in my haste to
escape, I began to run through the streets of London. I ran past the
shops and houses and churches of this place, feeling oddly
dispossessed. These structures, these trees, this air were not mine.
Nothing here, not even the affections of the woman that I loved,
belonged to me. I ran as fast as I could, for as long as I could,
succumbing finally to exhaustion, my perambulations relegated to a
series of limping skips that matched the jerky gyrations of my
wounded heart. I moved past a little park that reminded me of
Gramercy Park back home, and I thought again about leaving
England as soon as possible. Surely there was no reason for me to
stay now. And this time I didn't contemplate Rome and Paris, but
home. Home, Billy boy. I didn't understand why, but my very
presence here seemed to offend. My anger was leading me to
conclude that hidden in Willie Wilde's and his mother's rejection of
me was a prejudice against my foreignness, my Americanness,
against the symbol of who I was—not who I actually was or what I
had done. Of course, I had no evidence of this claim, none
whatsoever; they claimed to object to me and my desires on purely
personal grounds. As they saw it, I stood in the way of their family's
pride and progress. But then isn't all bias rooted in some personal
fear? So let them hate me, I thought. I couldn't change who I was or
what I wanted. If the Wildes couldn't bring themselves to love me and
if they would see to it that I couldn't love whom I desired to love, I
decided that I should retreat from their territory. And I made a
covenant with myself, William, in my rage—oh, I was suddenly
quite mad with an irrational resentment—that no Gable should ever
fraternize, as it were, with any Wilde!*

*I admit that these thoughts are comical in retrospect, but unless
you experience a similarly painful dismissal, a rank renunciation—
and I hope you never will—you can't possibly imagine the tumult of
emotions, emotions so powerful as to turn one into a caricature of
oneself, a laughable rendering of one's being, recognizable but with
too much nose, too much chin; or as in my case—in the throes as I
was of my panic, my Wilde paranoia—too much enmity, too much
woe. Perhaps it was some ugly inner visualization of myself, some*

unpleasant picture that I sensed needed refinement that set me on a direct path to Mr. Whistler. Was I just a wobbly, unfinished figure of a man in search of beautification? Or maybe it was simply that, in light of the afternoon's proceedings, Mr. Whistler was now my only real friend in all of London.

When he opened the door to his studio—monocle at attention; white tuft of hair shining silvery atop his forehead (so many times I've wondered if he painted that color there himself for effect); thick mustache wrinkling with perturbation at his having been disturbed, then widening with bemusement, I could only imagine, at my own palpable and more severe discontent—I couldn't help but observe that the man who had composed many masterpieces of serious portraiture, including pictures of Thomas Carlyle, his mother, his friends, and himself, had turned comic caricature into a way of life. His smile disappeared, and he walked away from me without saying a word. He crossed the room and resumed work on a canvas near the back wall of windows. I walked over and sat on the floor in my usual spot and, for several minutes, in silence, watched him paint. He made what appeared to be long horizontal lines with a very fine brush of black paint. His motions had a slight tremble until his hand reached the canvas, whereupon they created seemingly straight streaks or curves perfectly suited to the task. For the moment, I forgot about my cares and let his confident air soothe away my own unevenness. Watching him, I breathed a sigh of comfort. After a while, curious about his subject, I asked, "What are you drawing?"

Without hesitation, without ceasing his stroking of the canvas, Mr. Whistler said, "The same thing I am ever drawing—the conclusion that I am a genius."

At first I gasped in amusement. I held the breath at the back of my throat for a moment, waiting for the laughter to come, but it did not. Instead, the slow exhale, an expulsion of joy, deflated my mood. A sense of desolation overwhelmed me, and what should have been a burst of laughter manifested itself as an explosion of tears. I couldn't see Mr. Whistler through my veil of misery, but surely he must have started with surprise at my sobbing. Not all of my tears were for me; some were for him and his isolation, which, yes, he had chosen, but it seemed to me that a pretty picture—even one of one's mistress—was no substitute for a happy, love-filled life. His sharp

*tongue had garnered him far more enemies than my gentle missteps
ever would me. All he had were his paints and his wits. A great deal,
one could argue convincingly, yet somehow not enough. But, then, I
had nothing. Who was I to pity him? I had nothing—except him, it
would seem, for when I gathered myself and rose up from the
prostrate position into which I had sunk on the floor and opened my
eyes, there he was, bending down to me, hand stretched out,
presenting me with a brush. It was both a gift and an invitation. As I
began to reach up for the offering, I saw the black brush pinched by
his fleshy, paint-speckled fingers; the curve of his arm, covered by the
long gray sleeve of his smock; and behind that, against the backdrop
of pale yellow walls and the white rectangles of windows and their
panes, a fuzzy Jimmy Whistler, whose face, even out of focus, was
plainly and freshly swept with delight. This composition fixed itself in
my head instantly and indelibly, being as it was the very picture of
possibility. And I knew that as long as I held that image in my mind,
I'd be in the possession of hope. Art and hope, the lone exceptions to
the law of impermanence! Youth and love perish, but art and hope
endure.*

*And so I painted a picture of Mr. Whistler handing me that
brush. It's here in this room with me now. You should see this place;
it's filled with my attempts to paint into immortality the things I want
to keep. The Thames at night, arrangements of lilies, various scenes
of Mr. Whistler's studio, Constance. I've only sketched her in faint
pencil, afraid to cast too darkly "the shadow of my greatest defeat."
But, as I stated at the outset, the truth is that her memory is felt in all
of my work.*

*There: I've just touched my canvas with red to the tune of her
laughter. A blush of contentment now lightens my subject's cheek.
Many years from now when I look upon this painting I'll glance upon
that scarlet splash and hear the perfectly melodious sound of her joy,
the first sound I ever heard her make, the sound that shall remain for
me the symbol of her. I hope this is an omen that Oscar Wilde will
someday make her very, very happy, but even if he somehow fails to
do so, for me she will ever be laughing. This is the thing about
Constance that will remain constant.*

*I've been at work on this canvas for two weeks now. It's a new
subject, a difficult one, a little portrait of myself. It's the same Baxter*

you remember, William, only with a newly sprouted mustache, thin whiskers on his chin, and a woman's laughter eternally ruddying his cheek with a kiss.

Love,
Baxter

Poor Baxter, Traquair thought, wounded in the war of love as well. No envy necessary. Only pity. Someday soon he would share with Baxter the details of his relationship with Miss Trenton. Even while living far apart, he and Baxter seemed to be living lives of inextricably interwoven destinies. With this idea he climbed into bed, thinking further, as he dozed, that there might be something in their common blood that had doomed both their hearts to disaster.

Traquair awoke in the middle of the night in a panic, troubled by thoughts of kisses and disaster, caresses and corruption. Foremost on his mind was the kiss he had shared with Oscar. He had thought before, without articulating it, that there had been something sinful in the kiss. But, no, that was not it. Even if the kiss had been sinful, that was not his worry. He knew from Oscar that sin did not destroy innocence; it merely accentuated it. In this respect, the mission of sin was a holy one. So, no, that was not his concern.

It was his mother's enlightening tale that had brought new meaning to something Mr. Gable had told him—to everything Mr. Gable had ever told him—that had made clear not his sin, but his *crime*. He kept repeating to himself Mr. Gable's warning about the dangers of Oscar Wilde: "William, Wilde is a foreigner. A foreigner in the extreme, I might add. Do not be fooled by his language. Just because you can understand his words does not mean that he is one of us. . . . We've raised you to be an American. We will not hear of your being corrupted." Now Traquair understood the crime of the kiss. Mr. Gable's language presented him with the means of comprehending the obvious wrong he had done. He thought about how Oscar had pronounced the Declaration of Independence a profoundly flawed document, challenging the validity of its chief tenet that all men are created equal—and Traquair had accepted Oscar's argument. And today when Oscar had told him that, on the train from Atlanta, he had in fact shown Oscar the true meaning and absolute correctness of his faith in inequality, thereby freeing him, Traquair had allowed himself to be seduced by the confession. Traquair trembled now as he traced the methodical progression of his fall. *"We've raised you to be an American,"* Mr. Gable—his true father—had said to him sternly. Traquair knew now that, no, it was not the sin of the kiss that bothered him; it was the *treason.* Not the shallow, nationalistic variety Mr. Gable wanted him to be wary of committing, but the very opposite. He had actually committed some smaller but infinitely deeper crime, *crimes,* against himself, crimes against the republic of the individual. And not just with Oscar, but with others as well! He thought of his mother and Mr. Gable, his uncle and Mae, himself and Oscar, the near-disaster of him and Miss Trenton, Baxter and Constance, all the couplings he could think of, both the improper and the supposedly proper. Everyone and anyone else! Treason, he thought. *Treason.* To enunciate the word was very nearly to spit. How one betrayed oneself when one began the pursuit of another. How base a denial of the perfection of one's own individual being. Even as miraculously complete a personality as Oscar Wilde was tempted to reach out and embrace the offerings of the other side. That kiss! That desperate, treacherous kiss! Didn't Oscar know? No—it seemed the one thing he did not know. Using the sensitivity that Oscar had bestowed upon him, Traquair intuited that this failing would be Oscar's downfall, the thing of which Jefferson Davis had tried to warn him. What Oscar did not know—and what Traquair promised himself never to forget—was a terrible truth: that, in a sense, every kiss is an act of sedition. Every act of love conspires against the constitution of the solitary self.

THE TOME
1936

T HE BOOK was heavy. From this simple fact Traquair might have predicted its failure. Any book that weighed this much must be filled with lies. Truth defies gravity. It resists elaboration. Even the biggest truth, thought Traquair, is never cast more clearly than in the smallest of forms: the single sentence. The gut of truth never hangs over its belt. Its finger is never too thick for its ring. Chairs do not creak when it reclines. That is, perhaps, truth as a man. As a book, it does not give the reader's wrist an ache. A book whose heft does bring the reader physical discomfort is invariably fiction. The Bible would be more believable, Traquair thought, if it were not always presented as a ton of truth. Some of its individual books had real validity and vision. What was it Oscar Wilde had said when asked what he had learned from the Bible? Traquair searched his memory. Oh, yes: *"I've learned what every writer should learn from the Bible: All good books end with revelations." That* was certainly the truth, but this book—this fat, well-intentioned, lighthearted but heavy-handed tome that at present sat upon Traquair's lap—while it purported to be the truth, was not.

Oscar Wilde Discovers America, the book was called. It was a 450-page chronicle of the year—more than a half century ago—that he and Oscar had spent together. Traquair had been so excited when he had read about the publication of the book in last Sunday's *New York Times Book Review* that he had rushed right out to buy a copy. And he never rushed out to do anything these days. In fact, at seventy-five years of age, with little energy and even less enthusiasm, he never rushed, period.

The book's promising title had in it more truth than its authors knew—how could they have known?—and certainly more than they delivered. Oscar had actually mocked the discovery of America on numerous occasions. Some of his remarks on the subject had been reported, others had not. Traquair best remembered a rather brutal remark Oscar had made sometime early in their travels: "Columbus's discovery of America, it is widely acknowledged, was an accident; what goes unacknowledged is that the accident was fatal." Like many things Oscar had said, it was a clever line. But also like many things Oscar had said, it was *more* than just clever. It meant something.

Who were the authors of this new Oscar Wilde book? Traquair wondered. Who was this Lloyd Lewis and who was this Henry Justin Smith? A note about their previous works was the first thing in the book after the title:

> *by the same authors*
> CHICAGO: THE HISTORY OF ITS REPUTATION
>
> *by Lloyd Lewis*
> SHERMAN: FIGHTING PROPHET
> MYTHS AFTER LINCOLN
>
> *by Henry Justin Smith*
> DEADLINES

From these titles Traquair speculated, reasonably, that the writers were historians, biographers, literary gossips, and, finally, journalists. Just as he'd suspected: professional liars. Traquair had heard Oscar utter words that skewered such men in any of their incarnations. Historians: "Call all historians Ahab—the grand thing they seek is but prey for the kill." Biographers: "In their enthusiasm to re-create life, biographers are like Frankenstein, and their creations are just as monstrous." (Was that the exact phrasing Oscar had used?) Gossips: "Every legend is born the younger twin of boredom." And journalists: "At the hands of journalists, supposed recorders of fact, I am steadily transformed into a fiction." There was your fighting prophet, Mr. Lewis!

But then, why fault Lewis and Smith? They couldn't have known these things. Oscar had either spoken these lines to only one or two others, or whispered them to Traquair as they had traveled together all those years ago.

It was 1936 now. That had been 1882, when Traquair had been but twenty-two years old. He looked down at his hands, which were still gripping the thick book with grandfatherly indignity. (Why had the book frustrated him so?) Traquair's old hands startled him. These were not the same smooth, brown hands that had once forged Oscar Wilde's autograph, the hands he had expected to see when he had looked down just now. Not even the neglected winter hands of his youth had disturbed him as much as this assembly of crooked appendages. Whatever the shortcomings of *Oscar Wilde Discovers America,* the book had managed to transport him back to an earlier time, another century, when he had been just a few years removed from boyhood. In the hours of reading the book, Traquair had remembered the dashing young adventurer he had been during his time with Oscar. The trains. The hotels. The great cities: Philadelphia, Boston, Washington, San Francisco. The Atlanta fiasco. Oh, God. Lewis and Smith had got that one right with their reprint of the article that had run in the Atlanta *Constitution!* Oscar had been furious. Just furious. Traquair laughed now at the memory of the scene. But hadn't he, too, been shattered by the episode, becoming feverishly ill only a few days afterward? Hadn't his own reading of the *Constitution* article—a simple if somewhat biased journalistic account of a small, personal tragedy—shocked his system, revealing an unsuspected and embarrassing frailty? Maybe. Traquair still wasn't quite sure what had happened to him on that train from Augusta, landing him in that bed in Charleston.

Ah, but what a grand old time he had had with Oscar. During the year Traquair had known him, Oscar had been large and confident. He had been vibrant and generous, cunning and curious, inventive and forgiving. And how Traquair had followed his lead, both literally and figuratively. Throughout their travels he had been Oscar's constant shadow. He had come to view this as his role. Some had called Traquair overprotective and obsequious—in print, no less. Are these not the traits of one's shadow? he had often mused to himself in response to such criticism. He had been hired to be Oscar's valet, but he had become much more. The bag toter, sure. Oscar's trunks had given Traquair fits, but somehow he'd managed to move them from trains to carriages to hotels across the country and even through Canada. Yes, he had been the sentry at Oscar's hotel room door. All of the guests—gentlemen and pesky reporters alike—had had to maneuver past Traquair to gain Oscar's presence. He remembered his success with great pride.

But he had also been Oscar's companion. The late-night conversations in the hotel rooms after Oscar returned from countless dinners given in his honor were unforgettable; those little but large talks had remained the most important dialogues of Traquair's life, where Oscar Wilde had called him "Tra" and where Traquair had called him "Oscar," where Traquair had heard and uttered things he'd never heard or uttered again, except in the privacy of his memories. Like any man's shadow, he had moved synchronously with Oscar, in back, in front, at his side, as the spotlight of the poet's celebrity had demanded, had allowed.

Traquair was now an old man. The quick look at his hands, too weak even to muster the energy to toss away an offending book, was proof enough of that. (Were his brittle bones and his tender, mealy flesh the main reason the book seemed to weigh so much? Could truth, if the actual weight of the proposition itself really mattered, be dependent upon the strength and salubrity of the observer? Did truth's rigidity, like the body's, rise to a peak and then naturally decline with time? If so, then wasn't time's indiscriminate march onward immoral? Old-man questions, he rebuked himself.) Traquair was old—but in his mind Oscar Wilde had remained the youthful twenty-seven-year-old of 1882. Oscar's face had not become wrinkled and distorted with shame and disgrace. His hair had not thinned. He had not become fat with untruth. He had never even died, really. The image in Traquair's mind, when he thought of Oscar—which was often—was the same one the photographer Napoleon Sarony had captured during the year of the American tour, one print of which Lewis and Smith had had the uncharacteristically good instinct to publish here at the front of their book. The old hands turned a page and held down the frontispiece portrait of the young Oscar Wilde. Traquair, the shadow, had aged; Oscar, the man in the picture and in his mind, had not.

Traquair was sitting alone in his one-room apartment in Harlem. He wanted to stand, so he began to talk himself into the task. Usually, he could move about well enough, but after sitting for so long reading he always had to coax his legs into action. The negotiation would take about two minutes. He wanted to walk over to open his door so he'd be able to hear Sarah's radio from her apartment at the end of the hall. She played the Saturday afternoon jazz program he liked. She'd open her door, the music would come out, and everybody on the floor would be grateful. The neighbors would bring their chairs out into the hall and sit around chatting and smoking. Traquair didn't do that. In fact, he disapproved of the practice altogether. The congregating threatened to turn the whole thing into a ritual. And ritual was the religion of redundancy. He could tolerate the voices outside his door, though— as long as they remained at levels too soft for him to know exactly what they were saying. The muffled voices, meaning obscured, gained a kinship to music, which, while the most evocative of art forms, was still marvelously mute. That was a big part of the charm of music, its refusal to acquiesce to the literalness of language. Human beings, Traquair thought, should hum and mumble more. Louis Armstrong would have understood what he meant. Louis already knew; he was changing the world with that scatting business.

Traquair heard the latch at his door jiggle, which meant someone else had opened his or her hall door. The music came, soon. He had so wanted it to be Sarah's door opening that the faint music seemed to take longer to reach him than it should have. He stood up quickly now (his legs were ready), and as he walked slowly to his door, he was still clutching *Oscar Wilde Discovers America* to his chest with his left hand. He swung the door open wide to feel the big-band sound rush him whole. The force of the orchestra (he had no idea who was playing) felt like a sudden Santa Ana. Blinking his eyes as if to provide a lashy shield from a spontaneous funnel of dust, he felt an ache for the West, for California specifically, which, when he'd seen it years ago, had seemed a new and welcoming paradise. He could never predict what effect the music would have on him. Sometimes he wound up in Japan with a headache and an inexplicable and, sadly, unsustainable erection. Once a jolt of Duke Ellington had opened his window, letting in a bird who turned out to be a genie with a sense of humor but with no wishes. Traquair never knew exactly what to expect when he opened his door on Saturdays; he knew only that the impact the music had on him would be complete, both physical and emotional, like a bath in the short term, or like, so he imagined, love in the long. Hoping for a clearer view of the Pacific, he stood there for a few seconds more. When it didn't come, he pushed the door back until it rested about a foot from being closed.

Turning to face the room, Traquair found the bed more inviting than his chair. He hated the sound of his slippered feet on the hardwood floor. How bothersome friction could be. That was why, despite its important and irrefutable contributions to pleasure, it remained on the list of things that one would most like to avoid. With effort, Traquair picked up his feet a little higher to quiet the noise of his shuffle. Still holding the book, he climbed into the bed, whose soft mattress sank at the provocation of even his slight, if long, form. He fell back with a groan and breathed in the lilac he used to scent his pillows. Traquair believed that not only were pillows the repositories of one's dreams and, as such, deserving of lavish care, but, more practically speaking (and this was what a person could say to the inquisitive acquaintance who caught him scenting his linens), pillows touched one's face with greater frequency and for far longer durations than did anyone or anything else, save the air, which if not particularly fresh was, nevertheless, beyond one's control. His pillowcases were of an elaborate olive-green damask design, made from a fabric he had found about eight years ago in a small tailor's shop on 125th Street. The tailor's eyes had grown wide at Traquair's suggestion for the material; the tailor, Mr. Kandinsky, had planned to use it for scarves, ties, and jacket linings. He hadn't made anything else in years, he had told Traquair, embarrassment in his voice. And when Traquair had returned to pick up his pillow slips, Mr. Kandinsky had surprised him with a complete set of matching sheets. He had complemented his new bedding with a heavy, rust-colored quilt and with dark green curtains whose nearly visible warmth had often soothed him into slumber. The rest of his room was decorated with books neatly arranged on his writing table and on three shelves on the wall above (he thought of this space as his library), an oak armoire, two lamps—including a bedside light with a pearly white and gold glass shade—a small Indian rug with blues and reds at the foot of the bed, a miniature blue and white china vase on each of the two windowsills (the curtains were usually sashed open, but they were closed now), and a large portrait of Gloria and Henry Traquair that hung above his bed.

Traquair muttered something to himself as he began flipping

through the pages of *Oscar Wilde Discovers America* again, searching
for something without even realizing it. He came to the last line of the
book, which rather ambitiously purported to represent precisely what
Oscar was thinking as his ship, the *Bothnia,* began to steam back
toward England on the morning of December 27, 1882. The words
Lloyd Lewis and Henry Justin Smith quoted, Traquair had learned earlier when he had checked the notes, were actually excerpted from an
article by Oscar called "The American Man," and it featured his most
cynical view of the American: "For him Art has no marvel, and Beauty
no meaning, and the Past no message."

Traquair closed the book with a loud clap and, much to his discomfort, let it rest upon his lap. Reading it had made him nostalgic for
1882. Even with the book closed, the images of the times he had had
with Oscar were still lit in his mind, dancing to the music wafting in
from the hall. With an atypical swiftness and clarity, as if imitating his
page-flipping motions from just a moment ago, his memory raced
through the years that had transported him from the then and there of
1882 to the here and now of 1936.

Baxter had returned from Europe in the spring of 1883 with a full
beard, looking ten years older and assuming the pose of an artist. The
newness of his appearance had distracted Traquair, lessening ever so
slightly the emotional impact of embracing him, for the first time, with
the knowledge of their actual brotherhood. Baxter would never come
to know the truth about their kinship, or if he did, they never discussed it. Traquair had delivered the scarf he had promised, a bright
yellow one with red fringe. Before heading back to Europe (where he
would spend the rest of his life, in imitation, Traquair had always
believed, of James Whistler), Baxter had spent a couple of months at
home, during which time he had painted the portrait of Traquair's parents that now hung over his bed. He was in London in 1895 and
attended Oscar Wilde's three trials. He sent Traquair several letters
and sketches from the courtroom, and he described witnessing Oscar's
descent from the heights of English society and the literary world to
the depths of scandalous disgrace and prison as "rather like watching a
falling star, rare and spectacular." Oscar's two sons and his wife, Constance, had left London in shame. Baxter had written to Traquair,
"She'll still be ever smiling for me, but the world, which is more real-
istic than I, shall paint of her the very picture of sorrow." Over the

years, Traquair had sometimes thought of visiting Baxter, who lived in Paris now, but he never did. In the end, he was content to think of Europe as Baxter's, and America as his.

Moses Traquair had placed John into apprenticeship at his construction company. The arrangement had lasted for two or three years before John had taken off for someplace south of San Francisco; no one was quite sure where. Moses and Summer had raised Little Johnny as their own child, and he had ultimately taken over the family business. Traquair had kept in touch with his uncle until his uncle's death, but he had never traveled back to the West.

Neither of his parents—Gloria and Henry—had ever spoken to him again about the mysterious circumstances of his conception. Their relationships with him did not change, but they seemed to be more outwardly loving toward each other during their last years together. He had gone to his grave in 1898, and she to hers one year later, both guarding secrets—she, a truth; he, unknowingly, a lie.

Mr. Gable had outlived them both, even getting married again in 1905 to a woman thirty years younger than himself. By the time he died in 1909, Traquair thought they had a tacit understanding of their kinship, though Mr. Gable had never made any explicit acknowledgment. (At Traquair's mother's funeral, however, Mr. Gable had whispered to him, "Don't worry, son. You still have me.") Mr. Gable left a messy, dated will, but his wife instituted the payment of a small but adequate annual stipend to Traquair for the rest of his life, a gesture that had often made him consider that maybe even she knew the true nature of their relationship.

Much to Traquair's delight, he and Jefferson Davis's daughter, Winnie, had kept in touch. She had sent him a note thanking him for giving her the confidence to introduce herself to Oscar. "Meeting him has changed my life," she had written. "Now I am certain that I will be— that I *am* an artist!" She had indeed gone on to publish three books. The first was a biographical sketch of Robert Emmet, a book whose title, *An Irish Knight of the 19th Century*, Traquair always thought had in it a nod to Oscar Wilde. The dramatic circumstances of the book, however, the organization of what would be a failed civil rebellion, seemed to have been chosen for reasons much closer to home. The tragedy Traquair had uncomfortably sensed for Winnie when they had talked together in her father's library cottage had eventually come. In

1887 she visited Syracuse, New York, where she fell in love with an attorney named Alfred Wilkinson, who, as fate would have it, was the grandson of Samuel May, a well-known abolitionist. Winnie had written to Traquair about Alfred's visit to Beauvoir to ask Jefferson Davis's permission to marry her. "I was naughty and eavesdropped on the beginning of their conversation," she wrote. "Alfred made his intentions known quickly. In response Father said, with some playful cynicism in his voice, 'Ah, marriage. The Great Union.' It was the single funniest remark I've ever heard him make. He and Alfred shared a good laugh about that. He's invited Alfred to stay for a few days. I believe Syracuse may be my destiny. Something other than Memphis, as you promised when you were here." But Syracuse was not to be Winnie's destiny. While Mr. Davis did ultimately acquiesce to the marriage, family friends and supporters of the Southern Cause, including some veterans of the war, were outraged that the Daughter of the Confederacy would consider marrying a Yankee. A flustered Winnie determined not to bring such dishonor to her family and called off the marriage. In fact, she never married; neither did Alfred. At the age of thirty-four, she died of complications from malaria. Traquair treasured his signed copies of her novels, *The Veiled Doctor* and *A Romance of Summer Seas*. Both of the books had been written after she had dissolved her engagement to Alfred and both, Traquair thought, contained the ache of complex and forbidden love.

Thoughts of Theda Trenton still quickened his heartbeat after all these years. She had married and moved to Boston, and occasionally the society columns mentioned her visiting New York to attend this or that party. She eventually gained a reputation as a minor suffragette. Sometimes he remembered kissing her hand in St. Louis and feather-brushing her cheek with his shadow when he had seen her in New York. But somewhere in his mind he was still standing at the edge of a park downtown waiting for her. All of these images he accepted with the wistful resignation of that former general he and Oscar had met in Memphis; thoughts of Theda were but remnants of the war.

Oscar. He and Oscar had never seen each other again. Oscar had sent him a letter after their last meeting, asking that they not burden each other with apologies or words of gratitude. "The language of passion is unutterable," Oscar had written. And he had asked that Traquair not see him off. "I do not want your last vision of me to contain, as its background, the blank mass that is that dreaded ocean." Even when Oscar had come back to America in 1883 to open his play *Vera,* which would fail badly, Traquair had not seen him. Traquair's only real contact with Oscar over the years had been through his reading of Oscar's many works: the poetry, plays, essays, fairy tales, and his favorite, Oscar's only novel, *The Picture of Dorian Gray,* which, when it had appeared in the early nineties with its sinning but eternally youthful protagonist who comes to a crashing, revelatory, wretched end, Traquair had taken as confirmation that he had been right to resist the charms and logical progressions of Oscar's kiss, to forget the pleasures of the girls in the back rooms of the various dens he had visited. Inspired by his nightmare notion that to act upon the impulse of desire was a form of treason, Traquair had chosen to lead a life of celibacy. Since that passionate night with Oscar, he had reserved his kisses for his relatives, his platonic friends, and the phantoms in his dreams. When Oscar's own Dorian-like transgressions were exposed and he was ruined and sent to prison, Traquair again felt justified in having committed himself to a life of abstinence. He felt pure. He had lived a good life.

He had never fully embraced Oscar's notion that he was a tragic figure. Had he a larger ego, had he a more Wildean sense of himself, perhaps he would have analyzed the darker parts of his past and reached more dramatic conclusions. Oscar, no doubt, had he been Traquair, would have proclaimed America not merely a great work of art, but a great tragedy. And Oscar would have declared himself the hero of that tragedy, America's Hamlet, America's Othello. But Traquair did not possess such a grand sense of who he was. Maybe, he had concluded over the years, there was something about his beauty, his particular beauty that, in the end, was tragic, as the very thing—*the way he looked*—that had delivered to him so much special treatment, so many privileges, so much, including, he was sure, the love of Oscar, the beauty that had ushered him into the realm of what he desired, was also what had denied him the thing he wanted most: Theda. He had to admit that there was something tragic about that.

Traquair had become a teacher—history, of course—mostly in the upper levels of instruction. During his last twenty working years, 1909 through 1929, he had been invited back to Bowdoin, his alma mater, to teach American history. (Yes, he had revisited the Maine coast on many occasions and let himself be sensuously splashed again and again by the ocean that Oscar hated but that he loved and that, he told himself, loved him back.) For four semesters in the late twenties, because of his own history, he was also asked to teach a special course in the English department called "The Comedies of Oscar Wilde." The course was always filled to capacity, with Traquair gaining a reputation for peppering his lectures with anecdotes about his travels with Oscar, making him something of a campus celebrity among the more liberal set.

A celebrity? Traquair laughed to himself. He, a celebrity? *Oscar Wilde Discovers America* again made the full weight of its 450 pages felt upon his lap. All those pages and so little of him. A celebrity! Few men had ever been faced with such a massive documentation of their own insignificance. The book was not only a paean to the legend of Oscar Wilde; it was a long essay on the anonymity of William Traquair. To him it was not just a tome but a tomb.

Yes, reading the book had incited within him a certain weariness of spirit, an inclination to question his worth. His mood was so incompatible with the music coming into his room from the hall that it took on an even greater prominence. It was a mood of death—and the music was so filled with life. Death was what he was feeling like now. (Death, death, death. He knew it was coming to him soon. Some part of him even wanted it. Daily, even before he had started reading the book, he had thought of death. He had thought of death for years.) The weight of the book pressed harder into his lap now, into the very center of himself. It seemed to be threatening to smother him, to snuff out what tiny flicker remained of his life's flame. And then he thought: A book that encourages death is too ambitious for its own good. A book that destroys its readership assures its own irrelevance.

He heard his own laughter ring out at this remark as his hand instinctively and affectionately rubbed the cover of the book. And then, in the very next moment, his hand slapped the book in anger.

Yes, he knew why he didn't like *Oscar Wilde Discovers America*. It wasn't that the book was entirely without merit; it offered an altogether entertaining summary of the events of 1882. And it wasn't because the book weighed a ton and had its share of mistakes. He disliked the book because *even though* the book weighed a ton, it all but left him out. When it bothered to refer to him at all it was as "John" (an uninspired, made-up name, as admitted finally, if quietly, by Lewis and Smith, in their index, where they had placed quotation marks around the lying moniker), or as "the Negro valet," and once as the "liver-colored valet"! Liver-colored! He hated that that old rumor still had currency. It had its roots in the story from that Sioux City paper, which, ironically, had given Traquair some of his best coverage. He wasn't liver-colored at all, at least not most of the year. Only after about two months of winter did he lighten to a hue that might unimaginatively and insensitively be called liver. From April to November, Traquair saw himself as being his more natural color, something approaching a deep auburn. And now this inaccuracy was set indelibly in book form; he would forever be remembered—as if three or four or however many paltry little mentions (eight to be exact—he had counted) would gain him any lasting fame—as liver-colored.

But, really, he was in no position to protest, Traquair admitted to himself. He alone had accepted the role of shadow. How could he truly fault Lewis and Smith? Men more gifted than they had tried and failed miserably to describe the color of shadows (the inventor of puce he thought on this point a particularly egregious offender), while others had gone hoarse trying to call their proper names. Yes, it was obviously challenging work, attempting to humanize an adumbral presence.

And so he allowed now that the book had entranced him, as it was probably capable of entrancing no one else. If the book had not been written about him, it had been written *for* him; he was its most precious reader. Only he could read the book and completely project himself into the story the way writers always want their readers to do. That was rather easy to do when there you were on page 153 and page 204 and page 211 and—even without being indexed, even doing things you hadn't actually done or looking a little bit different from the way you saw yourself—on pages 169, 275, 372, 373, 382. Oscar had said something in New Orleans about the creation of a "fantastic patchwork portraiture." That phrase—one with which, Traquair thought, Oscar had predicted the rise of the art form of collage—was a good description of the image of himself the book had helped him piece together in his mind.

Traquair heard the music still streaming into his room from the hall and remembered that Oscar, obliquely but definitively, had also predicted jazz: "But, as America is the noisiest country in the world, I predict a new music, and your noise will, of course, be in the music. And should your new art in fact be a *great* music, it will be the sound of art dying." Was jazz the sound of art dying? If so, then it was a more appropriate accompaniment to his mood than he had realized. Contemplating that now—he heard some strangely contorted saxophone solo in the midst of a lovely big-band performance, some haunting meanderings around the melody that did seem to suggest that the loss of something was being lamented—made him, a dying old man, feel a certain kinship to the music that he had not felt before. He continued to entertain the thought that jazz was the sound of art dying, though he had decided many years ago that art had died on November 30, 1900, along with Oscar Wilde, who had told him once that when the man who symbolizes something dies, so does the thing for which he stands. Traquair indulged himself now with the conceit that he, like jazz, made a difference, that his old role as shadow to the Apostle of Art and his own quivering but still vital existence had somehow bought art a little extra time.

Under the influence of this egotistical impression (he allowed himself, finally, this minor indulgence), Traquair felt the need to be physically closer to the music, his lone ally in the struggle to sustain the life of Oscar's great, nearly forgotten cause. He wanted somehow to touch the music, and he wanted it to touch him. It seemed to promise a sensuous alternative to the passion he had denied himself for decades.

With less effort than usual, he threw back the bedcovers and stood up. He would go out into the hall and, in the company of his neighbors, listen to the music. If their chatter started to bother him he would tune them out, pretend he couldn't hear them; they wouldn't care. They would think he was hard of hearing or that he was going through some minor episode of senility. Old age had its advantages. He would endure the presence of the others in order to be closer to the music.

As he started to walk toward the door, he realized he was still clutching *Oscar Wilde Discovers America*. The book, so heavy moments ago, had a weightlessness now. He tossed it back onto the bed, where it nestled itself among the ripples and thick folds of the green damask sheets he so loved. Traquair thought that the book—a simple thing, thick and black, with its title, authors, and publisher embossed in gold letters on its spine—looked like it belonged where it had settled, and he knew he would return to it over and over again for the rest of his life, however brief a period that might be. The book reminded him a great deal of that Sioux City article with its nearly fictional rendering of who he was and what had really happened, and he remembered how he had concluded years ago, back in 1882, that a fictional him was better than no him at all. The book's flawed but somehow thrilling documentation of his existence and its simultaneous implied argument against the significance of his existence were realities he was drawn to examining. Wasn't the struggle to reconcile those two issues really all that most men have to counter the quotidian: that life is special but that one's own life, ironically, is not? Was that the final paradox? He knew he would never tire of wondering about that. As he turned and began to walk toward the well-lit hall, his neighbors and the music, he understood that though he was not special, though he was not like Oscar or any other great man or woman, he had a reason to live. No, not merely a reason; life, for him, was an imperative born of his relative insignificance.

He walked a little faster now, in response to the music and to the Wildean truth that had just fully rejuvenated him: Only the immortal can afford death.

SOURCES

Two main sources provided important information for the writing of this novel: *Oscar Wilde* by Richard Ellmann and *Oscar Wilde Discovers America* by Lloyd Lewis and Henry Justin Smith. Kevin O'Brien's *Oscar Wilde in Canada* was also helpful. Lori Curtis at the University of Tulsa's McFarlin Library, which houses Mr. Ellmann's papers, overwhelmed me with her generosity in searching for and supplying me with all of the crucial references to Wilde's American valet to be found in the collection: newspaper articles, including the invaluable Sioux City article that provides one of the few substantive physical descriptions of the valet I could uncover ("young," "likely-looking," "intelligent face," and "light mixed liver") and the Atlanta *Constitution's* coverage of the sleeping-car incident that occurred on the night of the Fourth of July; and copies of Mr. Ellmann's typed notes.

Some of the books that provided background information for the development of other characters in this novel include: *Mrs. Oscar Wilde* by Anne Clark Amor; *The Escapades of Frank and Jesse James* by Carl W. Breihan; *The Life, Times and Treacherous Death of Jesse James* by Frank Triplett; *Jefferson Davis* by Clement Eaton; *Jefferson Davis: A Memoir by His Wife* (Varina Howell Davis); *The Rise and Fall of the Confederate Government* by Jefferson Davis; *Jefferson Davis Gets His Citizenship Back* by Robert Penn Warren; *Varina Anne "Winnie" Davis* by Tommie Phillips LaCavera; *The Veiled Doctor, A Romance of Summer Seas*, and *An Irish Knight of the 19th Century* by Varina Anne Jefferson Davis; *James McNeill Whistler: An Estimate & a Biography* by Frank Rutter; *The Life of James McNeill Whistler* by E. R. and J. Pennell; *The Gentle Art of Making Enemies* by James McNeill Whistler; and many others.

Perhaps the most significant revelation in all of my reading came in Mr. Ellmann's notes for his biography of Wilde. The name the biography applies to Oscar's American valet is probably not accurate. In the notes one discovers the mention of a W. M. Traguier, who was the promoter of Wilde's lecture in St. Louis. "Traquair" is almost certainly a misuse and misspelling of "Traguier," an error made, perhaps, in a later transcription of Mr. Ellmann's notes. Mr. O'Brien in *Oscar Wilde in Canada* refers to the valet as Stephen Davenport, though he does not indicate his source. And, as elaborated upon in this novel, Lewis and Smith call the valet "John." At any rate, it was the inventive "error" in the Ellmann biography that, for me, created the character, opening the door to this fiction—which has little to do with reality—so Traquair he is and shall be.

The words and actions of the twenty-seven-year-old Oscar Wilde, as set forth here, are also almost entirely fiction. The thoughts and language I attribute to him are based on the manner and meaning of his recorded expressions: essays, lectures, plays, his one novel, the fairy tales, quotations from eyewitness accounts, and letters. What one can attribute directly to Wilde are: the famous customs declaration of his genius; the Gilbert and Sullivan remarks and quotes from the first New York lecture; the lines of poetry about his sister; the quotes from the St. Louis lecture; and the soup-kettle remark about the Tabernacle. In many instances, however, I have taken great license. For example, there is no evidence that Wilde actually predicted jazz, but here are the three comments he made that inspired my fictional claim that he did:

1) While in New Orleans (essentially the home of jazz and absolutely the home of the great, symbolic figure of jazz, Louis Armstrong), Wilde, as indicated in this novel, really did expound quite elaborately upon the artistic potential of the Negro. The *Daily Picayune* paraphrased some of his commentary: "One must go to Asia and Africa for picturesqueness in human costume and habits. In America he had found it only in the Indians and in the negro, and he was surprised that painters and poets had paid so little attention to these matters, and especially to the negro as an object of art."

2) Later, in Atlanta, Wilde said: "It should be—the south—the home of art in America, because it possesses the most perfect sur-

roundings; and now that it is recovering from the hideous ruin of the war I have no doubt that all these beautiful arts, in whose cause I will spend my youth in pleading, will spring up among you."

3) Wilde rarely spoke about music, but he told the Omaha *Weekly Herald*: "If ever America produces a great musician, let him write a machinery symphony. . . . But first they must abolish the steam whistle." Jazz musicians and composers would ignore Wilde's command and actually incorporate the sound of the steam whistle into their American symphonies.

On a related topic, the matter of art dying, Oscar Wilde, upon returning to England, said: "When I was in America, I did not dare to tell America the truth; but I saw it clearly even then—that the discovery of America was the beginning of the death of Art. But not yet; no, not yet!"

ACKNOWLEDGMENTS

Joy Harris and Alexia Paul of the Joy Harris Literary Agency are the reason this book is a book. Gillian Blake and Rachel Sussman at Scribner are the reason this book is a better book. I am grateful to them all.

A. J. Verdelle and Joe DeSalvo delivered the latest edition of Oscar Wilde's letters to me at a crucial moment, which helped ignite the transformation of the novel. It's impossible to overstate the significance of Marie Brown to me and a generation of young (or at least once young) writers. And I thank Josh Feigenbaum for his continued support of my work.

Finally, I owe many thanks to my friends and family, who since 1995 have tolerated my obsession with Oscar, especially Susan Mock and Bo Gallup, who are responsible for the appearance of Bowdoin College in this novel and for the notion that a place, such as Maine—or all of America for that matter—might be a metaphor for love.